NEW HAND

L.A. WITT

A BLUEWATER BAY STORY

RIPTIDE
PUBLISHING

Riptide Publishing
PO Box 1537
Burnsville, NC 28714
www.riptidepublishing.com

New Hand

Cover art: L.C. Chase, lcchase.com/design.htm
Editor: Chris Muldoon
Layout: L.C. Chase, lcchase.com/design.htm

ISBN: 978-1-62649-695-8

First edition
December, 2017

Also available in ebook:
ISBN: 978-1-62649-694-1

NEW HAND

L.A. WITT

TABLE OF CONTENTS

CHAPTER ONE

JESSE

S*omething came up. Not gonna make it. Sorry. :(*

"My ass." I rolled my eyes and slammed the phone facedown on the bar next to my nearly finished Coke.

A few chairs down, a bearded dude in a flannel shirt gave me a look. It was a look I knew well. The kind that telegraphed in no uncertain terms that he wanted to enjoy his beer and his baseball game without being afraid I might shower him with glitter or something. Most nights, I'd give a sassy hair toss, cross my legs, and shoot him a flirty grin. I mean seriously—Bluewater Bay was knee-deep in queers thanks to *Wolf's Landing*, and even dive bars like the Olympic Sports & Alehouse weren't safe from the likes of me. If he couldn't cope with a queen at his bar, he was in the wrong town.

But I wasn't in the mood to fuck with him. Not after Charlie's text message. I twisted on the barstool, angling myself away from Beardy McHomophobe, and stabbed an ice cube with my straw. I glared at my phone. Even though I couldn't see the screen, Charlie's text was seared into my brain.

Something came up. Not gonna make it. Sorry. :(

I sighed, shoulders drooping along with my mood. The routine of *Jesse meets boy, boy likes Jesse, boy finds out Jesse is HIV-positive, boy loses interest in Jesse* was one I'd been familiar with for a long time. It didn't always happen—I'd had plenty of hookups, friends with benefits, and boyfriends who were well aware of my status—but it happened enough to still make me dread the inevitable "Before we take this further . . ." conversation. I just hadn't expected Charlie to be like this.

"Refill?" The seriously sexy voice pulled me out of my thoughts, and I looked up to see a bartender watching me. And . . . I had to stare.

I'd been coming to this bar sporadically for ages, but I hadn't seen him before, and that was a face I *would* have remembered. A face, a pair of dark eyes, a set of shoulders—

I cleared my throat and nudged my glass toward him. "Sure. Thanks."

"What're you drinking?" God. That voice. Low and rumbly and *hot*.

"Um." What *was* I drinking? Crap. "Just a . . ." Alcohol? Nah. That would only make me more depressed because oh, right, I was in the process of being stood the fuck up by someone who thought I was a leper. "Coke."

He nodded and took my glass. As he put some ice in a fresh one, I stole the opportunity to take him in. He was easily in his forties, if not a little older. There were some lines on his face that even the bar's low lights didn't smooth over. The gray hair seemed oddly out of place. He wasn't young, but he seemed grayer than he should've been. No, not gray—*white*. He still had plenty of his natural dark hair, but he had streaks and sparkles of snow white, especially at the temples and along his part.

It didn't look bad on him, though. Quite the opposite. *Striking* was the word that came to mind.

So that's why people dig silver foxes. Holy shit.

Right then, his eyes flicked up to meet mine, and he handed me the Coke.

"Thanks." I took the glass, mildly disappointed he let it go before I could "accidentally" let our fingers brush.

He didn't walk away. The place wasn't exactly crowded. The bearded dude was still glowering nearby, and there were a few guys watching a baseball game down at the other end of the long bar with another bartender keeping an eye on their drinks. Most of the tables and booths were empty. Not surprising—it was the middle of the week and it was still early yet. So the bartender probably didn't have a lot to do except hang out and wait for me to need another refill. Fine by me, as long as he didn't mind me checking him out.

I took a drink and tried not to notice the way *he* was trying not to watch me suck on the straw. Our eyes locked. He colored a bit in the dim light and turned his head, clearing his throat but not exactly hurrying away from me.

"Just you tonight?" He winced, like he'd been trying to say something to break the ice and now felt like an idiot for blurting out the question. Not that it was a terrible question, but he seemed to regret throwing it out there.

And that . . . actually put me at ease. In fact, his subtle awkwardness was kind of endearing. Maybe because I thought a fortysomething bartender who looked so smooth would *be* that smooth, and the fact that he wasn't . . . I decided I liked it.

I played with the straw in my Coke. "I'm being stood up, actually."

His eyebrows climbed. "Seriously?" I might've been imagining it, but I could've sworn he gave me a not-so-subtle down-up. When our eyes locked again, he blushed—nope, hadn't imagined it. Clearing his throat, he focused intently on wiping a phantom smudge off the bar between us. "I, uh . . . I'm sorry to hear it. Can't imagine why someone would . . ." The blush deepened, and damn—shy looked almost as good on him as gray hair and lines.

Charlie who?

And with that, my evening was suddenly looking up again. I'd been expecting—or at least hoping—to get laid tonight. The fact that there happened to be an incredibly hot man right there behind the bar—and one who wasn't *necessarily* straight—was just damn good luck.

I took another sip and ran my tongue around the tip of the straw for good measure. He swallowed but didn't look away. Instead, he looked me right in the eye, and when I grinned, he shivered. Oh yeah. Dude was queer. Fuck yes.

Absently chasing an ice cube with the straw, I said, "You just start here? I come here all the time, but I've never seen you."

He nodded. "A week ago." He glanced around, a self-conscious smirk drawing my attention to his full lips. "Still learning the ropes."

I shrugged. "You had me fooled."

Chuckling, he met my gaze again. "Fortunately, a Coke on the rocks is pretty simple to make."

"'Coke on the rocks.'" I laughed. "I like it."

He just smiled.

I took a sip. "You new to town? Or just the bar?"

"Town." He didn't offer anything further. "What about you?"

L.A. WITT

"Well, ask any of your coworkers—I'm not new to this bar."

He laughed.

"And not to town either," I said. "Been here . . . almost six years now."

"Yeah? Where'd you move from?"

"Seattle."

His eyes lit up. "Really? Me too. What part?"

"Grew up in Mountlake Terrace, and I was living in Ballard, but it was too expensive to stay."

The bartender's lips quirked. "Yeah, that area's not cheap. I was in Madison Park. Just outside Capitol Hill."

"Ah, my favorite neighborhood." I grinned.

He chuckled. "Yeah. Mine too. So, is that what made you leave Seattle? Cost of living?"

"That, and my uncle lived here and was having some problems getting around and taking care of his place after he fucked up his hip. He got it replaced and does just fine now, and he ended up moving to the Tri-Cities, but I liked Bluewater Bay. So, I stayed." Pausing, I drummed my fingers on the counter and realized just how long my answer had been. "Sorry. You probably didn't need the whole autobiography."

"Nah, it's okay." The bartender's smile came back to life, and I decided I liked that too. A lot.

"Well, since you're new, you might as well get used to seeing me in here." I offered my hand across the bar. "Jesse Connelly."

He took my hand, shaking it firmly. "Garrett Blaine." As he released me, he said, "So you're a regular." There was a sparkle in his eyes that suggested he wasn't at all unhappy about that.

Warmth flooded my face. "Yeah. I probably come in here once or twice a week. When I'm too lazy to open my own beers."

Garrett laughed. He started to say something, but then glanced toward the other end of the bar and frowned. "Shit. Duty calls. I'll be right back."

"I'll be right here."

He smiled, then went to help the other customers, giving me one hell of a view of that jean-clad ass. Oh fuck yeah. I could absolutely get

4

on board with finding out how that silver fox looked in nothing but tangled sheets.

Shivering, I pulled my attention away before I gave myself a hard-on. My own jeans were a little too tight for that.

Without thinking about it, I picked up my phone to look at the time. And of course, I had another message from Charlie. More than one, actually.

Look, I'm sorry. I know it sounds awful. The timing and all. After what we talked about. But that's not it at all!

Come on, Jesse. Let's talk. Please?

You there?

I hated the sick feeling that coiled in my gut. Even more, I hated that it was as familiar as Charlie's postrejection backpedaling. *Sure*, it wasn't because of what we'd talked about. And he totally hadn't kissed me on the cheek this afternoon instead of on the mouth when we'd said goodbye after lunch.

I glanced at the bartender's back, and my heart sank into my queasy stomach. Flirting was fun, but . . . ugh. I didn't have it in me to hook up with anyone tonight. Charlie had left me feeling gross and raw. Like the least-desirable thing on the planet. Usually, I could steel myself for the possible rejection and just be matter-of-fact about it. I was upfront, possibly to a fault: "Full disclosure—I'm HIV positive." Then they'd either be cool with it or they wouldn't be, and the night would go from there. There was no reason to believe Garrett would follow Charlie's example.

But on the heels of a rejection from someone who was supposed to be a friend, I wasn't ready to chance a second dose. Not tonight.

Sighing, I stared into my drink. The way I felt right now was exactly why I didn't usually date friends. Not unless they knew my status before we started any kind of flirtation. I much preferred meeting someone for sex, telling them upfront I was positive, and letting the chips fall where they would. Rejection wasn't fun, but there was no point in waiting a few dates to tell someone. I'd learned the hard way—repeatedly— that getting to know a guy first would only make his rejection more disastrous. He'd be pissed that I'd waited so long, and I'd be hurt because I'd be invested in him. I'd actually care what he thought of me.

So when I met guys online and on hookup apps, they knew I was positive before they knew my name. It was in my profiles, for God's sake. Probably kept a lot of guys from responding to me, but that was fine. Better to nip it in the bud than deal with someone I actually liked trying to tactfully step into the friend-zone.

Charlie . . . he'd been different. My status had never come up because we'd just been buddies. We'd met at a Magic: The Gathering tournament two years ago, and we'd geeked out together over comics and gaming. I hadn't even realized he was gay until recently. Then he'd moved from Portland to Bluewater Bay for an assistant job on the *Wolf's Landing* set, and suddenly we were living near each other. And *then* last night's drunken *Call of Duty* had happened, one thing had led to another, and we'd made out on my couch until I'd finally made some weak excuse about needing to be up early for work.

And all damn morning, we'd melted each other's phones with racy texts and promises. I'd felt guilty for not saying, *Dude, before we continue . . .* but it hadn't seemed like something I should tell him over the phone. So while we'd had lunch today, I'd told him. Over the next few hours, the texts had cooled considerably, and our plans to meet at my place had changed to meeting here for a drink so we could talk, and now . . . this.

I glowered at my phone for a moment before typing out a message. *I don't think there's anything to talk about. You were gung ho until I mentioned my status. Way to make a dude feel sexy.*

My throat tightened at that last line. I'd meant it as an admittedly petty swipe but ended up hitting myself in the gut instead. Being rejected by some stranger? I could chalk that up to ignorance. And it wasn't like a guy was obligated to have sex with me if he didn't feel safe. I was fine with that. But a friend? Man. That hurt. Like, don't sleep with me if you don't want to, but don't be a dick about it.

Movement pulled my attention away from the screen, and my heart flip-flopped as Garrett reappeared in front of me.

"Sorry," he said with a lopsided smile. "It's like they expect me to actually work while I'm here."

I laughed despite the heavy, sick feeling in my gut. "Jerks."

"I know, right?"

"My bosses do the same thing. And it's not fair because I work around comic books and shit. Let a boy read, you know?"

Garrett chuckled. "You work at a comic shop?"

I nodded, gesturing over my shoulder at the street outside, as if that somehow indicated all the shops along the road. "I'm the assistant manager at End o' Earth." Heat rushed into my cheeks. "Not that being an assistant manager of a comic book shop is anything to write home about."

"Why not?" Garrett chuckled. "I'm assuming you earned it."

"Yeah, but still. Not exactly VP of a Fortune 500 company, right?"

"Who needs that level of stress, though?"

"True."

He held my gaze, but only for a second. Then he shook himself. "Nothing wrong with not working for a company like that. Corporate America isn't for everyone." As if for emphasis, he started wiping the immaculate bar with a blue towel.

I studied him. There was something odd about him. About the way he carried himself. About his expression. Like he was holding some cards I wouldn't have noticed at all if he hadn't been keeping them so tightly against his vest. And that made me curious about him.

The silence between us stretched on. He didn't leave, and I wondered if he was expecting me to pay my tab and get the fuck out. Which was probably a good idea. There was no point in sticking around if my date wasn't showing up.

At least, there hadn't been until this good-looking bartender had dropped out of the sky.

Thumbing the condensation on my glass, I looked up at Garrett. "Is it, uh, okay if I stay here for a while?"

"Stay as long as you want."

"Thanks. I promise I tip well."

He gave a soft laugh and waved his hand. And there it was again—that smile. I didn't want to be attracted to anyone right now, and I sure as shit wasn't going to make any kind of move tonight, but I could still enjoy a gorgeous man's gorgeous smile.

After a moment, his brow pinched and his eyes were full of sympathy. "So he really stood you up?"

I arched an eyebrow. "'He'?"

Garrett jumped, and some color slid out of his face. "Uh. Shit. I'm sorry. I . . ."

"It's okay." I laughed quietly and gestured at myself—skinny jeans, meticulously styled hair, and all. "I guess I do kind of give that vibe, don't I?"

"Uh . . ." He blinked like he had no idea how to respond to that.

"Relax. Literally no one was surprised when I came out." I winked. "Honey, they don't make 'em much gayer than me."

Garrett studied me uncertainly, but then he laughed. "Still. I didn't mean to be presumptuous."

"It's all right. And to answer your question, yeah, he stood me up." He shook his head. "Sorry to hear it."

"Thanks. What sucks is this isn't just some asshole I found on Grindr. He's a friend." I sighed, giving my phone a look. "Or, well, *was* a friend."

"Damn. That's rough." He studied me, and the question in his eyes was so obvious he might as well have asked it out loud.

"Let me guess—you want to know what happened?"

Garrett blinked but shrugged. "You don't have to answer."

"That's part of being a bartender, isn't it? Listening to people bitch about their drama?"

He chuckled. "It does break up the monotony a bit."

"Better than sitting at a desk all day, right?"

A subtle flinch, like I'd nudged a nerve. He shifted his weight. "Something like that, yeah. So if you feel like talking, I'm happy to listen."

"Thanks." I hesitated. There was no need to announce my status to Garrett. I wasn't trying to get him into bed, so he didn't need to know, and I still stung from the last time I'd tipped my hand. Even a nose-wrinkle from a stranger would've been too much right now.

So I kept that detail to myself.

I took a sip of my Coke, which was quickly getting watered down by melting ice. "The short version is that we've been friends for a while, and he moved to town recently. We started, you know, making noise about hooking up, and that was the plan tonight, but . . ." I shook my head, "I guess he didn't want to after all."

"So he just stood you up?" Garrett's eyebrows rose. "And he's your friend?"

"*Was* my friend," I muttered into my straw. "It's . . . I mean, it's complicated." *Bullshit.* "Long, stupid story." *Also bullshit. Except the stupid part. It's definitely stupid.* "Anyway." I looked up at him. "I really should get out of your hair. I'm just sitting here bitching at you about the dick I'm not getting."

"You're not in my hair." He shrugged. "Stick around if you want to."

I . . . I *did* want to. Going home and being alone and pathetic didn't sound appealing. Hunting someone else down for a roll in the hay sounded exhausting, not to mention demoralizing in my current mood. About the only thing that sounded good was staying where I was and talking with Garrett.

Garrett, who was probably just humoring me so I'd leave a good tip.

"You're sure?" I sounded like a little kid. Ugh. "Even if I'm not drinking?"

"You *are* drinking." He gestured at my glass.

"You know what I mean."

"Yeah, and no one else needs to know that's not a rum and Coke."

I eyed him, then my drink. "Oh. True. Well, as long as you don't mind me sitting here and feeling sorry for myself?"

Garrett gave me a smile that almost made me forget how gross Charlie had made me feel.

"You can hang around here as long as you want," he said. "Long as you don't mind keeping a bored bartender company."

At that, I couldn't help smiling back. "Deal."

CHAPTER TWO

GARRETT

"Holy crap." Jesse looked at his phone, eyes bugging out. "It's one thirty?"

"Is it really?" I checked the ugly neon Michelob clock on the wall. Sure enough, it was one thirty. "Wow. Time flies, doesn't it?"

"Yeah, it does." He pushed the barstool back. "How much do I owe you?"

"For a few Cokes? Not a hell of a lot."

Jesse chuckled as he took out his wallet. "Seriously. How much?"

I was surprised at the disappointment in my gut as I rang up his modest tab. When I put the bill on the bar between us, that disappointment sank deeper. Jesse's presence had made my shift fly by like it had been nothing, and I wasn't ready for it to be over. But what was I supposed to do? Suggest we go grab coffee at one of the few all-night restaurants in town? Because that wouldn't be weird or creepy.

Jesse handed back the bill with his Visa on top of it, and I went through the motions that were still somewhat awkward and clumsy. This job had a learning curve like any other, and even though I'd tended bar in my twenties, I was still getting the hang of everything at this place. Plus, the credit card machine was kind of an asshole, taking its sweet time processing, but I was okay with that tonight. Pathetic or not, I didn't object to the sluggish machine keeping Jesse here a minute or two longer.

While it lingered on *Transmitting . . .*, I stole a couple of glances at him. He stood out in a place like this. Hell, he probably stood out anywhere he went, but especially in a dim sports bar. Queer-friendly town or not, I had to admire a gay man who strolled into the Alehouse like he owned the place and made absolutely no attempt to conceal how femme he was. Femme men didn't usually turn my head, but the sheer ballsiness of unflinchingly swishing past a group of lumberjacks hunched over their beers? That was hard not to notice.

And once he'd had my attention, I couldn't deny he was hot. He was unabashedly himself. He was funny. Damn right, I was attracted to him.

Thing was, I hadn't felt so much as a tingle of attraction in ages. And it had been so long since I'd been attracted to someone and actually considered acting on it, the feeling was completely and utterly alien. Not bad, but not entirely good, either. While arousal zinged along my nerve endings, guilt roiled in my stomach.

Is it too soon?

My mind wasn't sure.

My body, however, had already decided it was absolutely not too soon. Not if I had a shot with someone as hot as Jesse. Which I probably didn't—he'd been flirty, but he seemed like the kind of guy who flirted with everyone. And what better way to distract himself from being stood up? No point in reading too much into it.

Eventually, the machine spat out the receipt, which I handed across the bar along with his card and a pen. "There you go. Just need a signature from you and we're all set."

He smiled as he took them from me. I always hated when people hovered while I was signing a receipt, so I cleared away his empty glass and ran the dish rag across the bar to catch a few stray drops.

Jesse finished with the receipt, laid the pen over it, and offered another smile, this one a little shy and a lot cute. "Thanks for humoring me tonight. This beat the hell out of moping around at home."

"Don't mention it. Passed the time for me too."

"True." He paused, lingering like he might say something more, but then he tucked his wallet into his pocket and took a small step back from the bar. "Okay, well. I guess I'll see you next time I come in."

"Looking forward to it." And I really was. That was kind of an auto response all bartenders developed after a while, but I meant it.

"Me too." Another smile, and he inched toward the door. "Anyway, I'll . . . I'll, um, I should take off."

You don't have to do that.

But I just nodded, and we held each other's gazes for a few seconds before he turned to go. Heart thumping, I watched him until the door swung shut and he was gone. Then I released a long breath and got back to work as my stomach fluttered with all kinds of feelings I hadn't had in recent memory.

When I went to close out his bill, I had to do a double take at the receipt, and I nearly jogged after him to let him know he'd made a mistake. A ten-dollar tip on a twelve-dollar bill? But before I could chase him down to correct it, I saw the note he'd scrawled underneath: *Srsly—thanks. I needed this tonight.*

I stared at it for a moment, then looked at the door, which had long since closed behind him. I wondered if he had any idea how much *I'd* needed this tonight. After a couple of hellish years and a few weeks of awkwardly adapting to a new town, I hadn't realized how much good it could do me just to spend an evening in amiable conversation with someone. Most of my relatively recent human contact had been with people who struggled to hold eye contact or figure out what to say. Or worse—couldn't hide their pity.

As I finished closing out Jesse's bill, something in me relaxed, and it was something that hadn't relaxed in way too long. Tonight had been a few hours of desperately needed *normal*. Of shooting the shit and enjoying the company of a friendly and possibly flirty stranger. That was oddly comforting after having resigned myself to grief; soul-crushing loneliness; and the never-ending, if well-meaning, sympathy from people I knew. One-time thing or not, this evening was the first glimmer of hope I'd had that "things will get better" was something more than an empty platitude.

Not long after Jesse left, I helped my boss, Don, close down the bar, then walked out to my truck. All the way back to my apartment, my mind was on Jesse. I liked chatting with people at the bar, and it was rare to have someone show up who wanted to talk to me for any length of time. Not unless they were drunk to the point of incoherence, anyway—and the whole smiling and nodding so they didn't know I couldn't understand them act got old fast.

Jesse hadn't been drunk. Hell, he hadn't touched a drop of anything besides Coke. He'd been quite obviously irritated and hurt over getting stood up, but instead of diving into a bottle and drinking himself stupid, he'd passed the evening with . . . me. Whenever I'd had to walk away to take care of someone else, he'd patiently waited until I'd come back, and we'd pick up our conversation right where we'd left off. Next thing I'd known, it was damn near last call.

The evening had been fun, but driving home now, I was unsettled. Maybe *unsettled* wasn't the right word. What I was feeling, it wasn't necessarily bad, but it was weird. Not something I'd expected when I'd clocked in eight hours ago.

I was . . . Shit, was I *really* attracted to Jesse?

One look at him in my mind's eye, and goose bumps prickled my arms. Oh yeah. I was attracted to him. How could I not be? He wasn't just hot—he was magnetic. A presence that was impossible to ignore.

I'd noticed him the moment he sauntered into the Alehouse. Because that was apparently how he moved. Jesse didn't walk—he sauntered. Maybe that was the only way to move in skinny jeans. Sean had certainly had a distinctive strut when he'd worn his. The memory of my husband stung, so I tamped it down and focused on the man who'd hung out at the bar for most of my shift.

Jesse had kept his head high when he walked—sauntered—and even when he'd been sitting at the bar. Probably to keep the long bottle-blond fringe out of his eyes. Whenever he had lowered his head—usually to scowl at his phone—he'd had to brush his hair back or at least toss it out of his face when he'd looked up again. It was such a smooth, practiced gesture, he probably hadn't even known he was doing it. I had, though. Even now, my fingers curled on the wheel at the thought of brushing his fringe out of his eyes or just letting the long strands slide between them.

And shit—I'd just missed my turn.

In my defense, I'd only lived here for the past three weeks. Small as Bluewater Bay was, it was still new and unfamiliar. I'd missed this turn twice the day I'd moved in, so I just told myself it was lack of familiarity with the town this time too.

On autopilot, I parked beneath my apartment complex, got out, and headed upstairs, mind still full of that cute blond with the wicked sense of humor and those intense blue eyes.

Chatting the evening away with him turned out to be a double-edged sword. As I walked up the stairs, his absence was as conspicuous as his presence had been at the bar. No wonder I hadn't objected when he'd wanted to stick around for a few hours. My boss got annoyed when people didn't order food or alcohol, but damn, the company had been nice.

And now it was gone.

At my front door, I sighed and found the right key on the ring. I put it in the lock, turned it, and pushed the door open. Same as I did each night after work. It was becoming a habit—one of those things I could do without much thought—but I couldn't say I was entirely *used* to it. Part of me wondered if I ever would be. Every time I walked into this place, a shiver went through me. Tonight was no exception. In fact, the chill was more pronounced than usual.

It wasn't that the apartment was cold or unnerving. It just . . . It wasn't *home* yet. My shit was all here, and I'd started putting a few things up on the walls to break up the sterile monotony of the place, but it didn't feel like home. It was too busy being empty and different.

As I locked the door behind me, I wondered for the millionth time if coming to this town had been a good idea after all. If I'd jumped the gun and moved too soon. After all, everyone had warned me not to make any major decisions for at least a year. Don't sell the house. Don't change jobs. Don't relocate. Don't get rid of anything, not even that hideous foldout bed in the guest room.

Maybe that made sense to everyone, but *everyone* didn't understand why I couldn't keep living in that house. And while I was at it, why I couldn't keep living in that town or keep working at that job. Everything had to go. None of it could wait an obligatory year to make everyone else feel better. At least I'd gone through the motions of selling the house, finding a new place, landing another job, giving my two weeks' notice, and all that other noise, even though I'd wanted nothing more than to walk away. *Everyone* was lucky I hadn't just tossed in a match and left.

Fact was, it had all reminded me too much of Sean, and not the good times I'd had with him. No, just the end. The long, agonizing months before that fucking disease had finally won. When being home had meant watching him slowly dying, and being at work had meant feeling guilty over not being with him. Plus, there'd been that crushing grief because he hadn't been there with me so we could pass in the halls and swing into each other's offices or have lunch together like we'd done since we'd started dating. Like we'd both figured on doing for years to come.

Nine months after Sean's death, I'd left Seattle and hadn't looked back.

"Okay, maybe don't wait an entire year, *but don't you think you're rushing into this?"* Fiona, my younger sister, had asked when I'd told her.

"Probably, yes. But the alternative is sitting here driving myself crazier. The sooner I get out of here, the better."

"But what are you going to do out there?"

"Scott says he knows someone who'll hire me as a bartender." I'd paused. *"I have to go. If I stay here, I'm going to lose my mind."*

She hadn't argued after that.

And now here I was.

Bluewater Bay wasn't exactly the other side of the world, but it was far enough to give me the change of scenery I desperately needed. No too-familiar skyline to make me cry in traffic. No Seahawks Stadium to take me back to the night we'd gotten engaged. No Mount Rainier in the background to remind me of when he'd still been strong and healthy and we'd taken that long, miserable, but somehow satisfying hike to the peak. Maybe someday I'd go back up there. See if our names were still in the book at the top.

For now, I was hunkering down on the north end of the Olympic Peninsula for . . . I didn't know how long. A while. Maybe a year or two. Maybe ten. However long it took to . . . Fuck, I didn't even know. Get over him? That wasn't going to happen.

Breathe again. That would be enough. Stay here until I could breathe again. Because I didn't think I'd really done that since my husband's diagnosis.

Not until . . .

Until tonight.

As I leaned against my apartment door, my head spun. Fuck, I *was* breathing again. I'd connected with someone, if only for a few hours, and . . . Yeah. Breathing.

I closed my eyes and exhaled slowly, taking a moment to savor this unfamiliar feeling of not being weighed down by grief. Oh, the grief was still there, and depression was still an invisible anvil on my shoulders, but the weight was lighter tonight. Still heavy, still painful, but not as immovable as it had been the past several months.

And all because a cute blond kid was stood up tonight. Funny how things work out.

I opened my eyes and pushed myself off the door and farther into my empty apartment.

Though I was nowhere near unpacked, I had finally finished arranging my furniture, and the place didn't feel as claustrophobic as it had when I'd moved in. The couch and entertainment center seemed to expand the living room walls, giving me a bit more elbow room, though this apartment could only feel so big, especially after the three-bedroom house I'd lived in before . . .

Before I'd moved here.

I slung my jacket over the back of the couch, dropped my wallet and keys on the counter, and continued down the short hallway to the bedroom, all the while trying to ignore how cramped the place still felt. I hadn't lived in an apartment since my college roommates and I had wedged ourselves into that godawful shithole twenty years ago. It would be different now, though. Once I got used to the place, it would be different. No roommates, for one thing. Plus it was a much nicer complex. A little small, but I wasn't sure I could deal with more empty space than a two-bedroom apartment had to offer. Not until I'd fully adjusted to being on my own again. Baby steps.

While I changed out of my work clothes, my mind wandered back to Jesse. How did my evening with him fall into line with the baby steps I'd been taking? Had he strolled into my life, given me a desperately needed breakthrough, and then moved on? Most likely. And that was okay. It was what I needed. What he'd needed too, apparently—Jesse had been lonely and I'd been grateful for the company. Maybe we'd been a little flirtatious here and there, but it didn't have to mean anything beyond two guys passing an evening together.

It was a good thing, I told myself. It meant there was hope that my libido might come back. If I could feel attraction, then maybe I could eventually work up whatever it would take—courage? strength?—to act on it. And if I still had the capacity to be attracted to someone, maybe there was a chance I could connect emotionally too. Even if it didn't happen anytime soon, the possibility of it happening at all was a relief.

Right now, I didn't need to do anything except enjoy the fact that tonight had happened. Let the mental image of Jesse make me grin like an idiot. Let the thought of his smile give me goose bumps. Let our evening at the bar wake something up in me that had seemed like it was dead and gone. Everything else would happen in time if it happened at all.

Baby steps, I reminded myself. *Baby steps.*

My best friend, Scott Fletcher, lived in Bluewater Bay—that was why I'd picked this town for my new start—and he came over the next night to see how I was settling in. He'd offered a million times to help me unpack, but I insisted on handling it myself. I was still drowning in a sea of boxes, but I'd started making some headway, and I'd finish it all eventually. The bedroom was unpacked. The kitchen was . . . not.

Fortunately, the good Lord had given us a thing called pizza delivery, and in no time, a couple of medium pepperonis were on their way. When they arrived, we ate like college kids: with paper plates and using boxes as tables. I'd also been to Your Daley Bread—the general store up the street—earlier to get the basics, and there'd been enough room in my basket for a six-pack.

I handed Scott a cold beer. "So where's Jeremy tonight?"

"Working. Any time Anna leaves the house, he's gotta be there."

"That must get tiring for both of them. And you." Jeremy was the bodyguard for one of the bigwig directors/producers at the *Wolf's Landing* set in town, so he was constantly busy.

"Eh." Scott shrugged as he took a swallow of beer. "I knew what I was signing up for. And she's a bit of a homebody these days anyway, so he gets a lot more nights off now."

"That's a plus. Does he still like the job?"

"Oh yeah." He chuckled. "I'm pretty sure he and Anna keep each other in line."

"Somebody has to, right?"

"Exactly."

I just laughed.

As we continued shooting the breeze, I propped one foot up on an unopened box, resisting the urge to groan as I rubbed at an ache in my knee. Go figure—I'd spent the day very carefully lifting with my legs so I didn't fuck up my back, and now my knee was pissed off. When the hell had I gotten old? No telling, but it was going to make tomorrow's shift *loads* of fun.

From the other end of the couch, Scott studied me, and I knew the question was coming before he said it. "How are you doing?" There was no point in pretending he was asking about my knee.

"I'm . . ." I stared into my beer, "I'm getting out of bed every morning. That's something, right?"

"It is. Not a small something, either."

From anyone but him, I might've taken that as an empty platitude. Except Scott understood. In fact, it hadn't been just the job and the promise of an escape that had drawn me to Bluewater Bay. If there was anyone on the planet who could understand what I was dealing with, it was Scott. He was a counselor by trade, and he'd spent a lot of time with me in Seattle during my husband's final months, but he also knew firsthand what it meant to lose a partner.

Though the deaths of our respective husbands couldn't have been more different, Scott and I got each other in ways no one else seemed to. Especially since Sean and Nathan had both been much too young. I suspected that in the last year, Scott had seen a lot of his past in my present. His world had dropped out from under him in the blink of an eye, and mine had gone in a slow shatter until the splintering crash at the very end, but we'd both been to that dark, broken place. The fact that he'd made it to the other side had been the only thing to pull me through some of the worst moments.

After Nathan's death, Scott had never been the same, but he *had* finally found some happiness again. First in his life on his own and in his career, then with Jeremy, the man he'd been engaged to for a while now. I just tried not to think about the fact that it had taken him a good twenty years to get there.

Not that I was in any hurry to find another partner. All I wanted was for the pain to stop. Or lessen. I'd take that.

Since last night with Jesse, it had been better. And worse. And better. I was hopeful now that there was a light at the end of this long dark tunnel, but I also felt guilty for being attracted to someone. I was ashamed of how much Jesse had been on my mind since he'd left the bar, but I was encouraged by it too. I felt better, but did I have any right to? I felt worse, but did that make any sense?

There was really only one thing I was sure of these days, and that was that grief was a roller coaster. The kind of twisting, turning, not-entirely-stable roller coaster no safety commission would ever approve, but somehow got built anyway, and once you were on it, you weren't getting off until—

"Garrett?"

I shook myself and met my friend's gaze again. "Sorry."

"It's all right." Scott grimaced sympathetically. "Spacing out sometimes is part of the process too."

"Great," I muttered into my beer. "At least that's normal."

"It will be for a while." He paused. "So, you got the job down at the Alehouse?"

I nodded, grateful for the subject change. "Yeah. I started last Monday. Could've done it sooner, but I wanted a little time to get a handle on all this shit." I gestured at the boxes with my beer bottle.

"Makes sense. Are you absolutely sure you don't need a hand with what's left? I'm happy to help, and I know Jeremy would be too."

"I think I've got most of it." Gingerly kneading my knee, I added, "I'll keep it in mind, though. Thanks."

While we grazed on the remnants of the pizzas, Scott's eyes kept darting toward something, and after a moment, I realized he was looking at my left hand. Probably at the third finger. Which was bare. The tan line was hardly visible anymore.

When he caught me catching him, he cleared his throat. "I'm, uh, surprised you took your ring off." He paused, then quickly added, "A lot of people hold off. Part of the grieving process, and . . . anyway. I just noticed, that's all."

I thumbed the divot the gold band had left. "I stopped wearing it a couple of months before he died. It, um . . . I lost too much weight, so the ring kept sliding off."

Scott gave a slow nod. "Yeah, I noticed you'd dropped a few pounds." His eyebrows pulled together. "Are you doing okay? Healthwise?"

I nodded. "Better, yeah. Another couple of months of this"—I held up the half-finished pizza slice—"and I'll probably be back to my fighting weight."

"Good. Good." Scott smiled faintly. It faded, though, and he quietly said, "You know if you need anything, all you have to do is call, right?"

"Yeah. Thanks." I debated telling Scott about Jesse, but ultimately decided against it. Scott would analyze it because that was what he did, and I wasn't sure I wanted it analyzed. It was probably nothing anyway—just a momentary connection to help me snap out of my funk. Besides, I'd enjoyed it, and I didn't want it picked apart.

So I let it go, and we kept working on the beers and pizza.

Scott left a while later, and I was again alone in my new apartment. At least it didn't feel quite so empty now. I'd put a few more pictures up too, which went a long way toward making the whole place seem less like a sterile void.

I let my gaze drift to a framed photo of a ferry silhouetted against a purple and orange sunset. Sean had taken it during an outing to Mukilteo Beach when we'd been dating. He'd rarely gone anywhere without his DSLR around his neck and had refused to use his phone for anything other than the odd snapshot or selfie. It hadn't been good enough for *real* photography.

Maybe not, but I had some gorgeous photos on my phone that I'd taken when he wasn't looking. More and more, I was glad I'd grabbed those stealthy candids.

There weren't any photos of him or us on the walls yet. That would come with time. For now, the ferry and sunset were enough. It wasn't the only picture I'd put up today, but it was like a focal point in the room. A comforting one. Enough of my past that I didn't feel completely lost, and enough of Sean that I didn't feel completely alone, but not so much that I cracked under the weight of it all.

Gazing at it now, I decided I was going to be okay. New place. New town. New job. Plus an old friend nearby I could lean on. The adjustment was going to take time, and there was still plenty of grieving to be done, but yeah, I'd made the right move. This was where I needed to be. It was all right that it would be a long road. I had someone here who'd been down it. Someone who could reassure me—from experience—that things would get better. He'd made it, and so would I.

And as a bonus, someone else had sauntered into my world, shocked my libido back to life, and given me a ray of hope I hadn't known I'd needed. Moving on wasn't just some pipe dream anymore. For the first time, it felt like something that might happen.

I took a deep swallow of beer, then toasted the photo with the bottle.

I'm gonna be okay, Sean. Just like I promised.

CHAPTER THREE

JESSE

"Hey, boss lady?" I poked my head in through the open doorway of Lydia's art room in the back of the comic book shop. "Could you please do something about your husband before I kill him?"

Lydia looked up from her electronic drawing pad. "Well, if you're going to, I wouldn't want to interrupt."

I glared at her. "You want to be the one to tell Ian?"

Her lips quirked, and then she groaned as she pushed her chair back. "What's he doing this time?"

"Just being..." I flailed my hands in the air and groaned.

Laughing, she walked past me and called out, "Simon, why are you upsetting the help?"

"Hey!" I huffed.

She glanced over her shoulder and winked.

"Bitch," I muttered.

In the shop, she halted with her hands on her hips.

Simon stood in the middle of the mess he'd been making by the shelves of role-playing games. His eyes flicked from me to her, and then he rolled them before going back to turning my carefully arranged display into an unmitigated disaster. "Oh, come on. It's not that bad."

"Simon. Sweetheart." She approached him carefully like she would a skittish animal. "What are you doing?"

"I'm putting the Mars III books and expansions closer to eye level. They're damn near on the floor, so nobody is seeing them, and if we don't start moving more, the company's going to pull our distributor status."

I cleared my throat. "So you're going to drop the D&D packs down below eye level?"

"People will find D&D," Simon said. "They come in here looking for it. Mars III?" He pointed at the packages surrounding his feet. "We need those where people can see them because otherwise they don't even know they exist."

Lydia turned to me. "He does have a point."

"I know." I sighed. "I know, and . . . Okay, look. If you want to redo a display, be my guest. But must you do it half an hour before closing time? Because we both know you're going to fuck it up, and I'm going to have to *un*fuck it."

She smothered a laugh and shifted her gaze to her husband. "And *he* has a point too."

Simon shot her a good-natured glare. "I'm not that bad."

"Of course you're not, sweetheart." She patted his arm. "But maybe now isn't a good time. I mean, Jesse's right—it's almost closing time, and we're going to be a madhouse tomorrow, so we can't afford to have a display all . . ." She gestured at it.

"Tomorrow?" Simon furrowed his brow. "What's tomorrow?"

Lydia and I both groaned. She face-palmed.

Before I could tell him, he grimaced. "Oh shit. The *Space Villager* expansion."

"Uh-huh," Lydia said.

Simon sighed, and when he turned to me, his cheeks colored a little. "Okay. Okay." He showed his palms. "You were right."

"I know." I scowled at the mess. "But what about all of this?"

Lydia glanced back and forth between us. "Tell you what." She faced me, eyes full of *Please don't be mad*. "You go ahead and take off for the night, but we'll still pay you for the full shift. Then tomorrow morning we can both set up the *Space Villager* display before the hordes show up for the launch."

I pursed my lips. "So you want me to come in early?"

Her brow pinched. "Could you? I'll buy coffee."

I shot her my best petulant look. "Good coffee? From Stomping Grounds?"

"Of course." She gave a long-suffering sigh. "I'll even get you one of those blended abominations you like."

A grin tried to come to life, but I fought it hard, the corners of my mouth probably visibly twitching. "With whipped cream?"

"Yes. *And* chocolate sprinkles." Her forehead creased. "So, I'll see you at seven?"

Seven? God. Even chocolate goddamned sprinkles couldn't get me out of bed before nine. But Lydia's *pretty please?* face could, so with a melodramatic sigh, I nodded. "Fine. Seven." I wagged a finger at her. "But if they skimp on the sprinkles this time—"

She laughed. "I'll make sure they don't." Turning a bit more serious, she added, "Thanks, hon. Now get out of here." She gestured at the display she and Simon would be putting back together tonight. "I don't want any witnesses."

Simon's eyes widened.

I just laughed and went in the back to get my jacket and keys. It was a relief, not having to stick around tonight. Coming in tomorrow morning would suck donkey dick, but it was better than me and Simon butting heads after a long shift, especially over something like displays.

And the fact was, I was a sucker for Lydia. I adored her. All she had to do was bat her eyes and say *Pretty please*, and . . . fuck my life, but I'd come in at three in the morning if she asked me to. She was like the big sister I'd never had and could never say no to.

For that matter, I'd pretty much bend over backward for Simon too. As much as we could drive each other crazy, he was a damn good guy, and he generally did have his shit together at the shop. When it came to things like finances, he was always on point. He'd even helped me with my taxes a few times, and when I'd bought my car last year, he'd come with me and strong-armed the dealership into giving me a way better deal. I loved the guy. I really did.

His wife and boyfriend were the creative ones, but Simon had the occasional moments of . . . well, attempted creativity. He'd get a hair up his butt and decide to "improve" something, which meant I'd be getting overtime that week while I unfucked it.

There were days when I'd get a headache from rolling my eyes at him, but I wouldn't trade this job for the world. He and Lydia were great people and solid bosses. I just wouldn't be me if I didn't butt heads with my boss once in a while. Or if I didn't do my level best to drive Simon insane.

So tomorrow morning, I'd be here at ass thirty to help make sure the displays were pristine and perfect in time for the *Space Villager* fans to show up and trash the place. Okay, that wasn't entirely fair. The gamers weren't destructive or anything, but when a new game or expansion released—especially *that* game—they'd crash through the front door as soon as we turned on the Open sign, and they'd descend on End o' Earth like a hurricane of enthusiasm. A few casualties were inevitable.

I smiled to myself as I walked out of the store. Never a dull moment in that place, and I wouldn't have it any other way.

On my way to my car, I hesitated, then looked back over my shoulder. Not at the comic book store—at the Alehouse.

It was a Friday night. Garrett was undoubtedly working—they usually had all the bartenders working on Friday and Saturday nights. Would it be weird if I wandered in for a beer? Wasn't like I could stay late tonight, but . . . one beer? Maybe two?

I chewed the inside of my cheek. I was a regular. No one would look twice if I walked in. Well, aside from some of the other regulars who didn't particularly like me prancing all over the place's masculine vibe, but fuck them. I just didn't want Garrett to think I was stalking him.

Oh what the hell? If showing up twice in the same week made me a stalker, then half their clientele qualified, because the same people were in there pretty much every time I came in. I wasn't convinced they ever left. Granted, they weren't there to ogle one of the bartenders, but still. The alternative was going home and depressing myself on hookup apps, because Charlie's bullshit still stung.

Just the thought turned my stomach to lead. I hadn't even been able to look at the apps the last couple of days because I couldn't get the other night out of my head. From experience, I knew it would be a week or two at least before my skin stopped crawling.

My gaze drifted to the Alehouse again, and I gnawed my lip. Hanging out with Garrett that night had staved off that feeling. I'd still been hurt and angry, still wanted to choke Charlie for making me feel gross, but talking to the hot bartender had tempered all that shit. Garrett had been exactly what I'd needed, and I'd been lucky enough to be in the right place at the right time to find him. Was I an idiot for thinking Garrett would want another round of talking while I drank? I swallowed, suddenly nervous. Suddenly shy. Suddenly full of reasons why I was pathetic and stupid and needy and—

And really, really curious about the man who'd salvaged my fucked-up evening with a sexy smile and endless conversation.

Fuck it. Wasn't like I had anything to lose.

So I took a deep breath and headed for the Alehouse.

CHAPTER FOUR

GARRETT

The Alehouse had a rhythm to it, even on chaotically busy nights like this, and I was confident I'd found my groove. The bar was getting more familiar, and I was struggling less to remember where things were. When I needed something from the back room, I could usually find it without much trouble. I didn't have to hunt down the margarita salt or ask my boss—again—where we kept the cocktail straws. I had my station set up the way I wanted it, with the bottles in my well arranged so I didn't even have to look at the labels when I reached for them. I'd learned how low I could let my ice bin get before I damn well better go get some more.

Most of the things I'd learned from my college bartending days had come back too. I could still mix quite a few drinks off the top of my head instead of checking the computer for the exact recipe. During the week, most people just ordered beer anyway, but on the weekends, we attracted more than just the usual sports bar clientele. That crowd ordered Long Island Iced Teas, daiquiris, Kamikazes, Sex on the Beaches, and plenty of shit I'd never heard of. At first, I'd been overwhelmed and worried I'd never keep all the drinks straight, but I was doing all right. And anyway, I was pretty sure I'd botched a couple of Hurricanes earlier tonight, putting in a little too much spiced rum and completely forgetting the lime juice, and I hadn't heard any complaints.

I paused between mixing drinks and dabbed some sweat from my forehead with a towel I kept handy for that purpose. Then I started pouring the three drinks table five had ordered, repeating the names in my head as I went.

Beam on the rocks. Dirty martini. Neat Scotch.

Even as I poured the Jim Beam over the ice, more orders were coming in, so I added them to my mental list.

Dirty martini. Neat Scotch. Whiskey sour. Miller Light.

Just like in my college days, the busy nights were a blessing. Made the time go by so much faster than wiping and rewiping the bar, glasses, and every other surface. Time to lean, time to clean, after all.

Not tonight, though.

Dirty martini—done. Neat Scotch. Whiskey sour. Miller Light.

I handed off the martini, the Beam on the rocks, and the neat Scotch to the server, and kept going as another patron ordered a Guinness.

Whiskey sour. Miller Light. Guinness.

The door opened like it had a million times in the last ten minutes, and I looked over.

And my hands stopped.

Jesse.

Whiskey sour. Miller . . . Light? Or was it High Life—crap. Light. It was Light. And then a Guinness. Right?

I shook myself and focused on pouring and mixing. Or, well, I did until I glanced up again and saw him coming toward my section of the bar. Though it was a busy night, most people preferred booths and tables, so there were quite a few open barstools. He could have taken any one of them, but he walked right past them like he didn't even see them and took the last empty seat at my end of the bar.

"Hey." I flashed him a quick smile. "Give me a sec."

"No rush." His smile erased the orders I'd been repeating in my mind. Didn't just scramble them—completely erased them like they'd never been there at all.

For a few panic-filled seconds, anyway. My brain recovered, and . . .

Whiskey sour. Miller Light. Guinness.

Once those were done, a few more orders came in, and I managed to keep them straight as I slowly adapted to Jesse being here. His presence tingled at the edges of my awareness even when I wasn't looking at him, and every time I did glance his way, that tingle became a crackle. Somehow, I didn't drop a drink or fuck up an order.

As I put a couple of beers up for the waitress to take to a table, I glanced at Jesse. "What can I get you?"

"Uh..." He jumped like I'd just put him on the spot. "I'll..." He shook himself. "A Coke on the rocks is good. Thanks."

Well, that was easy enough. I wondered briefly why he came into a bar so often if he apparently didn't drink, but I didn't have time to give it much thought.

I couldn't stop to chat after I'd put the Coke in front of him. Not with so many drink orders coming my way. He didn't seem to mind, though. And he wasn't exactly focusing on the game on TV or looking at his phone. Every time I glanced at him, he was watching me.

Mercifully, there was a lull after a while. It wouldn't last long, but I'd take it, and as soon as I was sure everyone had their drinks, I stopped in front of him.

"Sorry about that," I said.

"Sorry? About doing your job?" He shook his head. "It's cool. Don't worry."

I couldn't help smiling, and probably looked like a fucking idiot, but whatever. "Well, it's good to see you."

He smiled back, and even the neon glow couldn't mask the color blooming in his cheeks. "Yeah. You too. I, uh..." he cleared his throat, "Got off early. Thought I'd come in." Beat. "For a drink."

"Well, you're in the right place." I smirked as I gestured at the rows of bottles behind me. "We do drinks here."

Jesse laughed, and... wow. I hadn't realized my heart was capable of somersaulting like that, never mind just because of a shy smile and a soft sparkle in someone's eyes. Well, okay, I had known it was capable. Just didn't think I'd ever feel it again.

Holding up his glass, he said, "I might get something stronger after I finish this one." He glanced around the bar. "Except you'll probably get busy again soon, so maybe I should go ahead and order it."

I shrugged. "It's up to you. Just, fair warning—the orders come in waves sometimes, so don't take it personally if I have to dash off."

"I won't. I promise," he said. I must not have looked convinced, because he added, "We get rushes over at the shop too. I get it."

"Gonna guess your clientele isn't usually shit-faced, though." I made a subtle gesture toward a couple of guys who were probably getting cut off soon.

Jesse laughed. "Not drunk, no. But sometimes stoned. Or high as a goddamned kite."

I raised an eyebrow. After a glance around to make sure no one needed me, I said, "Sounds like you've got some stories."

"*Oh*, yeah." He trailed his fingers up and down in the sweat on his glass. "You want to hear them?"

"Stories about people being high in a comic book shop? You better believe it. Do tell."

Mischief glittered in his eyes. "Well, we had a guy come in a while ago, and he was absolutely tripping balls on something. He's a regular, but whatever he was on that day?" Jesse whistled and shook his head. "Might've been spice or shrooms or something, but whatever it was, that was some powerful shit."

"Yeah?" I grinned, leaning on my hands on the bar. "How'd that go?"

"It was fine at first. He was sort of spacing out and wandering around muttering to himself, but then he got to the display of sculptures. We—" He paused, lips quirking. "We sell sculptures by Ian Meyers, the guy who does the mini sets they blow up on *Wolf's Landing*. Anyway, they're really realistic. So this dude is out of his head on whatever, and he stops in front of that display." Jesse laughed heartily. "He was *convinced* they'd come alive."

"No shit?"

"No shit."

"So what did he do? Freak out?"

Jesse nodded. "He started clawing at the case and screaming at us that we needed to open it. That they were going to suffocate and die. Next thing we know, he's bawling on the floor that we're killing the dragons."

My jaw dropped. "Wow."

"Yeah. And I mean, we were all kind of rattled after that. High as he was, he could've really hurt himself or done some damage, you know? But he came in a few days later to apologize, and when we told him what he'd done, he thought it was funny. So . . ." Jesse raised his glass. "If he can laugh about it after the fact, so can I."

I chuckled. "Fair enough."

"My boss doesn't think so, though." Jesse grimaced. "The sculptor is his boyfriend, and he seriously panicked when he realized the guy was trying to break down the case." Into his glass, he muttered, "Thank God Ian wasn't there, or he'd have had a coronary."

"I might've freaked out too if I thought someone was about to 'liberate' my work."

"Me too. But it wasn't my shit, so . . ." He flashed a wicked grin.

I laughed. "Why do I get the feeling you keep your boss on his toes?"

"Me?" He put a hand to his chest and shot me one of those innocent looks that only the perpetually guilty could master. "I have no idea what you're talking about."

"Uh-huh." Jesus, he was adorable. And mischievous. No doubt a handful for whoever he worked for, and probably anyone else in his life. He reminded me of my husband in that respect. Sean had been a pistol and—

And I didn't want to think about him tonight, because I was feeling too good to let grief take over. The familiar heavy weight of the past year started pressing down on my shoulders, and I mentally flailed in search of a safer topic.

Across the bar top, Jesse brought his drink to his lips but stopped short. "You must have some stories from working in a place like this."

Somehow I kept my relief under the surface as I nodded. "A few, yeah."

Eyes locked on me, he took a sip. As he lowered his glass, he said, "Well? Let's hear 'em."

I chewed the inside of my cheek, running through the dusty old memories of my previous life as a bartender. "Nothing very exciting has happened at *this* bar." *Nothing yet, anyway, but if you keep coming back*—I muffled a cough. "Back when I was in college, though, I worked at a club in Seattle. Near the UW. And that place could get pretty wild."

Jesse tilted his head, raising his eyebrows expectantly.

I gave the Alehouse a sweeping glance, and when I was satisfied no one needed me right then, I started talking. "It was the usual shit, you know? Watching drunk people make asses of themselves. Trying to break up fights. My boss used to get bitchy when someone came into the place smelling like weed, but I didn't mind at all. Stoners aren't nearly as violent as drunks."

He nodded. "I believe that." His eyes darted around the room. "People don't get too crazy here, do they?"

"You tell me." I smiled. "Sounds like you've been coming here longer than I have."

"Okay, fair. And no, I've never seen anything all that wild in this place." He sipped his drink. "Well, except during a football game."

I groaned. "I am so not looking forward to football starting."

"Yeah. God help you if the Seahawks are having a shitty season."

"Uh-huh." I rolled my eyes. "When I worked at that place in the U-District, we had people who'd go crazy over the Huskies and the Seahawks. I mean, that was back when the Seahawks still sucked, so things didn't get quite as intense when they lost, but all it took was a couple of trash-talking Raiders or Steelers fans . . ." I shook my head.

Jesse grimaced. "Well, now that the Seahawks are playing decently . . ." He waved a hand at our surroundings. "Good luck."

"Yeah. Thanks." I glanced past him just as one of the waitresses was approaching the bar. "What do you need?"

"Three Coors and an order of medium wings with an extra side of bleu cheese."

"Got it." To Jesse, I said, "Give me a minute."

He nodded.

I sent the wing order back to the kitchen, then poured the beers and put them on the bar for the waitress to grab. Once she was on her way back to the table who'd ordered them, I faced Jesse again. "Sorry about that."

"You should be!" He scoffed haughtily. "Abandoning a conversation for two whole minutes to *do your job*. What the fuck, dude?"

I laughed, rolling my eyes again. "Uh-huh. So, stories . . . Oh! There was the time an ex-girlfriend crashed a bachelor party."

Jesse sat up, grinning. "Oh yeah?"

"Yep. They were pregaming before they went to the strip club down the block, but then his ex-girlfriend and her friends come wandering in. She's drunk, he's drunk, and the next thing we all know, they're screaming at each other about . . ." I waved a hand. "Hell, they were slurring so bad, I have no idea what they were actually saying. But she started crying, and he started crying, and that was right about the time the fiancée showed up."

Jesse's eyes bugged out. "Holy shit. Really?"

"I'm not even sure who called her and tipped her off, but she came storming in like she was ready to kill someone. It took two bouncers to hold her back, and one of them ended up needing stitches."

"Whoa." His jaw dropped. "What'd she do? Shiv him with a busted bottle?"

"Her engagement ring, actually. While she was trying to get to her fiancé, she backhanded the bouncer with that big rock." I gestured at my face, drawing an invisible line along the cheekbone. "Tore him up good."

Jesse shuddered. "Ouch. So what happened after that?"

"I don't even know, to be honest. I took the bouncer to the ER to get sewn up, and by the time I came back, you'd never know anything had happened." The memory made me laugh. "I was behind the bar and back to work for five minutes before someone stirred up some more chaos."

"What happened?"

I stared at the bar between us for a long moment as I tried to knock the dust off those memories. Finally, I shook my head. "I don't really remember. It's been a long time. That *might've* been the night we had to do the Heimlich on a guy who tried to swallow an eight ball, or it might've been—"

"Whoa, whoa, whoa." Jesse put up a hand. "Back up a sec. Someone tried to swallow an eight ball?"

Chuckling, I nodded. "That . . . actually happened a lot more often than you might think."

He stared at me incredulously.

I shrugged. "College town."

That got a sharp laugh out of him. "I guess what happens in the U-District, stays in the U-District."

"Unless it ends at the hospital, but yeah." I paused. "You know the U-District, then?"

"Yeah. When I lived in Ballard, I spent a lot of time in that area: the U-District, Green Lake." He smirked. "The People's Republic of Fremont."

I laughed. "Oh God. You know they still have that sign up, right?"

"Of course they do." Jesse smirked. "Pretentious fucking hipsters."

And didn't that describe the neighborhood of Fremont to a T.

I was about to make a comment about Fremont and its insufferable inhabitants, but some empty glasses a few seats down caught my attention. "Be right back." I took care of the refills, then returned to Jesse. "Sorry. Anyway . . . yeah. I'll try to remember some of the crazier stories from working in that bar. It's just been a few years."

His eyebrow rose, as did one corner of his mouth. "Define 'a few.'"

"Not to someone who was probably in kindergarten around the time I signed my first mortgage," I said dryly.

Jesse's wicked grin made my spine tingle, and he narrowed his eyes over the rim of his glass. "Oh, come on. You're not that much older than me."

I inclined my head, eyeing him.

He sipped his drink and smiled. "Okay, I won't try to make you *feel* old."

"Too late." I winked, and damn if he didn't squirm on his barstool.

He took another drink. "So tell me some more stories about that bar. It must've been entertaining as fuck, working in a place like that."

"It was. I can't say there was never a dull moment, but it could sure be interesting." I paused. "We had a lot of really shitty guys come in there, though. The ones who'd hit on women who were so obviously uninterested it was painful." I clicked my tongue. "I broke up a *lot* of those conversations by asking the guys why they were harassing my girlfriend."

Jesse straightened. "Seriously?"

"Yeah. They'd back the hell off as soon as they realized she belonged to another guy." Scowling, I shook my head. "Shouldn't have taken that, you know? But at least he'd be out of the poor woman's hair."

"Smart," he said with a slow nod. "Bet that earned you a few tips."

I laughed, nodding. "Yeah, it did. And half of them ended up asking me out too. Which . . ." My heart sank a bit at the memory. "That was actually how my coworkers figured out I was gay."

Jesse's eyebrow flicked upward.

I shifted my weight. "They saw me turn down enough hot women over the course of a year, they finally confronted me and asked. And . . . I told them."

He leaned in a little. "How did that go?"

"Not as bad as I'd expected. My coworkers didn't care. Not even the ones who I thought would have an issue." Scowling, I sighed. "My boss, however . . . Let's just say I'm pretty sure that's why I got fired."

"Fired?" he squeaked. "Really?"

"Different era. I probably should've just kept my mouth shut. I knew how my boss felt about . . . well, about guys like us."

Jesse's lips thinned and he huffed. "I think I'd have thrown something at him."

A laugh burst out of me. "Yeah, I'm pretty sure you would have. You don't seem like the type to take crap from people."

"Neither do you."

I sobered and gave the bar around us another glance, less to look for empty glasses and more to avoid his scrutiny for a second. When my gaze returned to his, I said, "Twenty-one-year-old me took a lot more crap than forty-two-year-old me does."

He gave me a subtle down-up. I couldn't decide if it was an appraising look or . . . or something I couldn't begin to read. He met my eyes again, and his smile screwed with my blood pressure again. "I can understand that."

Goose bumps prickled under my shirt and up into my scalp. Resisting the urge to squirm under his gaze, I said, "Time and experience do that, I guess."

Jesse's laugh was dry, bordering on wicked. "God help anyone who fucks with fortysomething me, then."

"Oh yeah?"

"Mm-hmm." He winked. "I've been told I'm 'challenging' already."

Is that right? I cleared my throat. "Good. That's good. Keeps people from walking all over you."

He snorted. "Yeah, people try, but they don't get very far. Which probably drives my bosses insane."

"Always does," I said with a laugh.

We bantered on about jobs and people and the odd story about workplace hijinks when they came to us. I moved away a few times to deal with customers, but just like I'd done the first time he'd come in here, I gravitated right back to him as if that was the obvious place for me to spend the evening.

All too soon, though, Jesse checked his phone and sighed. "I should go. I have to be at the shop extra early tomorrow."

My own disappointment surprised me, and I quietly said, "Damn."

"Tell me about it." He groaned. "They want me there—like physically *there* in the *shop*—at *seven*. In the *morning*." He clicked his tongue and shook his head. "They're slave drivers, I'm telling you."

I laughed. "Cruel bastards."

"Right? But at least the boss lady promised to bring me my favorite coffee, so . . ." He shrugged, and when he met my gaze, that wry little smile made the room ten degrees warmer. "I guess it's okay." He paused. "Do you mind me coming back another night?"

My heart did things I wasn't sure it had ever done before. Flippy, fluttery things. "I, uh . . ." I cleared my throat. "Sure. Of course." Damn it. I'd sounded way too eager, so I quickly added, "We love regulars."

Something in his expression fell, as if that wasn't the answer he'd been hoping for. With a slightly less enthusiastic smile, he said, "I'll probably go home and crash tomorrow night, but you'll see me again." Some hopefulness grew in his eyes as his forehead creased.

"I'm looking forward to it."

That brought back the missing enthusiasm, and I very nearly let go a sigh of relief that I hadn't fucked up that second chance.

"Okay. Well." He motioned toward the door. "I'll get out of your hair. But I'll see you soon."

"See you soon."

And yeah, I was definitely looking forward to it.

CHAPTER FIVE

JESSE

"**I** had an epiphany on my way to work." I clutched my travel mug as I waited for Lydia to unlock the shop's back door at stupid thirty the next morning. "It's a goddamned travesty that Starbucks doesn't have 7-Eleven sizes for their coffees."

She glanced at the mug in my hand. "That thing's practically a Super Big Gulp already. What more do you want?"

"I don't know." I took a sip. "A bucket, maybe?"

She laughed. "That's just what I need." She pushed the door open and waved me into the dark shop. "You and Simon bouncing off the walls from drinking coffee by the bucket, especially after I get you that monstrosity I promised you."

"We'd be awake, right?"

"Uh-huh." She locked the door behind us as I flipped on the lights. "And by the way, I'll swing into Stomping Grounds during lunch and get you that ... thing you drink. Just didn't have time this morning."

"Whatever." I made a disgusted noise before taking another sip. At least she'd texted me to let me know she'd been running late, so I'd had time to get myself some coffee, rather than letting me show up and find out there was no vat of sugar and caffeine waiting for me. After that disaster last winter when I'd tried to quit drinking coffee, she and Simon both took my addiction seriously—no one wanted to share space with an undercaffeinated Jesse.

While Lydia shut off the security system, I went to the shop floor, steeling myself to check the display Simon had been fucking with last night. To my surprise, it wasn't a complete wreck. She and Simon had apparently made a modest effort to do some damage control after I'd left, and the shelves he'd dissected were more or less organized now. Not quite to my standards, but it would do for the moment.

My boss appeared beside me. "How does it look?" There was a hint of trepidation in her voice. She and her husband called the shots around here, but it was no secret how much of a diva I was about displays.

"Not bad." I sipped my coffee as I turned to her. "No bloodstains on the carpet, either, so you guys didn't kill each other. Well done."

Laughing, she rolled her eyes. "Oh, come on. *You* two would've killed each other. Not us."

Okay, she had a point. The woman had infinite patience with both of the men in her house—her husband and their boyfriend, Ian—and had probably spent their long evening chatting while they'd reassembled the display. Hell, Ian might've even come by to help after he'd gotten off work. The packages and figurines were displayed artfully enough to suggest his influence.

So it was all good. I'd reorganize this later when I had more time, but the shop was in working order, nobody had throttled Simon, and I had coffee. Yep. All good.

"All right." She pointed toward the back room with her chin. "Let's get to it."

We dragged two of the big folding tables from the back and set them up in the corner of the shop closest to the door. This area was always empty unless we were having an event. It was one of Simon's crazy ideas—he'd had us rearrange the entire shop a few months ago so this area was wide open. We used the space for gaming tournaments, as well as for signings or release events.

The idea was to draw people in so Hunter Easton could sign their Wolf's Landing books or one of the actors could sign a photo, and then have them stand in a line that strategically snaked between the aisles in case they wanted to make an impulse purchase or three. It was incredibly effective. My coworker Dexy and I were always amazed at how much additional stuff people would have by the time they made it to the cash register. Simon might have been weirdly impulsive about when to wreak havoc on my displays, but he was damn savvy about getting merchandise into people's hot little hands.

That principle worked pretty well for game releases too—the more merchandise people walked past en route to the register, the more likely they were to have a sudden craving for the most recent Magic: The Gathering expansion or the latest and greatest Wolf's Landing swag.

Once the tables were out and draped with the plastic tablecloths provided by the game studio, we hauled out the boxes containing the expansion going on sale today. We were going to be busy, no doubt about that. *Space Villager* was a wildly popular MMORPG, and though the expansion was available online, there were some limited-edition figurines and swag packs for people who bought their expansions in stores. The hardcore fans wouldn't miss it.

As I sliced through the tape, I glanced outside. At least twenty people had already gathered outside, noses pressed against the glass, eyes wide and eager. Nearly all of them were decked out in *Space Villager* hats, T-shirts, and even sneakers, and most of them were clutching *Space Villager* travel mugs. Behind them, more fans were trickling down the sidewalk to join the growing crowd.

I suppressed a grin. Or at least tried to. Beside me, Lydia snorted.

"What?" I feigned innocence.

"You're going to end up on YouTube one of these days. You know that, right?" She was practically vibrating with barely contained laughter.

"I keep hoping." I let the grin happen. "Imagine what that would do to the shop if I went viral."

She covered her mouth, laughing harder. "You do you, baby."

"Oh. I will. I *so* will." Clearing my throat, I put the box cutter aside and casually turned so I was more or less facing the wide-eyed crowd outside. I made an exaggerated gesture out of opening the box, then dramatically turned away and shielded my eyes like I'd opened the Ark of the Covenant.

Lydia snickered. A few people outside laughed.

"One of these days," she said, "you really need to do this when Simon is here."

"Why? So he'll believe you when you tell him?"

"Yes! Exactly!"

"Nah." I shook my head. "I'd rather let him see it on YouTube." Okay so it wasn't intentional, but somehow the timing had always worked out so my other boss didn't bear witness to my prerelease setup shenanigans. Whenever Lydia insisted to him that it was true, I denied it, and he had no idea who to believe. If she tried to film me, I'd stop and do my job with nothing but decorum and professionalism.

No camera or Simon, though, so I leaned down to slowly—no, *seductively*—remove one of the *Space Villager* boxes, and held it up just enough to give the people outside a peek of its corner. Just enough to reveal the distinctive logo. Hand to God, a few of them licked their chops. Looking right at them, I made a big show of withdrawing the box as I ran my tongue across my lower lip. I locked eyes with a random person outside and slid my fingers up and down the colorful box like I was feeling it up. I snapped my hips to one side. Then the other. I sashayed toward the empty display, stretched out my arm, and dramatically placed the box in the middle of the table. A few people rolled their eyes, but most of them laughed or even applauded.

"You sure you don't need some music?" Lydia asked.

"Nope. I got this." And then I let loose, dancing like I was in a club as I took one box after another out of the package, turning the act of unpacking and arranging game expansions into the most ridiculously provocative maneuver I could manage without falling on my ass. Hey, if people were going to stare at me like a zoo animal while I set up a display, I was sure as shit going to have fun with it. And hell, it kept them entertained. I'd stood in enough lines like that—showing up at the crack of dawn for the latest game release—to know how fucking boring it could get.

The crowd outside was getting bigger by the minute, and with more people watching me, I played it up even more. I didn't even have to break my stride to open up the next shipment—Lydia took care of that for me before disappearing into the back and leaving me to it. The people outside egged me on—not that I needed it—and before long I was sweating like crazy and smiling like a fool while I swung around boxes of *Space Villager* like burlesque props. I seriously fucking loved my job.

"Jesse?" Simon's voice spun me around. He was watching me, arms folded across his chest and one eyebrow climbing his forehead. The expression on his face was probably supposed to be stern, but the way the corner of his mouth twitched, he was fighting really hard against a smirk. "What're you doing?"

"Um." I cleared my throat. "Unpacking the *Space Villager* expansions?"

"Uh-huh." His eyes flicked toward the crowd, who were laughing hysterically as I was "busted" by my boss. "I see."

"I told you he enjoys setting things up." Lydia appeared from between two aisles. "I swear this is half the reason people come all the way from Port Angeles and Sequim on release days."

Simon laughed, shaking his head. "Carry on, then."

"Oh." I winked. "I will."

Release days were chaotic as fuck, but they were fun. The enthusiasm that could knock over shelves and scramble displays was also infectious. Everyone chattered with everyone else about *Space Villager* and the rest of the shop's merchandise. I was literally getting paid to gush about games and comics and Wolf's Landing with people who were willing to line up at seven in the morning to get their hands on a game expansion. Didn't matter how tired I was today or how early I'd had to roll my ass out of bed—I felt great.

And I felt even better when Ian showed up with coffee from Stomping Grounds, especially since he was carrying a gigantic plastic cup overflowing with sprinkle-covered whipped cream. Technically Lydia was supposed to be the one to bring me my coffee, but I wasn't going to split hairs about her delegating it to her boyfriend.

I clasped my hands in front of me, mouth watering at the sight of the blended triple mocha. "Oh, you saint. Gimme, gimme, gimme."

"Only because your boss told me to." Ian tried to look put out, but we both chuckled as he handed me the cup. He wiped the condensation from the cold drink off on his jeans, then went to give Simon and Lydia their coffees. It wasn't unusual for him to bring them coffee, and it had become a running joke between us that he would bring some for me when I started living and sleeping with him like they were. Not that I would've been opposed to the idea. Dude was smoking hot.

But he had his hands full with them, and I had my hands full of sweet caffeinated bliss, and God yeah, this was a damn good day. I didn't even mind that I'd have to run an extra mile this afternoon to make up for some of the thirty-two million calories in every blissful gulp of—

"Hey, Jesse?"

I turned around and froze. Two words, one look, and my good mood ditched me. My skin started crawling and my stomach was suddenly heavy, my body weighed down by bone-deep fatigue.

Charlie hated *Space Villager*. He'd repeatedly expressed his disgust at how amateurish he thought the graphics were, which was ridiculous since the graphics on that game made *reality* jealous.

He wasn't here for the expansion, and my good spirits were gone. *Zero to "fuck my life" in point six seconds. Impressive, you dick.*

I took a breath. "What do you want?"

"I want to talk." He slid his hands into his pockets and looked at me through his lashes like the pitiful prodigal hero of a bad romantic comedy. "About the other night."

I pursed my lips. "No."

He straightened. "What?"

"I'm working. I don't have time for this." I motioned toward the throngs of people in the shop. "Especially not today."

"Well, don't you have a break or something coming up?"

I caught Simon's eye. His brow creased. He was fine with any of us having visitors in the shop as long as they didn't disrupt things, and he had precisely zero tolerance for anyone harassing us. His eyes said nothing if not, *Want me to kick him out?*

Yes, please. Or even better—have Lydia do it.

But I couldn't ask them to do that for me.

"We're slammed today," I reminded Charlie. "It could be a while."

He shrugged. "I can wait."

I didn't even try to hold back the frustrated groan. I'd hoped he would tell me never mind, walk out, and never come back. Should've known I wouldn't be that lucky.

"Let me talk to my boss," I muttered and stepped away before he had a chance to speak.

Simon left Dexy to handle the register. "What's going on?"

"He wants to talk." I ran a hand through my hair and sighed, wishing like hell my giddy, happy mood would come back. It felt like it had never been there at all. "Do you mind if I take my break?"

Simon glanced around the shop. "We've got things under control right now."

"But if you get busy again—"

"Then we'll handle it." He touched my shoulder. "If you need to go take care of something..."

"I don't know if I have time to dump his body in the strait."

Simon snickered and gave my arm a little squeeze. "Go. I mean it—we've got things under control."

I chewed the inside of my cheek and looked around. The *Space Villager* rush had died down enough for Simon, Lydia, and Dexy to keep things under control, but there would probably be another rush after lunch. If I was going to do this, I needed to either do it now or wait until my shift was over, which would mean spending the whole damn day fuming over it. Might as well get it over with.

"Okay. This shouldn't take long."

Simon nodded. No smart-ass retort about how it had better not take too long if I knew what was good for me, and I didn't like that. I needed this to be a minor enough thing for my boss to make a snarky remark or tell me it could wait until after work.

But he didn't, and I had to deal with it, so I slipped out the back with Charlie. The alley wasn't my favorite place in the world for this shit, but no way in hell were we doing this out on the sidewalk. I'd let customers watch me throw off my dignity and turn a setup job into a near striptease. They weren't going to watch me fighting back tears.

I wasn't even sure about doing it out here where one of my coworkers might hear something through the door. I knew how thin that door was—Simon and Ian might've thought they were being stealthy back here on that rare occasion they'd ducked outside, but oh, no. This boy had heard everything.

At least they were always doing something hot. This was going to be at best awkward, at worst a knock-down, drag-out screaming match.

So we walked a ways down the alley until we were almost to the road. We were behind a coffee shop now, and it was one of those really loud ones where they had to shout your mispronounced name over the music, chatter, and machinery. If anyone in there could hear us out here, I supposed we deserved to be heard.

We halted, and Charlie took a deep breath like he was about to launch into a rehearsed spiel.

"Why don't you just say it?" I growled. "We both know why you stood me up."

He stared at me, mouth still open. "I . . . Jesse, it wasn't—"

"Yeah, it was." I folded my arms tightly across my chest and shifted my weight. "Don't think I didn't notice how you wouldn't kiss me when you left earlier that day. I'm not stupid."

The blank, slack-jawed stare held for a second, but then he exhaled and shrugged. "Look, it was a shock, okay? What did you expect me to do?"

I blinked. "Uh, I don't know. Maybe something besides turn into a douche-nozzle?"

Charlie scowled. "Come on. It caught me off guard, you know? It's kind of a shock to find out you were making out with someone with HIV."

I pressed my lips together, trying like hell not to let fly everything that was coming to the tip of my tongue. When I was sure I could control my vocabulary and my tone, I quietly said, "Do you even know anything about HIV?"

"Of course." He shifted with obvious discomfort. "Which is exactly why I put on the brakes. That's some serious shit, you know? I didn't mean to hurt your feelings, but—"

"For fuck's sake." I pinched the bridge of my nose. "Charlie, you're a gay dude. You have sex with other gay dudes. How do you not know . . . I mean . . . how do . . ." I groaned in frustration—mostly because it was illegal to Batman-slap some sense into him—before I started ticking off the points on my fingers. "It's a manageable disease now. My viral load's undetectable. We could go *bareback* if we wanted to. There's—" I was about to make another point, but the way he turned green at the mention of going bareback halted me midbreath.

Throwing up my hands, I shook my head. "Forget it. I don't even know why we're talking about this." I turned to go.

"Jesse, come on." He grabbed my elbow to stop me. "Look, I'm sorry."

"Yeah, sure you are. So if I wanted to put you up against the wall and kiss you like we did that night on my couch . . .?"

He swallowed, the green in his face not fading in the least.

"That's what I thought." I jerked my arm away and kept walking. He didn't stop me this time.

I was barely halfway to the shop before he was deleted and blocked on my phone. Later, I'd do a little scorched earth with his social media presence too, but I needed to get to the shop and get back to work. There could be another rush at any moment, and Simon would have a stroke if he was short-handed. Or whatever. I just needed to be somewhere Charlie *wasn't*.

Shuddering, I jerked open the shop's back door. I shouldn't have come out here with him. I should've told him to fuck off and been done with it.

Instead of heading right to the busy shop floor, I paused to pull myself together. There was a lot of noise coming from the front, so another rush had probably started, and I prayed like hell everyone was too busy to come back here. I didn't need them seeing me fighting the urge to either cry or be sick. It didn't matter how well I knew the reality of my own disease; being reduced to a human biohazard was always an emotional sucker punch. One I'd never be fully prepared for, and one that would never *not* hurt.

Footsteps caught my attention, and I sniffed sharply before turning to see Simon stepping into the back.

He stopped and studied me. "You okay?"

I forced back the lump in my throat and nodded. "Yeah. Just, uh . . ." I waved toward the door. "Someone who won't be coming around again."

"That good or bad?"

I didn't have an answer. Charlie could take a long walk off a short pier for all I cared, but it still hurt like hell to know my friend was gone. To know he was grossed out by me. It didn't even matter how many guys I'd known—and slept with—who were aware that HIV wasn't fucking Ebola. All it took was one. And when that one was a friend . . .

Simon inclined his head. "Hey. What's going on?"

"Nothing." I brushed past Simon with a terse, "I'll be fine."

He sighed but didn't say anything.

And I was anything but fine.

CHAPTER SIX

GARRETT

"**G**arrett? You with me?"

I shook myself and turned to Scott. He eyed me from one of the folding lawn chairs on his condo's balcony. I was sitting in the other, and suddenly I didn't know how long I'd been staring out at the woods behind the complex.

Sitting up, I cleared my throat. "Sorry. I guess I zoned out."

He chuckled, gesturing with the joint we'd been sharing. "C'mon. This stuff isn't *that* strong." As if for emphasis, he took a drag and held in the smoke as he offered me the joint.

I waved it off. Apparently I'd had enough. Except I didn't think it was the weed. Normally, it didn't do much except lighten my head and relax me. I'd get a little stupid—take longer to pull thoughts together and longer still to articulate them—but that was about it.

So, no, I was pretty sure it wasn't the weed that had my mind floating away from Scott's balcony.

Scott turned his head and slowly blew out a cloud. "You're somewhere else today." He studied me through the thin smoke, narrowing his eyes a bit like I took some serious concentration. "You want to talk about it?"

I had to think hard about the question, and again, it wasn't the weed. Scott was one of the few people I could talk to about anything, especially my grief. Maybe it was his training as a counselor or the fact that he'd lost a partner too. Or it might've just been the way he was—he'd always been easy to talk to, even in the days before he'd gotten his training or experienced this kind of grief firsthand.

So if there was anyone I'd jump at the chance to talk to on those days when the grief tried to double me over, it was Scott.

Except the grief wasn't the . . . well, it wasn't the *central* issue today. Sean was never far from my thoughts and neither was the emotional shrapnel he'd left behind.

At the forefront of my brain, though, was Jesse. Twice he'd come into the Alehouse, passing the time at the bar and sipping a Coke while we talked about nothing.

I glanced at the smoldering joint, debating if I needed or wanted another hit. I'd probably had enough. Maybe. I'd give it a few minutes before I—

"You don't have to talk," Scott prodded cautiously. "You're just, uh . . . kind of out of it."

"Happens when you get me stoned, idiot."

He rolled his eyes and chuckled. "Yeah, okay. Your tolerance is easily as high as mine. Not buying it."

I laughed. Sitting back, I let my head rest against the sliding glass door. "There's, um . . . there's a guy."

Scott's chair creaked, and when I turned, he'd sat up. Eyebrows climbing nearly into his hair, he said, "Go on."

I looked out at the woods again. "I met him when he was in the bar one night. He was getting stood up, and we ended up talking until last call. And then he came back. To see me."

"Is that a good thing?"

"I'm . . ." I exhaled, my throat still burning from the smoke. "I think so, yeah." I faced him again, not sure how he'd respond.

A smile spread across his lips. "Well good." He watched me for a few long seconds, either studying me or giving his next comment a chance to break through the haze. "You think he's into you?"

"I . . ." It wasn't just the weed slowing my brain down. Even stone-cold sober I'd have struggled to answer him with any kind of certainty. "Maybe?"

The smile turned to a lopsided grin. "Or maybe I should ask: are *you* into *him*?"

I was nodding slowly even before I realized it. "I thought it was just friendly at first, but the way it made my night when he came in the second time . . ." I sighed, realizing a second too late how stupid I sounded. I was seriously a breath away from swooning.

So, of course, my conscience picked that moment to dump an icy bucket of guilt on top of my mood. I rubbed my tired eyes.

Scott's chair creaked again, and he put a hand on my knee. "You're worried it's too soon, aren't you?"

Lowering my own hand, I looked at him. "Am I that transparent?"

He shrugged, his expression completely serious. "I don't know about that, but I've been there, you know?"

I nodded again. My thoughts threatened to start wandering again, and I shook myself, not sure if it was the marijuana or just my own screwed-up head that had carried me away for a moment, and not sure how long I'd been gone. Clearing my throat, I sat back. "Sorry. But yeah, I'm . . . I don't know. *Is* it too soon?"

Scott half shrugged. "You're the only one who can make that decision."

"I'm not sure I'm ready to be trusted with a decision like that quite yet."

He gave my leg a squeeze. "If you're not ready, don't."

I pulled in a deep breath, tasting the faint sourness of lingering smoke on the air. "What if that means I'm letting a good thing pass me by?"

"Do you think you are?" Stoned or not, he was in therapist mode. No doubt about that. Analyzing this and me just like I'd known he would. I hadn't been ready for that the other night, but I welcomed it now—nothing like a joint and a half-baked counselor to sift through the jumbled shards of my mind.

"I don't have a clue. It's . . . I don't know." I scratched the back of my neck. "All he has to do is walk into the bar, and I've got butterflies." Hell, even saying it out loud sent them fluttering. "A *lot* of butterflies."

Scott smiled serenely. "Sounds like there's something happening, then."

"So what do I do?"

He shrugged. "Let it happen."

I searched his eyes. "But what if he's waiting for some kind of signal from me? I sucked at flirting even back before . . ." I swallowed. "You know me. Most of my relationships started with the other guy making a move. Or, you know, both of us being too shit-faced to care how smooth the other was."

Scott gave an intoxicated laugh. He'd witnessed me meeting a couple of my ex-boyfriends, and he couldn't explain any more than I could how things had progressed beyond slurred introductions and clumsy dancing to moving in together. Apparently, I was a hell of a lot more charming when I was drunk.

Sighing, I let my head fall back so I could stare up at the sky through gently swaying evergreen branches. "Maybe I should take up drinking again."

"Won't do you much good with this guy. If he comes into the bar and you're working, you can't be drinking."

"Point. Probably shouldn't come in on my off days and drink either."

"Exactly." He was quiet for a moment. When his chair creaked again, I watched him sit up and fold his hands in his lap, the lighter between them. "When he comes to the bar, what do you two do?"

"We just talk."

"What about?"

I shrugged. "Anything. Kid's kind of a comic nerd, so—"

"Whoa, wait. *Kid*?" Scott inclined his head. "How old *is* he?"

"I don't know." He'd said, hadn't he? "In his twenties, maybe? Can't be any older than thirty." It took a second—probably the weed this time—but the pieces fell into place in my head, and I exhaled. "Probably the same age as Sean. Give or take a year."

Scott said nothing.

Sighing, I looked up at the sky and branches again. "I wasn't looking, but damn . . . he's had my attention since he showed up at the bar the other night. He's cute as hell, and talking to him definitely makes my shifts go by faster."

"'Cute'? I've only ever heard you describe one other man you were interested in as 'cute.'"

I pursed my lips.

Scott's chair creaked. "I'm assuming he's not 'cute' in the grizzled biker manner of speaking."

I laughed. "No. I don't think Jesse could be further from that description."

"Mm-hmm."

I turned my head and arched an eyebrow. "What does 'mm-hmm' mean?"

He shrugged. "You tell me."

"Don't play counselor, Scott. If there's something on your mind, say it."

He watched me for a moment. "Just . . . you've always had a pretty distinctive type, you know? Right up until you met Sean."

My chest tightened, but I waved a hand. "What can I say? He showed me the light."

Scott didn't laugh. "I just want to know as your friend, not a counselor—are you into this guy because he really interests you? Or because you're trying to replace—"

"I couldn't replace Sean if I wanted to," I snapped.

Scott showed his palms. "I know. I know. But I guess what I'm asking is, are you looking for a real connection with someone new? Or are you looking for something you lost?"

"I'm not looking for anything. He was just . . ." I gestured as if Jesse were sitting right in front of us, "*there*. And the connection just happened. It had nothing to do with Sean."

"Okay." Scott nodded. "You know I'm only asking because I don't want you to get hurt, right?"

"Yeah, and I appreciate it. I really do." Sitting back, I exhaled. "But Jesse . . . he's not Sean." Though the more I thought about it, the more I got the feeling Jesse and Sean would've either been best friends or mortal enemies. Those tended to be the options when two people were so alike.

My skin prickled at the thought. It was stupid, though. The fact that Sean and Jesse were both on the feminine side didn't mean they were *alike*. Sean had hated being dragged into comic book shops. Jesse worked in one. It really meant nothing that they had some similar mannerisms, and exuded a similar charisma just by walking into a room, and had—

I shook myself again and threw a glare at the joint we'd mostly finished. Man, did that stuff make me space out. "I guess I'm nervous about dating again, and about . . ." *What if I am replacing Sean?* I waved my hand again. "Everything."

"It's all right," he said quietly. "And for what it's worth, no matter what, it's going to be terrifying the first time you date someone. Whether it's tomorrow or twenty years from now. So if you're freaking out, that doesn't necessarily mean you shouldn't do it. All it means is you're a guy sticking his neck out there and hoping he doesn't get hurt again."

Funny how "hoping he doesn't get hurt again" took on a whole new meaning these days. All my life, that had meant not wanting to be cheated on or lied to or deserted. What I wouldn't have given for that definition to still be the first one to come to mind.

I sat up and looked at him. "Good to know I'm not grieving wrong, then."

"No. You're not. And you're not moving on too soon or the wrong way or . . ." Scott absently turned his lighter over between his fingers. "If you click with this guy, you click with him."

"Except Sean hasn't been gone that long." *Why does it feel like he's been gone forever?*

"Garrett." He reached over and gave my forearm a firm squeeze. "If you're not ready to move on, then don't rush it. But if you are ready?" Another squeeze, gentler this time. "Let it happen. Don't do yourself the way I did."

I shuddered. It had taken Scott twenty years to find Jeremy after Nathan had been killed. I was pretty sure he'd gotten laid regularly, but he'd been too afraid of losing someone again to let himself get close to anyone. For two decades, I hadn't understood. For the last year? Oh yeah. I got it. The thought of going through this kind of hell twice was enough to give me more nightmares than I already had. I believed I could fall in love again. I didn't have nearly as much faith in my ability to go through this kind of *grief* again.

So maybe that was why I was worrying myself stupid. I was trying to find little pieces of Jesse that matched up with Sean so I could say, *Nope, he doesn't stack up*, and have a reason to move on, because that would hurt a hell of a lot less than what might happen. Which was probably totally irrational, but rational kind of went out the window when you'd watched your husband's casket get lowered into a hole in the ground.

"Like I said," Scott's voice pulled me back from my increasingly dark thoughts, "it's up to you if it's too soon or not. If you feel like it is, then by all means, don't push. But if you're ready, don't let anyone tell you you're not. Or that you shouldn't be."

Nodding, I swallowed. Then a heavy feeling settled in the pit of my stomach. "What if I think I'm ready, but I'm not?"

"That's okay too."

"But I don't want to hurt him, you know?"

"I know you don't. And I think most people would understand. Just be honest with him. If he's someone worth dating, he'll stick around as a friend anyway, and maybe you can make it work down the line."

I nodded again but said nothing. I didn't mention how my husband had weighed in on the possibility of me dating again after his death. I wasn't sure why I didn't bring it up. Maybe because the conversation had been excruciating in the moment, and even now, the thought of it made my throat tighten. Or maybe because I was afraid if I told Scott, he'd tell me in no uncertain terms I was being an idiot by holding back with Jesse. Which didn't make a lot of sense— Scott was never forceful with his advice—but nothing made much sense these days, so what the hell?

And for that matter, I didn't want to dissect the subject any further. I'd see how things went with Jesse. Not much more I could do right then. Maybe I was ready. Maybe I wasn't. Maybe I *was* latching on because he reminded me of Sean. And maybe he was just an incredibly attractive guy who probably had better things to do than spend time with a shell-shocked widower twice his age.

And maybe, just maybe, I was too fucking stoned to figure any of this out.

Turning my head toward Scott, I asked, "So how goes the wedding planning?"

Scott groaned. "If we're going to get into that topic . . ." He picked up the paper and weed and started rolling another joint.

I laughed. "That bad?"

"That bad." He scowled. "The guest list keeps getting bigger, which keeps making everything more complicated, and . . ." He paused to lick the edge of the paper to seal the joint. "I swear to God, half the *Wolf's Landing* cast and crew will be there."

"Oh, star-studded. Nice."

He shot me a glare. "Says the man who doesn't have to feed, accommodate, and entertain two hundred people and counting."

I gaped. "Two hundred? Seriously?"

He muttered something, then put the joint between his lips. He lit it, pulled in a deep drag, and held his breath as he passed the joint to me. I took some in too and held it until my eyes started watering. Then, slowly, we both exhaled. Renewed calm immediately settled over me. How much of it was the actual drug and how much was psychological, I had no idea, but it was pleasant either way.

Scott took the joint back and took another hit. After he'd exhaled some more smoke, he said, "It'll be fine. It's just . . . chaotic right now."

"I believe it." The memory of my own wedding and all the planning leading up to it made me seriously sympathetic. For once, it didn't make me sad either. That was probably the weed.

We leisurely smoked and talked as the midafternoon turned into early evening. He didn't have any appointments at his family counseling practice, and I didn't have to work tonight, so we had every intention of spending as much of today as possible reliving our high school stoner years. By the time I clocked in tomorrow afternoon, my head would be as clear as it ever was these days, weed or no, and I'd be able to do my job with ease.

This wasn't something we did all the time, and we were careful not to smoke in the house or at all when Scott's fiancé was home. The company Jeremy worked for had been cracking down on everything stronger than caffeine or NyQuil ever since one of their employees had fucked up on the job thanks to *being* fucked up on the job. Not good for a bodyguard. So, he couldn't partake anymore, and we made sure not to do it when he was there so he didn't get smoke on his clothes. And because it was just mean—those longing looks he'd give us while we smoked were kind of a buzzkill.

When Jeremy was at work and neither of us had to be anywhere for a while, though? Game on.

Eventually, Scott's phone buzzed, and when he looked at the screen, his glazed eyes lit up. "Looks like Jeremy's on his way."

"Party's over?" I asked with mock disappointment.

He laughed and offered me the mostly smoked joint we'd been slowly working on for the last two hours. I shook my head. He took a shallow drag, then snuffed out what was left of the joint. We sat out there for a while, until Scott was sure Jeremy would be home momentarily, and then went back inside. We both still smelled like marijuana smoke, so Scott changed clothes while I swapped my T-shirt for one I'd brought with me for this exact purpose. I put the smoky one in my car, then joined Scott in the living room.

Not long after, Jeremy came home, grabbed a beer, and sat beside Scott on the couch. He gave his fiancé a quick kiss, then made an exaggerated gesture of sniffing him. Grinning, he said, "You two been having fun?"

"What?" Scott eyed him innocently.

Jeremy rolled his eyes. He wrapped an arm around Scott's shoulders and kissed his cheek. "Stoners."

"Hey," I said. "Don't judge us."

"Oh, I'm judging you." He shot me what was probably supposed to be a glare, but all three of us laughed.

As we all sat there and talked—mostly Jeremy filling us in on his day—I was more relaxed than I'd been in a long time. Not high and loopy, but grounded. Collected. Like I always was after Scott had helped me get my thoughts in order.

I also felt better about Jesse and what might happen there. I didn't need Scott's permission to think about dating or hooking up with someone, but the advice helped. He was a good sounding board. Someone to remind me I wasn't disrespecting my late husband's memory.

Jeremy started to get up, jostling me out of my thoughts. "I'm getting some iced tea. Either of you want any?"

"No, thanks," I said.

Scott shook his head. After Jeremy had left the room, Scott faced me and offered a friendly smile. As he did, I realized he never smiled at me with pity. Not like everyone else who knew me. There was empathy there—and sympathy —but mostly he was soft and kind. A friend who knew I still existed as something besides a grieving widower. Up until recently, even I hadn't been so sure about that part.

"Thanks," I said, then realized I hadn't given him any context. "For the talk earlier."

"Any time. I just hope I didn't muddy the waters or anything for you."

"No, you just gave me some things to think about."

A moment later, Jeremy came back in and sat beside Scott with a glass of iced tea in his hand. They exchanged one of those looks that were forever passing between them. They were so ridiculously in love, and even the trials and tribulations of planning an ever-growing wedding hadn't begun to temper that. I was glad. Especially after all these years, Scott deserved to be this happy. And maybe that meant there was hope for me down the line too.

"You want my honest opinion right now?"

I looked at Scott, thinking he was asking Jeremy, but he was looking right at me. I straightened. "Oh. Um."

I hesitated. Even Jeremy fidgeted a bit, eyeing his fiancé. Scott was usually the type to just give his opinion, so that question was his warning I might not like what he was going to say. Or that I might not be ready for it.

I was curious, though, so I nodded.

Scott glanced at Jeremy, then met my gaze. "If Sean were here now, he'd be reading you the riot act for not already having that kid's number in your phone."

My gut clenched. Shit. No wonder he'd warned me. And he was right too. Sean had pretty much told me exactly that. "Even if he isn't my usual type? Or he's a bit too much like . . ."

Gnawing the inside of his cheek, Scott seemed to think about it for a moment. "Look, I'm not suggesting you marry the guy. But obviously there's some sort of chemistry or a connection. Maybe that's what you need right now. Just don't lose sight of the fact that you're still grieving, okay?"

I nodded. I moistened my lips, then offered a tight shrug. "And yeah, I know Sean would want me to pursue this, but I think he'd also be okay with me being cautious right now."

Scott's expression softened. "Probably. And I am too, believe me. Just . . . I guess what I'm saying is, be careful, but that doesn't necessarily mean to fight this or ignore it." He paused. "You *are* interested in him, right?"

I chewed my lip, mulling over the question despite the blazing neon *FUCK YES* inside my head, before I finally nodded. I'd already told him so, but it felt weird, acknowledging I was interested in a man. Like I had no right to be putting my sights on someone this soon, never mind someone who kind of hit the notes Sean had. At the same time, it was this huge relief that I still *could* want someone.

"Then go for it," Scott said with an encouraging smile. "And good luck."

"Thanks. I'll probably need it." I laughed dryly. "I'm not exactly the king of charm, you know."

They both laughed. Fortunately, they also let the subject go.

As the conversation moved on to other subjects, Jeremy rested his hand on Scott's leg, and a flurry of emotions jumbled together in my chest. I missed that kind of contact. For the last several months, I'd found myself hyperaware of the lack of Sean's hands on me or his absence beside me, but tonight, I caught myself longing for the contact itself. Maybe that meant I was finally accepting that I'd never have Sean against me again. Or maybe it was because someone else had piqued an interest I'd thought had been gone forever.

Not that it mattered. The bottom line was that there were wants and desires in me that were waking up again, and there was a man who was waking them up.

Whatever this was that had my heart fluttering every time I so much as thought of Jesse—and going utterly crazy whenever I saw him—wasn't something I could ignore. I didn't want to rush it or force it to happen faster than it wanted to, and I wanted to be careful, making sure I really was in this for Jesse and not someone to fill in for Sean.

My mind kept circling back to that last bit, but I dismissed it again. Jesse wasn't Sean. He couldn't be if I wanted him to be, and I didn't *want* him to be. I liked *him*.

And maybe I needed to make the effort to telegraph that to him. Not that I'd been all that great at communicating that sort of thing in the past. Hell, Sean and I never would have made a connection at all if Jose Cuervo hadn't scrambled our brains one fateful night.

With Jesse, there was no company party to give us an excuse to get shit-faced enough for a clumsy bathroom fuck, so I needed to figure out some other way to let him know he had my attention.

And maybe I had an idea . . .

CHAPTER SEVEN

JESSE

The day after Charlie torpedoed my good mood, I was still in a funk. I'd made it through the rest of my shift on autopilot. I'd slept—sort of—and still felt like shit. Even disinfecting my computer of all traces of Charlie hadn't helped. It had been kind of cathartic, but . . . meh.

Thank God I had my job to keep me busy, and it was definitely going to keep me busy today. The bosses must've known I needed something to occupy my hands and brain, because they'd left a long to-do list for me and Dexy. That or they just needed all this shit done. Either way, I wasn't bitching.

List in hand, I stepped out onto the shop floor in search of Dexy, who I found doing some paperwork by the cash register. "Hey, Dex." I gestured toward the back. "Boss-people said one of us needs to put out the new comic book issues, and one of us needs to rearrange the window display. Your choice."

Her lips quirked. "You're better at the displays, so I'll take care of the comics."

"Hooray!" The comic task was insanely tedious, and everyone knew I loved putting stuff in the windows. Probably more than I should have, from what my bosses had said, but whatever. Shelving displays were fun. Windows? Fuck yeah. And at least this was something creative, which had a shot at eventually cracking through the shittiness that had been weighing me down since yesterday. It hadn't cut through it yet, but once I was knee-deep in my project, I had no doubt I'd . . . well, maybe not feel great, but better.

Feeling a little less like shit on Charlie's shoe, I went into the back and put together a box of supplies. I had a few ideas for how I wanted to set this one up. Simon, Ian, and I had built some Wolf's Landing scenes out of LEGOs a few weeks ago, and they'd just been waiting for a chance to be displayed. Especially the one Ian had done of the World Tree. Trust him to make something cool to put my interrogation room and Simon's "some shit going down in the forest" scene to shame.

With Dexy's help, I moved the LEGO World Tree to the window. No way in hell could I move that thing myself, and we all would've had kittens if I'd dropped it. I was pretty sure Ian was still traumatized from his actual set piece being destroyed by a couple of stuntmen horsing around on the *Wolf's Landing* set, and I didn't want to be the one to tell him about a casualty like this.

Once the World Tree was in place, I made another trip to the back to get my box of supplies and the LEGO sets Simon and I had built. I checked to make sure I had everything, then hoisted the heavy and somewhat imbalanced box into my arms.

As I crossed the shop floor toward the window, the door opened, and out of habit, I looked.

Just in time to see Garrett walk in.

And damn if the box of display supplies didn't slide right out of my hands.

Of course, I instinctively tried to catch it instead of letting it drop straight down. I got one hand under it, the other not so much, and instead of landing upright, the box somersaulted. Shit went *everywhere*. In the space of two seconds, the gray industrial carpet was littered with office and craft supplies, figurines, a strand of Christmas lights, and at least a million LEGOs. Plus the Altoids tin I used for pushpins had come open, so there were colorful pins scattered all over the place too.

Yeah, that was so what I needed today.

Our eyes met over the mess. Garrett raised his eyebrows like, *Uh, what now?*

I made jazz hands. "Yay! Confetti!"

He snorted. "I must be just in time for the party."

"Yes, you are." Chuckling despite the warmth in my cheeks, I bent to pick up what was left of the LEGO interrogation room I probably should've glued together like Simon had suggested. But seriously, who glued LEGOs together? Where was the fun in that? Besides, now that it had broken, I'd have no choice but to rebuild it. On company time. God, I loved my job.

To my surprise, Garrett crouched beside me and started helping. He collected the rolls of two-sided tape and some markers and put them in the box. Then he held up a pair of scissors. "They let you use these?"

"Hey!" I laughed and held out my hand. "I'll have you know they let me use all kinds of sharp shit."

"Probably against our better judgment." Simon's voice turned both of our heads. He surveyed the mess. "What's ... uh ..."

"It's part of the new display." I held up a handful of LEGOs and some pushpins. "We make people walk over LEGOs and thumbtacks, and if they make it, they get a discount."

His eyebrows rose.

"What?" I shrugged. "I saw it on Pinterest."

Garrett snickered as he carefully picked up some pushpins and collected them in his other hand.

Simon gave me a *really?* look—I got those daily—then rolled his eyes and showed his palms. "I don't even want to know. Holler if you need a hand." With that, he returned to the back, where he'd been working on payroll or something.

Garrett and I made quick work of containing the disaster, then we both stood. I toed the box aside, and now that I wasn't distracted by cleaning up the floor, I realized ... Garrett was here. In the shop. And sometime in the past few minutes, between the moment he'd walked in and now, that disgusted and disgusting feeling from yesterday's confrontation with Charlie had dissipated, replaced by something a lot stronger and a lot more pleasant.

It was the first time I'd seen Garrett in the daylight. The white in his dark hair was less dramatic now. There must've been a black light somewhere in the bar that had picked out the white and made it seem more striking. The dim light of the Alehouse had also muted some of his features, and while his gray was subtler, the lines on his face were more pronounced now, adding a few years to him I hadn't noticed before. He'd said he was forty-two, but he looked a few years older than that. Why that made him even more attractive to me, I had no idea, but I wasn't questioning it.

The multicolored neon hadn't done his eyes a damn bit of justice, either. I'd sworn they were just an unremarkable shade of brown. Here in the sunlight that poured through the shop's front windows, they were a richer color—almost coffee black with some warmer undertones. Holy fuck, but a man could get lost in eyes like that.

Which I was doing.

By way of staring.

Like an idiot.

I cleared my throat. "Um. So. This is unexpected."

"Yeah, I . . ." He slid his hands into the pockets of his jeans and looked around the shop. "You mentioned you worked here, and I realized I've never been in before. I was curious about it." Some tension crept into his posture. "That's, um . . ." His eyes flicked back to me. "That's not weird, is it?"

"No, no. Not at all. Just a surprise." Okay, it was kind of weird, but not in a bad way. "So are you into comics?"

I fully expected a sheepish shrug and an admission that he hadn't picked up a comic since he was ten, but he actually nodded. "They're mostly in storage right now until I find a bigger place, and I haven't kept up with some of the more recent series, but I've got a pretty solid collection."

"Yeah? Marvel or DC?"

"Both. And I'm kind of a sucker for the indie stuff too."

Somehow, I didn't swoon. "Oh, a man after my own heart." I added the wink before I could stop myself, and the sudden pink in his cheeks told me it had come across a lot more flirtatious than I'd intended it to. But he didn't seem hostile to it, so I made no apologies. A guy who could reset my mood after I'd spent twenty-four hours feeling sorry for myself over whatshisname? Oh yeah, I'd flirt and I'd fucking *own* that shit.

Clearing his throat, he looked around the store. "I did some D&D when I was a teenager too, but all the games are so . . ." He eyed the RPGs. "They're all so different now."

"We have D&D. I didn't think you were a gamer."

"Well, like I said—when I was a teenager."

"I didn't think they had RPGs in the 1930s."

"Hey now. We had to have *something* to pass the time during the Depression."

I laughed. "Well played."

He chuckled and surveyed the shelves around us. "You a gamer?"

"Fuck yeah, I'm a gamer."

Garrett grinned, meeting my gaze. "Yeah? What do you play?"

"Anything I can get my hands on. I love first-person shooters."

"Me too." He grimaced. "Some of them give me a bit of motion sickness, but hey, that's why God gave us Dramamine."

"That's hard-core. PC or console?"

"All of the above."

Oh Lord. Oh *Lord.* My mouth had gone dry, and I had no idea what to say without sounding like an idiot. How often did hot older men stroll in here with a love of comics and no snobbishness about gaming systems? *Oh Lord.*

His gaze halted on a shelf up by the register. "Wow, you guys have a ton of Wolf's Landing gear."

"Yeah, my bosses work directly with the author and the production studio, and now that they've got all the licensing shit squared away, we get all the good stuff." I nodded toward the street. "Marlina next door gets pissed since she's running the actual Wolf's Landing shop, but tough shit. My boss is buddies with Hunter Easton, so . . ."

"Nice." Garrett shifted his gaze to the display of Wolf's Landing hardcovers. "I keep meaning to read the series. My—" He stopped so abruptly, I was surprised his teeth didn't snap together. Then he muffled a cough and said, "My sister's into it, and she's been trying to get me to read them. Says the show is much better if you read the books first."

"It is." I motioned toward the shelves. "I can hook you up." Glancing over my shoulder, I added in a hushed voice, "Don't tell my bosses, but I can give you a discount too."

"I heard that," Simon's voice came from somewhere in the back.

"Damn it. Fucker's got bat hearing, I'm telling you."

Garrett laughed. "Something about bosses."

"Right?" I rolled my eyes.

Still smiling, Garrett looked at the books again. "Oh, the copies are signed?" He tugged one off the shelf and gently opened the cover to reveal the signature. This was one of the early books, so it only had Hunter Easton's autograph; the later books were signed by both him and Kevin Hussain. Garrett hummed and gave a slight nod. "Okay, I'm in." He held up the book. "You get a commission?"

I nodded.

"In that case." He gestured at the display. "Why don't I pick up the whole series?"

I straightened. "Really?"

"Yeah. You know, so when I finish one, I can dive into the next." His expression suddenly had a mixture of shyness and playfulness. Like he was joking about his motive, but also didn't want me to get weirded out that he was buying the entire set—the entire *signed hardcover* set—after finding out I'd get a commission. Self-consciousness was a strange look on him. He usually seemed pretty sure of himself, so that hint of vulnerability was—

Oh, who was I kidding? It melted my little black heart. As if I weren't already putty in his hands.

I cleared my throat. "Oh, um, I almost forgot. Hunter and Kevin—er, Kevyan come in once a month or so for signings. Next time they're here, you should come! Get your books—well, they're already *signed*, but you could get them personalized." A second too late, I realized how stupidly excited I sounded.

Before I could rein back the enthusiasm, though, Garrett smiled. "Remind me when we get closer." He gestured at the books. "Couldn't hurt to get him to put my name in them, right?"

"No, not at all. And you'll love the guys. In fact, if you come in a bit before or after the signing, I can introduce you to them instead of having you wait in line."

His smile broadened. "I like the sound of that."

"Cool. I'll keep you posted."

"Sounds good."

Part of me still wanted to tense up and wait for the other shoe to drop. For him to take it back and tell me I was an idiot for thinking he'd actually come to the shop to see me, the authors, or anything else. But that didn't make sense. He never seemed like he was humoring me. I could say something stupid—deliberately or otherwise—and he'd roll with it. I'd never once seen *easy, kid* in his eyes, and that said something. It was almost like he . . . *liked* the side of me that seemed to annoy everyone else.

And my little black heart melted a little more.

I helped him carry the books to the cash register. As I rang them up and he pulled out his wallet, Garrett did a double take. "Holy shit. Magic: The Gathering?" He picked up one of the starter decks off the rack. "They still make this game?"

"You know it?"

"Yeah. One of my roommates in college taught me to play." He hung the deck back up. "I can't even remember the last time I played. I've probably forgotten everything."

"You'd be surprised. I know guys who learned when it first came out in the mid-1990s, then picked it up again years later and played it just fine. I mean, as long as you know the basic rules, you just follow the directions on the cards."

He seemed to consider that for a moment. "True. I don't remember it being all that complicated."

"Well, it didn't use to be. They've, uh, added to it."

"Yeah? You play?"

I nodded. "We have tournaments here, actually." I nodded toward the tables, which were currently empty. "I play in them whenever I'm not working."

Garrett glanced at the tables, lips pursed. Then he tossed a starter deck and some boosters on top of the books.

As I scanned them, I said, "If you ever want to play, say the word. I've got plenty of decks at home." And why did my heart start pounding as soon as I'd asked? It wasn't like I'd suggested we go on a date or something.

But as he always seemed to do when I'd said something that sounded stupid to me, he smiled. "I might take you up on that." He paused, then added, "If you don't mind me being a little rusty."

"Sounds like fun. I'll go easy on you." I very nearly cringed. Every other thing I said to him came out sounding like it could be seriously misconstrued.

God help me, but the man winked. "You don't have to do that. I'm pretty sure it'll come back to me."

"Yeah. We'll see." I chuckled, hoping he didn't notice how jittery I suddenly was as I rang up the cards and books. If he did, he didn't say anything.

After he'd paid and I'd bagged everything, I handed it all over the counter.

"Thanks," he said. "This should keep me busy for a while."

"You'd be surprised—most people blow through Wolf's Landing in no time."

"We'll see." That hint of shyness materialized again in the slight dip of his chin. "I'm, uh, not that fast of a reader."

"Well, at least you can stretch it out for a while. I blazed through the first four books in two weeks, and had to wait *months* for the next one." I sighed dramatically. "It was torture, I'm telling you."

Garrett laughed. "I'm sure. Okay, well, I'll let you get back to work." He paused. "You coming by the bar tonight?"

I am now. My heart sped up. "You want me to?"

Our eyes locked. For a few seconds, we were both silent, the awkward tension of an unspoken dare hanging between us.

Then he swallowed. "It's always good to see you."

I moistened my lips. "I'll be there after my shift, then."

His face lit up. "Looking forward to it."

You and me both.

He left, and before the door had even swung shut behind him, Dexy appeared beside me, craning her neck to watch him go. "That your new boo?"

"My 'new boo'?" I rolled my eyes. "Seriously?"

She smothered a giggle and elbowed me. "I'm kidding. We both know he has to be your insatiable sex toy for a few months before he gets upgraded to boo status."

"Dex!"

A gruff laugh from behind us turned me around, and I found Simon smirking at me.

I wagged a finger at him. "Not a word."

"What?" He put up his hands and batted his eyes. "I said nothing."

"Uh-huh."

Dexy snorted. "Simon says . . ." She pointed at the window. "That dude is Jesse's new boo."

Simon laughed harder. Dexy giggled.

I just rolled my eyes. "I hate you both."

But deep down, I kind of hoped they were onto something.

CHAPTER EIGHT

GARRETT

J ust as I'd hoped, Jesse was here this evening. He took his usual barstool and nursed a Coke on the rocks while we shot the shit in between me filling drinks for the smattering of other customers. He'd only been in here a couple of times, but I'd already decided I loved it when he came to the bar. Now we had even more to talk about. Video games. Obscure comic series no one seemed to have heard of. The ever-more-complex game of Magic, which I was suddenly itching to play again. The time flew by, and even the odd belligerent drunk or stubborn keg tap hadn't put a damper on my mood.

Before I knew it, it was last call.

To my surprise, though, Jesse didn't seem to be in a big hurry to take off. He took his time settling his bill, and there was still some Coke left in his glass.

As I wiped down the bar, he glanced at me. "Will your boss get mad if I hang out until you close?"

My hand stopped. "I . . . No. Of course not." Clearing my throat, I continued mopping up the scattered crumbs and water droplets off the hardwood. "Can't imagine it'll be all that exciting for you."

He smiled. "I'm pretty sure I can keep myself entertained until you're done."

I was tempted to ask what the plan was after that, but the words got lost in my throat. Did this mean something? Was he as interested in me as I was in him? I was afraid to ask, thinking I'd send him running. Like the moment was a flock of easily startled pigeons just waiting for a reason to fly off in a panic.

Or maybe that was just me.

"I'm, uh . . . I need to take care of a few things in the back room. Won't be long."

"No rush." God. That smile.

I took the bag of trash out from under my station and ducked through the doorway that led to the kitchen and the break room. At the end of the hall, I leaned out another door to toss the bag in the dumpster. When I stepped back inside, Don was there. He glanced into the barroom, gaze landing on Jesse, and an amused expression curled his lips. "New friend, eh?"

My cheeks burned. Don's expression was gentle, though. He wasn't getting on my case, just playfully ribbing me. And maybe there was even something more there. After all, he knew why I'd come to Bluewater Bay.

"Um. Yes, sir." I cleared my throat. "He's . . ."

He clapped my shoulder. "Get out of here, Blaine. I'll see you tomorrow."

"Are you sure?"

"Go." He nudged me toward the door. "Hailey and I can finish up here."

Don wasn't terribly generous with the early dismissals, so I wasn't going to argue. I grabbed my coat and clocked out. When Jesse and I made eye contact, I nodded toward the door, and he followed me outside.

The night was cool and smelled like pine trees and saltwater, and it was a nice switch after being in the stuffy barroom for the last several hours.

"So, um." I turned to Jesse. "Where are you parked?"

He gestured down the road. "At the end of the block."

"You, um . . ." I hesitated. "Mind if I walk with you?" I felt stupid asking. He was the one who'd stuck around.

Jesse smiled. "Not at all."

As we started walking, I slid my hands into the pockets of my jeans. He did the same. We both looked straight ahead, neither saying a word as our steps fell into sync. It had been a long, long time since I'd been a nervous teenager walking through the halls of my high school next to someone I'd been crushing on, frantically trying to work up the courage to say something before the bell rang, but I was pretty sure that had felt a lot like this.

My pulse was all over the place. It had also been ages since I'd made a move on anyone. Especially sober. How did we *do* this? And was I misreading all his signals? Or giving off the wrong ones myself?

Then Jesse cleared his throat and broke the silence. "You don't mind me coming in every night and hanging out until you close, do you?"

"Mind?" I shook my head. "Why would I mind?"

"I don't know." Jesse stared at the ground and shrugged. "I just didn't want you thinking I was stalking you or something."

"Did it seem like I was stalking you when I showed up at the comic book store?"

His lips quirked. "No. It was . . ." He paused, and a smile came to life as he turned toward me. "It was actually really nice. Especially after the shitty day I'd been having."

"Really? You seemed like you were in a good mood."

"I was." He stopped, and when our eyes locked, he whispered, "Because you were there."

My heart skipped. I had no idea what to say. Judging by the sudden red in his cheeks, he didn't either.

Jesse dropped his gaze and pushed his hands deeper into his pockets. "I, um . . . It was kind of a rough day. Yesterday, mostly, but I still felt like shit today." Pulling in a deep breath, he looked at me through his lashes and offered the faintest half shrug. "Then you were there. And the day . . . didn't suck anymore."

"Oh." That was all that remained of my vocabulary. I watched him, lips parted and eyes wide, not sure where to go from here.

The red in his cheeks darkened, and he cleared his throat as he rubbed the back of his neck. "I'm sorry. I'm, uh, not exactly smooth when it comes to this stuff."

"That makes two of us. I never was good at this part."

Our eyes locked. The air around us seemed to freeze in place. My heart slammed against my rib cage. Something about our words amped everything up. Like we'd acknowledged this wasn't just a friendly walk to his car. That "this part" wasn't my imagination, and something might . . . *happen*.

Yeah. It might happen. And I wanted it to.

With my heart in my throat, I took a half step closer. Jesse pulled in a breath, tensing a little—I swore I could feel his pulse surge—but he didn't move away.

Calling on every bit of courage I had, hoping like hell I wasn't about to screw everything up, I reached for his face. Jesse tensed again, inhaling through his nose, but he still didn't pull away. When my fingertips brushed his cheek, we both froze.

Voice unsteady, I said, "I, um ... I haven't done this in a long time."

"Yeah?" He ran the tip of his tongue across his lip. "How long?"

I couldn't help staring at his lips. "Too long." Not since the last man who—

This time it was Jesse who narrowed the space between us. His shirt was almost brushing mine. One firm breeze and our clothes would touch. But there was no wind. If we were going to get any closer, one of us would have to do the work.

As I inched toward him, Jesse lifted his chin. He might as well have been giving me a literal green light, but nerves kept me from getting all the way there. The heat radiating off his body warmed my skin through my clothes, and there was no misinterpreting what the next step would be, but I . . . Fuck, I couldn't. My stomach fluttered and my pulse was going crazy, and I silently begged him to—

His hand met my chest. Palm flat. Fingers splayed. Panic shot through me as I envisioned him shoving me back, but he didn't. He slid his hand higher, over my thumping heart, and when his fingers brushed my neck, I sucked in a hiss of breath.

He didn't stop. His hand curved around the back of my neck, nearly dropping my knees out from under me, and then his other arm went around my waist, and the pavement rocked under my feet, and—

We kissed.

Softly. Just lips pressing against lips. No moving. No breathing. Nothing except letting this gentle, earth-shaking moment linger. I didn't know if he was waiting for me to get my feet under me—if he knew how badly I *needed* to get my feet under me—or if he was just savoring the unhurried contact, but I didn't argue.

After a while, Jesse tilted his head and let his lower lip drag across mine. I wrapped my arms around him, and he sighed as he deepened the kiss. There was nothing rushed about his kiss or his touch.

Even his breathing was slow and impossibly controlled, whispering across my cheek in soft, warm gusts.

I was lucky I remembered to breathe at all. For a lot of reasons, I hadn't let myself think about what it might be like to kiss a man again. If anything, I'd figured I would feel guilty and reluctant and hesitant as hell, but I didn't. I definitely hadn't expected it to feel so . . . *right.* Like this was happening in the exact moment and in the exact place with the exact man it was *supposed* to.

And I hadn't expected to want to break down in tears right there in his arms from the sheer relief of being touched. Up until this moment, I hadn't realized how much I'd been starving for physical contact with another man. Jesse's fingers sliding through my hair, his chest pressed up against mine, his slim torso in my arms—the sheer heat and presence of him made my emotions go haywire. I hadn't thought about getting intimate with anyone in ages, and now I couldn't believe I'd gone so long without.

He touched his forehead to mine. We were both out of breath, trembling a little and panting like we'd been making out instead of just letting a soft kiss linger.

"I've been wanting to do that for days," I breathed.

"Yeah?" His voice sounded uneven.

"Yeah." I stole another one. Briefer. Lighter. No less mind-blowing. When I broke away, Jesse's smile was sweet and serene, his eyes heavy-lidded.

"If it's not obvious," he whispered, "I really like the way you kiss."

My pulse went haywire again. "Do you?"

"Mm-hmm." He drew me into another kiss, and this time there was nothing brief or light about it. He was bold and insistent, sliding his tongue past mine and gripping my scalp tight enough to make it sting. Whatever caution either of us had brought to the table was gone now, and we gave in to the need for something deeper and hotter.

All at once, though, my nerves surged back with a vengeance. Sure, I'd made it this far without spontaneously combusting, but I wasn't so sure I was ready to fall into bed with someone. From here, sex seemed like a potential minefield, one I didn't know if I could tiptoe through tonight. Not without tipping my hand and showing some emotions and baggage that would probably kill the mood for Jesse. I should—

He broke the kiss abruptly. Our eyes met again, and we were both totally out of breath, staring, trembling. There was panic in his expression that mirrored my own, but hell if I could figure out where it had come from. Was he just picking up on mine? Or was there something on his mind too?

"You okay?" I asked.

"Yeah, I . . ." He licked his lips and dropped his gaze. "This wasn't how I thought things would play out tonight."

"Same here." Though now that it had happened, it made sense. Of *course* we'd wound up kissing under a streetlight beside his car. How else could the night have gone?

Still avoiding my eyes, he chewed the inside of his cheek. That subtle panic radiated off him. I couldn't begin to tell what it was all about, but it did nothing to alleviate my own.

I cleared my throat. "Listen, um . . . we don't have to go any further than this."

His head snapped up. "What?"

"I'm . . ." I shifted uncomfortably, which made me brush against him everywhere we'd been softly touching, and I had no idea how my brain didn't short-circuit from that alone. "I've been out of the dating pool for a while. Whatever this is—whatever we're doing—would . . . would you be opposed to taking it slowly?"

The tension in his features softened, and he tilted his head. "Opposed to— No. No, definitely not." As he exhaled, I didn't miss the distinct relief in his eyes and his posture. "I think I'd rather go slow too."

It was my turn for a relieved sigh. "Okay. Good. Good. Then . . ." I struggled to find the words. "We, um . . ." Well, shit. Where did we go from here?

Jesse loosened his embrace. "I should go anyway," he whispered. "I have to open tomorrow."

I nodded, disappointment and another wave of relief vying for dominance in my chest. "Yeah. You, um, coming by the bar tomorrow night?"

He searched my eyes in the low light. "If you still want me to."

"Are you kidding?" I cupped his face and traced his prominent cheekbone with my thumb. "That's been the highlight of my day lately."

Pink bloomed in his cheeks, and that adorable smile curved his slightly swollen lips. "Really?"

I nodded. "You're good company."

Jesse laughed softly, shyly, and my knees liquefied. "I'll be there, then."

I shouldn't have been that relieved, but I was, and I almost let it show. "Can't wait."

His smile was quick to form, but even quicker to fade, and he searched my eyes. "You don't mind stopping now, do you? I mean, this isn't too slow, is it?"

"Too slow?" I blinked. "Because we're not already fucking over the back of a car?"

Jesse laughed again, more color deepening in his cheeks. "Well, I . . . I mean . . ." His humor faded, and he stared at the ground. "I just mean . . ." He chewed his lip.

"Jesse." I touched his chin and tipped it up. "Relax. I need things to go slow right now. Like . . . really slow."

He looked in my eyes. The question was there, but he didn't ask. Maybe he was afraid if he asked why I wanted to keep it slow, I'd ask why *he* did. And I didn't push because I wasn't ready to explain things. Tonight felt too damn good to weigh it down with grief and guilt.

After a moment, he swept his tongue across his lips. "Maybe we could start with . . . I don't know. A date?"

"Really?"

He blushed even harder as he smiled, and his eyes darted away. "Why not?"

"It sounds like a good idea to me." I smoothed his hair. "I don't know this town very well. Any place you recommend?"

Jesse swallowed. "Not offhand, but I can come up with something and let you know."

"Okay. I'm looking forward to it."

"Me too." He pushed himself up and kissed me again. "I'll see you sometime tomorrow."

I smiled. Then I pulled my phone out of my pocket. "I should probably get your number, then."

"Oh. Right. Good idea." He took out his phone too, and we exchanged numbers.

As we pocketed our phones, I said, "I'm off at eight tomorrow. That's not too late to go out, is it?"

"Not at all."

We held each other's gazes for a moment before I turned to head back up the street to my truck. It was just as well we hadn't stolen one more kiss. Every time we touched, I was more and more in favor of taking things further, and I wasn't entirely sure that was a good idea. He wasn't pushing for it, which I appreciated more than he probably realized. If a kiss overwhelmed me this much, sex would be way too much.

All the way back to my truck, I grinned like an idiot. I hadn't felt this good in far too long, and I didn't even feel guilty about it. If the guilt came crashing in later, I'd deal with it.

But if only for tonight, I felt amazing.

CHAPTER NINE

JESSE

What the fuck was I thinking?

All the way home, that thought hammered itself into my brain. How had we gotten even the least bit physical without me telling him? I'd been too caught up in the moment to stop and think, that was how. Usually, by the time I made it that far with a guy, they knew my status. I always made sure of it. I wanted him to know before he touched me so if he did decide he had a problem with it, at least my skin wouldn't crawl quite so much. I always told them. *Always.*

Except this time. And the last time. Fuck.

It wasn't like this thing with Garrett had come out of nowhere, either. From the moment I'd realized there was more going on than a sympathetic bartender humoring a regular, I'd known there was a chance the flirtation could actually go somewhere. I'd told myself over and over I'd tell him when the opportunity presented itself, even though I knew—holy shit, I fucking *knew*—from experience that the best approach was to just put it out there and be done with it.

But nooo.

Berating myself, I parked in front of my apartment and shuffled inside. Without even bothering to toss my wallet and keys onto the kitchen counter, I went into my bedroom, flopped onto the bed, and stared up at the ceiling. My lips still tingled from Garrett's kisses— God, he was good at kissing. Like, *mind-blowing* good. Once I'd given him the go-ahead for more than just lips-on-lips, he'd explored my mouth with this quiet enthusiasm, taking his sweet time as he'd teased my tongue, and his lips had moved languidly against mine. If that was a sneak peek of the things he'd do to the rest of my body once we got naked, sign me the fuck up *right now*.

Except...

Except.

I closed my eyes again and cringed. There was no way in hell I'd get into bed with a man unless he knew my status, and on the heels of Charlie's reaction, I was terrified of showing that card to Garrett. Especially now that I really, *really* wanted Garrett. It would've been a lot easier to tell—and be rejected by—Mr. Random Bartender than Garrett, the amazing kisser I'd been getting to know for the last week. And I *would* have told him at the first inkling of attraction. *Would* have.

But I hadn't. How could I have been so stupid?

Except, when would I have told him? In the beginning when I'd been raw and hurting after Charlie? Or when we'd started getting into that gray area between being kind of friendly and kind of flirty? When was it too soon and when was it too late?

God, fuck you, Charlie, for making me feel disgusting.

Not that it mattered. Blame Charlie, blame myself—nothing changed the fact that I still had to tell Garrett. I was scared to death to face him. Just the thought of seeing him tomorrow night turned my stomach.

He wanted to take things slow. Fine. So where did, *By the way, I'm positive*, fit into that? When would it be too soon? When was it too *late*? Was it already? Fuck, it had been too late before he'd even kissed me. Except, when I realized that kiss was about to happen, my mind had blanked of anything that wasn't how those full lips would feel against mine or how my body would fit against his broad, solid frame (amazing and perfectly, it turned out).

Damn it. This was exactly why I told guys upfront—I sucked at finding the right time once I'd gotten to know them. But I didn't go around announcing it to everyone I encountered on the off chance we might decide to have sex in the future.

Should've just slipped it into conversation at some point while we'd been talking about other shit. Or told him exactly why Charlie had stood me up instead of blowing it off as the guy being an asshole. It would've been the perfect opportunity to put it out there and let Garrett decide how he felt about it.

But nooo. My dumb ass had to hold off until we'd already blown past the point of obvious mutual attraction, and now I had to find the thing I hated the most—the right moment to put this out there—and hope he didn't turn into an asshole like Charlie had.

I shuddered. I didn't think I could handle that kind of rejection twice in rapid succession. Not from guys I'd gotten to know enough to give a shit about.

Fuck.

"Earth to Jesse?" Dexy waved a hand in front of my face.

I shook myself and turned to her. "Hmm?"

She cocked her head. "You're a space cadet today. What's up?"

"Nothing. Nothing. I'm . . ." I searched for a topic to pull us away from this train of thought. Clearing my throat, I motioned toward the back. "Has DHL been here yet? We're supposed to get a shipment of—"

"No, they haven't. Don't change the subject."

I scowled at her. "I'm fine, okay? Just . . . didn't sleep much last night."

Normally, that would get a smirk out of her, and she'd ask what his name was. But from the lift of her eyebrows and the creases in her forehead, she could read far enough between the lines to know I hadn't been up banging someone all night.

"Everything okay?" she asked.

I shrugged. "I guess. It's . . . kind of a long story."

She studied me, chewing the inside of her cheek, and I suspected she was debating how far to push. We were friendly, and we talked about all kinds of shit, but we weren't tight enough to delve into the really personal stuff. Sometimes I had a hard time knowing where the line was, and she was probably trying to figure it out right then too.

Sighing, I broke eye contact. "Don't worry about it. I'm, uh, going to go make sure the outgoing shipments are ready to go."

Dexy hesitated but apparently decided not to push. "Okay. Let me know if you need help."

"Will do." I slipped through the back door to the table where we boxed up anything that needed to be shipped. Usually stuff going back to manufacturers for various reasons, and occasionally things people had ordered but couldn't pick up in person. I was in luck—there were three piles of merchandise with shipping instructions on top of them. That would keep me busy for ten or fifteen minutes.

While I boxed everything up and filled out the labels, my mind was almost entirely fixated on last night. And tonight. Oh fuck. Tonight.

I shuddered as I set the packing tape aside. I so wasn't ready to face Garrett and tell him the truth. It was a familiar sick feeling. I'd once described it to someone as being comparable to getting ready to smash my hand with a hammer. I knew that the sooner I did it, the sooner it would be over, and I knew that the anticipation was sometimes a hell of a lot worse than the result, but it still took a lot to make me finally swing that hammer and be done with it.

I paused between shipments and rubbed my eyes. When I finally told Garrett and he took the news like a civilized adult, I'd feel like an idiot for holding back like this.

Or when he ran for the hills, I'd feel like shit for swinging the stupid hammer.

I needed to tell him. I needed more time.

I needed this over with. I needed to breathe.

Finally, cowardice won me over, and I texted him: *Boss needs me for a double shift. Can we postpone till tomorrow?*

My stomach somersaulted. It wasn't lost on me that I was sort of doing to him what Charlie had done to me. I was avoiding him in the name of avoiding an uncomfortable conversation. Ironically, my status was still the crux of that conversation; Garrett just didn't know it, and instead of him steering clear of me because he didn't want to be infected, I was doing it to him because I didn't want to be rejected.

My phone vibrated.

No problem. I'm off tomorrow, so we can meet earlier if you want.

Relief and apprehension mingled in my chest. Okay, I'd bought myself some time. Not enough, but . . . it was something.

And what difference would it make besides giving me one more night to lose sleep? Either he'd reject me or he wouldn't. Why not just get it over with?

Because rejection hurts more than wondering if it'll happen.

I wiped a hand over my face and cursed into the silence. My status didn't rule my love life. It just meant this one awkward obstacle whenever I met someone new. After that, we either kept seeing each other or we didn't, and that was pretty much the end of it being an issue, but damn I wanted to keep seeing him. Now that I knew how he kissed, I wanted to get him naked, like, *now*. Most guys—myself included—would be impatient at this point. Take it slow? No, thank you. Whenever things started getting physical, I wanted *all* the physical. In fact, aside from tonight, I couldn't remember the last time I'd kissed a man and not taken him to bed that same night. Except . . .

My chest tightened.

Except Charlie.

Charlie, who was chill about most things. Charlie, who was a good kisser. Charlie, who was sweet and kind and understanding. Charlie, who'd stopped wanting me the moment he'd realized I was positive.

Charlie, who was the reason I was terrified to tell Garrett.

I shook the thought away. Just because Charlie had been a twat-waffle about it didn't mean Garrett would. I was overthinking it. Garrett was mature and intelligent. As much as I'd liked Charlie, I had to admit that maturity wasn't his strongest point. Okay, so he'd probably say the same about me since I lived and breathed comics and role-playing, but *he* lived for the nights he could go out and get shit-faced, even though he definitely couldn't afford them. Not on top of a swank apartment, mountains of student loans, and out-of-control credit cards. Despite having a high-paying job, he'd been evicted from two apartments since I'd known him.

The thought gave me pause. As much as we'd gotten along, maybe I had dodged a bullet there. As a friend, Charlie was fun. As a boyfriend . . . maybe not so much.

Garrett, on the other hand, seemed a bit world-weary but rational and even wise. Shit, no wonder he'd grabbed my attention after Charlie. They were polar opposites, which meant I was worrying about nothing. Garrett was way too together and rational to react like Charlie had.

I pushed out a long breath and rolled some tension out of my shoulders. I'd bought myself a little time to pull myself together. Tomorrow night, I'd tell him. It would be okay, and we'd pick up where we'd left off *last* night.

And, dear God, please let him be as good in bed as his mouth told me he is.

CHAPTER TEN

GARRETT

I stared at myself in the bathroom mirror.

I'm really doing this.

I'd shaved. Put on a steel-gray button-up. Done as much as I could with hair this short. It was just as well Jesse had postponed things. Since I had tonight off, I had more time to put myself together. Freak out a bit, but also put myself together.

I'd given up on the tie, and not just because the part of my brain that knew how to tie them had skipped out on me for some reason. A tie just seemed too formal. We were meeting for dinner. There wouldn't be white linen tablecloths or wine presentations.

Just two guys.

On a date.

Because that was what this was—a date. An *actual* date.

Oh fuck. What am I doing?

Staring down my reflection, I gulped. The guy in the mirror didn't offer up any words of wisdom, just a face full of all the nerves I'd been trying to pretend weren't really there.

Forget nerves—I was scared shitless, and I wasn't completely sure why.

I couldn't even hide behind the worry that my late husband would be hurt to know I was already getting involved with another man. No, Sean had made sure I didn't have that bunker to shield me from my own cowardice.

Though I'd mostly blocked out the memory while I'd been smoking with Scott, it came back in full force now, and there was nothing I could do but let it fill my mind and take me back. It had been in the early months, before the disease had started gaining the upper hand, back when my husband had still been vibrant and lucid. I'd never forget standing there in the kitchen, loading the dishwasher, when Sean had walked in with *we need to talk* in his eyes.

"I need you to promise me something," he'd said after convincing me to abandon the dishes and sit down on the couch with him.

I'd flinched hard, and God, I hadn't wanted to have that conversation. Not then. Not ever. I couldn't imagine he had either, but he'd recently started accepting the fact that he wasn't going to see thirty, and he'd started preparing both of us. So whenever he'd sat me down like this, I'd known damn well it would be something related to the end, and I hadn't been ready to think about that. Maybe he'd accepted his mortality, but I hadn't. In some ways, I probably never would.

Sean had needed it, though. No matter how much it tore me up each and every time, I'd promised myself I'd have a million of these conversations with him if they brought him some peace before he . . . before it was over.

I wasn't ready, though, when he took my hand and whispered, "Promise me you won't turn away happiness after I'm gone."

My mouth went dry. "What?"

He swallowed, holding my gaze even though it seemed to take a monumental effort. "It's up to you when you start dating again, and—"

"Sean. Don't." I shook my head, trying not to get violently ill. "I don't even want to *think* about that. Not now."

"I know. And I don't either. But I need . . ." He bit his lip and dropped his gaze, staring down at our hands, which were clasped so tightly together it was getting painful. "Please. Just listen to me."

I took a deep breath to pull myself together. "Okay. I'll listen." I steeled myself against how bad this was going to hurt, but there was only so much emotional armor a man could put up.

It was Sean's turn for a deep breath, and as he pushed his shoulders back, he met my eyes again. "When someone comes along, if he's good to you and you're into him, just . . ." His expression was filled with so many things I couldn't read, and his voice was barely a whisper: "You decide when you're ready, but just promise you won't let *me* get in the way."

My heart stopped. I stared at him, unable to speak.

"If . . . if you meet someone, and the only thing keeping you away from him is me . . ." He met my eyes. "Like you feel guilty, or you think I'd be angry that you're moving on . . ." Sean shook his head. "I want you to know right now that I won't be. I *want* you to be happy, Garrett, and if a guy drops out of the sky after I'm gone . . ." He swallowed again, and his voice shook as he whispered, "Don't say no to him because you think I'd want you to."

"Sean . . ."

"Please," he'd whispered. "Promise me. I want you to be happy."

In the bathroom of my tiny Bluewater Bay apartment, I broke eye contact with myself and swiped at some unwelcome tears. This wasn't the time.

That conversation a lifetime ago had been excruciating, but now, even as my heart ached at the memory, I was glad we'd had it. I could practically hear Sean standing next to me, gesturing in Jesse's general direction and yelling, *Oh my God, go for it! What are you waiting for?* In fact, I could see him giving Jesse an appreciative down-up, then smirking at me and complimenting me on snagging a guy that hot.

The thought made me laugh, which helped me put a stop to the tears. Trust Sean to be able to make me feel better when I was freaking out about going on a date.

It was ironic how everyone had thought that as young as he was, he had to be entirely too immature for someone my age. That couldn't have been further from the truth. Immature didn't spend the last year of his life making sure everyone who loved him was ready to let him go. Not that it had been remotely possible to be prepared—the moment of his death had torn something out of me that would never come back—but damn if he hadn't tried like hell, all the way to his very last waking breath, to make sure the rest of us had peace.

I closed my eyes and exhaled. The thought of moving on was still hard. And admittedly, it was beginning to ignite some guilt and self-loathing deep in my chest. The prospect of sleeping with Jesse had my mind twisting in on itself in search of justification and permission. The thought of going on a date had reopened all the wounds and given the grief a second wind.

Going out with Jesse meant Sean was really gone. The last several months had been peppered with moments and milestones that had meant the same thing, and each one hurt in a new and unexpected way. Getting bills in the mail with only my name on them. Watching his car disappear down our street with its new driver at the wheel. The first Christmas without Sean putting on a Santa hat and entertaining our nieces and nephews with made-up carols. How long would it take for that to stop happening? Fuck if I knew.

I stared at myself in the mirror again. Yes, it hurt to remind myself he was gone, but I was still here. Jesse had reminded me that I was still alive and that I could feel things again that weren't grief and loneliness. I still keenly felt those things, but there was also desire, excitement, attraction, and . . . *want.* I actually *wanted.* I wanted to see where things with Jesse could go, and I wanted him. Not the memories he sometimes triggered of my husband. *Him.* Kissing him the other night had almost ripped me to pieces because I'd suddenly been aware of just how starved I'd been for intimacy, and now I wanted more of that.

I wanted more, and if I played my cards right, there'd be more tonight.

And not a moment too soon, I decided. It wasn't like I'd ever given myself a designated mourning period. I'd never decided to wait six months or a year or two years. There'd been no point because I hadn't seen myself ever looking at another man. Even if I'd known intellectually that I'd probably move on sooner or later, it had been impossible to consider. Laying down a time frame had made about as much sense as drawing up an emergency escape plan from a house I'd never seen before.

I gave my reflection one last look and set my jaw. I could do this. Scott had given me a sanity check, and I took his advice to heart. Who better to offer me some guidance than a licensed counselor who was a widower himself? And he'd given this his blessing.

I nodded sharply at myself and walked out of the bathroom to get my wallet and keys. Nerves were okay tonight. I'd have been worried if I didn't have them. But chickening out? Not a chance. I wanted to see what could happen with Jesse. It was too soon to call it anything, but it wasn't too soon to recognize that tingle of attraction. Or to act on it. I was in no hurry to push this thing forward. I just didn't feel the need to rein it back.

In the living room, I ignored my roiling stomach and thundering heart and kept right on walking. Out of the apartment. Down to my truck. Then I drove, and I didn't let myself think about bailing anymore. I was doing this and that was final. Maybe I'd fuck it up somehow, but I was going. I sure as shit wasn't standing up a man who I'd met because he'd been stood up by someone else.

On the way into downtown Bluewater Bay, I forced back another wave of fear that desperately wanted some attention. I held the wheel firmly and kept driving. I was *doing* this. I wanted to, and anyway, if I refused to give love a shot on the off chance tragedy might strike twice, there'd be hell to pay in the afterlife. I could see Sean standing at the Pearly Gates, arms crossed and head cocked in his classic *you done fucked up* fashion, ready to inform me of his disappointment.

The thought actually made me laugh again, with more feeling than earlier. Maybe that was a good sign too.

In town, as I walked from my truck toward Il Trovatore, the Italian restaurant Jesse had suggested, someone called my name. I stopped in my tracks, looked around, and found Jesse heading up the sidewalk toward me. He waved. I waved back.

Okay. We're doing this.

He stopped at the corner, facing me from one end of a crosswalk.

The signal changed to Walk.

Jesse started toward me.

And I waited.

Here goes . . .

CHAPTER ELEVEN

JESSE

The hostess seated us against the far wall of the warmly lit restaurant and handed us a couple of menus. After she'd taken our drink order, she left us to peruse the selection.

"So what's good?" Garrett asked.

"Don't know. I've never been here."

He arched an eyebrow. "Haven't you?"

"Nope. A friend recommended it, but I have no idea what they're good at."

"Fair." He glanced at the menu. "I haven't had a bad meal in this town yet, so maybe my luck will hold out."

I laughed. "You *haven't* lived here very long, have you?"

"Nope."

"Give it time."

"Yeah?"

"Trust me."

"Noted."

We shifted our attention to the menus. I skimmed over it, but all the words were jumbled. Or at least they didn't make it to my brain. They might as well have spelled out, *Tell him, tell him, tell him,* because that was all I could think about.

My gaze landed on one clear word: *chicken.*

Yep. That was me. Chickenshit.

My stomach churned. My fingers left little smears of sweat on the laminated pages I wasn't reading. I couldn't stop tapping my foot, and if it kept going much longer, the table was going to start shaking like we were having a séance. I hadn't taken a single bite or drink of anything, and I felt like something was stuck in my throat.

Fuck it. If I didn't get this off my chest, I would just keep feeling queasy. The mere thought of ordering made me want to hurl. Stupid nerves. Stupid bad experiences. Once bitten, twice nauseated as fuck.

There was no point in waiting until after we'd had dinner. So, taking a deep breath, I closed my menu and met his gaze across the table. "Look, um, there's something I think we should talk about."

Garrett's forehead creased. He closed his menu and folded his hands on top of it, as if to tell me I had his full attention.

Squirming under his intense, inquisitive gaze, my leg still shaking and not doing a damn thing to disperse this nervous energy, I struggled to hold eye contact. "The reason I wanted to take things slow last night, it's . . ." My tongue stuck to the roof of my mouth. "Before we take this any further . . ." This part hadn't gotten any easier with time. "I need you to know . . ." Fuck. This was all happening in the wrong order. It was all fucking backward. Guys were supposed to know this shit before I'd invested enough to actually hurt at the thought of watching them leave. I was supposed to be on a hair trigger, ready to bolt at the first sign of rejection, not already hurting at the thought of dropping that hammer.

Garrett's brow pinched. After a moment, he reached across the table and put a hand on my forearm. "What's on your mind?"

I glanced down at his hand, then pulled in another deep shaky breath. "To cut right to the chase, I'm positive."

He blinked, and his fingers twitched. "Come again?"

"I'm . . ." I swallowed. "I'm HIV-positive."

Time stopped. It always did right then, a single nanosecond stretching out while a million possible reactions played out in my head. A disgusted sneer. Shrugged acceptance. *"That's okay—me too."* Every possibility. And my body and brain flowed with preemptive relief, anger, hurt, nerves, and God only knew what else while I waited for that nanosecond to tick past so I could see how Garrett would take the news.

Tonight, reality played out unlike any of the mental movie screens.

Garrett? He *blanched.* His whole body slowly stiffened like it was turning to stone, and he stared at me like I'd just told him I had a bomb strapped to my chest with three seconds left till boom. Lips parted, eyes wide, he didn't speak. Didn't move. Didn't *breathe.*

With each heartbeat, the ball of lead in my stomach got ten pounds heavier. Under my clothes, my skin crawled. Even more under where his hand rested—not as firmly now—on my arm.

Yep. Definitely should have told him sooner. Charlie's response hadn't cut this deep.

"You know what?" I jerked my arm away and stood so fast I nearly toppled my chair. "Fuck you." Then I turned to go.

I made it three steps before another chair ground across the wood floor. "Jesse, wait!"

I didn't.

He followed me, and when I stepped out into the cooling evening, he reached for my elbow. "Just listen to—"

I wrenched my arm away again and spun around. "What part of 'fuck you' wasn't clear?"

He halted, eyes huge and mouth agape. "Jesse . . . I . . ."

"Don't." I shook my head and put up a hand. "Whatever you're going to say, I've heard it before, and . . ." Fuck. Now my voice was shaking. On the verge of cracking. "I really don't want to hear it from you."

Then I turned again, and this time I didn't go back. He didn't try all that hard to change my mind either.

Fuck him. I didn't need this shit in my life. I'd had enough of assholes like him, and besides, there were plenty of queer fish in the sea. Thanks to Wolf's Landing, a lot of those queer fish were here in Bluewater Bay. I knew from experience that plenty of them weren't ignorant assholes when it came to HIV.

I was just surprised—yet again—when someone turned out to be one of those ignorant assholes.

Especially when that someone was Garrett.

I didn't sleep that night. I'd tossed and turned, refusing to let myself cry even if I knew I'd exhaust myself and fall asleep. Alone in my bedroom, I was still too proud, too stubborn, and too fucking pissed off to let Garrett drive tears out of me. I'd given enough of those to Charlie.

In the morning, with another lament about the coffee shops in town not having Super Big Gulp sizes, I made it into work without crashing my car or faceplanting on the sidewalk. That was a start, I guessed. And I was clocked in. Earning my paycheck. Not really doing anything besides chugging coffee and breathing, but whatever. I busted my ass in this place. One day of feeling sorry for myself on company time wouldn't be the end of the world.

It wasn't fucking fair. In my entire life, I'd had sex with *one* person who I hadn't had to say those words to. *One.* After him, every single goddamned sexual encounter I'd wanted had been on the other side of an awkward conversation. Every relationship. Every screw. Every make-out session. It was like in order to get to any kind of intimacy, everyone else in the world just had to cross a concrete footbridge, complete with safety railings and streetlights, while I was over here hoping a strong wind didn't drop this rickety suspension bridge out from under my shaking legs. Sometimes it held. Sometimes it didn't. Every time, though, the sickening fear was there and it was real and sometimes it was fucking justified.

I was exhausted. I was just . . . so done.

"Jesse?" Lydia's voice startled me. I glanced at her, then down at everything laid out in front of me. I'd forgotten what the hell I was doing.

Unpacking a shipment of gaming dice. Right.

"Hey." I gave her another glance before reaching in to pull out a few more packs of the colorful twenty-sided dice. "I was just . . . uh . . ."

"You okay?"

"Yeah. Why?" I flashed her a quick and probably not very convincing smile.

Lydia exhaled. "Don't bullshit me, Jesse Brooks." Oh crap. When she broke out my full name, she wasn't fucking around. Especially not when she backed it with that look—same one she gave Simon or Ian sometimes when they were testing her nerves. "Tell me."

I swallowed. Admittedly, the pushiness and refusal to back down were comforting. She really did care, and she wasn't going to let me wallow on my own when we both knew I'd just bottle it up until it broke me. Plus she, unlike most people I wasn't planning to have sex with, knew my status. I'd confided in her about it a long time ago, and I didn't think she'd even told Simon.

I took a deep breath. "That guy I went out with last night? I told him. About my status. And he freaked out. Like . . ." I sagged against the stack of boxes and wiped a hand over my face. "I've never seen someone look as horrified as he did. I mean, some guys get all disgusted and won't touch me, but his reaction was . . . it was so weird."

Lydia grimaced. "Oh, honey. I'm sorry."

I slumped a bit more. "I get all kinds of reactions. His . . . Fuck. My skin is *still* crawling."

"I believe it. You said he's older, though, isn't he?"

I nodded without looking at her. "Fortysomething, I think. Forty-two."

"He *is* from a different generation, then. He probably still hears 'HIV' and thinks about what it was like twenty, thirty years ago."

"But he's a *gay guy*." I threw up my hands. "He can't be that out of touch, you know? Knowing how treatable and transmittable HIV is . . . that's, like . . . Being Gay in the Twenty-First Century 101."

She nodded slowly. "You're probably right. And either way, it's no excuse for him to be a dick-weasel to you." She put an arm around my shoulders and gave me a gentle squeeze. "It sucks. It really does. He sounded like a nice guy."

"Yeah. He did." And that was the worst kind. Especially since he'd still think of *himself* as a nice guy after this. After all, he hadn't been an asshole. He'd just been protecting himself. Making sure he didn't get sick. I couldn't be offended by a guy looking out for his health, could I?

My eyes stung, and I swiped at them.

She squeezed my shoulders again. "You want the rest of the day off?"

I shook my head. "No. I'm good. If I go home, I'll just wallow in it." I tapped my knuckle against one of the boxes. "This will keep me focused on something besides him."

"Okay. But if you need some time, even if it's just a long break, all you have to do is ask."

At that, I managed a smile. "Thanks. I really appreciate it."

She smiled back and gave my shoulders another squeeze. Then she went back to the sales floor, leaving me to boxes and my thoughts.

And, boy, were my thoughts swarming. Not surprising after two guys in rapid succession had acted like I was Typhoid Jesse. Maybe I needed a break from dating and hookups for a while. At least until the sting had faded.

Shaking my head, I went back to work, focusing on shipments and displays and inventories and whatever else could hold my attention.

When the alarm on my phone went off, I automatically reached for the little plastic case I kept in my back pocket and popped it open. I went through this same motion every day at the same time, but today, I paused. I stared at the pill between my fingers.

HIV was part of my life. Had been for a long time. When the diagnosis had hit, I'd been terrified of dying a slow, painful death, but thanks to medical advances, it hadn't been like that at all. I took the drugs, got the checkups, had my viral load tested regularly. It had altered my life about as dramatically as my dad's diabetes had—there were changes and risks and drugs, but I was still me and my day-to-day life wasn't much different than it would be if I were negative. Most days, no one would ever know I was positive if not for the daily pill regimen. Days when no one—myself included—noticed.

And then there were days like today when I couldn't forget.

I swore under my breath and tossed back the pill.

I'd be okay. I deserved better than someone like Charlie or Garrett, and there were definitely better guys out there.

But that didn't mean it didn't hurt right now.

CHAPTER TWELVE

GARRETT

J esse wouldn't return my texts. I suspected I was blocked already, and I didn't blame him.

Shit. How the fuck did I undo something like this? Even if I could reach him, was there anything I could say that would reach past all his anger? Because God knew he had every right to be that pissed.

In the moment, I'd been too off guard to understand his reaction. Reeling from an unexpected rush of emotions and memories. By the time I'd realized he was pissed, he'd been on his way out, and he hadn't stopped.

Sitting in my truck, I stared at my phone. It had been two days, and I'd been losing my mind ever since. I felt like an utter jackass. Even if he wasn't willing to see me again, I at least wanted to apologize. I wasn't about to stalk him, but . . . damn, there had to be some way to reach him.

And even if there was—then what? I didn't know if I could have explained myself that night, and I still wasn't sure I could explain myself now. I knew why I'd choked. The moment he'd said he was positive, I'd gone someplace else. To an office where I'd been surrounded by books and medical degrees, sitting in a hard chair in front of a gigantic desk and grasping a sweaty hand, staring into a pair of round glasses while "very little we can do" and "six months at most" and "we'll have to think about palliative care" echoed in my ears.

In the forty-eight hours or so since Jesse had stormed out of Il Trovatore, I'd been kicking myself and my wounded psyche. It didn't matter that I was well aware that the virus wasn't a grisly death sentence anymore, or that there was little to no risk involved in sex with someone whose HIV was properly managed. The words had snagged a cascade of deep-seated trip wires. The scared teenager who'd grown up gay in the 1980s and early 1990s had collided with the grieving widower who'd watched a different disease slowly consume his husband, and the possibility of going through something like that again had paralyzed me.

I gnawed my lip and gazed up the street at the sign above End o' Earth. I was out of options. Either I walked in there to talk to him, or I let this go. Chances were good we'd eventually cross paths in this small town, but if I wanted more than a cold shoulder when that happened, I needed to fix this *today*.

After a lengthy internal pep talk, I got out of the truck and headed up the sidewalk, but I balked outside the comic book shop. It was one thing to show up here when things were good. If I were pissed at him and he came strolling into the Alehouse, I would be furious. But how else was I supposed to get in contact with him?

Might be a good time to take the hint that he doesn't want *contact from you.*

I gnawed the inside of my cheek. It was worth a try. *One* try. If he turned me away, then that was the end of it.

So, whispering a prayer that he'd listen to me, I pulled open the door and stepped inside.

"Hello." The woman behind the counter smiled at me. "Is there something I can help you find?"

"Um. Yeah." I cautiously approached. "Is, uh . . . is Jesse here?"

In an instant, her expression hardened. "Who's asking?" Icicles hung off every word.

I swallowed. "Garrett."

Her eyes narrowed and her jaw tightened. "Yeah, I figured as much. He doesn't want to see you."

"I know. And I get it. But . . . what happened, it's not what he thinks. I just—"

The derisive snort told me Jesse had definitely filled her in on how things had gone down. There was no way she thought I was anything less than the world's biggest asshole.

I cleared my throat. "Look, can I just leave him a message? It's totally up to him if he wants to hear me out. If he doesn't, I'll let it go." I showed my palms. "I'll leave him alone."

She studied me, still cold but not throwing me out. "So if he doesn't want to hear it, or he decides not to accept your *apology*"—she spat the word like it was poison—"I won't see your face in my shop again?"

Oh shit. This was his boss.

I nodded. "No, ma'am. You won't see me again."

She watched me, eyes boring holes in my skull. I thought she might send me packing, but after a moment, she pushed out a breath through her nose, grabbed a piece of paper from beside the register, and slapped it down on the counter.

Wordlessly, I took a Deadpool pen from a Spiderman cup and started writing. Trying to, anyway. With her scrutiny and my nerves, there was no telling if I'd manage to come up with something coherent—never mind convincing—but after a few fits and starts, I had the most basic explanation. Short and to the point and hopefully enough, because it was the best I could do now.

Once I was done, I didn't bother reading it over. I'd only drive myself insane. Instead, I folded the note in half and handed it to her. "Thank you."

She glared at me, but she took the note.

I waited, not sure what I expected her to say. When she offered nothing, I took a step back from the counter and muttered again, "Thanks."

I was halfway to the door when her voice stopped me in my tracks: "You know you're not the first, right?"

Slowly, I turned around. "Sorry?"

She eyed me coldly, my note still in her hand. "He's been treated like shit for this for the same reason by plenty of guys. So whatever excuse you have?" She gestured with the note and tightened her jaw. "Don't hold your breath."

My heart sank even deeper. Lowering my gaze, I nodded. "I'm not. I just want him to know the truth. The rest . . ." I shrugged. "That's up to him."

Her expression didn't change, and she didn't offer any other commentary, so I continued toward the door. I didn't look back as I headed outside and started up the street to the Alehouse. The ball was in his court now.

Please, Jesse. Just listen.

CHAPTER THIRTEEN

JESSE

As soon as the door to End o' Earth closed, I pushed out a breath and sagged against the wall dividing the back room from the shop floor.

"You okay?" Simon asked.

I nodded. "Yeah. Sorry about that."

"Don't be." He gave my shoulder a gentle squeeze. "If you need a minute, you—"

"No, I'm good. I need to get back to work." I pushed off the wall, rolled my shoulders, and stretched some tension out of my neck as I repeated, "I'm good."

He eyed me uncertainly but didn't try to stop me from finishing my task so I could return to the floor. I appreciated the concern, just like I appreciated Lydia handling Garrett. For all we busted each other's chops, there were few people I could count on like Simon and Lydia.

I probably shouldn't have been surprised Garrett had come here. Thank God I hadn't seen him. I'd been happily putting together a box of comics so I could display them out front, when I'd heard *that voice*, and that had been enough. I'd frozen. Nearly panicked. Nearly *cried*. What the hell?

Fortunately, Lydia had handled the situation. She hadn't come back to grab me and have me deal with him. Thank God, because I didn't think I could face him right now. Not without going to jail or breaking down, and I wasn't sure which of those options was worse.

"Hey." Lydia appeared in the doorway.

"Hey. Thanks for . . ." I motioned toward the sales floor.

"Don't mention it." She showed me a folded piece of paper. "He said to give this to you." She held it up but didn't hand it over. "You want it? Or do you want me to just get rid of it?"

My first instinct was to tell her to nuke it from orbit. Failing that, put it through the shredder. *Then* nuke it from orbit. I had a feeling I knew what it was—an explanation. Some sort of excuse that would make it my fault or tell me how I'd overreacted. I'd heard it all before and wasn't interested in hearing it again.

But I was also a goddamned masochist, so I held my hand out for the note.

Lydia hesitated. She probably knew exactly what was going on in my head and was already bracing for impact. Still, she handed me the note.

Before I read it, I offered the closest thing I could muster to a smile. "Thanks again for standing up for me."

Her smile was also subtle, not to mention a bit sheepish. "Probably wasn't my place, but it was either that or bludgeon him with something."

That actually pulled a laugh out of me. "As long as you'd called me out from the back first so I could watch."

She gave my shoulder a gentle squeeze, but said nothing else. She walked away, leaving me to my note.

I stared down at it for a long moment, thumbing the crease. It was tempting to toss it or burn it or turn it into confetti. I'd already met my monthly quota for ignorant idiots justifying why they wouldn't touch me without a biohazard suit on. Why subject myself to another round of it?

My heart was in my throat, and I was afraid to read it. I wanted to hear him say it in person. Look me in the eye and fucking say it where he couldn't hide from how much he was hurting me and how pathetic his stupid excuse was. But then I'd actually *hear* his stupid excuse, and I couldn't crumple that up, toss it in a trash can, and set it on fire like I could with this note.

And why the hell wasn't I crumpling it up and burning it? I couldn't think of a single reason that didn't involve torturing myself with the ridiculous hope that he could somehow justify the other night. No, I knew better. I hadn't misunderstood shit. Maybe he thought he could smooth something like that over, but this wasn't my first rodeo. There was no way he'd written anything here that would make him any different than the men who'd come—and gone—before him.

So . . . fuck him.

I crunched up the note in my hand and tossed it. It bounced off the wall and into the trash can with a satisfying *thunk*.

Then I went back to work and didn't give the note another look.

I clocked out at the end of my shift and headed home. Even after a couple of reassuring pep talks from Simon and murderous comments about Garrett from Lydia, I didn't feel any better. My guts were still in knots and I was still grinding my teeth, but hey, at least I could go do that at home now. And there was alcohol there.

There's also alcohol at—

At the Alehouse.

My feet stopped. I was halfway to my car, but I turned around and glared at the Alehouse sign.

All damned day, I'd been thinking about the note I'd left crumpled in the trash can. I hadn't been able to make myself read it. Then Dexy had taken out the trash and the point had been moot, but the note was still on my brain. As much as I really didn't want to hear yet another explanation about why my status was so horrifying, this thing with Garrett didn't feel . . . done. It wasn't that I needed closure—it just felt like something else needed to happen. I groaned. Fine. *Fine.* I'd go hear what he had to say, and then I could hate him for real once he'd confirmed everything I already knew, which basically amounted to him being an ignorant asshole. At least then I wouldn't have to wonder or make it even worse in my head. Because I would absolutely do that.

With a string of profanity that would have horrified my mother, I shoved my hands into my pockets and headed back up the sidewalk toward the Alehouse.

I stepped into the neon-lit bar, and by the time my eyes adjusted, Garrett had already zeroed in on me. His expression offered nothing. Only that he saw me.

Well, no turning back.

My stomach roiled as I went up to the bar. Even more when he stood in front of me. Somehow I unstuck my tongue from the roof of my mouth and croaked, "Hey."

"Hey." He shifted nervously. "You got my note?" He sounded hopeful, but nervous.

"Yeah, I . . ." I chewed my lip and stared at a couple of drops of water on the bar between us. "I got it, but I, uh, didn't read it."

Garrett blinked. "You didn't?"

"No." I narrowed my eyes. "Whatever it is, you're going to have to say it to my face."

He flinched like I'd slapped him. I'd expected him to be annoyed that he'd have to repeat everything he'd written, but that flinch caught me off guard.

Without meeting my gaze, he nodded. "Okay. That's fair. Let's not do this in here, though." He motioned toward the potbellied bald guy at the cash register. "Give me a second to tell my boss I'm stepping out for a minute."

I nodded, gritting my teeth against the anger and dread. What was I doing?

But I didn't stop him. When he returned, he led me out the back door of the bar and into an alleyway. It wasn't one of those creepy piss-scented alleys like you'd find in New York or Seattle—just a narrow gap between the buildings with some cracked concrete, a closed dumpster, and a couple of lawn chairs next to a coffee can full of cigarette butts. And for that matter, it reminded me a bit too much of the talk I'd had with Charlie behind End o' Earth. Déjà vu all over again. Yay.

And you were expecting . . .?

I should've read the stupid note and been done with it. Why did I do this to myself? I shifted uncomfortably, glancing down the alley and wondering how quickly I could get to the end of it and be home free. A few feet away from me, Garrett folded his arms tightly across his chest. Not defensively—more like he was warding off a chill even though the night was kind of warm.

I folded my arms too and did nothing to temper the hostility in my posture. "Okay." I jutted out my chin and squared my shoulders. "Talk." *And make it quick before I decide I don't want to hear it.*

Garrett took a deep breath.

Before he could speak and before I could stop myself, I snapped, "You want to know why I was alone the night I met you?"

He blinked. "Uh... okay?"

"Because the guy I was meeting freaked out after he found out I'm positive." An ache in my throat warned that my composure wasn't as solid as I'd hoped. "He was totally into me right up until—" My voice cracked, and I clenched my teeth.

"Jesus," Garrett breathed. "So this was already a raw nerve."

"You think?" I growled. "And even if it wasn't, I mean, what did you think—"

"Jesse." He pressed the air with both hands. "Please. Let me explain myself. Even if it's not enough, I just need you to know why I freaked out. I promise, it's not what you think."

Well, I had said I would, so I gritted my teeth and tightened my arms across my chest. "Fine. Make it quick."

He swallowed. Then he pulled in another deep breath, hesitated like he thought I might jump in again, and finally spoke. "Before I moved to Bluewater Bay, I was married. To a younger man." His lips pulled tight for a second, and when he went on, his voice was unsteady. "He was... The thing is, I had fifteen years on him, and I just assumed—took for granted, really—that he'd outlive me."

Something cold somersaulted behind my ribs. I held my breath. This was not the direction I'd anticipated the conversation going, and I had no idea what to say.

Garrett moistened his lips. "We'd both pretty much expected that, you know? We'd planned for it. Made peace with it. We knew anything was possible, but chances were . . ." He made a *do the math* gesture.

My mouth had gone dry, but I somehow managed to whisper, "What happened to him?"

"Cancer." The word came out as a barely audible whisper. His Adam's apple bobbed, and he released a long breath. "He was so ridiculously healthy, we all joked at work that he should auction off his sick time for the rest of us to use. Then he . . ." His eyes lost focus. After a long silence, he shook his head. "Anyway. We knew the day he was diagnosed that it was a matter of when, not if. The doctors gave him six months at most, and they made it clear they were being generous."

"Oh my God," I breathed.

"He ended up holding on for eighteen." Garrett's sad laugh was almost as heartbreaking as what he was telling me. "Stubborn son of a bitch."

I stared at him in stunned silence.

Garrett sobered as he met my eyes. "I'm telling you this because . . . the thing is, the other night, when you told me you were positive, I . . . I panicked. But not for the reason you think."

My tongue stuck to the roof of my mouth again, and my heart slammed against my ribs.

He went on. "In that moment, all I could think of was when we found out Sean had cancer. When they . . . said it would kill him. And I . . ." A shudder ran through him. "The point is, it wasn't that I was disgusted or afraid you'd infect me if we fooled around. That didn't even cross my mind. It just triggered something. Took me back to a dark place. Combine that with remembering what it was like to grow up gay in the eighties and nineties, and yeah, I was scared, but it wasn't for myself. It was . . ." He pushed out a ragged breath. "It was for what might happen to *you*."

It took a few seconds, but the pieces fell together in my head, and somehow I found the air to whisper, "You were afraid of watching me die."

He hesitated but nodded. "I know it's stupid, and I know they've made leaps and bounds in how the disease is treated. I know things have changed, and the prognosis isn't grim like it used to be, but like I said, I'm from the era when it was a shit show. And I mean, we just met. It isn't like either of us has any idea where this"—he gestured at both of us—"could go. But like I said, I panicked. I went back to . . ." He swallowed. "That memory is still pretty fresh."

I didn't speak right away. I let it all sink in first. Eventually, I moistened my lips. "How long has it been?"

Garrett sighed. "He passed away last June. I . . . moved out here last month because I couldn't . . ." He rubbed a hand over his face, and good God, he suddenly seemed exhausted. Had he been that way all this time? "The bottom line is, I'm sorry."

I had no idea what to say. None. Not a clue.

Garrett cleared his throat. "So that's it." He looked in my eyes. "And to be clear, what you told me didn't make me want you any less."

"Really?"

He nodded. "You're the first person who's turned my head since my husband. I like you. And I . . ." He blushed a little and looked at the ground. "To be honest, I thought my sex drive was dead and gone until I met you, but I also didn't realize how badly I'd been needing just some *affection* until you touched me."

My knees almost buckled under the weight of his shaky words. I still didn't know what to say, but I had a feeling what he needed from me right then wasn't anything I could articulate anyway. Instead, I came closer and reached for his hand, first letting my fingertips graze his knuckles, then sliding my hand over the back of his.

For several long seconds, we both stared at that point of contact. Slowly, Garrett turned his hand over, and my heart raced as our fingers laced together. The heat of his palm against mine made my head spin. I'd come out here ready to let him have it for being an ignorant asshole, and now . . . this.

Garrett lifted his gaze. Our eyes locked, and he held my hand tighter. With the other, he reached across the void and cupped my face. "I am so sorry. I never meant to make you feel the way I did."

"No, I get it now." I ran my fingers through his hair. "Now I understand why you were trying to stop me when I left."

He nodded. "Yeah. And I mean it—I'm sorry. You deserved a hell of a lot better than that."

"Thanks." It was a dumb thing to say, but I didn't know how else to respond. "And you're . . . You really still want to . . ."

"Yes. Nothing you told me changes anything. I still . . ." Color rose in his cheeks. Uncertainly, he smoothed my hair, and a cautious smile formed on his lips. Looking at me through his lashes, he spoke in a husky whisper. "What can I say? You're fucking hot."

I laughed, and so did he, and the tension seemed to flutter away. Drawing him to me, I said, "You're not so bad yourself."

Garrett grinned, his expression still nervous but gradually relaxing. "So you're not opposed to hooking up with someone who remembers rotary phones?"

"Rotary what now?"

He rolled his eyes, and I laughed as I moved in closer.

"For what it's worth," I murmured against his lips, "I am absolutely not opposed to hooking up with you."

"Thank God for that," he growled and kissed me.

Holy fuck. I shivered hard enough to mess with my balance, then leaned into Garrett. Wrapping my arms around him, I opened to his kiss, and my whole body broke out in goose bumps as his tongue slid past mine.

There was something different about the way Garrett kissed me this time. I was used to a certain amount of tentativeness from someone who'd just figured out I was positive, but that wasn't it. In fact, it was the opposite. He kissed me hungrily and aggressively, like he'd been craving this since the other night. It was like he was more . . . not relaxed, but open. Guard down. Cards not tucked so firmly against his vest. If I'd thought for a second that he really did have a problem with my status, that evaporated in the heat of his kiss. No man who was afraid of being infected kissed me like that.

Moaning softly, he pressed me up against the cool brick wall, letting his erection nudge my hip. I broke the kiss with a gasp, and suddenly his lips were on my neck, and I thought I was going to melt right down the wall.

We'd talked about going slow, but suddenly that didn't feel like an option. It was almost like we'd both been putting on the brakes because of the things we hadn't said, and now that we'd talked, there was no reason to hesitate. No reason at all. At this point, I'd be lucky if I held out until we were in private.

"So, uh . . ." I gulped. "So much for moving slow, right?"

"You still want to move slow?"

"N-no."

Garrett lifted his head and brushed his lips across mine. "Neither do I."

"Except . . ." I struggled to find my breath. "You're still at work."

He stiffened, then swore, and I wondered if he'd actually forgotten where he was. "Damn it. I should . . ." He looked in my eyes. "I'm off in a couple of hours."

"I'll text you my address." I grinned, sliding my hands up the front of his shirt. "And when you're off work, I'll be standing by for some adult content."

He laughed. "I like the sound of that."

"Figured you would." I was tempted to move in for another kiss, but I had a feeling that would just keep us out here until he got fired. "I should let you get back to work."

Garrett scowled but nodded as he caressed my cheek. "If you're sure about me coming by later..."

"Completely." I grinned and turned to kiss his palm, then flicked my tongue across the center of it.

He shivered and licked his lips. "I'll be there as soon as I can."

CHAPTER FOURTEEN

GARRETT

I swung by my apartment for a shower and changed into some clothes I hadn't been sweltering in for the last several hours, then put Jesse's address into my GPS. Bluewater Bay wasn't exactly a huge town, so it wasn't at all surprising that his apartment was less than a mile and a half from mine. In minutes, I was parked in a guest spot and hauling ass up to his front door.

Ignoring my nerves—and good God, I had a few—I knocked.

The dead bolt clicked, ratcheting up my nerves by at least tenfold, and the door opened, and—

This was exactly where I needed to be.

Jesse met my gaze from across the threshold. We both stared for a moment, nothing but cool night air between us. He'd showered too, his bleached blond hair damp and a little messy. I was peripherally aware that his T-shirt had something snarky on it, but comprehending the words and the colorful cartoon meant pulling my attention away from his sparkling blue eyes, and that wasn't an option right now.

Jesse's grin hovered between shy and suggestive, and it edged toward the former as he stepped aside and motioned for me to come in. When he shut the door behind us, I thought I heard him pull in a ragged, nervous breath, but when he faced me, the shyness in his expression was gone. In seconds, my nerves were overshadowed by excitement and need. I could decide tomorrow if we'd moved too fast—tonight we weren't moving fast enough.

Grinning so wickedly he was damn near smirking, he stepped toward me. I thought one of us should say something, but I didn't know what, and he didn't offer anything. Instead, he locked eyes with me, and his hands followed my belt around to the small of my back as he lifted himself up to kiss me.

Oh yeah. This was definitely where I needed to be tonight.

I sighed into his kiss as I wrapped my arms around him. "Sorry I took so long."

"You're right on time."

And with that, we were kissing again, hard and deep and relentless. Jesse pushed me back a step, and I grunted as my shoulders hit the wall. He pressed against me, his body hot and his cock hard as he explored my mouth and overwhelmed me with *him*. I slid my hands down over his ass, reveling in the throaty moan that vibrated against my lips as I squeezed the firm muscles.

My God. Thirty seconds in his arms, and I was high. Turned on, shaking, and fucking *high*, and it was amazing. Jesus. The only times I'd really given myself over to anything pleasurable in recent memory had been when Scott and I lit up on his balcony, and that hadn't been close to this. The marijuana highs were great, but not like the taste of Jesse's kiss. The weed killed my focus. Left me too scattered to think.

I wasn't scattered now. Jesse pulled my focus to him, and he held it, narrowing my world to him and only him. To turning him on the way he'd effortlessly turned me on. Exploring him. Tasting him. Finding out exactly how he sounded when he came.

"We should go in the bedroom," he breathed between kisses. "It's a lot more comfortable than my couch, and that's where we're going to end up if we keep doing this." We weren't in a bedroom already? Holy shit.

I laughed and claimed another kiss before murmuring, "Lead the way."

Jesse nipped at my lower lip, then let me go, took my hand, and led me down the short hall. He shut the bedroom door behind us. I wasn't sure why I was relieved by the closed door. There was no one else in the apartment, so who cared? But with the click of the latch, the whole universe was sealed outside, and it was just him, me, a bed, and everything we could squeeze out of a night together.

In the quiet confines of the bedroom, before our lips had even touched, Jesse was tugging my shirt from the back of my waistband.

As his tongue slid past mine, his warm hands slid up my back, and I gasped hard enough to break the kiss.

Jesse froze. "What? What's wrong?"

"Nothing." I shook my head, laughing at my own reaction as I pulled him back in. "Just . . . haven't been touched in a while." It sounded stupid to my ear, but Jesse gave no indication it had sounded stupid to him. He kissed me again, slowly and languidly, and his hands continued under my shirt.

How was it that the simple contact of a man's hands on my bare skin could shake me to the core like this? It wasn't my first time with a man. Just my first time since the world had ended. Suddenly it seemed like even longer since I'd been intimate with someone, and my senses weren't just overwhelmed by Jesse's touch—they were overwhelmed by the need for *more*.

I mirrored him and pushed my hands under the back of his shirt. He arched into me, humming softly against my lips as his fingertips pressed into my skin. As his body heat radiated into my palms and through his clothes, my head spun. I inhaled his scent like it was a drug. Savored his skin and his warmth and his contours like I'd been at sea forever and he was dry land. My own thoughts were too stupidly poetic, almost making me laugh out loud, but I didn't care. For the better part of a year—more than that—I'd swung between pain and numbness, and suddenly there was this. My brain could make it all into whatever ridiculous poetry it wanted to as long as I had Jesse's smooth, sexy body against mine. And we weren't even naked yet.

I needed to feel and see more of him, so I pushed his shirt higher, and we broke the kiss and the embrace long enough to strip it off. Jesse peeled my shirt off too, and then we were tugging at belts and zippers, and somehow we toed off our shoes and . . .

My scrambled brain registered nothing except clumsy movement and cool air and hot skin until I realized I was pulling Jesse down onto the bed on top of me. Naked. Both of us. He sank onto me, hard cock grazing mine as soft lips descended on my neck. I closed my eyes and exhaled, tilting my head to offer more of my throat as I ran my hands up his arms and over his shoulders. Jesse took full advantage. He kissed from my jaw down to my collarbone, then back up the other side, all the while rocking his hips *so* subtly against me.

I lost myself in it. Completely. In want and heat and breathing and touching. From the moment I'd realized I was attracted to him, I'd been afraid this was happening too soon. Now that we were naked together, everything we did seemed long overdue. Like every inch of my body that hadn't yet been touched was aching furiously for a brush of his hand or a rub of his leg. I'd been aware of my loneliness before tonight, but now I could *feel* it as sure as I could feel the sheets under my back and Jesse's beautiful body stretched out on top of me. I could feel it, but it was falling away every time he kissed my neck or I ran my fingers through his damp hair.

When he found his way back to my mouth, I grabbed his hair and kissed him greedily, and the shudder that ran through him made him grind even harder against me. The subtle rocking wasn't so subtle anymore, the friction driving me wild. I wanted this to last all night, and I wanted to get off right now, and . . . fuck, I just wanted . . .

"I want you so bad," I said.

Jesse shuddered again, growling against my lips. "What do you want me to do?"

"Anything. Everything."

"Anything?" There was a teasing lilt in his voice, but a note of caution too.

"What do you have in mind?"

He moaned again and kissed me and barely broke the kiss enough to purr, "I want to fuck you."

My body responded like he was already buried to the hilt in me, and I arched under him. "Yes, *please*."

Jesse shivered hard, squirming against me. "Turn over."

One more kiss and we separated. I'd barely positioned myself on my hands and knees before the wrapper tore. The lube bottle clicked. Hoping he didn't notice my nerves, I gulped and willed myself to relax. I'd almost convinced myself there was no reason to be nervous at all when his hands curved over my ass, kneading the muscles. I closed my eyes. Every time he touched me, I was acutely aware of how long it had been since anyone had. Instead of exciting me, though, knowing he was getting ready to fuck me made me tense up all over. It felt like decades since I'd done this, and a million panicked thoughts skittered through my brain. Should we go slow? Would it hurt like it had the very first time? Did I still know how to relax and enjoy—

His tongue. There was nothing, and then there was his tongue, and I couldn't breathe as he drew gentle circles over my hole. All the panic vanished in favor of *Oh my God* and *Yes, more.* It had been way too long since I'd had sex, and even longer since I'd experienced this, and my elbows shook under me as my entire body threatened to collapse beneath the intensity of his soft, patient touch.

The panic was gone, and so was the tension. Everything ceased to exist except the pleasure of Jesse rimming me like he intended to do it all night. He was in no rush. His cock must've been painfully hard, and he'd sounded desperate to start fucking me, but that sense of urgency was replaced now by this languid and unhurried motion. His tongue was pure magic. Much more of this, and he was liable to make me come without touching my cock or being inside me.

"Oh God." I squeezed my eyes shut and let my head fall forward. "That's so good."

He moaned, his voice vibrating against my sensitive skin. Then his hand drifted between my legs to cup my balls, and I thought I was going to lose my mind. He caressed my cock and balls, licked all around my hole, and my entire body was hot and tingling and trembling. None of the sensations were *new*, per se—I was hardly a virgin—but everything was distinctly *Jesse.* Familiar and not. His soft but insistent tongue. His teasing touch. The echo of his sultry voice when he'd said he wanted to fuck me.

And if he didn't get to that part soon, I was going to be reduced to a pile of ash in a matter of minutes.

"C'mon," I pleaded. "Fuck . . . fuck me."

He swirled his tongue, then murmured, "Eager?"

"You think?"

He laughed as he pushed himself up, and his hand curved over my hip. Genuine concern filled his voice when he spoke. "Need me to use my fingers, or should I just—"

"Just go for it." I curled my hands around the sheets. "I can't wait."

He ran his palm from my hip to my side. "Just say so if you want to slow down."

"I will."

He shifted around behind me. There was another click of the lube bottle. The soft hiss of—I assumed—his hand stroking more lube onto the condom. Gently, he put some on me too, sliding a finger inside to make sure I was good and covered. The penetration made my head spin. Maybe I did need him to finger me first.

I rocked back against him, encouraging him to keep doing it. He laughed softly, but he didn't slide his finger free. He fucked me with it slowly, and when I could breathe again, he added a second. For what must've been hours, he teased me with his hand, scissoring his fingers to stretch me in between taking deliciously slow strokes. As impatient as I was to take his cock, this felt amazing.

After God only knew how long, he withdrew his fingers, and his hand materialized on my hip. "Ready?"

"Mm-hmm." I wasn't just ready for it now—I was hungry for it. Needy and desperate in ways I hadn't known in a long time. My dry spell had been no one's fault, but that hadn't made it any less painful, and it didn't make this relief any less profound.

Jesse guided himself to me. The pressure increased slowly, both of us taking long breaths as we waited for me to relax enough to take him.

"Oh God," he groaned even before I'd yielded to him. "This is . . . gonna be fast . . ."

I just nodded, leaning back against him, eyes watering as the head of his cock started to slide past the tight ring. I couldn't speak. Couldn't see. Could barely breathe. It wasn't just from the intense burn, though. It had just been so long. Too long. I'd been overwhelmed tonight by lips on mine and hands on skin and the weight of another man on top of me. Taking him inside me, knowing he wanted me—it was hard not to get emotional as too many months of physical isolation came to an end.

Jesse groaned again as he pushed deeper. He withdrew a little, then eased in farther, and the slide of his cock made my spine tingle. I couldn't tell if he was moving slowly to tease me or to keep from hurting me, but it had both effects. The stretch was intense, but not unpleasant, and the slowness drove me insane with the need to be fucked hard and fast.

"More," I finally croaked. "C'mon."

"More?" His hands drifted up and down my back, and he was panting already. "You want it hard?"

I nodded. "Please."

"Oh, baby," he murmured as he slowly withdrew. "I'm so not kidding—this is gonna be fast."

"Bring it."

He made a sound that might've been a laugh or just a delirious moan, but before I could give it much thought, he thrust into me, nearly knocking my arms out from under us. He did it again. And again. My arms weren't going to hold us up, but I didn't care. Every time he buried his dick inside me, I unraveled a little more, and I wanted to shatter. The pleasure was overwhelming, almost excruciating, and every thrust added more intensity, like layers of electricity, if such a thing were possible.

I squeezed my eyes shut, and a few hot tears slid down my face. Not just from the physical sensations, either. For months, I'd been constantly aware of that deep, painful sense of loss, but tonight was the first time I was aware of my grief like this. It seemed to be falling away, pieces sliding off my shoulders with every thrust like plaster knocked off a wall by a headboard.

There's life after all that grief, something seemed to be telling me.

Yes. Yes, there was. And holy fuck, after feeling like shit for so long . . .

"Oh God!" I cried out. "That's so . . . so good."

He whimpered. Then he slowed down. His weight shifted, and he pressed me down onto my stomach, and he stayed with me, molding his body to mine. Once we'd settled onto the mattress, he started moving again, rocking his hips as he kissed the back of my neck along my hairline. The soft brush of his lips turned me on as much as the slow, deep strokes he was taking inside me.

"Fuck," he moaned. "I'm . . . close, but I don't want . . . yet . . ."

"Want you to come." I pressed my forehead into the sheets. "Then we can do it again."

He swore against my neck and thrust just a little bit harder, his body shaking all over as he forced himself into me. My eyes welled up again as he moved. I was so close to coming, but as I fought back the tears, it kept my orgasm at bay too, and I couldn't breathe as I rode that line, as I hovered on the edge of breaking in every way, and then Jesse moaned in my ear, "Oh fuck, I'm gonna come."

I moaned too, my own climax closing in fast as his voice and body shook with arousal. I screwed my eyes shut, squeezing a few hot tears free in the same instant my orgasm jolted through me. I gasped, swore, and then he was burying his face against my neck and fucking me harder, deeper, riding me with erratic and needy thrusts until a hot breath rushed past my neck, and he shuddered.

Jesse sagged over me and exhaled. "Fuck . . ."

"Yeah. Fuck." I pressed my forehead into the mattress, struggling to catch my breath. "That was . . . so good."

"Uh-huh." He kissed my neck just below my hair and sucked in a sharp hiss as one last shudder rippled through him.

Then we were still. Just lying there. Just breathing. His skin was sweaty and feverishly hot, and mine probably was too, and I was pretty sure I could feel his heart pounding right alongside mine.

"You okay?" he murmured.

"Way more than okay."

"Good." He kissed behind my ear and pulled out, but he didn't get up. Instead, he burrowed against my neck again. "For what it's worth, I'm really glad you came by the shop."

The words jarred something in me. Everything from the last couple of days seemed like they'd been a dream or something I'd seen in a movie. The guilt, shame, and panic were distant memories. The nervousness about him confronting me? Gone. It was like this— panting and sweating in his bed—had been inevitable, but it hadn't been. One wrong word or lapse in courage, or Jesse not changing his mind after tossing the note, and tonight wouldn't have happened.

Somehow, everything had gone right, and we'd found our way to this.

"Yeah." I reached back to stroke his hair. "Me too."

Neither of us moved for a little while. We'd gotten out of his bed long enough to clean ourselves up, but ever since then, we'd just been lying here, kissing lazily and soaking up the afterglow. At one point, I thought he'd drifted off. I might've dozed myself.

"Still awake?" he asked.

I nodded, then pressed a kiss to his shoulder. "Mm-hmm."

"Me too." He paused. "Can I ask you something?" There was a hint of nerves in his voice. If I hadn't been fully awake before, I was now.

"About?"

He swallowed. "About your husband?"

My stomach somersaulted hard. "Um. Yeah. I guess?" I wasn't sure how that topic would affect the mood in the room right now, but I supposed there was nothing wrong with us being open and honest about things. "Go ahead."

Jesse shifted onto his side and lifted himself up on his elbow. "I'm just curious about him. Most guys I've dated, they've got exes, you know? And they're usually talking catty shit about them." He trailed his knuckles up my chest. "I've never been with someone who lost a partner the way you did. I guess . . . like I said, I guess I'm curious about him."

"What do you want to know?"

"Well . . ." His eyes lost focus for a second. "I guess the basics. How did you guys meet?"

I couldn't help smiling fondly at the memory. "We worked together, actually."

"So he was a bartender?"

"No, no." I shook my head. "I was an accountant before."

Jesse's eyebrows shot up. "No shit?"

"Why is that so hard to believe?"

"I don't know. I guess . . . I mean, I've only seen you as a bartender." He looked me up and down as he ran a fingertip across my stomach. "I'm trying to imagine all this wrapped up in a shirt and tie with a pocket protector and—"

I laughed and batted his hand away playfully. "Shut up. I did *not* wear a pocket protector."

"But . . . you're not saying no to the shirt and tie?"

"Shirt. Tie. Glasses. The works." I rolled my eyes. "I was an accountant and I looked the part."

"You wear glasses?"

"Mm-hmm."

He looked a little closer. "Ah. Contacts. Never noticed them before." A soft smile—a shy one—spread across his lips. "Now I want to see you in your glasses."

I laughed. "You'll get your chance, I'm sure."

"Good." He paused, then shook his head. "Anyway. I'm sorry. I . . . Crap, now I kind of feel like an ass. I was asking you about something serious, and—"

"It's okay." I slid my hand up his arm. "This is kind of nice, actually. It's been a long time since I've been able to talk to someone about him without focusing on . . ." I swallowed. "Focusing on the end."

"That must've been rough."

"It was. So, how we met." I laughed at the memory. "We were coworkers. I'd been with the company for about eight years when he started over in the marketing department. And I couldn't *stand* him."

"Really? Why not?"

I laughed. "Because he was way too fucking chipper at eight o'clock staff meetings."

"Oh my God." Jesse drew back, a hand to his chest and expression so horrified, I might as well have told him Sean had been a serial killer. "That's . . . ew."

"Exactly. Plus I took my drab, serious accountant persona seriously, and he was the exact opposite. Sean was . . . he was one of those people who came into a room, and you *knew* he was there. He wasn't loud or obnoxious, but he wasn't exactly a wallflower either. And that just grated on my nerves." I paused, then added, "He called himself the Queen of Marketing."

"Like, queen of the department? Or the entire profession?"

I thought about that for a second. "He'd probably say both."

"So what changed?" He paused. "I mean, if you don't mind talking about it."

"I don't. Like I said, this is nice." I took a breath and gazed up at the ceiling. "When our company hit its twenty-fifth anniversary, they took us out on one of those cruises in Puget Sound. I was, um, a little drunk."

"I'm going to guess you were more than 'a little' drunk."

"Oh, I was." I chuckled, rolling my eyes. "I don't drink much now, but I did back then. *And* there was an open bar. *And* I was surrounded by people who annoyed me."

"I can see why you were drinking."

"Yep. So there I was, grumpily getting shit-faced, and the next thing I know, Sean and I are on one of the outside decks, and I suddenly forgot he wasn't my type *at all*. Next thing after that, we were fucking in one of the restrooms."

Jesse's eyebrows shot up. "Really?"

My cheeks burned as I nodded. "Yep. Once I was drunk enough not to be annoyed by him or anyone else, I realized that good *God*, that man was hot."

"Nice," Jesse said with a soft chuckle.

I couldn't help grinning. "It was a little awkward at work on Monday, and we kind of avoided each other for a couple of days. Which wasn't too hard—it was a small building, but we didn't have to interact all that much. Then he came into my office and said we should clear the air. One very fast blowjob later, the air was definitely cleared."

"Wow. He came in and blew you at work?"

"Actually, I blew him."

Jesse straightened. "Really?"

I laughed. "Why is that such a shock? You don't think I like sucking dick?"

He shivered. "It's not that. Just . . . I don't know. I guess I have a hard time imagining you as the type to suck a guy off at work. Or maybe because if we worked together, I'd be fantasizing about sucking *you* off in your office."

It was my turn to shiver, which made Jesse grin.

"*Anyway*," I said. "We realized we liked fooling around, and it didn't take long for us to realize we liked each other too. A lot. It sounds crazy, but it wasn't two weeks before I knew I'd marry him." A pang of panic mixed with guilt hit me in the gut. I was in bed with another man telling him it was practically love at first fuck with someone else? Would this make things awkward?

But Jesse smiled. "That's kind of sweet, actually. And you were right."

"Yeah, I was." The guilt eased as I realized Jesse wasn't put off, and the more I thought about it, the more I also realized how good it was to be able to talk about Sean without feeling like my chest was going to crack open. The fact that I was naked in bed with another man seemed like it should've made me feel like an asshole, but it didn't. It was weirdly comforting, actually. Like a huge step forward. I wasn't at home wallowing in my grief, and I wasn't pretending Sean had never existed. Instead I'd found a happy medium that I hadn't imagined was possible. One where Sean was still gone, but I was still living my life. Still *enjoying* my life. The void he'd left would never completely close, but it felt less like something that would swallow me up and consume me.

"So, Sean wasn't your type?"

I shook my head. "Nope."

"So . . . what *is?*"

"Well, prior to him, I was always into really, really masculine types. I had a thing for bikers and military guys, and I had a perma-hard-on for the guys renovating my apartment in college."

Jesse grinned. "You have good taste. Did the workers on your apartment at least have the decency to walk around shirtless?"

"More often than not." I shivered at the memory. "Fuck, they were hot."

"Sounds like it." He trailed his fingers along my thigh and offered a devilish smile. "Are you not into guys like that anymore? Or did Sean just open your eyes to what it's like to be with someone this *fabulous?*"

Even as I laughed, a knot grew in my stomach. I turned onto my side, facing Jesse, and slid a hand over his waist. "He's the reason I decided a guy didn't have to be six feet of hairy muscles to be attractive, yes." I smiled despite that knot and pulled him a little closer. "But I'm pretty sure a certain hot, ballsy blond strutting into the Alehouse would've caught my eye no matter what."

He laughed too but seemed slightly uneasy. "Oh yeah?"

"Mm-hmm." I made an emphatic gesture of running my hand up and down his side and his smooth abs, and when he shivered, I murmured, "You think I'd have missed out on this?"

Jesse bit his lip, squirming under my touch. "I'm glad you didn't. 'Cause I like what you do with it."

"Me too. And to be serious, I do find you very attractive. On your own, not just because of him."

He was quiet for a moment, watching his own hand drift along my arm. "When you're with me, do you think about him or me?"

"You." I paused. "I mean, I won't lie and say he doesn't cross my mind all the time, but that happens whether you're there or not." I cupped his face gently. "But if you're asking who I've been wanting for the last few days, and who I hope is coming in whenever the Alehouse door opens . . . no question. It's you."

He searched my eyes, and his smile slowly formed. "That's all I need to know, then." He lifted his head, kissed me softly, and then rested it on the pillow again. "I don't want you to forget him or not think about him. Just as long as you're thinking of me as me and not 'that guy who's kind of like him.'"

"Not at all." I grinned cautiously. "Pretty sure you're one of a kind anyway. You're amazing."

Jesse clicked his tongue and rolled his eyes. "Please." He pretended to buff his nails on a shirt he wasn't wearing. "I'm awesome."

I snorted. "Yes. Yes, you are." We shared a long, lazy kiss, and though that knot had still set up shop in my gut, it wasn't so tight now. I hadn't lied to Jesse—Sean was on my mind a lot, but when we were together, it was all about Jesse. I wanted him, and even if I'd been all about hypermasculine men in my younger days, I couldn't imagine ever not being attracted to this sexy, feisty man.

After a moment, I drew back and met his gaze. "So while we're talking about heavy personal things, can I ask you something?"

Jesse rested his palm in the middle of my chest. "I'd be kind of a hypocrite if I said no, don't you think?"

I shrugged. "I don't know about that."

"Either way—shoot."

I studied him for a moment, then softly asked, "How long have you been positive?"

Jesse's lips tightened and his eyes flicked away from mine for a second. "Since I was sixteen."

I stared at him. "You've . . . had it since you were a *kid*?"

He nodded. "I got it from a boyfriend in high school. Tested positive two weeks before my seventeenth birthday." Sighing, he shifted around. "Happy birthday to me."

"So, you didn't go years without it being detected. That's a good thing, right?"

Jesse shrugged. "It's good because then I could get it treated and under control faster, but the irony of it is that I was diagnosed early because my doc was a homophobic jackass."

I raised my eyebrows. "How do you figure?"

He shifted again, perching on his arm like he was settling in for a lengthy story. "I got sick, and at first everyone thought it was the flu. But it wouldn't go away, so my mom took me to the doctor. She was terrified I had mono, but the doc figured since I was such a beacon of heterosexuality that he should test me for"—Jesse made air quotes—"'everything.'"

I cocked my head. "He didn't actually make that beacon comment, did he?"

"Not out loud, but I could tell by his attitude. My sexuality was visible from space even back then, so it's not like it took a rocket scientist to put two and two together. He asked if I was sexually active—and, oh my God, he was so disgusted when he asked—and I was too embarrassed to admit it in front of my mom. Besides, my boyfriend and I had broken up, so it technically wasn't a lie." He rolled his eyes. "Anyway, he took some blood, and when the results came back, he was the only one who wasn't surprised."

"Just because you're gay?" I growled.

"Yes and no." Jesse huffed out a breath and rolled onto his back, putting a hand behind his head and looking up at the ceiling. "I guess the symptoms I had are kind of a red flag. Muscle pain, swollen lymph glands, being fucking tired all the time—it's acute retroviral syndrome. When the virus is, like, settling in and the body is going haywire."

"Huh. I never realized it showed symptoms at all that early."

"It doesn't with everyone." He smirked. "Guess I was lucky—symptomatic HIV and an apparently not-so-subtle penchant for sucking dick. The perfect storm to get my doctor to test me."

"I guess homophobia is useful once in a while."

"Right?" Jesse chuckled softly but didn't meet my gaze.

I cupped his face and traced his cheekbone with the pad of my thumb. "I assume you've been treated since then too?"

"Oh yeah. The antiretrovirals were shitty for a while until the docs found the right dose and the right med, but thank God I was diagnosed around the time some of the newer drugs were coming out. Early on, it was pretty bad—the shit I took in the beginning was fucking miserable. But then the good stuff came available, and my dad had insurance that actually covered it, so things got a lot better. My viral load's been undetectable for years. Aside from the ARS there at the beginning, I've never really had any symptoms." He scowled. "Well, except for side effects from the drugs, but those have been all right for a long time too."

"Good. Good." I exhaled. "Man. I just can't even imagine. Seventeen..."

"Yeah, well. Sixteen-year-olds don't always do bright things. As my dad always says, play stupid games? Win stupid prizes."

Frowning, I caressed his face. "I don't think having sex as a teenager qualifies as playing stupid games. Hormones are what they are."

"They are, but..." Jesse sighed, lowering his gaze. "Thing is, I knew the risks. I went to one of those schools that actually taught about condoms and HIV and everything. But my boyfriend told me he was a virgin, and I stupidly believed him. And since we were both"—he made air quotes again—"'virgins,' we didn't need to use condoms. So, we didn't."

"Jesus Christ."

"That was about my reaction. Thank God I was diagnosed early, before I'd been with someone else, or I might've infected *them*." He shuddered.

I swallowed. "What about him? I assume you told him?"

"Of course." Jesse rolled his eyes. "Naturally, he accused *me* of giving it to *him* even though *he* was the lying manwhore, but at least he got tested and..." He waved a hand. "Hopefully he got treated and started using rubbers."

"Hopefully." I studied him. There were moments when Jesse seemed so young, almost boyish, but then there were moments like this where he seemed years beyond his age. Which I supposed made sense—getting that news when you were barely old enough to drive was bound to age someone. I didn't want to think about how almost-seventeen-year-old me would have coped. "You must get a lot of people who don't take the news well." I cringed. "I'm sorry I was—"

"Stop." He took my hand and brought it to his lips. "Quit beating yourself up. Now that I know what really went through your mind, you had every right."

"Still."

He kissed my fingers again. "It's fine. And yeah, the reactions can run the gamut. Doesn't bother some people. Others get weird about it. Guys I try to hook up with can either be cool or run screaming for the hills. And to be honest, if it bothers them, I think I'd rather they be a dick and run off." He fidgeted like the conversation was making him uncomfortable. "It's a lot easier to take than being in bed with someone who's trying really, really hard not to show how much you disgust him."

"I'm sure." I still felt like an asshole for how I'd made him feel that first night, but I didn't apologize again.

Jesse moistened his lips. "You want to know what hurt the most after I tested positive?"

I raised my eyebrows.

"My parents kind of freaked out, and they ended up letting it out to my grandparents. Which . . ." He sighed. "I wasn't thrilled about that part, but . . ." He waved his hand. "Anyway, the thing that hurt? My grandma wouldn't kiss me on the cheek anymore."

If it had been possible, my heart would have literally snapped in two right then. I didn't know what to say, so I just slid closer to him and draped an arm over his stomach.

He watched his fingers trail up my forearm. "Before that, she was one of those grandmas, you know? And I'd always hated it because she'd just grab my face and give me a huge kiss on the cheek, and she had this lipstick that was almost impossible to get off. But then when we went to see her after we found out I was poz . . ." He chewed his lip. "Up until then, I'd been really scared, and I was freaking out that I was going to die. And I'd kind of assumed nobody would want to sleep with me again, but I was totally okay with that at the time because that was how I'd gotten it, you know?" He swallowed. "But when my grandma wouldn't do the thing she'd done every time she'd seen me from the time I was an infant . . ."

I laced our fingers together. "I can't begin to imagine. And I can see why you took my reaction the way you did. I can't really think of a reason why you *shouldn't* have."

"Once bitten," he whispered. He was quiet for a few seconds before shaking himself and meeting my gaze. "You had no way of knowing, though, and I'm really glad you didn't let that be the end of it."

"Me too."

"I know you're not disgusted." He ran his fingers through my hair. "Some guys will humor me enough to kiss me until they can tactfully bow out, but they're sure as hell not going to bottom without a second thought."

I squirmed at the memory of taking his thick cock. Caressing his cheek, I said, "They're idiots."

He met my eyes and a smile slowly formed. "I'm glad you didn't turn out to be one of them." Inching closer to me, he snaked his arm around to my back. "'Cause I kinda like what happens when we end up naked."

I laughed as goose bumps sprang up all over my body. "Yeah. Me too." As his thigh brushed mine, I sucked in a sharp breath. "Maybe we should do this again."

"Go another round tonight?" He lifted his chin for a brief kiss. "Or see each other again after this?"

"Yes."

Jesse laughed softly and kissed me for real, and I slid a hand up into his hair as he slid his tongue into my mouth.

Yeah, we were definitely doing this again.

And not just tonight.

CHAPTER FIFTEEN

JESSE

"I'm going to go out on a limb," Lydia said with a smirk, "and guess you and your boy made up last night?"

I glared at her over my coffee cup. "Don't you have . . ." I flailed a hand in the general direction of her art room. "Arting to do?"

"Oh yes. Plenty. But it can wait until I've finished giving you a hard time about limping in here with your eyes barely open."

"I'm not limping." I stretched a bit, wincing at the ache in my left hip. If I was this sore after three very athletic rounds in my bed, I could only imagine how Garrett felt today. The guy was plenty fit and limber, but he'd bottomed all three times. And he had like fifteen years on me. He had to be feeling it today. I just hoped he agreed that all the aches, twinges, knots, and stiff spots were *so* worth it.

Lydia cleared her throat, drawing my attention back to her. "You're aware that you're grinning like an idiot, right?"

Well, now that she mentioned it . . .

I coughed and schooled my expression. "I have no idea what you're talking about."

"Uh-huh." She laughed, but then she turned serious. "You guys did work things out, though?"

I nodded before taking a deep swallow of coffee. "There was, um . . . He was right. There was more to the story."

Her eyebrow arched the same way it did whenever I tried to bullshit her. "After what you told me, I'm a little hard-pressed to believe he had any excuse."

"He does." I rolled my stiff shoulders. "He's . . ." I hesitated, not sure how much I should tip Garrett's hand to my boss. "Just trust me, okay?"

Lydia pursed her lips.

"*Trust* me," I insisted, putting up my hands. "I don't want to go into detail because I don't want to share his business, but he made sense, and he also spent the whole night apologizing." I paused. "Well, when he could talk, I mean . . ."

She snorted and rolled her eyes, and her expression softened. "Okay. As long as you guys are on the same page."

"We are."

"Good." She finally smiled. "I trust your judgment. Just be careful, okay?"

"I will. Now get to work before the boss catches you slacking off."

Lydia laughed. "Brat." Then she went into her art room and I got to work. As I was straightening a display that some marauding kids had jostled, my phone buzzed. I glanced around. My bosses didn't mind me texting on the clock as long as I didn't abuse the privilege, but I didn't need someone glancing over my shoulder if things got racy. Which they hadn't yet with Garrett, but after last night, I suspected they would.

Safe from prying eyes, I checked the message.

Can barely move today. Do it again? ;)

I shivered. Racy texts, right on schedule. *When/where?*

He responded before I'd even pocketed my phone. *Have to work late tonight, but I'm off tomorrow. Want to try that Italian place again?*

My heart fluttered as I wrote back, *Definitely. Esp if we go somewhere afterwards. ;)*

As long as "somewhere" means getting fucked like that again.

Oh. It does. It absolutely does.

It was weird to walk back into Il Trovatore with Garrett. Our first attempt at a date in this place had ended in disaster before the breadsticks had even arrived. Judging by the texts we'd been exchanging since yesterday, this attempt would end with bruises and orgasms. Just the way I liked it.

I suppressed a shiver as I took my seat. We were three tables over from the place we'd sat before. Another couple was at that table, gazing at each other lovingly while they talked over wine and steaks.

We did have the same waitress, though, and she gave us a wary side eye as she came to take our drink orders. I tried not to look as embarrassed as I felt. It wasn't like we'd made a huge scene the other night. I'd gotten up, made it halfway through storming out before Garrett had tried to stop me, and then finished storming out. I had no doubt people had noticed, and Garrett must've been *mortified*, but it wasn't like we'd had a screaming match in the middle of the dining room or something.

The waitress must have caught on fast that all was well between us now, because by the time we'd finished ordering our drinks, she'd visibly relaxed. It wasn't like we were the first couple to make a scene in public, then show up again like nothing had ever happened. Okay, we weren't exactly a couple, per se, but she didn't know that.

I didn't mention her reactions to Garrett. The less said about the other night, the better.

After we'd ordered dinner and gotten our drinks, I met his gaze across the table. "So, how are you settling into living here?"

"It's . . . an adjustment. The lack of traffic is a bonus."

I laughed. "Oh yeah. And the traffic has actually gotten a lot worse since *Wolf's Landing* showed up."

"Worse?" His eyebrow arched. "Than what? An old lady in a station wagon?"

"Basically."

Garrett smirked. "Oh, that must've been a hardship for all of you." He put a hand over his heart and sighed. "Going from two cars on the road to six."

"*Seven,*" I corrected. "In a town this small, that makes a difference."

Our eyes met, and we both laughed.

"Well, horrendous traffic aside," he said, "I do like it. It's a switch, but I like it."

"It's a nice little town. That's why I'm still here."

"I can see that. I don't know if I'll stay in that apartment, though. It's okay, but . . ." He wrinkled his nose. "I don't know. It just feels temporary, if that makes sense."

"Yeah, I get you." I took a quick drink, and as I put the glass down, added, "If you do decide to move, places are a lot cheaper outside of downtown. Especially outside the city limits."

"Not much to rent out there." He absently thumbed the edge of the placemat. "I'm not sure I want to buy anything quite yet."

"Understandable. I'm actually thinking of buying later this year. I've got money saved up for a down payment and all that, but I'm waiting until after the networks announce their cancelations."

Garrett cocked his head. "Why's that?"

"I've been hearing rumors that *Wolf's Landing* is getting canceled after this season. If it does, there's going to be a *huge* exodus from Bluewater Bay."

He grimaced. "Could mean a nasty blow to the economy."

"I know, and it'll probably be rough for a while, but Forks recovered after Twilight left, so . . ."

"Fair point. Hmm. I hadn't thought about waiting to see if the show's renewed. I'll keep that in mind."

"At least right now, everything in this town revolves around the show. There's a reason the newspaper includes the ratings every week."

Garrett whistled. "Seems a little precarious, basing an economy around something that could go away overnight."

"If you think about it, any town's economic base could implode." I shrugged. "Everett and Renton are pretty diverse, but let's face it—if Boeing ever closed, the whole western half of the state would be in a world of hurt."

"That's true. Very true." He paused, idly playing with the edge of his placemat. "So I've heard a lot of people say Bluewater Bay is small enough, everyone knows someone involved with the show." His eyebrows rose, silently asking for confirmation.

"Oh yeah. Definitely. I actually know a lot of people because the cast and crew come into the shop all the time. In fact, that's how I heard about the cancellation rumors. A couple of the actors were grumbling about it the other day. I hope it's not true—the ratings are still good, and they're not even halfway through the books—but it's really expensive to produce. So, we'll see." I paused. "Filming goes on hiatus pretty soon, and Carter's leaving for a couple of months to shoot a new film. Levi just came back from shooting another film in Canada. Everyone's hoping that'll put the two of them back on the radar of the mainstream audience and hopefully draw them to *Wolf's Landing*." I stopped again, realizing I'd been rambling. "Sorry, I'm—"

"Don't apologize." He smiled. "You really do get the inside scoop on this stuff, don't you?"

I laughed. "Well, like I said, the cast and crew come around a lot. Plus Ian—my bosses' boyfriend—works on the set. So, we hear a lot of it. And Carter was at almost every gaming tournament while Levi was gone. Poor guy was going crazy."

"And now *he'll* be gone."

I nodded. "So I figure we'll see Levi around the shop more."

Garrett straightened. "Oh really?"

"Mm-hmm. Carter's gotten him into gaming, and he's as much a comic book dork as any of us."

Garrett blinked, lips parting. "Levi . . . is a gamer? And into comics?"

"Yep." I grinned when the pieces came together. "You've got a bit of a crush, don't you?"

He instantly blushed and cleared his throat, glancing shyly around the restaurant as if someone might have overheard.

"Dude." I waved a hand. "I don't know many gay men who aren't into him. And Carter, for that matter."

"Carter's hot and all, but Levi?" Garrett shivered. "Good God. I've been into him since the first Chad Eastwick movie."

"Who hasn't? But, uh, don't ever mention that to him."

"Why's that?"

"Levi has, shall we say, a love-hate relationship with Chad Eastwick. The character put him on the map, but it also got him typecast for a long time."

"Ah." Garrett gave a slow nod. "That's why he retired for a while, isn't it?"

"Yep. So it's kind of a sore spot for him."

"Duly noted. Not that I expect to meet him anytime soon."

"Honey." I flashed him a wide grin. "You hang around me, you'll end up meeting him. Especially if you play cards at the shop."

"Oh. Good to know." He paused. "And actually, I might do that anyway. Believe it or not, after I came by the other day, I dug out my collection of Magic."

I sat straighter. "Did you?"

He smiled, the expression caught somewhere between devilish and sheepish. "I haven't played in a while, but going through the cards, the rules came back to me pretty fast. I mean, I might still be kind of rusty, but . . ." He half shrugged as he reached for his glass. "I've definitely got the itch to play again."

"Oh really? You want to play sometime? With me, I mean?"

Garrett's smile made the room spin. "Hell yeah. If you can handle getting your ass handed to you by an old guy, that is."

I sputtered. "It's gonna be like that, is it?"

He just winked.

Chuckling, I said, "Let's do it. I've always got a few decks ready to roll. So, you know, whenever you're game . . ."

He grinned over the rim of his glass. "Bring it on."

"Oh, I will."

"You must have a hell of a deck," he said. "Having an employee discount on cards, and getting all the latest expansions . . ."

"I do, yeah." I paused, suddenly a bit sheepish. "I, uh, probably shouldn't work at a comic and game shop, honestly. I'm lucky my paychecks make it out the door."

"But you get a discount, right?"

"I do," I admitted, "but I still probably spend more at the shop than I would if I wasn't there forty hours a week."

"Eh." Garrett shrugged. "It's obviously stuff you love, and if you've got enough money saved for a down payment on a house, I don't think anyone can judge you for indulging in comics and games."

I couldn't help smiling.

Right then, the waitress returned, balancing a large tray on her arm and shoulder. She carefully set our plates in front of us—chicken cacciatore for me and a delicious-looking eggplant parmesan for Garrett.

"Can I get you gentlemen anything else?" she asked.

Garrett looked up at her. "Could I get another Coke, please?"

"Of course." To me, she asked, "What about you, sweetheart?"

"I'm good, thanks."

She left, and Garrett shifted his attention back to me as we dug into our food. "So working at the comic book shop—is that a long-term job for you?" He sounded cautious, like he was curious but also worried he might offend me.

"Don't know." I sliced off a piece of chicken. "Originally, it was supposed to keep me in the black while I was taking care of my uncle, but it's turned out to be a pretty good job. They pay me well, the hours are flexible, and it's actually kind of fun. So." I shrugged. "Sometimes I think I should be doing something else. Sometimes I think I'll stick with what I'm doing."

Garrett nodded as he chewed. After he'd taken a drink from his nearly empty Coke, he said, "It's hard to find a job you like that pays the bills. I don't think there's any shame in sticking with it any more than there's shame in moving on to something else."

The comment surprised me. I was automatically defensive about my job because so many people had given me shit for still working in retail—especially this flavor of retail. They'd either condescend to me about how I needed to get a real job, or pat me on the head and be equally condescending about how if I was happy, that was all that mattered. But Garrett hadn't sounded like that at all. Both options were perfectly viable in his mind, and he didn't try to nudge me in either direction.

So why the hell was I suddenly self-conscious about my career choice?

Heat rushed into my cheeks, and I stared down at my food. "Sometimes I do think about finding something more . . . I don't know, respectable?"

"Why?"

Sighing, I met his gaze. "Because I'm not sure I want to go to my ten-year reunion and tell all my classmates I'm selling comic books for a living."

Garrett's eyes widened.

I shifted. "What?"

"Your . . . ten-year reunion?"

"Yeah. It's next year."

He groaned and pinched the bridge of his nose, and when I realized why, I laughed.

"Did I just make you feel old?"

"*So* old." He chuckled before taking another bite. The waitress finally showed up with his fresh Coke, and he took a sip as he met my gaze again. "In all seriousness, I wouldn't worry about how your life or your plans look to people you went to high school with. It's your life.

If you're happy with what you're doing, and it's providing what you need, you're ten steps ahead of more people than you realize."

I nodded, not sure how to respond.

"A lot of people plan their lives out carefully and do all the things they're supposed to," Garrett went on, "and then realize it isn't what they want after all. Or life throws them a curveball. I went to college right after high school, got a job as an accountant as soon as I graduated, and did the Monday-through-Friday, nine-to-five corporate gig—401(k) and all. And now I'm pouring drinks in a sports bar." He shrugged. "For me, it was because my circumstances changed. Maybe you just decide you want to do something different, or figure out what you've wanted to do all along. There's nothing that says you won't find your calling when you're forty, or that your calling is even a career. My sister works a soul-numbing job and throws the rest of her energy into what she's passionate about."

"Which is?"

"Painting. She's amazing, and she's even got some pieces on display in an art museum, but she's never made enough to give up her day job. And she's fine with that. Her art is something she does because she loves it. So, maybe your calling is something like that."

"Huh," I said quietly. "Maybe I just haven't figured out what it is yet."

"Maybe not."

Our conversation continued wandering through hobbies and jobs and things we'd done and things we *wished* we'd done. As we talked, it struck me how Garrett could offer advice and wisdom without talking down to me. Yeah, he had quite a few years on me. Yeah, he had more life experience than I did. But nothing about his comments made me feel like I was being lectured or patted on the head. Hell, he'd listened to my insights about the Bluewater Bay real estate market; most people treated me like I was a kid who should just focus on selling comics and making rent.

That wasn't Garrett's style, though, and I liked that about him.

I had a feeling that, as I got to know him better, I'd like a lot of things about him.

The first time we came to Il Trovatore, we'd barely lasted five minutes. Tonight, we more than made up for it. Long after we'd finished eating, we were still sitting there, talking about anything and everything until our very patient waitress started dropping hints that they'd be closing soon. By the time we'd settled up the bill and headed out, it was nearly one in the morning, and they locked the doors behind us.

Garrett glanced back with a sheepish grin. "Hope that tip was enough to make up for taking a table for that long."

"You tipped her almost thirty percent. I think we're good." He'd insisted on paying for dinner tonight, wanting to make up for our disastrous first date. I hadn't argued, but I'd made him promise to let me pay when we went out again tomorrow.

We'd both parked in the lot around the corner, and we walked in comfortable silence to our cars. We reached mine first.

I turned to him and grinned. "So, what now?"

Returning the grin, he wrapped his arms around me, not a trace of self-consciousness in his expression despite being out in public. Not that there were many people awake at this hour, but still. And dear God, I loved it.

"'What now?'" he repeated. "Don't you mean, 'Your place or mine?'"

"Mm-hmm." I snaked my arms around his waist. "I'm pretty sure we both know what happens once we get there."

"Yeah, we do." He slid his hands into my back pockets and pressed me against the car door, caging me in and pinning his own hands behind me. "I'm just not sure I can wait that long."

My breath hitched. The smoldering desire in his eyes damn near rendered me speechless, but I managed a pathetic, "Oh yeah?"

"Yeah. I haven't been able to get you out of my head."

"Likewise." I ran my fingers up the back of his shirt under his jacket. "I really want to get you into my bed again."

"Oh, you will." He grinned as he leaned in closer. "But first . . ."

One kiss, and I was grateful for the car and his solid body keeping me upright. I loved how Garrett kissed. I loved how he kneaded my ass through my jeans and teased my tongue with his and pressed his hardening cock against my hip.

The hint of wine in his mouth made the whole night real. Not just this moment, but the entire evening. How long had it been since I'd gone on a real date with someone and then ended up fooling around? Usually this kind of kissing only happened on Tinder hookups or in a back room at a bar. Not after I'd spent hours talking about everything with a gorgeous, intelligent man who just got more interesting by the minute.

"If I haven't mentioned it," I murmured, lips barely leaving his, "I love the way you kiss."

"Likewise." He teased the corner of my mouth with his tongue. "And if *I* haven't mentioned it, thanks for giving me another chance."

I grinned against his lips. "Well, you *were* pretty persuasive, especially once we got into bed."

Garrett laughed. Then he kissed me again, and the kiss deepened as his hands drifted from my pockets to the small of my back and then up under my shirt.

He broke the kiss and dipped his head, and the instant his lips brushed my neck, my back arched off the car door. I held on to his shoulders, squeezing my eyes shut and tilting my head as his warm lips skated across my skin. I was painfully hard now, my mind full of pornographic fantasies of everything we'd be doing if we weren't out in public. And . . . we needed to be someplace that wasn't in public because I needed to have him bent over something, taking my dick until we were both wrung out and spent.

"We should get back to my place," I breathed as he slid a hand between us. "Or yours. Don't care. I just . . . Oh fuck, Garrett . . ."

"We'll get there." He nibbled my earlobe and kneaded my cock through my jeans. "But I've been keeping my hands to myself for the last few hours, and now I need . . ." He trailed off into a moan as he rubbed me harder.

When he started fumbling with my belt, I gasped. "What are . . ." I ran out of air. And thoughts. Somehow, I managed to grab his wrist, and his hand froze, a finger still hooked under the leather.

"You want me to stop?" he asked.

"Not even a little. But we're not far from . . . We could . . ." His thumb slid over the head of my cock, and my vocabulary was reduced to, "Oh fuck . . ."

"Say the word and I'll stop." He trailed this thumb along my partially undone zipper. "Otherwise, we can go back to one of our apartments for round *two*."

I shivered hard and released his wrist.

He laughed, his breath warm on my lips. "Had a feeling you'd see things my way."

"You're pretty persuasive."

Another laugh, then another kiss, and his lips and tongue almost distracted me from the buzz of my zipper separating and the jingle of my belt buckle falling free. When his fingers wrapped around my cock, we both groaned.

Then he went for my neck again, and I was in heaven as he stroked my dick and kissed my throat. His hand was just callused enough to create some friction without being too rough, and that friction was underscored by the softness of his lips and breath on my throat. I gripped his shoulders, leaning hard against the car as he made the whole world spin. *I* was usually the aggressive one, not the one melting and trembling and holding on for dear life.

His lips left my neck. His weight shifted.

And then . . .

Fuck. Oh fuck. His mouth. I hadn't even realized he'd gone to his knees, but there he was—kneeling on the pavement, a hand braced on my hip while the other steadied the base of my cock. He focused on the head, then deep-throated, then focused on the head again. When his eyes flicked up to meet mine, I had to bite my lip to keep from crying out and giving us away to the whole town. As he ran his tongue slowly around the head, I stopped caring if everyone in Bluewater Bay—hell, the entire Olympic Peninsula—knew what was going on. The sight of him, the delicious sensations he licked to life on my cock—I lost all sense of shame or decorum.

Moaning, I gripped the side mirror and pressed back against the car, curling my toes inside my shoes as his lips slid up and down my cock. "Oh my God . . ."

He hummed softly against my dick, the vibration nearly turning me inside out. I could've stood here all night, letting him work his magic like this, but damn if I was going to last. Not when I'd been half-hard all day just thinking about sleeping with him tonight, and not when his mouth was so goddamned talented.

"Oh shit," I breathed. "Garrett, I'm gonna . . . gonna come. Fuck . . ."

I thought he'd stop—a lot of guys did even though swallowing was safe—but instead he doubled down, stroking harder and taking me so deep I must've been hitting his gag reflex. My eyes rolled back and my spine arched off the door. "Fuck!"

I came hard, thrusting into his mouth as much as the awkward position allowed, and Garrett didn't quit. His lips, his tongue, his hand—he kept going and going until I couldn't take anymore and somehow blurted, "*Stop*."

He eased off and stood, and the instant our eyes met, he gripped the back of my neck hard and kissed me, his mouth vaguely salty. I grabbed onto the front of his shirt for something to hold on to, and kissed him back just as eagerly. My head was spinning from my orgasm and the fact that I hadn't even begun to catch my breath, but . . . whatever. If I passed out, it wasn't like I was going anywhere.

Garrett slid his hand up into my hair and made a soft, almost inaudible sound against my lips. Kind of a growl, kind of a moan—whatever it was, I took it to mean he was enjoying himself. If that didn't give him away, the subtle twitch of his fingers against my scalp and the languid way he kissed me were pretty convincing hints.

After a while, Garrett broke the kiss, and while I gulped in air—holy fuck, I was *still* out of breath—he grinned. "So. My place?"

"Y-yeah. Your place."

CHAPTER SIXTEEN

GARRETT

"**C**an I ask you about something?" Jesse met my gaze from across the table at Flat Earth, the pizzeria he'd been dying to introduce me to. "If, um, you don't mind one of those 'you come from a different generation' questions."

"Well, now I'm definitely curious." I peeled a piece of insanely hot pepperoni off my slice of pizza, and just before I popped it in my mouth, added, "Go ahead."

He took a bite of his pizza, washed it down with a swig of Coke, and sat back, wiping some grease off his fingers. "You said before that you lost your job because your boss didn't like gay people. And I know that happened a lot more back then."

"Back when we were all riding horses and had to fetch water from the well every morning."

Jesse snorted, rolling his eyes. "Yeah, yeah, yeah. Anyway." His expression turned more serious. "How did your family take it? Knowing you were gay?"

"They took it better than some of my friends' parents did, let's put it that way."

His eyes widened.

"One of the first guys I dated was kicked out of the house after his mom found a gay porno in his room when he was seventeen. That happened to a lot of guys I knew, actually." I picked another pepperoni off the pizza. Still hot. "So, I was lucky. Mine weren't thrilled, but they came around after a while, and they've actually adored a lot of my boyfriends. And my husband." I paused to eat the pepperoni. "How about yours?"

Jesse shrugged. "Eh, it wasn't like they hadn't figured it out before I told them. They were basically like 'Yeah, and?'" He laughed. "My coming out was pretty anticlimactic."

"That's good, though." I smiled. "It shouldn't be a big deal."

"I know, but after I'd worked up to it for six months, you'd think they could've . . . I don't know, at least acted surprised."

I chuckled. "Those bastards."

"I know, right?"

We nibbled our pizzas for a little while, and I decided he had good taste in pizzerias. I was definitely not leaving here without one of their refrigerator magnets so I could call for delivery.

After we'd both gone through a few slices, I sat back, soda in hand. "I have to say, with families and acceptance and all that—the gods favor no one. My family was great. Should've known that would mean in-laws from hell."

Jesse grimaced. "Oh yeah?"

I nodded. "They weren't homophobic or anything. Hell, they went to Pride with Sean from the time he was a teenager. They just didn't like *me*."

Jesse cocked his head. "Why the hell not? Have they *met* you?"

"Yeah. That was about the time they decided they didn't like me."

His eyebrows climbed his forehead. "What did you do? Sacrifice a goat at the dinner table?"

I snorted. "No. But they took serious exception to Sean being with someone so much older. Or rather, with someone so much older being with their son."

"You were, what, fifteen years older?"

"Yep."

Jesse shrugged as he pulled another slice of pizza from the pan between us. "So what was the big deal? I mean, that's about the same as us, isn't it?"

"Give or take a year, yeah." I sighed. "The thing is, they thought I was taking advantage of him. I mean, they never said it to my face, but I could read between the lines. And Sean told me a few things they'd said." Shaking my head, I rolled my eyes again. "His mom and sister were both convinced I was using him, but for different reasons."

"I'm going to guess one of them thought you were using him for sex."

"That would be Mom," I muttered.

Jesse wrinkled his nose.

"I know, right? But his sister was convinced I was just looking for someone to depend on me."

Jesse blinked a few times. "Come again?"

I exhaled, absently wiping some lingering grease from my fingers. "Because Sean was still finishing his master's, and I made the mistake of—within earshot of her—suggesting we move in together so he could quit his second job and focus on school. Somehow that came across to her that I was trying to erode his financial independence."

"That's kind of . . . nuts."

"It is, and it isn't. I mean, she meant well. She adored her brother, and the guy he dated before me was really manipulative and actually did try to make him dependent. So she was just being protective."

Some of the tension fled Jesse's posture. "Oh. Yeah, I guess that makes sense. Older sister?"

I nodded. "He was the youngest of four, and there were six years between him and his next sister. So he was the baby of the family, and they all protected him like grizzly bears."

"Wow," Jesse whispered. "That must have been rough on them—all of you—when he . . ."

I swallowed hard. "Yeah. We actually did make peace while Sean was sick, though. I think part of it was because he encouraged us to, but also, I think they realized I genuinely did care about him. If the fourth or fifth time my mother-in-law found me asleep on the floor in Sean's hospital room didn't convince her, I don't know what would."

He glanced at his pizza like he wasn't so sure he wanted it anymore. "Man. I just can't imagine everything you guys went through."

"It wasn't fun," I said flatly. "Thank God they were all there, though. And Scott—my friend who lives around here—came over almost every weekend toward the end. So there was a lot of support." I paused, then cleared my throat and reached for another slice of pizza. "So that conversation took a depressing turn. We don't have to stick with this topic if you don't want to."

He laughed, sounding a bit relieved, but he shook his head. "No, we can talk about it if you want to."

"Not particularly." I sipped my drink. "Speaking of Scott, I should really introduce you guys one of these days."

"Oh yeah?"

"Mm-hmm." Goddamn this pizza was good. "If you don't mind hanging out with a marriage counselor who's also a stoner."

Jesse laughed for real this time. "Seriously? He has to smoke to stay sane at that job or something?"

"Well, maybe, but he's been a stoner as long as I've known him. That's how we met—smoking in the woods behind our high school."

"And you've been friends ever since," he singsonged. "The magic of weed."

I chuckled. "Yeah, basically."

His eyebrow arched. "You still smoke?"

"Occasionally."

The eyebrow rose higher, and so did the temperature of my cheeks.

"Okay, pretty much whenever I hang out with Scott unless his fiancé is there. Isn't fair to smoke in front of Jeremy when he can't smoke."

"Job?"

"Yep. So what about you? You smoke?"

"I haven't in a long time." He gestured dismissively. "Never really did much for me."

"That's okay." I grinned. "More for the rest of us."

"Right. Like that shit's endangered in this state." He nodded toward the front counter. "I'm going to get another soda. You want anything?"

"Nah, I'm good. Thanks."

He got up with his empty glass, and as he walked past, he gave my shoulder a gentle but obviously deliberate nudge. I just smiled before going for my pizza again.

I didn't know if it meant anything that I could talk about Sean and my in-laws and his death, and it was almost like normal conversation. Jesse didn't seem to mind, and it didn't make me feel like falling to pieces as much as it would've a few weeks ago.

Maybe that meant I was moving on.

Maybe there was hope for me yet.

As Jesse and I found our groove, two things became very obvious very quickly.

One, we were basically inseparable. Lunch breaks. Late dinners. Long nights. Any chance we had to be together, we were.

And the other thing? We were going to annoy the shit out of waitstaff at every restaurant we went to.

We were both polite and we tipped well, but without fail, we'd get lost in conversation and wind up closing the place. Not even two weeks into this, we'd started giving servers a sheepish heads-up that we'd probably be there a while and promising to tip extra for taking so much time. It didn't help that my work schedule—and to a lesser degree, Jesse's—meant we didn't usually sit down to eat until late, so we were lucky to get out of any restaurant before midnight.

This evening, for a change of pace, we weren't going out. I had the night off and Jesse would be done at six, so I was cooking for us. At least then we wouldn't have to feel guilty about occupying a table until sunrise. Plus, Jesse had made a comment about finding culinary skills incredibly attractive, and who was I to pass up an opportunity to make the guy swoon?

It had been a while since I'd cooked for anyone but myself, and I was more excited than nervous. It was like breaking out of a rut and taking another step back into the land of the living.

As a bonus, it pushed me toward unpacking my apartment a bit more. I still had way too many unopened boxes cluttering the whole place, and I also needed to dig out some kitchen things so I could cook. So I spent the morning digging through boxes I'd been avoiding for the last month. Though I'd unpacked the bare essentials early on, the more specialized cookware and the dishes that didn't look like glorified paper plates had been MIA. While I was at it, I finished unpacking the boxes of clothes that were still stacked in the bedroom and even cleared out the one marked *DVDs*, which had been doubling as an end table for the last couple of weeks. If Jesse was going to be here for more than just a roll in the hay, the least I could do was make the place look a step up from a bachelor pad.

All the boxes were explicitly labeled, but during the move-in, some had wound up stashed in the wrong places because I'd gotten tired of doing anything beyond dragging the damn things into the apartment. In between taking out cookware I hadn't seen in ages, I stumbled across a large box marked *PHOTOS*.

One look at it, and my heart jumped into my throat. I might as well have been able to see every single picture tucked away inside that box and the albums within, and it was like my brain was trying to process all of them—and the vivid memories associated with them—at the same time.

I had other things to do, though, so I ignored the box of pictures. Or, well, I tried to. Even after I'd found what I was looking for and dug out the spices and utensils I needed, I kept gravitating back to the box marked *PHOTOS*. It wasn't like I didn't know what was in it, but I suddenly had this overwhelming urge to look through it.

While the sauce for the enchiladas simmered, I turned back to the box on the kitchen table. With my heart in my throat, I pulled out one of the albums.

I grew up before the digital age. Taking pictures during that time had involved little yellow boxes of little black canisters containing little rolls of film, which had to be loaded, wound, and then taken to the drug store to be developed. There was no instant gratification. If you fucked up a picture, you didn't know it until later. Nothing was uploaded seconds after it was captured.

So when digital became the big thing, I'd dug in my heels . . . for a while. Once the quality had caught up to—and ultimately surpassed—film, and once the cost had come down so far it seemed ridiculous to even consider film, I'd jumped on the digital bandwagon without a second thought. And like so many people, I'd taken to keeping photos on my phone and my computer, not bothering to have them printed.

My husband, however, had inherited his mother's adoration of photo albums. I wasn't sure if he'd ever used a thirty-five millimeter camera in his life, or if digital had simply been the way of the world by the time he knew what photography was, but he'd been diligent—nearly obsessive—about getting his favorite photos printed. Not just printed, but displayed in frames and, of course, albums.

He hadn't been a scrapbooker, per se—he didn't like embellishments and flourishes. No whimsical stickers or cutesy borders. Just simple acid-free albums, each photo carefully arranged in chronological order to tell the story of a weekend in Victoria, an afternoon at Pride, or the hilarious comedy of errors that had ensued while we'd helped my dad fix the roof on their cabin at Lake Chelan.

The album's pages creaked softly as I turned them. I paused on a picture of the two of us on my parents' deck. Must've been at a barbecue or something, since we were both wearing shorts and sunglasses, and we each held a brown longneck. Budweiser for me. For him, some microbrew I couldn't name.

We were standing against the railing, both looking at something outside the frame. We were laughing. At what, I couldn't remember. Maybe the antics of a niece or nephew. Maybe my sister had said something ridiculous and probably inappropriate for mixed company. Whatever it was, we'd been caught on camera, frozen in time with huge smiles and my arm draped loosely around Sean's waist. He was tucked into the crook of my shoulder, head tilted like he'd been leaning on me up until something had drawn his attention.

My heart thudded as I gazed at the photo. I couldn't help running my fingers over the protective clear plastic, as if that might somehow take me back to that moment.

In the photo, my left arm was around Sean, and the sun had been positioned just right to glint off my wedding ring. Here in my kitchen, I absently thumbed the divot where the band had once been on my third finger.

I remembered staring at this photo—among others—in the weeks after Sean's diagnosis, and again after he'd died. I couldn't say if I'd been torturing myself or trying to memorize him and our life together before he was gone, only that I hadn't been able to stop myself.

Tonight was the first time since Sean's diagnosis that I'd seen these photos without breaking down. My throat was thick with emotion, and my heart hurt as I looked from one picture to the next, but it wasn't that soul-wrenching grief that had become way too familiar.

That feeling tingled around the edges, but it was more like a habit now. Something I felt because I expected to feel it.

That realization was oddly encouraging. Clearing my throat, I turned the page. It still stung to wade through the memories of my marriage, but I definitely felt better these days. No one and nothing could ever replace Sean, but maybe moving on wasn't as impossible as it had seemed in those devastating early days.

I sighed and gave the stove a glance. Nothing seemed to need my attention, so I faced the album again, idly thumbing the red leather cover.

I'd used all these photos and books to wallow in my grief before. Now it felt a bit more . . . objective? Like I was checking in with myself, seeing where I was emotionally, and gauging that based on how I responded now versus a few months ago. And I liked the result. I liked that even though I was still sad and I still missed that man like crazy, I didn't feel so fragmented and lost anymore.

It occurred to me that this was the first time I'd gone through our photos since I'd started seeing Jesse. There was a place in the pit of my stomach that should've swelled with guilt right then, but . . . it didn't. Yeah, it was surreal to be looking back on my marriage and the man I hadn't had nearly enough time with, but I didn't feel ashamed or guilty about having someone new in my life. If anything, it loosened a knot that had been there for months. The knot of apprehension that the rest of my life would be a miserable, grief-stricken existence.

Exhaling slowly, I closed the album and went to check the pot on the stove. Of course, my mind stayed with the photos. I expected it would be there for a while.

In the weeks after Sean's death, I'd gone to a widower support group in Seattle. They had been good people, and though I'd been nervous about joining a group of straight men, they'd welcomed me without blinking, along with another guy who'd lost his longtime boyfriend. It wasn't homophobia that had ultimately driven me out. In fact, I was pretty sure I'd have kept going except at the third meeting, one of the guys had brought up his new girlfriend. He'd lost his wife four years prior, and started dating this woman within the past year. He was talking about getting married.

I'd never gone back to the group after that. I'd resented the hell out of them for talking about new partners. Replacements. We'd lost our spouses, not wrecked our cars.

Looking back now, I understood. The man had been alone for three years when he'd met his current girlfriend. He wasn't running out before his wife was cold in the grave. My grief had been raw while his had had time to heal.

And now *mine* had had time to heal, and there was a new man in my life. Was this thing with Jesse something that would last more than a few weeks? No way to know. But that was okay. I liked being with him. I liked talking with him. I liked the sex. Even if we fizzled out in a month, I'd enjoy it now, and I'd enjoy the hell out of knowing I still had the capacity to be someone's lover.

The lack of guilt and shame caught me almost as off guard as my attraction to Jesse. I hadn't gone looking, so maybe that was why I didn't feel bad about it. I hadn't even realized anything was happening until it was *well* past the point of *maybe he's into me*. It almost felt like I'd stumbled backward into this and, once I'd regained my equilibrium, decided it felt *right*.

A knock at the door brought a smile to my lips. He was on time, as always. I quickly checked the pot on the stove again, glanced at the box of photos on the table, and went to let him in.

When I opened the door, he grinned at me, and goose bumps sprang up all over my skin. I loved the effect he had on me. Every time I saw him, I wanted him more than I had the last time. Forget the novelty wearing off—the more I knew what he was capable of in the bedroom, the more time I wanted to spend there with him. Though I knew it was entirely possible this was a short-term thing, I sure as hell wouldn't object if he wanted to stick around for a while.

I shook myself, stood aside, and waved him in, and as he stepped past me, I caught him with an arm around the waist. He laughed, letting me reel him closer as I nudged the door shut with my foot.

"Miss me?" he murmured as our lips brushed.

"Always." I kissed him full on, and he moaned softly as he slid his fingers up into my hair. I loved how the world seemed to pause whenever we kissed like this. In a minute, we'd pick up the conversation and I'd continue cooking, but first . . . this. A long, gentle kiss with his strong, warm body pressed up against mine.

He broke the kiss just as gently and smiled. Then he sniffed the air. "Something smells amazing."

"Nothing extravagant. Just chicken enchiladas."

Jesse's face lit up. "Oh, you went all out, didn't you?"

"Well, I had to find some dish to keep you interested in case my lack of charm starts showing through."

He laughed, rolling his eyes. "Yeah, okay."

I chuckled. "Anyway, it still needs another . . ." I craned my neck to check my watch. "Twenty minutes or so."

"Good. Plenty of time."

"For . . . ?"

He slid his hands up the front of my shirt and grabbed handfuls of the fabric. "What do you think?"

I pulled him closer. "I think we should take this to the bedroom."

"I think we should."

CHAPTER SEVENTEEN

JESSE

I f not for the timer going off in the kitchen, I was pretty sure Garrett and I would have gone two rounds. One round was hardly a disappointment, though, and I had no doubt we'd wind up back in bed before the night was over. Assuming we didn't eat too much, that is, and as good as the kitchen smelled right now, that was a possibility.

Garrett—wearing jeans and nothing else—went into the kitchen to make sure dinner didn't burn, and I stared at the ceiling for a few minutes, grinning like an idiot. For the last two weeks, I'd pretty much spent my days fantasizing about the sex we'd be having once we were in the same room, and he blew those fantasies out of the water every time. I was starting to see why a couple of my friends were into older men. I'd teased Kevin about it a few times, but he'd always just given me a sly smile and insisted that nothing beat all the years of experience Hunter had accumulated before they'd met.

"Make all the geriatric jokes you want," he'd said with a shrug a couple of months ago. *"Whenever he's done with me, I'm* the one who *needs a damn walker."*

Carter had nodded sagely along with him even though Levi wasn't *that* much older than him. Kevin, Carter, and I were all roughly the same age. Hunter must've been pushing fifty by now, but Levi was in his . . . early forties, I thought. Maybe a touch older than Garrett.

Whatever the case, both Carter and Kevin had sworn up and down that nothing in the world beat sex with an older man.

Yeah, I could see that now. I leaned over the side of the bed and fished my phone out of my pants pocket. I wasn't even dressed yet, but couldn't resist shooting Kevin a text.

Dude. Older guys. You were right.

Then, grinning to myself, I got up. As I pushed myself to my feet, my hips were a little disjointed, but my legs stayed under me. They even did what they were supposed to do while I pulled on my jeans and walked from the bedroom to the kitchen, though I was pretty sure they were going to be stiff and sore tomorrow. Considering the shop had a bunch of shipments coming in first thing in the morning, there'd be no hiding it if I was moving a bit gingerly. Simon was going to have a field day with that. Which I supposed I deserved after relentlessly giving him crap about all the times he'd come in looking haggard and sore after a night with his wife and boyfriend.

I left the bedroom, and in the kitchen doorway, I stopped and stared.

Holy fuck.

Few things were sexier than a man cooking. A shirtless man with a bite mark on his shoulder and sweat still curling the ends of his hair? Oh sweet Jesus, yes. If dinner turned out to be as good as it smelled, this man might actually be perfect.

"Has anyone ever mentioned how hot you look when you're in the kitchen?"

He glanced over his shoulder, and he actually blushed. "Let me guess—you've got a calendar of shirtless men cooking, don't you?"

"I . . . Well, not for *this* year, but I may or may not have had one in the past."

"Uh-huh."

I snickered, but before I could comment further, my phone vibrated.

Pics or he isn't real.

I smirked as I watched Garrett at the stove, then snapped a shot of him. Oh good Christ, yes. "You mind if I send this to a friend?"

"Send what?" He turned around, and when he saw my phone in my hand, his eyebrow arched. Craning his neck, he repeated, "Send *what*?"

Hoping my face was the very picture of innocence, I showed him the screen.

He peered at it, then rolled his eyes and laughed. "And you're sending it to . . . who?"

"Just a friend who doesn't believe me when I say I'm nailing a hot older guy."

A laugh burst out of Garrett, and I regretted I didn't have my phone at the ready to get a picture of that too. He was sexy when he cooked, but he was gorgeous when he laughed. The way the corners of his eyes crinkled, the sort of lopsided smile—fuck, he was beautiful.

"All right, all right." He waved a hand at my phone. "You can send it."

"Sending it."

A moment later, Kevin replied, *Well done. ;)*

That message was quickly followed by, *Hunter agrees.*

"You'll be pleased to know," I said with a grin, "that Hunter Easton and Kevin Hussain think you're hot."

"Hunter East—" Garrett turned again, eyes wide. "Like, *the* Hunter Easton?"

"And *the* Kevin, aka Kevyan Montanari, yes."

He blushed again. "I didn't realize you had them on speed dial."

"You'd be surprised who I have in my contacts." I winked as I pocketed my phone.

"I'm sure." He paused to pour the cheese and sauce on top of the enchiladas. "Now that I'm getting into those books, I might have to get you to introduce me."

I grinned. "I told you I will. So you started reading them?"

He nodded, reaching for a couple of plates. "Not exactly flying through because I haven't had a ton of time, but I'm keeping the first book at work to read on my breaks. It's really good."

"Just wait until book three. I mean, they're all good, but the third one takes it to another level. And when Kevin starts writing with him?" I whistled. "Holy *shit*."

"Yeah?" Garrett glanced at me, eyes sparkling like he was as excited about the series as I was. "Hell, I might have to take some vacation time and binge-read them. Well, when I have some vacation time anyway."

I stepped closer and put my hands on his hips, resting them half on his waistband and half on bare skin. Nuzzling his neck, I murmured, "You really think you'd be spending that vacation time with your nose in a book?"

Garrett shivered, pressing back against me. "You make a good point."

"Mm-hmm." I planted a soft kiss behind his ear, then let him go so he could continue putting dinner together. "Actually, if you're seriously getting into the books . . ." I hesitated.

"What?"

"Well, there's a con coming up. In Portland. I'll be there at the End o' Earth booth, but . . ." I scratched the back of my neck, not sure why I was hesitating. "Do you want to come?"

"What kind of con is it?"

"Wolf's Landing–themed. It's pretty much a smaller, furrier version of Comic-Con."

Garrett laughed. "It's like Comic-Con? I'm sold."

"Really?"

"Yeah. I love cons like that. I've been to San Diego Comic-Con twice."

My jaw fell open. I'd known he was a geek, but something about realizing he'd made the pilgrimage to SDCC made *this* geek all tingly inside. "You have? Really?"

He nodded. "My sister and I try to go when we can actually get tickets and a hotel room within fifty miles."

"Wow. I've always wanted to go. I've been to Seattle and a couple of others, but never San Diego."

"If you get the chance, you should." He grinned. "Maybe Fiona and I can rope you into our cosplay."

My brain damn near short-circuited. He did cosplay? And he was entertaining the idea—hypothetical or otherwise—of including me? What? Somehow, I managed to say, "You do cosplay?"

"Uh, yeah. What's the point of going to Comic-Con if you're not going to dress the part?"

Be still my beating heart.

I wasn't sure when my mouth had gone dry, only that it had. "So what did you guys dress as?"

"The first year, we didn't really coordinate. She went as Captain Janeway and I went as Indiana Jones."

Oh Lord. Oh, oh, oh Lord. The mental image of Garrett dressed like Indiana Jones fried what little of my brain was still functioning.

Before I could stop myself, I paraphrased Kevin: "Pictures or it didn't happen."

He laughed. "I've got them on my laptop. I'll pull them up after dinner."

"I'm looking forward to them." I so was.

And now that I had photos on the brain, I noticed there was a stack on the table. Next to it was a box with *PHOTOS* scrawled in black Sharpie, and it was about half full of loose pictures and a couple of albums. My curiosity was suddenly almost irresistible—I was eager to know every little detail about his past and his life and who he was—but I held back.

Gesturing at the box, I said, "You've been busy."

"Oh." Garrett cleared his throat. "I was, um . . . just unpacking a few things earlier. Organizing a bit."

"So I see." I stepped a little closer, catching a glimpse of some snapshots that were probably from a vacation. Curiosity was quickly getting the best of me, but I refused to be rude. "May I?"

"Yeah, sure. Have at it." He didn't sound reluctant. A little guarded, maybe. I supposed that was reasonable.

I picked up a stack and carefully went through them. Almost immediately, I came to a picture of a good-looking guy, and my heart jumped. "Is this . . . ?" I held it where he could see it, my pulse pounding as I wondered if I was crossing a line.

Garrett looked at it, and from the flicker of pain across his expression, I knew the answer even before he nodded. "Yeah. That's Sean." He swallowed, and a smile slowly formed. "That was about three years ago, I think. When we took our nieces and nephews to Disneyland."

I shifted my attention back to the photo. Yeah, it was definitely Disney. There were hints of familiar cartoon characters and colorful architecture in the background, and a couple of blurry people with mouse ears on their heads. The picture was just Sean, though, close-cropped to include his head and shoulders and little else. Enough to see that he'd been pretty damn hot. Sandy-blond hair that seemed to be perfect even though, from the rustle of his T-shirt, he was obviously standing in the wind. He had just enough stubble to pass for a thin beard, and it emphasized the sharp angle of his jaw and perfectly framed the smile on his lips.

In his sunglasses, I could see Garrett's reflection taking the photo with a sleek silver camera.

"How long were you guys together?" I ventured cautiously, not sure if he was in the mood to discuss his late husband.

Garrett appeared beside me, dinner either under control or forgotten. "Almost five years. Married for three."

In the back of my mind, I ran the numbers, and my breath hitched. Hadn't he said Sean had lived eighteen months after his diagnosis? So they'd only gotten a year and a half to be married before they'd found out their time was short. Only three and a half years together at all. Shit. I couldn't even imagine.

"Thank God we were married, too," he said, almost more to himself. "And we were damn lucky our insurance company recognized same-sex marriages, so when he got too sick to work, he didn't lose his coverage. He just became my dependent." Garrett's gaze grew distant, and he exhaled. "You know I sometimes have nightmares about what would've happened if we hadn't been able to get married. How . . ." He swallowed. "How much treatment we wouldn't have been able to afford."

My tongue stuck to the roof of my mouth as the unspoken words resonated through the silent room: *How much more he would have suffered. How much sooner I would have lost him.*

I suppressed a shudder and quietly said, "I'm glad you guys had coverage." It sounded stupid, but I didn't know what else to say.

Garrett shook himself and met my gaze, and he smiled sadly as he wrapped an arm around my waist. "I'm sorry. I didn't mean to take this conversation down that road."

"No, it's okay." I tugged his hand around toward my stomach and gently wrapped my fingers around his wrist. "It's probably good for you to be able to talk about it. All of it."

"I know, but given what we're doing . . ." He chewed his lip.

"I'd be kind of an asshole if I said I didn't want you to talk to me about him. He was a huge part of your life. And so was . . ." I swallowed. "So was his death."

Garrett exhaled, breath gusting across the side of my neck. Then he pressed a soft kiss to my cheek. "Thank you. I'm . . . working through a lot of it, and I try not to fixate on it, but it'll probably come up from time to time."

"That's okay." I ran my thumb alongside his wrist. "Any time you want to talk, we can."

He kissed my cheek again. "Thank you." Then he released me and cleared his throat. "Ready to eat?"

I smiled, grateful for the break in tension. "Yeah, definitely."

As Garrett took care of dinner, I couldn't stop thinking about the photo of his husband. Something about seeing the man's face made the whole story real. Not that I'd thought he was lying or anything, but now I knew what Sean had looked like.

In the past, I'd seen photos of guys' exes, and I'd immediately been jealous. Comparing myself to the previous boyfriend, wondering how I stacked up against them.

Looking at Sean had just made me sad. I couldn't begin to imagine what it was like to lose someone the way Garrett had lost him, and I ached for him. For both of them. What must it have been like to come home from that doctor's appointment? It wasn't like I didn't have experience with medical news knocking my feet out from under me, but my doctors had immediately started in on treatment options and managing the disease. They'd assured me my long-term prognosis was good, and that HIV wasn't a death sentence anymore. And even then, I'd been scared shitless. I couldn't imagine walking out that day knowing I was going to die. Or knowing my partner—my husband— was going to die. How *did* you process something like that, as the patient *or* the partner?

No, seeing Sean's face didn't make me jealous. I actually felt a bit guilty for being with Garrett. It wasn't right that they weren't together anymore. It wasn't fair that an ugly disease had come along and stolen Sean away. I was thrilled to be with Garrett because he was an amazing man, but did that mean I was celebrating in some small way that Sean was gone?

Fuck. Dating a widower was a lot more complicated than I'd realized.

It occurred to me then that when I'd told him I was positive, I'd practically given him a flashback to his husband's diagnosis. Like he had PTSD from it. And maybe he did. I was no expert on the subject, but now that I thought about it, it seemed reasonable as fuck that someone who'd lost their partner like that could have PTSD.

Given how recently Garrett had lost Sean, that raised the question of how much he'd recovered. Not only if he'd recovered enough to be interested in a relationship with me or anyone else, but how much he had to put into one. If we were just going to fuck each other's brains out, I was totally game, but there was more than heat between us. Not love or some deep soul mate connection—just a softly glowing ember of something that felt like it could turn into a lot more if we put in the effort to fan it.

So . . . *did* we fan it? Was he in any place to even think about what this was or what he wanted it to be?

I surreptitiously watched him while he plated our food. Maybe it was time to talk about it. Get on the same page.

I didn't bring it up during dinner, though. Not while I helped him clean the kitchen, not when we moved into the living room with a couple of glasses of wine. I was actually a breath away from bringing it up as we made ourselves comfortable on the couch, but Garrett spoke before I could.

"So, you really want to see pictures of me at Comic-Con?"

Okay, so I had some burning questions, but maybe they could wait a *few* more minutes. "I absolutely do."

Garrett pulled up the photos. He'd been hot in the Hawkeye costume he'd worn his second year—Fiona had gone as Scarlet Witch—but he'd rocked the Indiana Jones look. The distressed white shirt that wasn't buttoned up all the way. The khaki pants that had seen better days. The leather jacket. The hat. The fake blood and bruises on his face. The scruff.

The—*gulp*—whip coiled on his hip.

"Wow," I said. "You really went all out, didn't you?"

He laughed. "My sister and I destroyed three shirts trying to get that look." He gestured at the screen. "You'd be amazed how hard it is to look like you've been dragged through the mud and run through the wringer without actually dragging yourself through the mud."

"How did you do it?"

"Ran it through the laundry until it was starting to fall apart. Used it as a rag to wash my car. Soaked it in coffee for a few days." He wrinkled his nose. "It was *clean* at the con, don't get me wrong, but the fabric was so fucked up it was itchy as hell."

I chuckled. "That's dedication."

He smiled and flipped through more photos from the con. In every one, he was smiling. No, not just smiling—laughing. And there'd been a lot less gray in his hair. It wasn't that long ago, either. I recognized some cosplay characters in the background, and they were from recent movies.

He had on his wedding ring, but I didn't ask where Sean was. Maybe Comic-Con hadn't been his thing.

Or maybe he'd been too sick.

No, I doubted that. Garrett looked much too carefree and enthusiastic.

I was curious but didn't ask.

After he'd been through the folder of Comic-Con photos, Garrett closed his laptop and set it on the coffee table. Then he draped his arm along the back of the couch, just above my shoulders.

My stomach flip-flopped. Now that I'd had a couple of glimpses into his past, I was itching to know what kind of future was in front of us. Or if there was a future at all besides burning up the sheets. Which was fine, of course—casual sex with a man as talented and hot as him? Fuck yes. But were there emotional lines I needed to know about?

Twisting a little so I was facing him, I swallowed. "Okay, I'm not going to be that guy who wants a commitment or whatever on the second date. But . . ." I chewed my lip and struggled to hold his gaze. "I guess given what you've been through, maybe we should talk about what we both want out of this."

Garrett fidgeted subtly. "That might not be a bad idea."

Our eyes locked.

You starting? Or am I?

Go ahead. No, you go ahead.

I took a sip of my wine just to wet my dry mouth. "I think I should follow your lead here. I'm open to pretty much wherever this thing wants to go, but I know you've been through . . ." Fuck, how to finish that comment.

"Yeah," Garrett cut in, "and I'm not going to blow smoke up your ass and tell you I'm completely over Sean. Or that I will be any time soon."

I nodded slowly. "So it's really your call."

He was quiet for a moment, gazing into his wineglass as if the liquid might offer up some wisdom. Finally, he took in a breath. "To be perfectly honest, I don't know." He took my hand, lacing our fingers together. "So . . . I don't have much of an answer for you except that I'm open to whatever this"—he gestured at both of us—"has the potential to become. I'm just not in any hurry, if that makes sense."

"Yeah, it does." I took another sip of wine. "If, uh, if we're going to keep doing this, it probably wouldn't hurt for you to get on Truvada."

He studied me. "That's that . . . anti-HIV med, isn't it?"

I nodded, my gut tightening as I waited for his response. Nothing made things sexier or more romantic than telling a dude he should be on a prescription drug if he wanted to keep sleeping with me.

He slid a hand over my thigh. "It might not be a bad idea. I can look into it."

I exhaled, nodding again, and quickly added, "I mean, even if you're *not* on it, I'm undetectable, so theoretically we don't even have to use condoms. But I know most guys prefer to use them. And I'm fine with that."

"We can cross that bridge when we get there. And we might as well get tested for everything else too." He paused. "I mean, you're the first man I've been with since my husband, and he and I were both negative for everything, but I'm happy to get the paper that says I'm all clear."

"Thanks." I was glad he'd volunteered it. It made me feel like an ass to insist on it, especially from a man who'd been married or celibate for the last few years, but I'd already been bitten once by someone who'd sworn up and down he couldn't possibly have anything. "And . . . we can still use condoms. Even if you're on it." As much as science had (finally) admitted that my odds of infecting Garrett were on par with my mom's cat learning to tango, that didn't mean Garrett would be game to skip taking precautions.

Garrett smiled, squeezing my leg gently. "Like I said, we'll cross that bridge when we get to it. I'm not opposed to the idea of ditching them as long as it's just you and me."

My heart skipped, and I wasn't sure if it was at the suggestion of being exclusive or at how he was unabashedly okay with having bareback sex with me. "Do you, um . . . do you *want* it to just be you and me?" Was two weeks too soon to be exclusive?

He studied me for a long moment, his expression giving nothing up. Finally, he took my hand and smiled. "I think it's a little early in the game for any kind of commitment, but how about this—if you want to hook up with someone else, just be honest with me about it?"

"And vice versa, right?"

His smile made my pulse go nuts, and he ran his thumb back and forth along mine. "I don't see me wanting to hook up with anyone else anytime soon, but yes, I'll be honest with you about it either way. In the meantime . . ." He set his wineglass on the coffee table. Then he took mine and did the same. Turning to me, he grinned. "I'm all yours tonight."

"Mmm, I like the sound of that." Especially the part where this not-entirely-comfortable conversation was over. Eager for a change of subject, I pulled him close, and somehow we segued seamlessly from an awkward minefield of a subject to . . . this. And I didn't think I'd felt this relaxed in his arms before. Everything was out on the table, and nerves I hadn't even known were there seemed to vanish as Garrett kissed me. It was like when we'd hooked up after he'd told me the real reason he'd balked, and things had just felt more open and honest.

"Should we take this into the bedroom?" he murmured between kisses.

"Hmm, I don't know." I dragged my lower lip across his. "I think we're fine right here."

Garrett just grinned, pulled me closer, and kissed me again.

CHAPTER EIGHTEEN
GARRETT

Kicked back on Scott's balcony, I closed my eyes and let the weed work its magic. This was the kind of high I remembered from my college days. Back when I couldn't imagine anything more stressful than exams or term papers, and a few lungfuls of sour smoke was all I'd needed to relax.

Since moving to Bluewater Bay, the hours I'd spent smoking with Scott had been a reprieve from the crushing depression. They had worked much like a painkiller taking the edge off a nasty injury—I'd still been miserable, but it had been temporarily bearable.

Today, it was more like a huge portion of the weight on my shoulders was gone. Like I was floating. Like I was actually *high* the way I remembered from my more carefree days: my head light and my body languid.

And if I was honest with myself, some of that lightness had been there even before I'd taken my first drag. Every time I went anywhere near Jesse, a little more heaviness slid off. Not enough to make me think my grief would magically evaporate, but enough to give me hope that I wouldn't feel like shit forever.

Across from me, Scott rubbed the bridge of his nose, his features still tight even though we were better than halfway through an exceptionally strong joint.

"You're too stoned to be this stressed," I said. "What's wrong?"

He laughed halfheartedly and sat back. Staring up at the sky, he sighed. "Wedding planning. That's what's wrong."

I grimaced. "Still?"

"It's not until December," he grumbled. "It's going to be happening for a while."

"Are you at least making headway?"

"Oh yeah. But it's two steps forward and three steps back. You get two things locked down, deposits paid and all that, and three others fall through. You know how it goes." Instantly, he winced. "Sorry."

"It's okay." I smiled as I set the joint in the ashtray on the plastic table between us. "Yeah, I do know how it goes. It's a goddamned circus."

"It so is." He closed his eyes again, but the tension lingered in his forehead. "This wedding shit is a nightmare." He scowled harder. "I mean, the planning part. I'm looking forward to it and all, and I can't wait until we're married, but damn, I'd forgotten what a headache it was."

"It'll be worth it in the end." Nostalgia crept in, reminding me of how frazzled Sean and I had been in the weeks leading up to our wedding. I'd never forget how I'd been tearing my hair out right up until the ceremony, and how the moment I'd laid eyes on him in that tailored tux, grinning with tears in his eyes, surrounded by all the people and decorations we'd spent months wrangling . . . it had been worth it. Every frustrating, expensive moment. I had no doubt Scott and Jeremy would feel the same way.

Scott gazed up at the trees. "It's weird, you know? This is my second wedding, but the first legal one." He smiled serenely, some of that tension fading from his expression. "Times have changed."

"Yeah, they have."

We were both quiet for a while. Long, comfortable silences weren't unusual with us, even when we weren't smoking, so it didn't bother me. I liked just being around him, and the tranquility of the woods behind his condo was almost as intoxicating as the weed. More than once, I'd considered getting a place in this complex when I eventually decided to buy instead of rent. Then I could sit out here and enjoy the scenery anytime.

Eventually, Scott spoke. "So how are things going with . . ." He paused. "Jesse?"

I released a long, relaxed breath. "Good. They're going really good. We're actually going out of town for a weekend soon."

"Oh yeah?" Scott straightened a little. "That's kind of a big step, isn't it?"

I shrugged. "Not really. I once took a ten-day cruise with a guy I'd just met."

"True. You did."

"This is just a weekend in Portland. Jesse's going to a big convention with the comic book shop, and he invited me along."

Scott's eyebrows rose. "And you're going?"

I nodded.

He smirked. "Just what you need—a reason to get back into role-playing games and comic books."

"Who says I ever got out of them?"

"Why am I not surprised?" He gave me a playful nudge with his elbow. "Nerd."

"Jock."

"Hey." He shrugged as he lit the joint again. "Social strata cease to exist in the stoner circle."

"Amen to that." I watched him take a drag, and couldn't help a fond smile. We'd come from wildly different social circles, but after a few sessions of getting baked off our asses together, we'd become good friends and had been ever since.

Scott lowered the joint, holding his breath as he offered it to me. My head was perfectly light, so I declined.

After a few seconds, Scott released the smoke as slowly as he'd inhaled it. "So things really are going well with this kid."

I winced at the reference to *kid*. "He's not *that* young."

Scott arched his eyebrow.

Rolling my eyes, I chuckled. "Fine. He's young. And yes, things are going great. I have no idea if it'll go anywhere or if we're just screwing around, but . . . yeah, it's good. He's even . . ." I stared at the white-painted floorboards of the balcony, studying some of the pine needles that had collected and were trying not to fall between boards.

"What?" Scott asked, reminding me I hadn't finished my thought.

I sat back in the chair. "He doesn't mind talking about Sean."

"Oh. That's a plus." He paused. "Do *you* mind talking about him?"

"It's a little weird when the subject comes up while we're in bed, but . . ." I considered it before shaking my head. "No, I really don't mind. It's not the most comfortable subject for either of us, but he seems to get that up until recently, Sean was a huge part of my life.

I can't say much about the last few years without mentioning him, you know?"

Scott nodded as I spoke.

"The other night," I went on, "I'd left some pictures out. He saw one and immediately realized it was Sean."

"And that didn't bother him? Seeing a picture of your husband?"

I shook my head. "If it did, he sure didn't let it show. He even asked about him a little."

"Which didn't bother you?"

"Not at all." I let out a long breath, feeling some more of that lightness pushing the dull heavy weight off my shoulders. "A few months ago, I don't think I would've been able to, but now . . ." I shrugged.

"Good. That's a really good sign." He studied me. "So you're holding up pretty well in general, then? It's a great sign that you're out dating again and that you can talk about Sean, but . . . *are* you handling everything okay?"

"Yeah, I am. Mostly. It's still hard, but I'm better than I was a few months ago. That says something, right?"

Scott smiled. "Says a lot, actually. Grieving shouldn't be rushed, but I'm glad to see you're getting out there again."

"Me too." I paused, gnawing the inside of my cheek. "Speaking of getting out there and dating again, I'm curious about something."

"Okay?"

I exhaled. "And this stays between us, all right?"

"Of course." The sudden worry in his tone made him sound closer to sober than either of us probably were. "What's up?"

I hesitated, uneasy about divulging Jesse's status to someone he didn't know.

Scott shifted, the lawn chair squeaking under him. "Everything all right?"

Meeting his gaze, I chewed my lip. "I'm just . . . I've been out of the dating loop for a while, you know? And . . ." I paused. "How much do you know about those new anti-HIV drugs? Truvada, that sort of thing?"

He blinked like he hadn't been expecting the question, then shrugged. "They're effective as hell from what I hear." His eyebrows lifted just enough to ask why.

"I mean, if I'm going to be dating again . . ." I fidgeted uncomfortably. "Is it worthwhile? Getting on it?"

"Can be, yeah," he said immediately. "I pretty much rec it to any of my clients who aren't in monogamous relationships. Jeremy and I talked about having an open relationship at one point, and if we'd gone through with that, we'd definitely both be on it."

I nodded. "Too bad they didn't have this shit years ago."

"No kidding," he muttered. "But it's a damn good thing we've got it now. I mean, I work with some serodiscordant couples who use it, and—"

"Sero-dis-what now?"

"Serodiscordant. Where one partner is positive and the other isn't."

Oh. Right. I had seen that term on some websites, hadn't I? I shot the joint a glare, then arched an eyebrow at Scott. "How the fuck can you still pronounce that while you're this high?"

He laughed. "Just don't ask me to spell it, all right?"

"Fair enough. Anyway." I made a *go on* gesture.

"Right. So. I work with a few couples, and pretty much all the negative partners are on PrEP and the positive partners are undetectable." He shrugged. "The meds are so effective now, the odds of infecting the negative partners are practically nil, even if they're not using condoms. Or PrEP, for that matter. A lot of the monogamous couples don't use it as long as the positive partner is undetectable."

I nodded slowly. That was what I'd gathered from reading online, and hearing it from him settled what was left of my nerves. I wasn't sure what else to say, but my head was getting clearer than I wanted it to be, so I picked up the joint and lighter.

Scott watched me silently. He didn't ask if or how the topic related to Jesse, which I supposed was his way of keeping Jesse's status ambiguous. As it stood now, I could easily have been asking because Jesse was positive *or* because we weren't monogamous and I wanted to be safe. I could've been asking because I'd read an article about it, or because I was ready to get out and play the field. There were plenty of possibilities that didn't mean Jesse was poz, and though Scott could probably read between the lines, he didn't push to confirm either way. I appreciated that.

As I blew out some smoke, I offered him the joint, but he shook his head.

"While I'm thinking about it, do you have a doctor in town yet?" he asked. "If not, I know one who's great, and I know for a fact she'll hook you up with a prescription."

I started to speak, then thought twice. Rolling my eyes, I said, "Let me guess—there are still some docs who won't?"

"Not without making you feel like a filthy whore who *deserves* to get AIDS and die, no." The bitterness in his tone startled me.

"Really? In this town?"

"Homophobes are everywhere." A wicked smirk spread across his lips. "I just remind myself how fucking miserable they've got to be in a place as queer as Bluewater Bay."

I laughed. "Good point. And yeah, I'll take that doctor's number."

"Remind me." He motioned toward the sliding glass door behind us. "I've got her card."

"Cool. Thanks."

"Don't mention it. By the way, if this guy ends up sticking around, we should do a double date or something."

"So you can grill him?"

"Something like that."

I just laughed. "Yeah. We'll see."

Maybe we would. I had no idea where things would go with Jesse, but . . . maybe we would.

CHAPTER NINETEEN

JESSE

G arrett was sexy as hell anyway, but when he took out his contacts and put on his glasses? Ohmigod. *Hot.*

When he was wearing glasses and grinning deviously as he shuffled a deck of Magic: The Gathering? Oh, fuck yes. We'd just made plans to play cards tonight, but the way he looked, he was one hundred percent getting fucked before I went home.

Since his kitchen table was occupied by some more boxes he'd been sorting through, we used his coffee table instead, with both of us sitting on the couch. It was easy enough to play side by side—we would just keep our hands angled so we couldn't see each other's cards, and lay out our battlefields next to each other. I actually liked it better this way anyway. When he played a card I wasn't familiar with, I would be able to read it without too much effort.

I took my own deck out of the small backpack I'd set next to his couch. "You ready to play?"

"Whenever you are." As if for emphasis, he put the deck on the table. "What color are you playing?"

"This is a green deck, but I usually play blue and white." I winked. "I won't unleash *that* deck on you while you're still rusty."

"Much appreciated," he said with a chuckle.

"What about you?" I nodded toward his deck. "What color?"

"Black."

"Huh. For some reason, I'd pegged you for a red-deck kind of guy."

Garrett grinned. "I have one of those too. But I do enjoy playing black."

"Fair enough." I finished shuffling and put my deck on the table. We each put out a twenty-sided die to keep track of our life points and set them with the twenty facing up. Then we drew seven cards. Normally when I played, players would look at the bottom card on each deck, and whoever had the card with the highest casting cost would go first. Since Garrett was getting back into the game after a long time, I let him go first to give him a head start.

He pursed his lips as he inspected his cards. It was cute, watching him study them like they were written in a foreign language. He tentatively laid down a Swamp—a land card he'd use to get mana so he could cast spells. Then he turned it slightly to indicate it was tapped, and cast a Throne of Bone. That was a pretty benign card. It just meant any time he cast a black spell, he could gain a point of life. Good thing we had more twenty-sided dice handy.

As we went back and forth, steadily building up lands and armies of creatures, I reminded myself he was still getting back into the swing of things. As tempting as it was to attack the crap out of him with my vast army, I went easy on him. I didn't even destroy that Throne of Bone despite the fact that he'd racked up an extra ten life points thanks to the little bastard.

Several turns into the game, Garrett put down *two* Nightmares. They were flying creatures—one that could only be blocked by other flying creatures—and their power and toughness were based on the number of Swamps Garrett had. And . . . he had a lot. And I didn't have many flying creatures because this deck was mostly things like Woolly Mammoths and Ironroot Treefolk, which were reasonably strong but definitely earthbound. Thank God I had a couple of puny Scryb Sprites that could at least take one for the team—they had flying, so they could each block a Nightmare and save me from being damaged, but they'd be dead.

Out came a third Nightmare, and I started getting nervous. Okay, time to stop going easy on him. Next turn, the kid gloves came off.

Garrett looked at the battlefield and took a breath. "All right." He dropped Terror cards on top of each of my Sprites, killing them. "And now I'm attacking you with two Nightmares, each equipped with . . ." He added an Unholy Strength to each of them, beefing up their power by two points.

He looked at me, a sly grin on his face like he'd been just *waiting* to unleash hell on me.

I scanned the cards in my hand. Then the ones on the battlefield. I had nothing. No way to cripple the Nightmares and no way to block them. "Fuck."

"So if you can't block my fourteen-point Nightmares . . ." He surveyed the cardboard carnage, and as he met my gaze, he smirked. "Looks like you're dead."

I blinked. For a moment, I stared at the cards, trying to find the piece he'd overlooked. The cocky mistake he'd made. The reason his entire onslaught fell apart like, well, a house of cards.

There wasn't one.

It was perfect.

"You . . . bastard."

Garrett snickered. "Beginner's luck?" The innocent lilt in his voice made me arch an eyebrow.

I eyed him as I started shuffling my cards back into a neat stack. "Okay, how long has it *really* been since you've played?"

"Um. Well." He cleared his throat, cheeks coloring as a suitably sheepish—and fucking adorable—grin came to life. "Maybe not as long as I told you before."

"Seriously?" I studied him. "Why did you tell me it had been longer?"

The grin faded a little, but the color in his face didn't. "I . . . guess I wasn't sure how to say that's how the accounting department spent our lunch breaks at my last job."

I stared at him. "You . . . and your coworkers . . . played Magic on your lunch breaks?"

He looked at me through his lashes and gave a little nod. "We did, yeah."

"Why the hell is that so hot?"

Garrett cocked his head. "Come again?"

"Don't know. Just saying—you were sexy before, but the mental image of you in a shirt and tie playing Magic with the other accountants is . . ." I pondered it, then nodded. "Yeah. That's hot."

"And here I thought telling you I was a Magic-playing accountant would ruin my image."

"Ruin it?" I shook my head. "Oh sweetheart. You have no idea how much I like this side of you."

He grinned. "You really like nerds, don't you?"

"Dude, I work in a comic book shop."

"Fair point." He laughed. "You're a dork."

"Uh-huh. And apparently so are you."

"Guilty." He shrugged. Then in a sultry voice, he purred, "So does that mean if we play enough Magic, you'll get turned on?"

"Oh, I'm already there."

"Are you, now? Well in that case . . ." He picked up his deck. "I say we play again."

"Fuck yes." I reached into my bag. No point in going easy on him now, so out came the blue and white deck. He also switched his cards out.

When the game started, he shot me a grin. "So, which outcome will make you harder? If you win or lose?"

"Don't know." I winked, biting my lip. "Guess you'll have to find out."

"Hmm, I guess I will. I just can't decide if I should go easy on you."

"*Pfft*. You know I like it when you don't go easy on me."

"Uh-huh." He glanced at me as he drew a card. "You better not go easy on me either."

A shiver went through me so violently, I was tempted to say forget the game. But I was intrigued by this. I loved his devilishness and his poker face, and I wanted to see where this went.

After several turns, we'd both amassed enough cards to start dealing some damage to each other. Garrett had knocked me down to twelve points, and I had him down to eleven. Creatures were piling up in graveyards almost as fast as they were coming out onto the battlefield.

And I'd have been lying if I said it didn't turn me on to watch him work. Not just because he was sexy and nerdy as he played Magic in glasses, but because I could see the gears turning. He was smart. He strategized. He had brains and used them, and that was insanely hot to my perverted little geek mind.

When it was my turn, I scanned the battlefield and tapped one of my creatures. "My Serra Angel is coming at you with her fully erect phallic sword of righteous justice—"

Garrett snorted. "Really?"

"What?" I shrugged. "And what are you gonna do about it?"

"Hmm." He stroked his chin as he eyed his cards. "Well since you killed my Dragon Whelp last turn, I don't have any flying creatures." He looked like he was trying—though not very hard—to suppress a smirk. "Looks like I'm taking it."

"Yeah. Yeah, you are." I slid a hand over his thigh. "You *take* that sword. You take it good."

Garrett didn't fight the smirk anymore. "Long as you brace yourself, because I'm about to come at you with my big . . . thick . . ." Leaning closer, he licked his lips and gestured at one of his artifact cards. "Wand of Ith."

I snorted and clapped a hand over my mouth. "Oh my God. Really?"

"Hey, you started it."

Yeah, and I didn't end it either. As we played on, the puns and innuendo just kept piling on top of each other. Anything with a sword, wand, or rod was turned into a phallic joke, as were creatures like my poor, unassuming Sea Serpent. Before long, we weren't even paying attention to strategy or even rules—all that mattered was which cards could be misconstrued into something dirty, until we were both collapsing into fits of laughter, tears streaming down our faces as we gasped for air.

Wiping his eyes and laughing, Garrett said, "I have never played Magic with anyone who could turn it pornographic."

"You should hear me playing D&D."

He burst out laughing all over again. "Oh my God. Do I even want to know?"

"That depends." I set my cards on the table and twisted toward him. Sliding a hand up his thigh, I adopted the most ridiculously "sexy" voice I could, and murmured, "Do you think you could handle me as your dungeon master?"

Garrett's lips parted, and he put his hand over mine. "When you put it like that, it does sound intriguing."

"Does it?"

"Oh yeah." He put his cards on the table, then pushed my hand higher on his leg. "Should I roll to see if we get naked?"

"Mmm, I think you should roll to see if you kiss me, first."

"I don't think I need a die for that." He cupped my face and kissed me. At first it was as playful as our game. Light, gentle, lips curving like were each holding back a laugh. Slowly, though, our lips softened. Our fingers dug in. A low moan thrummed between our mouths, and the game was forgotten. Garrett held me tighter and pulled me onto his lap. As I straddled him, his hands slid up my thighs and onto my ass.

All the bantering ceased. All the talking ceased. Hell, I was lucky I was breathing. As he kissed me and touched me and my hardening erection rubbed against his, I barely remembered where we were, never mind what we'd been doing.

I wanted to get naked and sweaty with him, but I had to admit, I was enjoying the hell out of this. Apparently so was he. His kiss was hungry and his fingers twitched as he caressed and groped, but he wasn't in a rush. If there was one thing I was quickly growing to love about Garrett, it was exactly what we were doing right then— being touchy and teasing without it actually being foreplay. Maybe this would end with us in bed and maybe it wouldn't, but it didn't *have* to. Even when the touches were undeniably sexual—like when he squeezed my ass or when I rocked my erection against his—there was no sense of urgency.

He was *patient*. That was it. He could enjoy making out and even some playful fooling around, but his point of no return was a hell of a lot further down the line than most men's.

"I think you're the first man I've ever known," he murmured against my neck, "to get a hard-on because of a game of Magic."

"Mmm. Maybe." I tilted my head to the side and bit my lip as his kisses gave me goose bumps. "Does this mean you'd be willing to play again?"

"If this is what you're like after you lose, you better believe it."

"Hey!" I laughed, and so did he, and his breath was cool and ticklish against my neck.

Then he nudged me back. "We should really take this someplace flat."

"Mmm, maybe with some lube and condoms nearby?"

"Except . . ." He licked his lips before drawing me back down, and just before our lips met, he whispered, "I kind of have you right where I want you."

I moaned into his kiss. Beyond that, we barely made a sound. Once in a while, a soft moan escaped someone's lips, or a low growl would send a shiver through both of us, but for the most part, the room was silent except for clothes brushing clothes. The sofa creaked now and then when we'd shift. The sounds of kissing had never turned me on all that much before, but they sure did now. Maybe because I'd never really focused on them before, but in the near-silence, every little sound drove me wild.

This wasn't what I'd had in mind when I suggested playing cards tonight. Hell if I was going to protest, though.

Barely breaking the kiss, Garrett shifted to stretch out on his back, and my body moved like it was taking cues from his brain instead of mine. I was on top of him now, my hips between his parted legs and my mouth still moving with his. His free hand slid up under the back of my shirt, and the warmth of his skin made me gasp. For as much of last night as we'd spent tangled up in each other, I held on to him and touched him and breathed him in like this was the first time we'd ever been in the same room. This time, last time, every time—didn't matter. He always had this effect on me. No wonder I was hooked.

He slipped a hand between us, and as he tugged at my belt, I shifted onto one arm and reached down to do the same for him. With a little fumbling, we managed to get belts unbuckled and zippers undone. I lifted my hips enough, and we quickly fell into a steady rhythm. I rocked gently back and forth, and we stroked each other, rubbed against each other, and even though I was out of breath and could barely remember what to do with my mouth, like hell was I going to stop kissing him.

He moaned like he was about to say something, so I lifted my head, but he grabbed the back of my neck and dragged me down again. Okay, then—he didn't want to stop kissing either. Fine by me.

I pushed my cock into his fist like I was pushing it into him, and I groaned as he squeezed just right to make my back arch and my toes curl.

Garrett moaned, thrusting up into my hand. His ragged breath rushed past my lips. "I'm . . . gonna come."

"Y-yeah. Me too." And before the words were even out, I was there, unloading on his hand and shuddering so hard I was surprised I didn't black out.

Beneath me, Garrett moaned again. His breath caught. And then he was coming too, jerking and gasping until we both sighed and collapsed.

"Oh my *God*," he slurred.

"Uh-huh." I lifted myself up on shaking arms and kissed him. "That was hot."

"Yeah it was." He brushed his lips across mine. "Is this going to happen every time we play Magic?"

I pretended to give it serious thought. "Yeah, probably."

"Good." He grinned, combing a trembling hand through my hair. "Next time you want to play, you just let me know."

"Oh, I will . . ."

CHAPTER TWENTY

GARRETT

"**W**hy did I think it was smart to go this route?" I grumbled at the steering wheel and the long line of cars ahead of us on Highway 16. The Tacoma Narrows Bridge was ahead, and everyone had slowed to a crawl as if they were all having flashbacks of that footage of Galloping Gertie from the 1920s or whatever. "Come on, people. The bridge doesn't flop around like that anymore!" I let my head fall back. "We should've taken 101. Or taken the ferry and come down I-5 out of Seattle."

Beside me, Jesse laughed. "Oh come on. This is Washington—traffic would've been shitty any way we'd gone."

I grunted softly. He had a point.

"In fact . . ." He tapped his phone a few times. "Yep. That's what I thought."

"What?" I craned my neck a little, but just long enough to see the colorful map on his screen. As per usual in this area, especially during rush hour, more highways than not were black or red. Nasty traffic as far as the eye could see.

"There's construction on 101," Jesse said. "It's a mess all the way to Olympia. Seattle looks so bad right now, I'm surprised the sidewalks aren't black and red."

I chuckled. "Funny. I haven't been gone all that long, and I've already gotten spoiled and forgotten how ugly the traffic is over here." Admittedly, I felt better knowing that there was nothing we could have done to avoid the congestion. "How does I-5 look through Tacoma and Olympia?"

"Like we might want to stop for dinner and wait some of it out."

"That bad?"

"Yep." He turned to me. "We're not in a hurry either way. I could eat, or I can wait, and it's not like we have to be in Portland by a certain time. So, whatever you want to do. You're driving."

"Let's see how we feel after we get across this stupid bridge."

"Sounds like a plan."

As we continued our crawl, I couldn't help feeling a subtle sense of déjà vu. And I knew where it was coming from—I'd had road trips like this. Where I'd have been grinding my teeth to dust with road rage, but my laid-back copilot knew just how to defuse me and make the act of sitting in traffic almost pleasant. Why was I not surprised that Jesse was that way?

I wasn't surprised, but I was admittedly kind of unsettled.

Because Sean had been that way.

That doesn't mean anything. Some people are just chill in traffic.

I sighed, hoping Jesse read it as frustration with the idiots in front of us instead of with myself. I was seeing signs that weren't there. So what if Jesse was laid-back in traffic? Playful in and out of the bedroom? Easygoing about damn near everything? Maybe that was just the kind of guy I liked now.

I was overthinking it as usual. Ever since Scott had pointed out some similarities between my late husband and my new boyfriend, my trigger-happy brain had been quick to pounce on anything about Jesse that remotely echoed Sean. Jesse laughed at something Sean would've laughed at, and kind of sounded like him? Red alert! Jesse stopped on the sidewalk to fawn over a dog like Sean would've? Sound the alarm! Jesse made a catty comment about a customer and rolled his eyes just the way Sean always had? Abandon ship!

Yeah. Overthinking it.

Except even this trip was familiar. Sean had gone with me whenever Fiona and I had done Comic-Con. She'd fly in, and he and I would drive. The con had never been his cup of tea, so he'd go off and do touristy things while she and I drowned in nerdiness, but the road trip? That was our thing. He'd let me drive because I was a terrible passenger, and I'd let him pick out restaurants because he'd always been better at finding the diamonds in the rough. Or at least the places that wouldn't give us food poisoning.

He'd gently tease me about my impatience in traffic, and somehow always knew what notes to hit so I'd laugh instead of getting even more annoyed. That was probably the only reason we'd made it through Los Angeles without me losing my shit. Just having him there beside me made the long drive pleasant. Kept me calm, made the time go by, made me a *little* disappointed when we'd reached our destination. I could have driven forever with him in the passenger seat. Just like I could drive forever with Jesse—

"Hey." Jesse nudged my leg. "You still here?"

"Huh?" I shook myself, and realized the car in front of me had started moving. I'd spaced out too long, and some jackass in a Prius squeaked into the space. "Damn it . . ."

I kind of expected Jesse to make a joke about me zoning out, but instead, he put his hand on my thigh. "You okay?"

"Yeah. Yeah." I rested my hand over his and gave him a quick smile. "Just, uh, trying to remember if there's any place worth stopping to eat in Tacoma."

He seemed to buy it, and picked up his phone again. "One way to find out."

I faced the road again, the uneasiness pulling harder at my gut. I was relieved he'd bought my explanation.

I just tried not to think about the fact that Sean would've responded the same way.

Rumors might have been flying that *Wolf's Landing* was about to be canceled, but the fandom was sure going strong. The convention center was packed. I doubted there was a place to park within five miles, so thank God Jesse and I had a room at the con hotel.

It wasn't quite the scale of something like Comic-Con, but few things were. Still, it was impressive as hell, and there was an enthusiastic vibe that pulled everyone in, even the significant others who'd started out looking like they'd grudgingly come along.

The booths and merchandise were endlessly fascinating. I couldn't believe all the different Wolf's Landing-themed items people had come up with. I'd heard that the studio and publisher had both initially wanted to be strict about licensing, but Hunter Easton had used his not-insignificant clout to insist on giving smaller companies and independent artists access to the brand. Jesse's boss Lydia was apparently making a killing off her art, and she was clearly not the only one. The gigantic hall was crammed with booths hawking toys, spinoff comics, clothes, art, costumes, and anything imaginable with the series' theme. Someone even had little werewolf ears that could be worn by small pets or babies. There was an interior decorator who had once been a set designer and now specialized in decking out entire rooms to look like sets from the show. I didn't imagine there was much demand for something like that, but she had a solid crowd around the booth, so what did I know?

There were panels and Q&A sessions going on in one of the other rooms, and long lines waited by the autograph tables. It wasn't just Hunter and the main actors, either. As I wandered around the con, I saw anyone even peripherally involved with the books or show getting mobbed for photos and autographs. One was suddenly swarmed with teenagers holding bound manuscripts, and it didn't take much to figure out she was Hunter's and Kevin's literary agent.

It was crazy and chaotic, but it was fun. The atmosphere was upbeat, just like I remembered from Comic-Con, and I eagerly soaked it up. People were genuinely excited about the series, and even the most introverted attendees could be pulled into a conversation with random people—myself included—about the books, the show, the people involved, the werewolf lore . . . anything. I was nearly late to lunch with Jesse because of an animated discussion with some cosplayers who were stunned to find out I'd only read the first book. Fortunately, they were almost religious in their refusal to let spoilers slip, so it made for an entertaining conversation without ruining the series for me.

Eventually, I broke away and hurried toward the End o' Earth booth, but it wasn't like Jesse was standing there tapping his watch. In fact, I probably could've continued my conversation awhile longer, because he and his bosses were slammed.

It was amazing to watch him in action, though. Jesse was in his element at the comic book shop, but here? Holy shit. He was made for this. Decked out in a Wolf's Landing T-shirt and a pair of wolf ears, with a cartoon wolf nose and whiskers painted on his face, he worked the crowd with practiced ease. Even when the mob was five deep, he had everything under control. Somehow, he always knew who was next even though they were just bunched up against the table with no actual line, and when things got really hectic, I swore he was simultaneously helping three or four people. When people started getting impatient or if a particular piece of merchandise was sold out, he soothed the tension with jokes. At one point, when even that didn't work, he started dancing wildly to some music coming from another booth, waving merchandise around and singing his various sales pitches or people's order totals. It worked—everyone was laughing too much to be pissed off.

Once in a while he'd pause for a swig from his water bottle, but otherwise, he never let on that all of this was taxing in any way.

"He's just like a swan," I could hear my old boss saying. *"Glides along perfectly on the surface, and makes it look easy because no one can see the feet paddling like gangbusters underneath."*

My boss hadn't been talking about Jesse, though. He'd been talking about Sean.

I quickly forced the memory aside. It bugged the hell out of me that my mind kept putting Jesse side by side with Sean. I made a mental note to smack Scott when I got back to Bluewater Bay; his concerns had obviously gotten under my skin, and now I was second-guessing myself—and my boyfriend—at every turn. Jesse wasn't Sean. Jesse was Jesse. End of discussion.

It was almost forty-five minutes before Jesse could bow out and join me. I didn't mind, though. Even when my brain was being ridiculous, I loved watching him work. His enthusiasm was infectious, and he was the very picture of competence, not to mention grace under pressure. If he ever went to work as a bartender, he'd be rolling in tips.

He took off his wolf ears, and as he broke away from the crowd, he wiped his forehead with the back of his hand. "Sorry about that. We got a bit busy."

"It's all right. You sure they can let you go?"

He glanced back, then shrugged. "Yeah. They should have a reprieve for a while, anyway." Motioning after the migrating crowd, he added, "Everyone's going to the preview of the season premiere. Which means the dining hall is probably deserted too."

"Perfect."

At the dining hall door, Jesse flashed his badge and tossed his hair. "Stand aside—I'm with the band."

The woman at the door rolled her eyes and waved us in. I chuckled, shrugging apologetically, and followed him as he strutted into the room.

The dining hall was comprised of a couple of adjoining conference rooms converted to a cafeteria of sorts exclusively for employees and merchants, and it was indeed empty. Jesse had explained to me on the way up that this had been Hunter Easton's doing. After the man behind Wolf's Landing had caught wind of people working at the con being unable to go get food for various reasons, he'd demanded the organizers set up something so no one had to leave the building or fight the long lines. No wonder everyone adored the guy.

"So when do I get to meet all the Wolf's Landing people you keep mentioning?" I asked as we got into the modest buffet line.

"Soon." He picked up a plate and perused the row of chafing dishes. "Everyone's been slammed because of the production schedule and getting ready for the con, but they'll all be on lighter schedules after this week." He glanced at me before scooping up some Spanish rice. "Come to the next Magic tournament at the shop, and I guarantee you'll be starstruck as hell."

"Oh yeah?" I chuckled. "Sign me up."

He winked. "I already did."

"Did you now?" I laughed as he handed me the spoon so I could get some rice.

"Yep. It was filling up fast, so . . ." He shrugged.

"I'd call you presumptuous, but I think you just know me too well."

Jesse flashed me a devilish smile that made my knees weak. "If you consider knowing you in the Biblical sense to be knowing you too well, then . . ." Another shrug, this one much more flippant. "Guilty."

I chuckled as we continued down the buffet line, pointedly ignoring my idiot brain's attempts to suggest how well *I* seemed to know *him*.

He isn't Sean. Stop it.

We found a table near the gigantic floor-to-ceiling windows and dug in. The food wasn't half bad—the pork was a touch dry, but otherwise, everything was seasoned nicely and not cooked within an inch of its life. They really did make sure their people were well taken care of.

"So, what have you been doing all day?" Jesse asked as he speared a piece of chicken.

"Browsing the merchandise, mostly. I did go to a couple of panels, but most of the good ones were full."

"Oh yeah?" He lifted his eyebrows. "Which ones did you go to?" He watched me intently as he took a bite.

"There was one a little while ago with the artists working on the graphic novels."

Jesse sat up, nearly choking. After he'd washed down his food, he said, "Oh, how was that? Did they have any previews?" He was practically bouncing with excitement.

I couldn't help grinning as I nodded. "Yeah, they had a PowerPoint with some frames and some of the concept art. It's going to be *amazing*."

Jesse sighed, damn near swooning. "I can't wait until they release the next one. Did they say when it's due out?"

"January."

He groaned. "Fuck. They're taking their sweet time, aren't they?"

I nodded.

"Bastards."

"Right?"

"So what other panel?"

"The Q&A with the stuntmen." I laughed, shaking my head. "That is a *wild* bunch."

"They kind of have to be," he said. "Have you seen the shit they have to do?"

"I saw a few clips during the panel, yeah." I whistled. "It probably shouldn't have been as funny as it was, but when they started rattling off all their injuries, they had everyone rolling."

Jesse snorted. "Little bit of schadenfreude?"

"Just a bit."

"What kinds of stories did they have?"

I thought for a moment. "Well, Levi Pritchard's double said he knew it was going to be a bad day when he had to dangle upside down from the jaws of a mechanical dragon. As he put it, it started out bad and just kept going downhill until he wound up with three bruised ribs and a dislocated shoulder."

Jesse grimaced, squirming in his seat. "Ouch!"

"No kidding. And then there was the time Carter Samuels's double almost lost an eye..."

How Jesse maintained his boisterousness through a twelve-hour day, I would never know, but when I came back to the booth around closing time, he was still being... well, Jesse.

Finally, his shift was over, and we headed up to the room to call it a night. The minute the elevator doors shut, the façade vanished. He sagged against the wall, closing his eyes and pushing out a heavy breath. It was like some unseen director had yelled, *Cut!*, and now Jesse didn't have to be *on* anymore.

I put a hand on his waist. "You okay?"

"Yeah. Just tired." He wrapped his arms around me, resting his hands on the small of my back, and kissed me. "You weren't bored today, were you?"

"No, not at all." *Especially not when I got to watch you in your element.* "I might've blown my budget already too."

"Already?" He laughed, sounding even more tired. "Do I need to confiscate your wallet?"

"Yeah, probably."

Haven't I had this conversation before? Yes. It means I need to restrain myself at cons, not that Jesse is channeling Sean.

I let him lean on me as the elevator continued its ascent. Even as we headed down the hall, he stayed against me, and ... I liked it. I didn't care if anyone saw us. Hell, I was kind of disappointed there wasn't anyone in the hallway *to* see us.

Yeah, this gorgeous man is here with me. Or I'm here with him.

Whatever. We're here together, and I couldn't be happier.

I keyed us into the room. Jesse gently freed himself from my arms, shuffled across the floor to the bed, and collapsed facedown on the comforter. "Oh my God."

I lay beside him and rubbed a hand up and down his back. "You sure you're okay?"

"Yeah. Just . . . peopled out."

"I can imagine." I kept my voice soft. I'd have been shocked if he didn't have a headache, and I didn't want to contribute to it. "Anything I can do?"

"Nah. You're good." He rolled partway onto his side and slid his hand over my thigh. "You're an exception to the 'I'm done with people' thing."

I smiled. "I should hope so, because I don't really have anywhere else to sleep."

He laughed, sounding even more tired.

"We'll just take it easy tonight." I smoothed his hair. "You hungry? I could order room service."

That brought some light back to his eyes. "That sounds good. You mind if I grab a shower?"

"Not at all. Let me know what you want to eat, and I'll order it while you're showering."

"Thank you." He smiled, cupping my face gently. "I hope you don't mind staying in tonight. I'm sure you didn't come all the way down here to hang out in a hotel room."

"No, I came all the way down here to hang out with *you*. And even though I wasn't working, I was at the con all day. I could stand to be away from people for a while myself." I caressed his cheek with the backs of my fingers. "Present company excluded."

"I feel special."

"As well you should."

Jesse curved a hand behind my neck and drew me in for a long kiss. "Okay. I'm gonna go get that shower."

"Okay."

After I'd ordered food, I stripped out of my clothes and lounged in bed. I could easily throw on a pair of shorts when the room service showed up. In the meantime, I intended to get as comfortable as possible.

Physically, that was easy. Mentally, not so much. I was getting hung up on things that weren't there. And even though I kept telling myself there was nothing to get hung up on, that didn't stop me from circling back to that ridiculous train of thought.

I was still wound up, but hopefully not letting it show, when Jesse was done showering. He did do a pretty good job of pulling my focus, though—it was hard to think about anything when he came strolling out of the bathroom in boxers and nothing else. The painted-on nose and whiskers were gone aside from a little smudge on one cheek, and his blond hair was finger-combed into some semblance of order instead of being meticulously styled. More like he needed it out of his face than he actually cared what it looked like. It was hard not to smile at that. There was something endearing about reaching a point in our relationship where he didn't feel like he needed to be flawlessly put together when he was around me. Some people thought that meant you didn't care anymore. I preferred to think we were just that comfortable with each other.

And just like that, the uneasiness evaporated. That was it. It wasn't Jesse that reminded me of Sean. It was our relationship. We were getting into a comfortable groove like Sean and I had. Okay, I could live with that. If our relationship was echoing my marriage, we were definitely doing something right.

"You order food?" He eyed me as if to ask why I'd bother getting undressed.

"Mm-hmm. It'll be an hour or so. Guess we're not the only ones with this idea."

"Damn. Well." He grinned. "Nothing wrong with relaxing until then, right?" He kicked off his boxers and joined me in bed, and I pulled the sheets up over us. As soon as he was settled, he rested his head on my shoulder. "Ahh, this is what I needed."

"Yeah?" I wrapped my arm around him and played with his damp hair. "Getting off your feet?"

"Mm-hmm. And this."

I smiled. "It's fun watching you work, by the way."

"Why's that?"

"You're just so . . . sure."

"How do you mean?"

"Like when you've got fifty people clamoring for your attention." I stroked his cheek as I spoke. "It's like you never missed a beat. I would've been tearing my hair out, but I don't think you even broke a sweat."

He laughed. "You want to know the secret?"

"Sure."

In a stage whisper, he said, "Name-brand deodorant."

I snorted and gave his head a gentle pat. "Dork."

He smothered a laugh and cuddled closer to me. "Nah, I just take it one person at a time. I freaked out at my first con, but Lydia taught me how to roll with it. And then I realized that if people are getting impatient and I start dancing around or acting like an idiot, they laugh. Then they aren't such dicks."

"I should keep that in mind at the bar."

"Well, you have the advantage of pouring alcohol down their throats."

"You'd be amazed how dickish people can be even when they're buzzed."

"Eh, yeah, fair enough."

"You're obviously good at what you do." I kissed the top of his head. "And what can I say? I just enjoy watching you."

"Pervert."

"Mm-hmm."

He laughed again, then lifted his chin and dusted a kiss under my jaw, and I couldn't help shivering. His lips curved into a grin against my neck. "Like that?"

"You know I do."

He did it again, more deliberately this time. I tightened my arm around his shoulders and tilted my head back to offer up more of my throat. He pushed his knee between my thighs and slid halfway on top of me. My whole body tingled with need—I loved the warmth of his skin against mine almost as much as I loved the softness of his lips.

His hand drifted downward, and as he trailed a finger alongside my erection, he singsonged, "Somebody's getting turned on."

I sucked in a sharp hiss. "Of course I am. I'm naked in bed with you."

"Mmm, I like the sound of that."

Trailing my hands up his sides, I murmured, "Thought you were tired."

"I'm exhausted." He lifted his head and met my gaze, his eyes filled with fatigue, but also something much stronger and hotter. "I think I can find the energy to fuck my man, don't you?"

I grinned. "If you're tired, we can always—"

He kissed me hard.

Well, if you're sure...

I wrapped an arm around him and returned his kiss, holding his lean, hot body against mine. I slid my free hand between us and started stroking him as he did the same to me. Our breath mingled between our lips, our soft moans the only sounds besides us rhythmically pumping each other's dicks.

His barely audible moans drove me on more than his hand did. I loved how much he was trembling, gasping, cursing. All day, he'd been the very picture of unflappable poise, and now he was falling apart, and that was breathtakingly hot. Exhilarating. Knowing he could keep himself together when he was under pressure, but chose to let himself go in my arms.

"You're almost there, aren't you, baby?" I whispered between kisses.

"Uh-huh."

"Good. Christ, you're hot."

He thrust into my hand and whimpered. "I'm gonna come," he murmured, thrusting into my fist and gripping my cock even tighter. "Jesus, Garrett, that's *perfect*. I'm gonna..."

"Oh God, me too. Fuck!"

Hot semen coated my hand and hit my stomach, and we both moaned and cursed as we kept working each other's dicks until we couldn't take any more.

We let go. Exhaled. Relaxed.

"That was fun," he murmured.

"It was." I grinned against his lips. "Do it again sometime?"

He laughed softly. "Fuck yeah."

I chuckled, kissed him, and sat up. "We should get some sleep after we eat. You've got a long day tomorrow."

"Ugh." He made a petulant noise but sat up too. "Fine."

"You'll thank me when you're not dead on your feet tomorrow."

"Yeah, probably." He stole another quick kiss and got up. We made quick work of cleaning ourselves off, then got back into the rumpled bed. I molded myself to his back, and he practically purred as he pressed back against me.

His voice was heavy and slurred with sleepiness as he said, "I'm really glad you came to the con."

"Me too. Especially since it means spending so much time with you." I kissed the side of his neck. "I'm going to get dressed. Food should be here soon."

He didn't answer. He was sound asleep.

CHAPTER TWENTY-ONE

JESSE

I forced my eyelids open and checked the time on my phone. A few minutes after seven. Definitely no hurry to be up, especially since I didn't have to be at the booth until ten.

And most especially because I was sprawled out in this giant rumpled bed with Garrett. I left my phone on the nightstand, rolled over, and took him in as the morning sun teased his features into view. He was so gorgeous. Not the type of guy I'd ever imagined myself with, but I wasn't sure what I'd imagined. It just made sense that this beautiful man with white in his hair and years on his face was the one I didn't want out of my mind or my bed.

Salt-and-pepper stubble dusted his sharply angled jaw, and holy shit he had lashes for days. When he was asleep, the lines in his face relaxed. All the tension eased, and he looked peaceful. Of course, most people did while sleeping, but it was such a switch from when he was awake. Seeing him like this, all relaxed and soft, I wondered how the first few months after his husband's death had been. Back when the grief had still been raw. Had he even been able to sleep?

I quickly pushed that thought out of my mind. I didn't want to think about how much pain he'd been in back then, or how much he was probably still in when he was awake.

Propping myself up on my elbow, I had to fight the temptation to caress his stubbled jaw. It was almost impossible to keep my hands off him, especially when we were in bed.

And the fact that we were here in this hotel bed made him that much harder to resist. Not just because hotel rooms invited all kinds of wild, inventive sex, but because he was *here*. He couldn't possibly know how much it meant to me that he'd come to the con. Even after I'd warned him ahead of time that I couldn't guarantee much in the bedroom—cons were fucking exhausting—he'd taken a few days off from the bar and tagged along to Portland. I'd be working, preoccupied, stressed, and tired, but he wanted to spend the time with me anyway.

Finally, I had to—I slid the backs of my fingers down his cheek.

He wrinkled his nose and grumbled. Then his eyelids fluttered. "Time is it?"

"Early."

He groaned, but his lips pulled into a tired smile as he opened his eyes. "There better be coffee brewing."

"There is." I traced the edge of his jaw with a fingertip. "Downstairs in the coffee shop."

He swore under his breath, but there wasn't much heat behind it. "Come here, you." He wrapped me in a bear hug, and I happily slid up against him. "What time do you have to work?"

"Ten. We've got plenty of time."

"Good." He kissed my forehead. "Maybe we can actually have a decent breakfast."

"Mm-hmm. And before we do that . . . you think that shower's big enough to fuck in?"

He chuckled sleepily. "You know, for someone who didn't think he'd want to fool around much this weekend . . ."

I nuzzled his neck. "I obviously underestimated how horny I'd be with you around."

His hand trailed down my side and under the covers. "You won't hear me bitching."

I laughed, but choked on it when his fingertips brushed my cock.

"So." His chuckle turned wicked. "About that shower . . ."

The shower was definitely big enough. Despite getting out of bed at a little after seven, it was almost nine before we finally left the hotel room. Totally worth it, though. And worth the ache in my hip that would probably be following me around for the rest of the day. If Garrett could still walk without complaining, so could I.

Fed, caffeinated, and pleasantly sore, we stepped into the convention hall to do some shopping.

As we wandered, I kept stealing glances at him. He'd skipped his contacts today, probably because the air in the convention center was so dry, and I still couldn't get over how sexy he was with his glasses on. But that wasn't the only thing I kept looking at. My gaze kept drifting toward his hand. After being so affectionate and sexy, it was kind of jarring to not be touching now. So why *weren't* we touching? Did I dare . . .?

If I was going to try to cross that line, this was probably the place to do it. Wolf's Landing and its fandom were about as queer friendly as you could get, so if there was any place we could get away with being affectionate in public, this was it. The only one who might have any objection was Garrett.

So, with no shortage of nerves twisting in my gut, I let my fingers brush his. When he didn't pull away, I did it again, and this time I allowed them to linger there for a second before letting them fall away.

Before I could make another attempt, Garrett slid his hand firmly into mine. He glanced at me, and we both smiled.

And . . . that was that. Neither of us said a word about it.

Of course, that didn't stop me from grinning like an idiot, but whatever. It had been way too long since I'd been with a man who was okay with public affection, and I'd missed it more than I'd realized. I wasn't into "get a room" levels of PDA, but this? Gentle contact that made it clear to everyone who cared that we were together? Fuck yeah.

We weren't joined at the hip after that, either. We'd let go to pick something up or flip through a book, or if one of us needed to sign a credit card receipt or something. Sometimes we'd go two or three booths before our hands would find their way back to each other, or an arm would slide around a waist. How was it possible I'd found a guy who was comfortable with exactly the kind of public affection I liked?

Another booth stuffed with spoof merchandise—and not just from Wolf's Landing—caught our attention and drew us in. While Garrett perused a rack of iPhone covers, I checked out a display of coffee cups. Not that I needed any more coffee cups, but I liked the ones with snarky slogans. Question was, did I want the one that said

This Wolf Ain't Landing Till He Gets Coffee, or the *If the World Tree Doesn't Grow Coffee, I Don't Give a Fuck*? Decisions, decisions.

Hands on my waist startled me, but only because I hadn't heard him coming. As he slid his arms around me and kissed my cheek, I leaned back against him.

He looked over my shoulder at the coffee cups in my hands. "Getting into trouble?"

"Shopping is not getting into trouble."

"Mm-hmm. Didn't you buy like four mugs yesterday?"

"I can neither confirm nor deny."

"Do I need to go up to the room and count?"

I tried to elbow him playfully, but he just laughed and held me tighter. "You're a dork."

"And you're going to need a bigger kitchen for all these mugs."

"Yeah, probably." I held them up so he could see the slogans. "Which one should I get?"

He paused to read them, and laughed. "Hell, why not get both?"

I twisted around a little, eyeing him. "Are you enabling me?"

"Maybe?" He flashed a grin that was probably supposed to look innocent.

I laughed, rolled my eyes ...

And bought both mugs. Bastard.

We continued through the con. As we walked, we were almost always touching. Sometimes holding hands. Sometimes arms around each other's waists. More often than not, he just had his hand resting on the small of my back, and I decided I loved that more than anything. It was possessive without being obnoxiously territorial. The gentle weight of his hand was comforting and kind of hot. Like a promise that while everything was calm and platonic right now, it would be anything but in a few hours.

Eventually, we meandered past the crowded section where the End o' Earth booth was set up. I wasn't at all surprised to see a huge mob in front of the tables and my bosses looking mildly panicked. My shift technically didn't start for another half hour, but they were slammed. Scowling, I turned to Garrett. "I should probably get to work. I think they could use the help."

He nodded. "Yeah. Good idea." He held out his hand. "You want me to take that stuff up to the room?"

I glanced down at my shopping bags. "You sure?"

"Of course. You need to work, and I have a key." He beckoned to me, and I transferred the bags to his hand.

"Thanks." I didn't move right away, though. "I'm working the booth until five, and since it's the last night, Simon and Lydia usually do pizza or something in their room later on. If you want to go."

"Sure." He smiled, thumb rubbing gently against mine. "I'm game for anything."

"Okay. Maybe we can go grab a light dinner or something first, since it'll be eight or nine before they're back in the room."

Garrett nodded again.

"All right. I'll see you in a few hours." I raised my eyebrows. "You sure you won't get bored?"

"'Bored'?" Garrett snorted. "Go bankrupt maybe, but I don't see myself getting bored."

I laughed. "Well, I can spot you for gas money if you blow your entire wad."

We locked eyes, both silently daring each other to run with the double entendre.

Finally, he just shook his head. "All right, you better get to work." He nodded toward the booth.

I glanced over. Yeah, Simon was getting frazzled, and even Lydia looked like she was nearing the end of her tether. Ian and Dexy were nowhere in sight, and with the crowd thickening by the second, yeah— they needed all the help they could get. "Okay. I'll see you later."

"Looking forward to it."

One quick kiss, one long look, and we separated.

As soon as I stepped behind the booth, Simon clapped my shoulder. "Oh thank God. Ian had to go to some studio thing, and we had to send Dexy to the office supply store, so it's been just us holding down the fort."

"Let me sign in on the time sheet," I said. "And I'm all yours."

And all through my shift, there was a cool spot on my lower back where Garrett's hand had been.

That evening, I'd been desperate to get out of the convention center. I'd had enough of fluorescent lights, recycled air, and yes, even Wolf's Landing. I was stiff and sore all over, but walking down the sidewalk was nice. The fresh air more than made up for the extra effort my legs had to put forth.

We grabbed some munchies and coffee from a food truck near a park and shot the breeze while we ate and walked. Eventually, we ended up by some shops, a lot of which were obviously geared toward tourists.

"My God," I said as we slowed in front of one. I arched an eyebrow at the snow globes, spoons, coins, postcards, T-shirts, oven mitts, paperweights, beer cozies, bookends, and Lord only knew what else. "How many different things can they put *Portland* on?"

Garrett snickered, letting the backs of his fingers brush mine. "About as many things as they can put *Wolf's Landing* on, I'm guessing."

"Fair point."

We exchanged glances and kept walking.

In front of a small jeweler, Garrett slowed, and we stopped so he could look at some Seiko watches in the window. While he checked them out, the display of magazines at the next shop caught my eye. I craned my neck, perusing the covers to see if anyone hot was featured this month. Levi was supposed to be on the cover of something soon to promote his new movie, and I was definitely grabbing a copy of that one when it came out. I didn't see it, though, and none of the other magazines on the rack had anyone or anything worth coughing up seven bucks for a copy. The latest superhero abomination was out soon, so half the magazines were focused on that, and some controversial Oscar-bait monstrosity was getting a ton of attention from—

"You got a problem, faggot?"

I jumped twice. First at the slur. Then at the realization it had been directed at me. I shook myself and met the gaze of a snarly guy in an Oregon Ducks baseball cap. "Sorry, what?"

"I fucking saw you staring at me." He faced me fully, puffing himself up as if he weren't already twice my size. "So, you got a problem?"

I gritted my teeth. Behind me, though Garrett didn't make a sound, his presence was suddenly . . . there. I glanced at him, ready to tell him to stay out of it, but there was nothing aggressive in his posture. It only took a split second of eye contact for him to tell me he had my back, but he wasn't stepping in.

Then I faced the asshole again. "What makes you think I was looking at you?"

He glared at me. "I fucking saw you."

All around us, heads were starting to turn. Conversations quieted. People stared.

I didn't take my attention off Asshole McDuck as I quickly assessed my options. Sarcasm and mockery could usually shut people like this down in a hurry, but even with a bunch of people around and my good-sized boyfriend behind me, I didn't want to gamble too much. Not when he had on a loose flannel overshirt that could easily hide something more dangerous than insecurities and a bad attitude.

I narrowed my eyes and gestured—with an exaggeratedly limp wrist, of course—toward the magazine rack. "Unless you're a copy of *GQ* with Steve Bancroft's face on the cover, I didn't even know you were standing there until you said something." I bit back an additional comment about *So who was staring at who, darlin'?* because I still couldn't be sure what was or wasn't under that flannel shirt. Sass wasn't worth the risk.

His lips pulled tight and he glared at me. His eyes flicked toward Garrett. Then scanned our surroundings.

Finally, with some grumbling that was probably a few more homophobic slurs, he rolled his eyes, turned on his heel, and stomped down the sidewalk.

All around us, everyone stayed tense for a moment before they slowly relaxed. Conversations started again. A few glances went his way, but otherwise, the world kept on turning as if nothing had happened.

I exhaled, trying to calm the jittery feeling in my stomach as the adrenaline began to ease.

Garrett put a hand on my back. On that spot that had been cool all day while I'd worked the booth. "You all right?"

I nodded, smoothing a hand over my shirt as if our altercation had ruffled my clothing. "Occupational hazard when you don't act straight enough."

He glanced in the direction the Ducks fan had gone. If looks could kill, that motherfucker would've dropped dead right there on the sidewalk.

I touched Garrett's arm. "It's okay. It's done."

"I know." He was still scowling, but as he turned to me, his expression softened. "You sure you're good?"

I nodded. "Yeah. And thanks for not jumping in."

At that, he actually smiled a little. Cupping my face, he said, "I know you can hold your own." His eyes flicked toward the space the guy had occupied, and the smile faltered. "If he'd lifted a hand to you, he'd have been shitting his own teeth, but . . ."

I laughed and put an arm around him. "I've never had a big strong protector. I kind of like this."

He eyed me incredulously, but then he laughed and kissed my temple. As we started walking back in the direction we'd come, he wrapped his arm around my shoulders. "I hardly think you *need* protecting."

"Still."

Keeping me close to his side, he said, "I'm your boyfriend. Not your bodyguard."

I had to smile at the words. Not just because I agreed, but because he'd actually said, *I'm your boyfriend,* out loud. I didn't give a damn if that made me a huge romantic dork. And getting all giddy and ridiculous about that was better than thinking about the confrontation, so I ran with it.

As we walked, we didn't talk much. That was fine. I liked our companionable silences, and anyway, my mind was still on the altercation with that asshole that had left me shaken. It happened sometimes, and even in progressive places like Seattle and Portland, it was a real and fucking irritating part of being a loudly gay man, but I didn't think anyone ever really got *used* to it.

If there was any silver lining to what had happened, it was the side of Garrett it had revealed.

Some guys seemed to think that because I was on the femme side, I needed a big bad protector to fight my battles for me. And yeah, if things got physical, I probably couldn't do much against someone built like a brick shithouse. But as long as it was just verbal, I could stand my own ground, thank you very much. I *hated* being defended. I hated the assumption that I needed or wanted someone else to valiantly step in and fight my battles for me. Something like that had actually been the end of one of my few relationships.

Tonight, it was like Garrett had known exactly what I'd needed— *let me know you have my back, but don't tag in until I need you.*

I stole a glance at him, and a fluttery feeling danced in my stomach. I had zero doubt whatsoever that he'd been serious about getting involved if things had turned physical, and just the rage radiating off him would quite possibly have made up for any difference in strength between him and McDuck. But he'd let me call the shots. I'd wanted a chance to defuse it, and he'd given it to me. I'd wanted to keep things from escalating, and he'd let me. A hotheaded guy could've stepped in, turned things into a brawl, and quite possibly found out the hard way if my gut feeling was true about what was hidden under that shirt.

I had to fight a shudder at the thought of Garrett getting hurt on my behalf, and I was once again thankful things hadn't gotten out of control.

As we walked, I held him a little tighter. With this man, I felt safe and supported, but also respected. Like he could let me stand on my own two feet, but was one hundred percent there if my balance wavered.

Funny how that made me want to fall in a very, very different way.

CHAPTER TWENTY-TWO

GARRETT

"**Y**ou did bring your cards, right?" Jesse asked after we'd returned to our room.

"Of course." I nodded toward my bag. "I know what happens when we play Magic, so you'd better believe I came prepared."

Jesse grinned. "Simon and Lydia said we're playing while we do pizza. The 'what happens after Magic' part will have to wait a bit, but . . ." He raised his eyebrows. "You in?"

"Sure. That sounds like fun. Even if I do have to wait for the *really* fun part."

A sly smile curled his lips as he wrapped an arm around my waist. "I'll make it worth the wait." He kissed me lightly. "Promise."

"Oh, I know you will. You always do." I claimed a deeper kiss, not to change his mind about waiting until later, but to let him know I was absolutely going to hold him to it. If his lips and tongue were to be believed, he liked that idea.

We'd be here all night if we kept standing here kissing, though. So, we pried ourselves apart, grabbed our cards, and headed down the hall to the room Simon, Lydia, and Ian were sharing.

Of course I was fully expecting to see the three of them there. It was a bit of a shock, though, when I realized there were a few more players tonight. Didn't matter that I'd known who some of the regulars were at the shop. Didn't matter that I'd known everyone at the comic book shop was friends with half of *Wolf's Landing*. There just wasn't much that could prepare a man for walking into a hotel room and finding Levi Pritchard, Carter Samuels, and Hunter Easton shuffling their decks and distributing munchies. Especially not when I'd been a shameless Levi Pritchard fanboy since his Chad Eastwick days.

Seeing him cross-legged on a bed in a pair of sweatpants and nothing else, shuffling a deck of Magic cards, shaved about twenty years off my life.

"Holy shit," I said under my breath.

Jesse shot me a smirk, and when he winked, I didn't have to ask if he'd known who would be here tonight. He took my elbow. "Guess I should introduce you—"

The door clicked behind us, and we stepped out of the way. In walked Kevyan Montanari—not that I instantly recognized him from all those Wolf's Landing interviews I'd watched or anything—with a stack of pizza boxes. "Food's here!"

"Yes," Jesse said. "Perfect timing."

Kevyan smiled. Then his gaze shifted to me, and his eyebrows jumped. "Oh hey, I was hoping I'd get to meet you this weekend." He gave me a very conspicuous down-up, followed by a lecherous grin. "We've heard a lot about you."

My cheeks burned.

Beside me, Jesse sighed with exasperation. "Shut up, Kev. I haven't given you *that* many details."

Kevin chuckled. "Aw, come on. I was just messing with him." He shifted the pizzas to his left arm and offered his right hand. "I'm Kevin."

Oh, I know who you are.

"Garrett," I said, though he obviously knew that too.

We shook hands, and he went to put the pizzas down beside the TV on the big dresser. Then Jesse introduced me to everyone else. I'd already met Simon and Lydia, but I hadn't met their boyfriend, Ian, until tonight. I managed to not make an idiot of myself as I was introduced to Hunter and Carter. Meeting Levi with some sense of dignity? That was a little more challenging. He obviously wasn't the young guy who'd played Chad Eastwick anymore, but time had been incredibly kind to him. There was also a big difference between seeing that lopsided smile on a screen or a poster and having it directed at you.

"Nice to finally meet you," he said as he shook my hand.

Nice . . . to finally . . . meet me?

I tried to speak, but choked. With a subtle cough, I regained my voice. "Yeah. Same."

Something sparkled in his eyes, as if he knew exactly how much I was struggling to be a normal idiot instead of a stunned fanboy idiot.

I stole a self-conscious glance at Jesse, fully expecting a little jealous side-eye, but he was grinning at me like he'd been waiting to see how I'd react to Levi. Not a hint of jealousy or insecurity. Which . . . no shit. Why would he be insecure? That wasn't like him at all. Why would I—

Oh.

Right.

Because while Sean hadn't been the type to flip his lid if I'd so much as looked at another man, he'd had his moments of uncertainty. That palpable doubt, like he thought I'd be tempted to jump ship.

Jesse didn't do that. He wasn't insecure like that. He wasn't Sean. Arguments could be made that I was an idiot, though.

After the introductions had been made, Simon and Lydia put some bowls of candy on the nightstand, and bags of chips were strategically placed on the beds. Nobody was drinking, surprisingly, but that was fine by me.

"Are we waiting on anyone else?" Lydia asked.

"Just us," Carter said. "Everyone else had other plans."

Levi scoffed with mock indignation. "What the hell could be more important than eating pizza and getting your ass kicked at Magic?"

"Well." Hunter clapped his shoulder. "You'll have to tell the rest of us about that last part."

"Shut up, Easton."

"We do need to get some more people here," Lydia said. "Especially some more women. Our card nights are seriously getting heavy on dudes."

"Uh-huh," Levi said. "And if I recall, that wasn't an issue until you made Natalya swear off Magic until the end of time."

"Who, me?" Lydia feigned offense. "Not my fault she wasted her Counterspell on a dumb Lightning Bolt and couldn't defend against a ten-point Fireball."

Simon laughed. "It was probably the cackling more than the card that put her off."

"Hey." Lydia waved a hand. "If she doesn't like shit-talking—"

"Oh God, please don't piss her off," Carter grumbled. "Do you know how painful it is when the stunt coordinator is in a bad mood?"

Levi snickered. Carter elbowed him, which didn't help.

"We could always ask them to come back," Ian said. "But you all know damn well we won't be playing Magic. Those two are hooked on Cards Against Humanity."

"And they're fucking awesome at it too," Hunter grumbled. "Especially Anna's bodyguard."

A laugh burst out of me. "Jeremy? Really?"

"You know him?" Hunter asked.

"Yeah, I've known his fiancé since high school. He's really that good at Cards Against Humanity?"

"Oh my God." Hunter whistled. "There is *no* beating him. *None.*"

"I think he cheats," Carter said. "No way in hell he always has the perfect card for every round."

I just laughed. It was surreal to be swept up in banter with people I'd only seen on camera. They were just normal guys though, here for a good time and some relaxation after a long, busy weekend. And I was definitely making a mental note to play Cards Against Humanity with Scott and Jeremy.

After we'd devoured two of the three pizzas and everyone had meticulously scrubbed all traces of grease off their hands, we settled in and started shuffling cards. We couldn't play one large game because there wasn't space. Not unless we wanted to sit on the floor, and none of us were that adventurous. Instead, we broke into small groups at the little table and on the gigantic king-sized beds. Simon and Ian cuddled up next to each other, playing against Carter and Jesse on one of the beds. Kevin and Lydia took the table for a one-on-one match.

And that was how I wound up on the second bed, facing off against Hunter Easton and Levi Pritchard, *and how the fuck is this suddenly my life?*

I glanced at Jesse as we settled into our respective games, and he winked. Oh right. This was my life because he was my boyfriend, and . . . *No, seriously, how is* any *of this my life?*

After Levi, Hunter, and I had been playing for a while, I surveyed the battlefield. "Okay. Well. I seriously never thought I'd say these words, but . . ." I tapped three of my creatures. "Levi, I'm attacking you with my Shivan Dragon and two Fire Elementals, both of whom are equipped with Whispersilk Cloaks, so you can't block them."

Levi grunted as he glared at my cards. "That dragon is flying, isn't it?"

"Yep."

He scanned his row of creatures, none of which had the ability to fly and thus couldn't block my dragon. Then he huffed sharply and picked up his twenty-sided die. "All right. What's the damage?"

"Um . . ." I counted it up. "Fifteen."

He blinked. "Seriously?"

"Yep."

"Fuck you." He scowled as he put his die down with the five showing. Our eyes locked for a second, and he gave me a wink as if to make sure I knew this was all in good fun. Which I'd known, but damn if that wink hadn't made my pulse race.

We both looked at Hunter. He pursed his lips as he looked at the cards we had laid out in front of us and the ones he had in his hands. Then he grinned and leaned down to tap two of his creatures. "First, I don't like that Shivan Dragon, Garrett." He tapped his Royal Assassin. "It's dead."

"Damn it," I grumbled as I put the dragon in my graveyard. "Fucking Royal Pain-in-the-Assassin." I made a mental note to destroy it my next turn.

Hunter chuckled, but he wasn't done yet. "Levi, I've got two Sengir Vampires coming your way. Both flying. So . . . eight points of damage unless that Northern Paladin of yours suddenly sprouts wings."

Levi shot him a murderous glare, rolled his eyes, and put his cards down with a heavy sigh. "Well, I'm out."

From the other bed, Carter said, "Told you that deck is weak when it comes to defending against flying creatures."

"Nobody asked you, peanut gallery."

Everyone snickered, even Levi as he collected his cards and started shuffling his deck.

Chuckling, Hunter cast a Terror, killing off the Vulshok Sorcerer I'd had every intention of using to kill his Royal Assassin next turn.

"Bastard," I grumbled as I tossed the card into my graveyard on top of the Shivan Dragon.

He grinned smugly. It didn't last, though. When it was my turn, a Lightning Bolt fried the Royal Assassin, and then I came at Hunter with a twelve-point Fireball followed by a two-pronged attack of unblockable Fire Elementals, all of which wiped that smugness off his face in a hurry.

"Damn," he said as we started reshuffling cards. "You're good at this."

"No kidding." Levi craned his neck. "Jesse, your man's banned from Magic nights."

Without missing a beat, asking for context, or even looking up from his own cards, Jesse said, "Not my fault you suck."

"Hey!" But Levi was laughing. To me, he said, "Good game. You don't have to go so easy on us, though."

"All right." I smirked. "I won't."

"Way to go, Pritchard," Hunter muttered. "Now he's going to fuck us both up."

I nodded. "Yep."

Levi rolled his eyes, and all three of us chuckled.

"Hey, Levi." Carter leaned across the gap between the beds, holding out his phone. "Message from the cat sitter. Looks like they're suffering terribly without us."

Levi took the phone and eyed the screen, and then the most adorable smile lit up his face. "Yeah." He laughed. "They're pretty miserable, aren't they?" He turned the phone so Hunter could see it, then so I could. On the screen, two enormous tabby cats were sprawled on their backs, paws up in the air and tails lolling off the side of a sofa.

"Holy shit, they're huge!" I said. "Maine coons?"

"Yep." He beamed like a proud dad before handing the phone back to his husband. "Two huge, spoiled, shedding Maine coons."

"You have no one to blame but yourself for the spoiled part," Carter said.

Levi just shrugged. "What's the point of having cats if you don't spoil them?"

Hunter chuckled. "And no cats on this planet are more spoiled than Link and Zelda."

"Your cats' names are Link and Zelda?"

Levi met my gaze, smiling. "Yeah. When they were kittens, their ears looked huge because of those tufts on the end, and they reminded me of Link on *Legend of Zelda*."

I laughed. "I like it. Man, I haven't played that game in years."

He perked up. "You played?"

"From the day it was released."

"Same." He was grinning widely now. "My parents practically had to confiscate the Nintendo to get me to put it down."

"Me too," I said. "It's a wonder I didn't flunk out of school."

"Thought I was the only one," Hunter said with a laugh.

Some snickering was coming from the other bed, and when I looked, I realized the younger guys were all trying to smother their amusement. I also realized they'd probably all been in diapers—assuming they'd been born at all—when *Legend of Zelda* had been released.

Hunter and Levi had obviously caught on too. Levi rolled his eyes and muttered something about "damn whippersnappers" and "get off my lawn." Hunter just threw a pillow at Kevin.

"Kids these days," I said.

Jesse shot me what was probably supposed to be a glare, but it lost its intensity when he couldn't suppress a grin. I returned it, and felt a little flutter at the realization that as overwhelming as it was to be playing cards with Levi Pritchard, it was fucking amazing to be going back to my room later with Jesse. How did I get so lucky?

"All right." Levi cleared his throat and pulled another deck of cards from the case beside him. "We ready for another game?"

"Don't know," I said. "You ready to get your ass handed to you again?"

He flipped the bird, then started shuffling his cards.

"Hey, Levi," Carter said. "You want to use my green deck?"

Levi's eyes lit up as he put his own cards aside. "Fuck yes, I do."

Carter dug around in the vinyl case by his feet, pulled out a thick deck, and tossed it to Levi. Levi caught it, and they exchanged grins before he freed the cards from their rubber band and started shuffling.

Several turns into the game, Levi drew a card off his deck, and his brow furrowed. "What the . . . Oh, son of a bitch." I thought he must've drawn a shitty card until I realized he was holding it away from his face and squinting intently. "Could they make the print a *little* smaller on some of these?"

Hunter and I laughed.

"You got one of the microscopic ones, didn't you?" I asked. Sometimes the cards had lengthy descriptions wedged into the text box, which meant an incredibly tiny font.

"Yeah." Levi scowled. "Microscopic fucking words . . ."

Hunter chuckled. He glanced over his shoulder toward Carter and Kevin, then slid a small case out of his pocket. Without a word, he surreptitiously pushed it across the comforter toward Levi.

I had to smother a laugh as I realized what it was. When Levi took off the top and saw the reading glasses sticking out, he shot Hunter a withering glare.

"Seriously?" he grumbled.

Hunter motioned toward the case. "Would you just hurry up and read the card?" he hissed. "Maybe before they"—he gestured at our respective significant others with his thumb—"realize any of us need *reading glasses* to play Magic?"

"Point taken." Levi glanced at Carter, then took out the glasses and quickly put them on. I had to admit, he didn't look too bad in them. Not that I could imagine him looking bad in anything.

As soon as he'd read the card, he took off the glasses and shuttled them back to Hunter, who tucked them away without further comment. I was damn near shaking with laughter by this point, watching the two of them try to be sneaky about reading glasses.

I got it, though. Such were the trials and tribulations of aging with a younger partner. I didn't imagine Kevin or Carter would be horrified by their husbands needing reading glasses, but it was probably a matter of pride for the older men. Between Jesse and my late husband, I'd been there, done that. Just as well I'd been wearing glasses since I was twelve, and thank God for seamless bifocals.

"Well that was needlessly complicated," Levi muttered and played the card. It was an artifact creature I'd never seen before, and Levi put three counters—Skittles, in this case—on top of it.

"What is that?" I asked.

"A Tetravus." He shook his head. "Long story short, those"—he pointed to the counters—"are one/one flying creatures. Or . . ." He picked up the card and squinted at the directions again. "They will be if I decide they are at the beginning of my next turn, I guess."

"What the fuck?" Hunter took the card and read it. Rolling his eyes, he handed it to me. "Well, all right, then."

I read the instructions, and yeah, they were more complicated than they needed to be. The counters were one/one flying . . . something. Whatever.

I gave the card back to Levi and watched him put it down on the comforter and replace the counters. Then I shook my head. "I don't understand that card, and therefore it must be destroyed." I dropped a Shatter onto the comforter. "Bye-bye, Tetra-whatever-you-are."

"Damn it." Levi tossed the card into the graveyard, then popped the Skittles into his mouth. "All that effort to read the fucker, and I don't even get to play with it."

"And now we know why men never bother reading the instructions," Lydia interjected from across the room.

"Woman," Simon said in a playfully warning tone.

"What?" She shrugged, glancing up from her cards. "Don't act like it isn't true."

"She's got you there, babe," Ian said.

"Traitor," Simon muttered.

"And you're outnumbered," Lydia singsonged.

Simon just smiled like a fool. Couldn't say I blamed him.

The games went on, as did the trash-talking, and I loved it. Not just the game and the proximity to Levi fucking Pritchard—*oh my God*—but everything. The relaxed atmosphere. The easy banter. The way no one seemed to think twice about bringing me into the fold. It was hard to believe I hadn't known a single person in this room a month ago.

Every so often, Jesse and I would exchange a glance and a smile. I liked that we didn't have to be joined at the hip. We were in the same room, lost in our own games and conversations, and we didn't need to glom onto each other at every opportunity. This morning, we'd shared plenty of public affection while we'd wandered the con, and when the night ended, we'd be cuddled up together in bed. That was enough for me.

I also liked that he didn't mind me sitting over here with a man I'd had a crush on for twenty years. It was easy to get insecure, especially early in a relationship, but he didn't object to me sitting next to a shirtless Levi any more than I objected to him sitting beside Carter. And, I reminded myself, that was one more subtle reason to separate Jesse from Sean in my head. Now if I could just ignore all the other—

Don't. Not now. You're having a good time and so is he. Just don't go there.

So I tamped down those thoughts—again—and focused on the cards in my hand.

As the night went on, Levi managed to win a couple of games, and Hunter suddenly brought out his A game to kick both our asses. We switched players a few times, and the evening flew by as we bantered over Magic.

Eventually, though, we started to wind down. As tired as we all were from the convention, we'd hung in there for a long time. Hunter and Kevin bailed around twelve thirty. Levi probably could've held out for another hour or so, but Carter was fading fast, so they took off just before one. We stayed a little longer to chat with Ian, Simon, and Lydia, then strolled down the hall to our own room.

Jesse looked up at me as we walked. "So, did you have a good time?"

"I just spent an evening playing Magic with . . ." I waved a hand behind us. "*Them.* You're damn right I had a good time."

Laughing softly, he put his arm around my waist. "I figured you would."

"Uh-huh. Though you could've warned me about who was going to be there."

"I could've." He nodded. "But what would be the fun in that?"

I gave him a playful glare.

"What?" He batted his eyes. "Come on. You wouldn't have been nearly as adorable if you'd known what was coming."

"Uh-huh. Well, I did have a great time." In front of our room, I wrapped my arm around his waist and kissed him softly. "Not just tonight, but at the con."

"Me too. I'm glad you came."

I smiled and leaned in for another kiss, and I wasn't at all surprised when it turned into a longer one. A deeper one. Jesse combed his fingers through my hair, and I didn't even know whose soft moans were whose.

"You all turned on from playing Magic?" he asked between kisses.

"No." I nipped his lower lip. "I'm turned on because I know I'm going to have you in bed all to myself."

Jesse hummed and slid his hands up my back. "So what are you going to do with me?"

"I've got a few ideas." I pressed him up against the wall beside our door, and he sucked in a hiss of breath. "Starting with getting you out of these clothes and ending with you covered in cum."

He shivered hard. "God, I love when you talk dirty."

"Yeah?"

"Uh-huh."

I leaned in and kissed him, pinning him to the wall with my hips.

"Our room's right there," he murmured. "Bed . . . condoms . . ."

"Mmm, we'll get there." I nibbled the side of his neck, grinning when he arched between me and the wall. I'd been perfectly fine sitting apart from him for most of the evening, but now that he was in my arms again, I fully intended to make up for lost time.

"Let's go inside," he panted. "I want you. Right now."

I took the key card out of my pocket and touched it to the reader. As soon as the latch clicked, I pushed open the door.

"Finally," Jesse murmured, and dragged me inside.

Somehow, I had the presence of mind to shut the door behind us.

After that, the only thing I thought about for the rest of the night was Jesse.

CHAPTER TWENTY-THREE

JESSE

"**I** just don't get how everything fits like a dream on the way down." Simon gestured at the rental van. "And then it doesn't fit after we've sold almost everything and have even *less* crap and—"

"Simon." I patted the air with both hands. "Calm your tits."

My boss glared at me, but he did push his shoulders back and take a few deep, cleansing breaths.

"It fits on the way down because we spent three weeks packing everything perfectly into boxes." I nodded toward the stack of not so perfectly packed crates crammed with shelves, racks, stands, and leftover merchandise. "Now we're all tired and we just threw it together, so no, it's not going to fit as nicely."

"Oh. Okay, I guess that makes sense." He took another breath like he was going to comment further, but then he abruptly turned away and coughed into his elbow.

A few feet away, Dexy and Lydia froze, heads snapping toward him as they nearly dropped the crate of books they'd been hoisting into the van.

When he coughed again, harder this time, I arched an eyebrow. "Simon . . ."

"I'm fine." He sounded raspy. Had he been already and I just hadn't noticed?

I pointed at him. "Tell me you're not sick."

"I'm fine." He put up a hand. "I'm just a little scratchy."

"Scratchy like the air is dry?" Lydia paused to help Dexy drop the crate unceremoniously into the van. "Or scratchy like *we're* all going to be sick as dogs by the end of the week?"

Simon didn't answer.

Lydia and I looked at each other, and we both groaned. Goddamn it. Simon always went down with the con crud first. If he was already coughing, then I had maybe two days before my life started getting miserable. Always worked out that way. If we made it home without Simon showing a single symptom, then we were all good. The second he started sniffling or coughing, it was just a matter of time before Lydia, Ian, Dexy, and I were sick too. In that order. Which meant we already had it, and I'd probably given it to Garrett, too. Fan-fucking-tastic.

Speaking of whom, Garrett strolled up to the van right then and glanced at each of us in turn. "There anything I can do to help?"

I was about to tell him we were good, but Lydia piped up with, "I don't suppose we could send you for coffee, could we?"

I glared at her, not sure how I felt about her conscripting my man for coffee detail.

Garrett, however, just smiled. "Sure. What does everyone want?"

We each gave him our order, which he jotted down in the notepad app on his phone since everyone wanted something crazy complex. Simon tried to give him the shop credit card, but he waved it away.

"My treat," Garrett said with a smile. "I'll be back in a minute." He paused, giving all the boxes a look. "Do you need my truck for some of this?"

Simon scowled at the boxes. "We . . . might, actually."

"Okay." Garrett nodded. "When I come back with the coffee, should I just pull in here?"

"That would be awesome." Simon smiled, looking for the first time all morning like he might not lose his mind. "Thanks. I really appreciate it. The coffee and the truck."

"No problem." Garrett gave me a quick kiss on the cheek, and with that, he was gone in search of coffee.

We all watched him go, and after a moment, I realized Simon was humming, which he didn't usually do. When I glanced at him, he stopped but smirked. The second I turned away, he started again.

And then I recognized the tune—"Jessie's Girl."

I smacked his arm. "Shut up."

He snickered. "What?"

"Simon." Lydia clicked her tongue. "Really? Get back to work."

He gave her a mock salute. "Yes, ma'am."

As he continued organizing crates, she rolled her eyes before turning to me. "For the record," she said with a smile, "I really like your man."

"Oh. Well." I wiped my brow and sighed dramatically. "What a relief."

"Hey, it should be. You know what happens when you're dating someone we don't approve of."

"Fair point."

She sobered a little. "To be serious, though, he seems like a really good guy, and Hunter and Levi were raving about him this morning. So, I approve."

I knew about Hunter and Levi, but I motioned toward Ian and Simon. "And they do too?"

Lydia smirked. "Oh, you could say that."

I arched an eyebrow.

She laughed. "Ian was practically swooning over him, and I think I saw little floaty hearts over Simon's head too. Can't blame 'em—he's *hot*."

"Oh, you three don't even know the half of it." I suppressed a shiver at the memory of last night. A weekend of exhaustion couldn't begin to temper the heat between us when we were alone, and once we'd made it back to our room, we hadn't stopped until neither of us could move. I was lucky I was useful at all for loading the van right now—there wasn't a muscle or joint in my body that didn't ache.

Worth it.

Garrett returned not long after with coffee and his pickup. I made sure the van was packed and divided the overflow between Ian's car and Garrett's truck. Then I went back in and did one last sweep to make sure we hadn't left anything at the booth.

After Lydia had finished checking out with the con organizers, we all hit the road. Dexy rode with Lydia in the van, and Simon joined Ian in his car.

I, of course, rode shotgun with Garrett, happily sipping the coffee he'd brought me, while he patiently wove through Portland traffic.

"Hope you didn't mind me ditching you this morning," I said.

"Nah. It gave me a chance to run through the booths that were doing some last-minute clearance. I, uh, *might've* spent some more money." Christ, he was adorable when he looked all sheepish like that.

"Oh yeah? What did you buy?"

He gestured over his shoulder.

I craned my neck, looking behind the seat. There was a plastic shopping bag, and a familiar logo peeked through the opening. Facing Garrett again, I said, "You bought more cards?"

He nodded, smirking even as he blushed. "I thought I'd try my hand at building a deck with some of the newer expansions. You know, so I can whoop your ass or Levi's."

I blinked. "I am not even joking when I say I'm getting hard right now."

Garrett laughed and put his hand on my thigh. "Well, then. Mission accomplished."

I chuckled. "So I guess that's a yes if I ask if you want to get together with everyone for another Magic night."

"Yes. Definitely."

"Good. Because Levi texted me this morning and said he had a blast playing against you, and Hunter definitely wants a rematch."

Garrett shot me a wide-eyed look. I thought he might've been a bit starstruck. "Seriously?"

"Mm-hmm. But Hunter says if you touch his Royal Assassin again, he'll make you regret being born."

Garrett barked a laugh. "Oh. Game on."

I just snickered. After I'd sipped my coffee again, I sighed happily. "Ahh, it's been a fun weekend, but now I guess it's back to the grind."

"Back to the grind?" He chuckled. "Seems like your normal shifts will be a cakewalk after the con."

"They will, but the cons are fun."

"True. Well, I've still got a couple of days off. My sister's coming up to visit and stay tomorrow night."

"Yeah?" I studied him, suddenly kind of uneasy. "So, I'll see you after she takes off?"

He glanced at me, then squeezed my leg. "I was hoping you'd have dinner with us. I think you'd like her."

"Oh. So you're . . . You don't mind me meeting . . ."

"Of course not." He patted my thigh. "If you've got time. I know your schedule's a bit tight when you get back."

"I can make it happen. Simon owes me a few favors, so just let me know when and where, and I'll be there."

"Great. I'll see what she wants to do and text you the time and place."

"Sweet. I'm looking forward to it."

As I sat down beside Garrett at Rockin' Surf and Dockn' Turf, I was shocked at how obvious the resemblance was between him and his sister. They had the same sharp features, the same dark hair—though his had grayed a lot more than hers—and the same mischievous eyes. He'd told me she was three years younger than him, but she looked closer to my age than his. I wasn't sure if that was because she just looked younger than she was, or because the last couple of years had aged Garrett faster than they should have.

"Jesse, this is my sister, Fiona. Fiona, my boyfriend, Jesse."

She shot him a look I couldn't read, but then put on a smile and extended her hand across the table. "Nice to meet you."

"You too. But . . ." I gestured at her hand. "I probably shouldn't. I've got a cold."

"Oh yeah. I can hear it in your voice." She grimaced sympathetically. "Poor thing."

"Eh." I shrugged as I took a tissue from the pack in my pocket.

Garrett shot me a concerned look. "You doing okay?"

"Yeah." I dabbed at my nose. "Just this stupid con crud."

"Con crud?" Fiona arched an eyebrow at her brother. "Did you go to a Comic-Con without me?"

"No, no." He rested his hand on my leg under the table. "I went to a Wolf's Landing con with him over the weekend."

She perked up a little. "Oh? I didn't realize you were into the series."

"I wasn't. But Jesse got me interested."

Her eyebrows quirked in a way I couldn't quite read, and her eyes flicked toward me. "Oh." There was slightly less enthusiasm in her voice now. "So you're a fan?"

I nodded. "I work at a comic book shop. We sell a lot of Wolf's Landing stuff, so I don't think I could *not* be into it if I tried."

She laughed slightly more than halfheartedly.

"He introduced me to more than the series," Garrett said with a grin. "Would you believe I spent an evening playing Magic with Levi Pritchard and Hunter Easton?"

Fiona's eyes widened. "Uh. No."

I took out my phone and scrolled to a photo. When I showed it to her, her jaw dropped.

"Hey!" Garrett craned his neck to look at the screen. "I didn't know you took a picture."

"My boyfriend was playing Magic on a bed with a half-naked Levi Pritchard. Yeah, duh, I took a picture."

Garrett chuckled, and when he saw the photo, he grinned. "Send me that one, would you?"

I thumbed a couple of keys. "Done."

"Thank you."

Fiona smirked. "Oh Lord. You introduced him to Levi? I'm surprised he hasn't fanboyed himself to death."

"You're not the only one," Garrett said into his drink.

I grinned. "It was pretty cute, watching him introduce himself."

Garrett side-eyed me, blushing.

I flashed a toothy grin and elbowed him playfully. "What? It was!"

He rolled his eyes.

As I turned to Fiona, ready to joke about her brother's ridiculously adorable starstruck face, I paused. She was watching him, and she wasn't as amused. Still smiling a little, not hostile or anything like that, but something was knitting her brow. The way she absently thumbed the edge of her menu added to the obvious uneasiness.

I couldn't decide if she didn't like me or if there was something else going on. I didn't ask, though. That was between Garrett and his sister.

So, while Garrett started telling her about the con, I popped a cough drop in my mouth and tried to ignore the tension.

Easier said than done.

CHAPTER TWENTY-FOUR

GARRETT

With my sister in town, the day promised to be busy but pleasant. Though my apartment wasn't much to look at, she'd never been to Bluewater Bay, so I planned to drive her around. Showing someone else around seemed like a good way to learn the town anyway, and I wasn't going to complain about spending some time with Fiona for once.

First things first—breakfast.

"I can already see why you like it here." Fiona looked around Main Street as we headed toward the Sunrise Café. "It's so much quieter than Seattle."

"That part definitely has some appeal. Being within spitting distance of Scott is nice too."

She shot me a smirk. "You two stoners have been hanging out, haven't you?"

I laughed, my cheeks heating up. "Maybe."

"Uh-huh." She rolled her eyes.

I held open the café's door, then followed her inside. Despite our banter, there was a knot of uneasiness in my stomach, and I didn't like it. There was some distance between us that hadn't been here when she'd arrived yesterday. I knew Fiona—she had something on her mind and didn't want me to know about it. Or she didn't know how to say it. Either way, it was going to stay wedged between us until she either brought it up or let it go, and the latter happened about as often as Halley's Comet putting in an appearance.

The worst part was I was pretty sure I knew what she was thinking about.

The shift in her attitude had happened while we'd been having dinner with Jesse. I hadn't noticed exactly when, only that she'd been different when we'd left the restaurant than when we'd arrived. We'd still chatted and caught up, but there was something . . . cool. Not quite cold, but chilly.

As we sat down, ordered coffee, and perused the menus, I stole glances at my sister, trying to get a bead on her. I knew the problem had to do with Jesse. I just couldn't figure out the angle. What wasn't sitting right with her?

It wasn't that I was dating. She'd been surprised to hear that I'd met someone, but not put off or anything. She'd seemed excited to meet Jesse. So something about *him* had rubbed her the wrong way. Hell if I knew what.

The last thing I wanted was a confrontation. I didn't see my sister very often now that I'd moved out here, and I didn't want to ruin her visit. But goddamn, this frosty edge to her mood was going to drive me insane.

"Everything all right?" I asked finally.

She met my gaze across the table, eyes wide with innocence. "Of course. Why?"

"Don't bullshit me, Fiona." I inclined my head. "You've been keeping me at arm's length ever since dinner last night."

She pursed her lips and broke eye contact.

"If there's something on your mind, just say it."

Staring into her coffee cup, Fiona pulled in a long breath through her nose. "It's about Jesse."

"Yeah, I figured. What about him?"

"Well." She chewed the inside of her cheek, studying me uneasily. "Don't take this the wrong way, okay? I'm just concerned about you."

I made a *go on* gesture.

Fiona straightened, pulling in a breath. "Are you really into him? Or is he filling the void Sean left?"

The question hit me in the gut. *So it's not just me.* But I played stupid anyway. "Come again?"

She swallowed. "He's a nice guy, okay? But he's . . . familiar. And that worries me."

I fidgeted uncomfortably. "Familiar, how?"

"Familiar like Sean." She drew back a little like she thought I might get pissed. "Some of his personality quirks, you know? I mean, the second he walked in, I thought of Sean. And when he opened his mouth, my first thought was that he sounded just like Sean."

I chewed the inside of my cheek, but didn't know what to say.

She tilted her head the way she always did when I was being dense. "You don't hear it?"

"I . . . Well, kind of. But . . . so what?"

The head tilt stayed, and she doubled down with an eyebrow lift.

"What?" I tried not to sound irritated, but I was. "Yes, they have some similarities, but—"

"They're not just similarities, Garrett." She exhaled. "It's not that he's identical to Sean. He's just . . . They're the same type, you know?" When I didn't respond, she went on. "You know damn well you used to have a very distinct type. *Every* guy you dated was this super manly tough guy. And don't think any of us missed how you used to ogle that same kind of guy when you were a teenager. That's how we all figured out you were gay in the first place! Honestly, the whole family was a little worried you'd marry an ex-con or a guy from a biker gang or something." She gave a soft, sad laugh. "So we were all surprised when you brought Sean home because he was so obviously *not* your usual type."

I almost laughed myself, but not quite. The shock and confusion on my family members' faces the day they'd met Sean had been priceless. "He kind of surprised me too. He actually annoyed the shit out of me at the office when we first met."

"I know." She nodded. "And really flamboyant guys were . . . Well, I always got the impression they did annoy you. So when you started dating Sean . . ." She played with the handle on her coffee cup. "I mean, you were so obviously in love with him, and we all adored him. We were just surprised is all." She swallowed before she met my eyes. "And . . . the thing is, Jesse's that same type."

I gnawed the inside of my cheek. I sure as hell couldn't argue. Though he was less so than Sean had been, Jesse was definitely flamboyant. He couldn't give two flying fucks what people thought of how he dressed, how he spoke, how he moved. I'd admired that about Sean, and I admired it about Jesse. The fearlessness. The unabashed comfort in their own skin. In that respect, Jesse hit a lot of the same notes Sean had, but he wasn't Sean. I didn't want him to be. I told myself it was that confidence that drew me in, and I'd convinced myself the familiarity had just been us settling into a solid relationship. But admittedly, Fiona had me second-guessing myself. Again.

"Yeah, Jesse's more femme than the guys I used to date," I conceded, but then I shook my head. "That *doesn't* mean he's replacing Sean."

"No, it doesn't." Her brow pinched. "But between that and his personality, it's hard not to wonder."

"How about taking my word for it?" I kept my irritation under the surface, but barely. Defensiveness wouldn't help my case. "Losing Sean didn't mean I lost my ability to think for myself."

"I know. I know. And . . ." She released a heavy sigh. "I'm just worried about you, okay? I want you to be careful. With yourself, and with him. You've coped with Sean's . . . with Sean being gone better than most people would have, but grief is still a thing, you know? And I don't want to see you getting hurt—or unintentionally hurting Jesse—because you're not as ready as you think you are to move on."

"So when do I get to say I'm ready?" It was a losing battle to keep the defensiveness out of my voice. "I'm happy when I'm with Jesse. Do you really want me to cut him loose and stay miserable for another year or two until—"

"No! That's not what I'm saying at all." She shook her head. "But he hasn't even been gone a *year*, Garrett."

"That year has been a lot longer than you think."

She flinched. "What does Scott have to say about Jesse?"

It took all I had not to roll my eyes. I adored my sister, and I understood she was just genuinely concerned, but the insistence on questioning my judgment—and wanting the input of my *therapist* best friend—was grating. "Are you suggesting I need a shrink's opinion before—"

"I meant from the perspective of someone who's been there."

"Okay. Fair." I tapped my nail on the edge of the table. "Either way, he's actually encouraged me to see where things go with Jesse. He's been there, done that, and thinks it's good that I'm trying to be *happy*."

"I want you to be happy too. I really do. And I know Sean wanted you to be happy." She studied me like she was debating how much she wanted to argue. Finally, she deflated and sat back. "Just . . . be careful, all right?"

I nodded. "Of course I will." I sounded sure, even to myself. But deep down, her doubts were starting to gnaw at me. *Am I ready for this?*

As I'd promised to do, I spent the morning driving Fiona around town. Since she was a huge fan of the books and the show, I took her on one of the tram tours of the *Wolf's Landing* production lot. Then we grabbed a late lunch, and afterward, we said goodbye and Fiona headed back to Seattle.

I tried not to think about our conversation too much. Or about those niggling doubts I'd been shooting down on a daily basis since before Jesse and I had left for Portland. Everything was going great with him. There was no reason to overanalyze it and see how it stacked up against some arbitrary time frame or how many perfectly common personality traits he and Sean had in common. So it hadn't quite been a year since I'd lost Sean? That didn't mean this thing with Jesse was too fast or too soon. So Jesse and Sean were similar in some ways? Jesse *wasn't* Sean.

Get it through your head, Garrett. Jesus.

I refused to let my conversation with Fiona put a dark cloud over my relationship, but I was suddenly itching to see Jesse. I always wanted to see him, but part of me was extra eager just to look at him and remind myself that yes, this thing we were doing was real. It had nothing to do with Sean and everything to do with Jesse being, well, Jesse.

Since I didn't need to be at the bar for a few hours, I wandered toward the comic book shop to visit him. And maybe to see how he was feeling after the way he'd sounded when he'd joined me and Fiona for dinner. I knew damn well it was nothing to actually worry about. A cold wasn't a death sentence for someone with HIV anymore.

But still. There was a part of my brain that could hear Sean insisting he was fine when he'd started losing weight for no apparent reason. He'd still been convinced it was nothing serious even while we'd sat in the waiting room minutes before his doctor had told us it was the opposite of nothing serious.

The voices from my youth were there too. You didn't grow up gay when I did without developing a deep-seated fear of AIDS, and that fear didn't magically vanish with the medical advances that had largely defanged the disease's effects. The fact that a person could live a long, normal life with HIV didn't erase the people I'd known who'd been diagnosed before treatments could spare them their slow, hellish deaths.

Those voices were there, but I was overreacting. I knew the facts. Ever since Jesse had told me he was positive, I'd been reading about HIV and the latest treatments. I wanted to understand it as much as I could, and I needed to convince myself that it wasn't the time bomb it had been thirty years ago. Nearly everything I'd read had told me the same thing—especially in someone like Jesse with an undetectable virus, a cold or something equally benign was cause for no more concern than it would be in me. Rest, fluids, and more rest, and he'd bounce back like anyone else.

Things were different these days, I reminded myself as the comic book shop came into view. Hell, now that we'd both been tested for everything else, we could have sex bareback if we wanted to, especially now that I was taking Truvada. That had been *unthinkable* in my younger days.

So why the fuck couldn't I stop worrying myself senseless after Jesse had coughed a few times yesterday?

Because I was an idiot who was ignoring everything I'd read. And now I was obsessing since it gave me something to worry about besides what my sister had said. All I needed was to drop in, visit him, see that he was just fine, and I could relax.

I pushed open the door to the shop. There were some teenagers perusing comic books on a shelf off to one side. The UPS driver was entering some information into his tablet while Simon nudged a stack of newly arrived—and slightly dented—boxes behind the counter with his foot.

After the UPS driver had left, Simon turned to me. I was about to ask if he could grab Jesse for me, but paused. Simon didn't look so hot. He had dark circles under his eyes, and his complexion was a few alarming shades whiter than usual. The skin around his nose was chapped and raw like he'd been using sandpaper for Kleenex.

"Hey, Garrett," he rasped. "How's it going?"

"Probably better than it is for you."

He laughed, which made him cough. "Con crud. Kind of hard to avoid."

I grimaced sympathetically. "Sorry to hear it."

"Eh, occupational hazard." He shrugged as he sniffled. "At least I didn't get it as bad as Jesse."

My heart stopped. "Come again?"

"Yeah, he got it bad." Simon shook his head. "Dumb shit came into work this morning, and I sent him right back out the door. Kid's way too sick to be anywhere but in bed."

My already-stopped heart fell into my feet. "How bad is he?"

"He could barely breathe, and I'm pretty sure he had a fever." Simon paused to cough a few times. "I think he might have the flu, to tell you the truth."

Ice water ran through my veins. "I'm, uh, going to go check on him."

Simon nodded. "Tell him I'm not kidding—I see his face here tomorrow, I'll let Lydia drag him home by his ear."

Any other time I might have laughed, but right then my brain was too full of worst-case scenarios. How sick *was* Jesse?

His apartment wasn't far, but it took forever to get there. Seemed like it, anyway. Finally, I was at his door, and I paused to collect myself—well, try to—before I knocked.

There was no answer at first. I considered calling him, but as I was taking my phone out of my pocket, some shuffling on the other side gave me pause. I pocketed my phone again and tried to school the worry out of my expression.

Jesse opened the door, and yeah, he looked like shit. His skin was flushed instead of pale. Exhaustion radiated off him, and if I wasn't mistaken, so did a fever.

"Oh my God," I said. "Are you okay?"

"Yeah. Just—" He turned away and coughed into his arm. A deep, hacking cough that brought to mind bronchitis or even pneumonia. When he faced me again, he looked like the effort of coughing had taken most of the energy he had left. Pressing his shoulder against the doorframe, he said, "Meant to text you, but I fell asleep."

"That's okay. Do you need me to take you to the doctor or—"

"Relax," he croaked, making a dismissive gesture even though it seemed like his hand weighed fifty pounds. "It's just the flu." He coughed a couple of times, then managed an even more pitiful, "I sound worse than I am."

I scowled.

He glared weakly at me. "I'm *fine*, Garrett."

I started to speak, meaning to ask if he was sure, but the look he shot me cut me off, so I changed tactics. "You mind if I stay with you? Just in case you need anything?"

He studied me, but then he gave a heavy shrug and stood aside to let me in.

He'd apparently holed up on the sofa. There was a thick quilt strewn over one end, and a couple of pillows stacked on the armrest. Some movie I didn't recognize was paused, and the coffee table was covered with DayQuil, NyQuil, a box of tissues, and a six-pack of Sprite that was missing two cans. An empty bowl with a spoon and a wadded napkin assured me he'd at least tried to eat something. Chicken soup, if I had to guess.

Jesse shuffled into the living room and dropped onto the couch. He moved the blankets a bit so I could sit down too, and he smiled weakly. "I won't say no to you staying, but fair warning—I probably won't be the best company."

I leaned down to press a kiss to his hot forehead. "It's okay." It definitely was. Seeing him sick like this set off too many alarm bells in my head. Even though my boss might not like it, I suspected I'd be calling in sick for my shift. I just didn't want Jesse out of my sight until he was well.

Or at least until he was cooler than the surface of the sun.

CHAPTER TWENTY-FIVE

JESSE

I felt like a bastard for it, but Garrett was driving me up a wall.

Two days into my wallowing, he had become a constant presence at my apartment unless he had to go to work. I mostly slept, and he slept on my couch because I was too hot to be within arm's length. The second I moved or made a sound, though, he was *right* there, offering water, meds, and rides to the doctor's office.

I probably should have found it endearing. There was something to be said for being waited on hand and foot, and for someone rushing around to take care of your every whim. It was one of the only perks of being sick.

And usually, I *was* grateful for that shit, but usually it didn't have this vibe to it. This . . . *grimness*. Though he didn't say a word, I could see it in the crease of his forehead and the way he'd hold his breath whenever I had a really bad coughing fit. As if I didn't already get that fleeting *oh shit what if it's* not *just the flu this time?* panic whenever I was sick even if I knew damn well my last CD4 count had been awesome and it absolutely *was* just the flu. Like I wasn't already freaking out because my viral load would probably jump, which was always unnerving even if it was just a blip. Being sick sucked enough *without* the constant feeling that the guy taking care of you thought you were going to keel over.

It's just the flu, dude. Back off.

Except even through the haze of an on-off fever, I knew that while it was the flu making me short-tempered, it *wasn't* the flu turning him into Super Nurse. I didn't have to ask and he didn't have to say, and I just did not have the patience for it. The flu was making me miserable enough. My whole body hurt. Some of that was left over from the con—moving heavy boxes, being on my feet for that long, and having wild sex at night had taken its toll—but the stupid microbe had added some serious aches to the mix. I couldn't breathe. Food sounded about as appealing as running a marathon in ill-fitting high heels.

So basically everything annoyed me. Including Garrett. Maybe when I was back to my normal healthy self, I'd feel like the world's biggest asshole for being annoyed with him, but I *wasn't* normal and healthy yet. I was bitchy and miserable, and having him flitting around, making sure I had tissues and water and more meds had me near the end of my chain. I almost snapped at him a couple of times, and when I felt myself getting close to doing it again, I finally said, as calmly as I could, "Garrett."

He stopped halfway to the kitchen and looked at me.

I pointed to the empty cushion beside me. "Sit."

He hesitated, but then joined me on the couch.

"Listen, I appreciate you helping me out," I said as evenly as I could. "But I need you to back off just a little. All this fussing over me and worrying like this makes me feel like I'm a lot sicker than I am." I dabbed at my nose for the thousandth time. "It's not the plague. It's *just* the flu."

He chewed his lip, and I could hear the argument coming from a mile away. I arched an eyebrow, and I suspected he could hear my counter argument coming too.

He sighed. "Okay. Just promise me you'll let me take you to the doctor if it gets worse, or if it doesn't get better in a couple of days."

"I promise. And don't worry—I keep tabs on my health. I'm not one of those stubborn idiots who won't see a doctor until they're too sick to move. I go to the doctor *when I need to*, okay? I've got an appointment tomorrow for a blood draw so they can check my viral load, and if it weren't for that, they wouldn't want me to come in at all. Can't take antibiotics because it's a virus, so . . ." I shrugged. "I'm doing exactly what they told me to do—taking it easy, sleeping, and drinking a ton of fluids. I'll be *fine*."

Garrett lowered his gaze, and he slowly released a breath. As he rubbed his eyes with his thumb and forefinger, I realized he looked as tired as I felt. "I'm sorry. I . . . I know you can take care of yourself." He reached for my hand and gave it a gentle squeeze. "I'm sorry."

"It's okay. And I kind of feel like an ass telling you to stop being nice to me." I laced our fingers together.

"No. You just don't want to be smothered. I get it."

I relaxed a bit. "Exactly."

He chewed his lip. Awkward silence lingered for a while, and I had no idea how to fill it. Then Garrett sighed.

"It's kind of fucked up, you know?" he said. "You spend your whole life around people who get colds and the flu, and it's not a big deal. Everyone knows how to take care of themselves. Then you take care of someone who can die of an infection at the drop of a hat, so you have to treat every cough and sniffle like a life-threatening emergency." He swallowed before he looked in my eyes. "You'd be amazed how hard it is to break that habit."

My heart dropped. Oh, goddamn it. I'd been grinding my teeth, convinced he was just freaking out because he'd been so worried about me getting the flu on top of having HIV. I hadn't even thought about the other reason he'd worry himself sick. And, fuck. Did that mean I'd called Garrett's late husband a stubborn idiot when I'd mentioned that I was smart enough to go to the doctor?

I rubbed my thumb along the back of his. "I didn't think about that. I'm sorry. I kind of feel like a dick now. I didn't even think about what you went through with him."

"Don't worry about it." He let go of my hand and wrapped his arm around my shoulders.

Closing my eyes, I sighed and let my aching body melt against him. "Thank you, by the way." I draped my arm over his stomach. "I do appreciate you trying to take care of me."

"Don't mention it." Garrett kissed the top of my head. "We'll figure all this out. How much is too much. Boundaries. All of that."

"Yeah. I know. Learning curve, right?"

"Exactly." His hand ran up and down my arm, and something settled in me. I'd half expected a fight, and God knew I'd come at him hard enough that he'd have been justified in snapping right back.

But he hadn't.

It was weird. I'd had fights with boyfriends before. When a fight got heated, odds were usually even that one of us would walk out and that would be the end of it. Not just the fight, but us.

Tonight could have easily erupted into a fight. I was sick and short-tempered. He was probably stinging from the raw nerve I'd stomped on. All the pieces had been there for this to blow up and get ugly.

But it hadn't. Not even after I'd served those pieces up and tossed them in his face. He'd listened to me, and he'd explained himself, and we'd landed here—snuggled together on the couch, his arm around my shoulders and his fingers absently playing with my T-shirt sleeve. I wasn't sure how to deal with someone who cared enough to not just throw up his hands and call time on things once they got heated. Someone who didn't decide my hot temper and impulsive mouth weren't too much to deal with.

The one thing I knew for sure was that I was relieved as hell that things had stayed calm. That he'd stayed here. Twenty minutes ago, I probably would have been momentarily thrilled to have him leave just because I'd felt smothered, but God, now I felt so stupid for even thinking that.

It was this weird feeling of simultaneously not wanting to fight with Garrett and somehow being sure I *could* fight with him and come out on the other side without one of us leaving. Like this thing we had wouldn't vanish the instant one of us raised our voices.

I don't want to fight with you.

I don't want you to leave.

I don't know what I feel because I've never felt this before, but . . .

I cuddled a bit closer to him and tucked my head under his chin.

Please, please don't let it stop anytime soon.

CHAPTER TWENTY-SIX

GARRETT

Jesse and I were both true to our word. While I did my best to keep my worries—rational and otherwise—out of sight, he took care of himself. He mostly slept for the first couple of days after our conversation, and when I came over after work on the third night, he was up and eating the soup I'd left in the fridge before my shift. He was still scratchy and congested, but he didn't seem to be aching as much, and the heat radiating off him was normal instead of alarming. The next day, he went back to work, and aside from a stubborn cough that hung around for another week, he was mostly back to normal.

The only thing lingering was the results of his bloodwork. The flu could bump up his viral load, so tests like this were routine. I tried to follow his lead and not stress over them. If they weren't cause for hand-wringing for him, then there was no reason—okay, no *rational* reason—they should be for me. So, as patiently as I could, I waited. The medical center here in Bluewater Bay was somewhat limited, so they'd had to send it to a lab in Port Angeles. That was only one town over, but God forbid these things happen quickly.

Though he was back on his feet, he didn't make any move to pick up where we'd left off in the bedroom. I didn't know if it was apprehension about his results, or if he still didn't feel quite well enough, but I didn't push. At this point, I was just happy to see him healthy again.

Almost two weeks after he got sick, the results were back.

"So?" I watched him uneasily. "What does it say?"

His heavy sigh answered pretty succinctly. "My viral load's up." He scowled. "I know it's just a blip, but it's always disconcerting when it happens."

"'It's always—' This has happened before?"

He shrugged. "I've been positive for years. It's bound to happen once in a while." He turned to me, and his features tightened. "Dude. Seriously. This isn't that big of a deal." He held up the test results. "For all I know, my CD4 count is back where it should be and my viral load is back to undetectable, but I have to assume I'm not until I get the next test back. It's not a catastrophe."

I glanced at the paper in his hand, uneasy. No, not just uneasy. It was the kind of gut-flipping feeling I remembered having when glowing dots on a CT scan meant that despite chemo and radiation, the tumors were growing. Or worse, spreading. I knew it wasn't the same this time, but tell that to my stomach.

Jesse huffed sharply. "Jesus. Yeah, it's disconcerting, but I swear, every time I mention my health is anything but perfect, you look like I just dropped some kind of bomb on you."

"I . . ."

We held eye contact for a moment before he swore and tossed the results on the counter. "Okay, if we're going to keep doing this," he said, voice taut with anger, "we need to get on the same page about that." He stabbed a finger toward the discarded paper. "It's part of being positive. If you can't live with it, then—"

"Whoa. Whoa." I showed my palms. "Easy. I worry about you. That's all."

"We talked about this," he snapped. "I had the *flu*."

"And you're immunocompromised!"

Jesse swore softly. "Come on. Remember how I said I'm usually the last person at the shop to get sick? Doesn't that say something?"

He had a point, so I nodded. "All right. Yes. It does. But you tried to go to work with a fever. How is that taking care of yourself?"

"Oh, I don't know. Maybe by making sure I can pay my *rent* so I'm not living in a cardboard box? And hey, while I'm at it, so I still have *health insurance*?"

I exhaled. "So you work yourself into the ground, get even sicker, and have to take even more time off?"

His jaw tightened. He took a breath like he was about to speak, but paused. Then he let that breath out. Shoulders sinking and features softening, he met my eyes. "I don't want to fight about this."

I swallowed. "Neither do I."

"Then we need to lay down some boundaries. Like you said when I was still sick." He took my hands in both of his. "I meant what I said before—if we're going to do this, you've *got* to give me some breathing room when it comes to my health. I've been positive for a long time. Ten fucking years. I know what I'm doing, okay?"

I pursed my lips.

Before I could speak, he went on. "I know you've been through hell because of your husband, but every time you jump, it gets me worried too. I'm . . ." He gulped, eyes hovering between angry and pleading. "I'm more than this disease, all right?"

My stomach somersaulted again, though not for the same reason. "I know you are. And I'm sorry." I squeezed his hand. "Just . . . be patient with me. After Sean . . ." *Oh hell, I am so not going there right now.* I swallowed. "I'm trying. I promise. But you know it's just because I care about you, right? Just like when I was a little too enthusiastic about taking care of you?"

He nodded, gaze down. "I know. I . . . I know." Sighing heavily, he ran a hand through his hair. "I guess I just need to know you see me as more than some fragile thing that's going to break in a strong wind. And every time this comes up, I'm worried . . ."

I stepped closer and put a hand on his shoulder. "About what?"

Jesse chewed his lip and obviously avoided my eyes.

"Talk to me, Jesse." I squeezed his shoulder gently. "Whatever it is. This is all part of that learning curve, remember? Figuring out boundaries and all?"

He nodded, exhaling. "I just . . ." He shifted his weight, still not looking at me. "It makes me worry you only see a disease when you look at me. And that it's only a matter of time before it turns you off."

"Turns—" I almost choked on the word. "God, no. That's the last thing that ever crosses my mind." I touched his cheek. "You turn me on so much I'm lucky I can concentrate on anything else."

He looked up at me, chin still down.

"I was worried about you. That's all." Caressing his cheekbone, I added, "I'm sorry, I just really care about you, and I was afraid—"

He nodded. "I know. And . . . I wasn't mad about that part. Just . . ."

"I understand." I moved my hand to his hip as I cautiously came closer, and when he didn't draw back, I murmured, "I'll work on it. On taking your word for it that you're all right."

He searched my eyes, and after a moment, he started to slowly relax. "Well, um . . . now that I'm not sick, we can . . ." He nodded toward the bedroom, but his eyes flicked back to something else. When I followed their trajectory, I understood—the test results.

"Relax." I kissed him again and nudged him a step closer to the bedroom. "I'm not worried if you're not."

Jesse chewed the inside of his cheek. Then he exhaled sharply. "Okay. And goddamn it, I was totally going to suggest we could start going bareback too."

"Really?"

"Yeah. I mean, all our other tests are negative. So." He shrugged. "We don't really need condoms, you know? Or, well, we didn't." Rolling his eyes, he cursed softly. "Fucking viral load."

Pieces fell together in my head, and I suddenly understood why we'd still been sleeping separately even since he'd recovered.

I touched his chin again and lifted his head so he was looking at me. "Is this why you haven't wanted to do anything the last week?"

He winced, lips tightening, and his eyes darted away.

"Jesse," I whispered. "Were you afraid . . ."

The tight line of his lips thinned even more, and his cheeks colored. "After I told you my viral load might come back up . . . I was afraid to suggest doing anything because . . ." His color deepened as his voice trailed off.

"What kind of assholes did you date before me?"

His head snapped up and he eyed me, clearly startled by the question.

"I knew you were positive before we ever hooked up," I whispered. "We don't even need to change anything because we've been careful from the start, you know?"

Jesse swallowed.

"When the new tests come back, we can talk about ditching condoms. But that doesn't change anything right now. We were using condoms before you got sick. We'll keep using them now. It's no different. Long as you're fucking me like you always do, I'm game for anything."

He searched my eyes, brow creasing.

I wrapped my arms around his waist. "And quite honestly? The second you're up for it, let me know, because I have been going out of my *mind* wanting you the last couple of weeks."

That brought a relieved smile to Jesse's lips, and after a couple of seconds, that morphed into a ridiculously sexy grin. He pressed up against me, running his hands up my chest. "Have you?"

"I have." I wrapped my arms around him and pulled him against me. "And I know things have been a little tense, and I've been driving you crazy, but—"

He kissed me. Hard.

Message received: *Shut up and drive me crazy for real.*

I held him close and kissed him back just as hard, sliding my hands into his back pockets as I pressed my swelling erection against him. The low moan vibrating between our lips told me he definitely felt it, and he pushed back with his own cock.

When he broke away, panting hard, his forehead was feverish against mine, but not the way it had been two weeks ago. "You know, my bed feels a bit too big when it's just me."

"Yeah?" I kneaded his ass through his jeans. "Should we go make it feel smaller?"

His lips curved into a grin against mine, and then his tongue was in my mouth and I forgot all about beds and rooms and places and . . . God, I'd missed this. I'd missed *him*. He'd been right here—close enough my proximity had annoyed him—but there'd been some space between us, and now that space was gone.

Jesse broke the kiss. "Bedroom," he panted. "Now." He took my hand and led me down the hall. We shed our clothes, made sure there were condoms and lube in reach, and then tumbled onto the mattress and picked up where we'd left off.

No, that wasn't right. In the other room, we'd been much more subdued. Not in a hurry at all. Lying in his bed, naked and hard and out of breath, there was nothing subdued about us. I pinned him down, kissing him hungrily, and he hooked a leg around me as he rubbed his cock against mine. He dragged his nails across my shoulders, through my hair, up my sides. Sometimes they burned. Sometimes they almost tickled. God, I loved it. All of it. Everywhere and every way he touched me.

The more we made out and groped each other, the more we trembled and groaned. The feverish hunger between us was intoxicating; all the desperation of the very first time combined with all the familiarity of two men who'd been together before—not only did we need each other so bad it hurt, we knew exactly how to turn each other on.

And suddenly tasting his mouth wasn't enough. I wanted to taste him everywhere. I broke away and started down his neck, and he rewarded me with a helpless moan as he arched off the bed. The heat of his skin against my lips nearly turned me inside out. Fuck. *More.* It had only been two weeks, if even that, but it had felt like forever, and I couldn't resist exploring him like it was the first time all over again. I kissed and stroked every inch of his smooth, gorgeous body, pausing now and again to sink my teeth in just so I could hear him gasp. Flicking my tongue across his hipbone. Gently biting his nipple. Kissing the inside of his knee. Nothing and nowhere was off-limits as long as he squirmed and cursed and pleaded for more.

As I neared his cock for the twelfth time, he kneaded my scalp, and there was some insistent pressure behind his hand. Some subtle— but not—guidance.

I licked his skin and purred, "Something you want, sweetheart?"

He moaned. "Garrett..."

"Talk to me." I couldn't hide my grin, so I didn't try. "Tell me what you want."

He forced out a breath, then lifted his head and looked down at me with a mix of arousal and aggravation gleaming in his eyes. "I want you to suck my cock."

This time the moan came from my lips, and I kissed just above his groin as a shiver went through me.

"I'll suck your cock," I said. "Long as you fuck me good and hard after."

The response was a soft whimper, followed by, "Oh yeah."

He bit his lip and watched me kiss closer and closer to his erection. When I was less than an inch away, I realized he was holding his breath.

"Don't pass out," I said, making sure my own breath whispered across his dick. "I don't want you to miss any of this."

"Then quit— Oh *God*."

Eyes locked on his, I ran my tongue from the base of his cock to the head. He watched, eyes wide and lips apart, as I teased up and down the entire length. When I reached the base again, I lapped at his balls while I stroked him with my hand, and he sank back to the pillows with a strangled moan. His hips lifted slightly, then again, like he was fucking the air. Or like he wanted to fuck my mouth. "Jesus . . ."

I took the head between my lips, and when he lifted up again, he pushed deeper into my mouth, releasing a ragged sigh as he did. My own balls tightened, and my cock got even harder, as if I were the one being blown. Groaning with pleasure, I gave him more, stroking him and teasing with my lips and tongue as he slid in and out of my mouth.

"Fuck, you're so good at that," he ground out. "Oh God, Garrett . . ."

The sound of my name gave me goose bumps. Something about that, about knowing he was still here enough to remember I was the one doing this to him, was *hot*. So I gave him more. I gripped him tighter. Swirled my tongue around the head. Squeezed with my lips. He was damn near thrusting now, hips jerking as he pushed his cock into my throat. Whatever he was saying, I didn't understand it anymore, but I was pretty sure it was profane and peppered with attempts at my name.

Abruptly, he grabbed my hair and growled, "*Condom.*"

He didn't have to tell me twice. I let him go and sat back on my heels, and we both lunged for the nightstand. Between the two of us, we made short work of getting the rubber on and slicking it up.

"How do you want me?" I asked, still out of breath.

"On your back."

I did as I was told, parting my legs for him. He pushed them farther apart as he guided himself in. He was more forceful than usual, but he watched my eyes, probably searching for signs of discomfort.

The only discomfort here was the lack of his dick buried inside me, so I curved a leg around behind him and pushed his ass with my heel. "C'mon. *More.*"

"More?" Jesse's eyes danced with lust and playfulness. "What if I want to tease you?"

I exhaled. "Oh baby, I need . . . C'mon . . ."

"Look who's begging now." He withdrew a little. "How the mighty have fallen, hmm?"

I bit back a growl. "Shut up and fuck me."

Jesse laughed. Sitting upright, he held on to the backs of my knees and thrust hard. *Deep.* I yelped in surprise, and yeah maybe a little pain, but it felt so good I thought I was going to black out. He did it again. Then again.

"Like that?" he asked through his teeth.

"So much." I squeezed my eyes shut and tried to breathe as he pounded me relentlessly. "God, yeah, Jesse."

"You're so hot like this," he said. "I'd take a picture, but this is much more fun."

I laughed, and holy hell, I felt drunk. I looked up at him, then reached for him. "C'mere, you."

He let go of my knees. I grabbed the back of his neck, pulling him down and me up, and we met in the middle in a messy, hungry kiss. He kept thrusting, and we kept kissing, and it was sloppy and desperate and fucking perfect. He didn't need any kind of rhythm as long as he didn't stop. He was on top of me and in me and kissing me—what more could a man ever want?

A tremor straightened his spine. He broke the kiss with a groan, pushed himself up on his hands, and fucked me like a man possessed. No rhythm. No finesse. Just eager, frantic hunger as he started to fall apart. "Oh Jesus . . . Garrett . . . I'm—" The sound he made was primal, almost pained, as he forced himself all the way in and shuddered. His hips jerked, and he tried to get even deeper, and then he sighed and collapsed over me, panting and shaking. I wrapped my arms around him to bring him all the way down.

Jesse pulled out, but didn't get up. Without even lifting his head off my chest, he reached between us and started stroking me.

I gasped at the contact. Holy fuck, I was close. *So* close. Breath coming in sharp, rapid huffs, I kneaded his hair and his shoulder. My hips couldn't move, not with him still resting between my legs, so all I could do was lie there and let him jerk me.

"Oh yeah, baby," I breathed. "Yeah, just like . . . yeah . . ." I squeezed my eyes shut, held my breath, tried like hell to thrust into his fist, and—

Abruptly, he moved. Before I could make sense of it, my dick was enveloped in tight, wet heat, and when his tongue swirled the head, I saw stars. Just a couple of licks, a couple of pulls, and I was gone, coming so hard I almost levitated off the bed, and Jesse moaned and hummed as he kept me going with more strokes, more teasing, until I begged him to stop.

He did, and I collapsed onto the bed. A moment later, he was over me, kissing me languidly with my cum on his tongue.

Only for a moment, though. "Gonna get rid of the condom." He brushed his lips across mine. "Don't move."

"Not . . . not going anywhere."

He laughed softly and stole one more kiss before he got up.

I couldn't say if I passed out or dozed off or what, but when I opened my eyes again, his head was on my shoulder, his warm body pressed up against mine under the sheet.

"Did I fall asleep?" I murmured.

"Mm-hmm." He kissed under my jaw. "Think I did too."

"Oh."

"And hey." He lifted up enough to look in my eyes. "Look at that—the bed doesn't feel quite as small anymore."

Chuckling, I cuddled closer to him. "Just in case, we'd better stick to the middle." I kissed his temple and murmured into his hair, "So we don't fall off."

Jesse laughed and held me tighter. "You're a dork."

"Birds of a feather."

"Okay, fair enough." He kissed me softly. "That was insanely hot, by the way."

"What? Falling asleep?"

He snorted, rolling his eyes. "Yes, Garrett. Falling asleep."

I laughed and smoothed his messed-up hair. "And yes, it was hot. Crazy hot. Which is not exactly a surprise when you're involved."

He grinned, but there was a sudden hint of shyness in his expression. Or maybe it had been there before and I just hadn't noticed.

"What's wrong?" I asked.

"I . . ." He chewed his lip. His eyes lost focus for a moment, but finally flicked up to meet mine again. "It really doesn't faze you, does it? The test results?"

I cupped his cheek. "Why would it?"

"I guess I was worried you wouldn't want to . . . you know, while my count was up."

"We're being as safe as I was during the days before the meds you're on were even invented."

That eased some tension in his features and his shoulders. "That's true. I don't know." His cheeks colored as he avoided my gaze. "I guess it's a good thing we hadn't started going bareback, right?"

"I don't think it would've made much difference, would it?" I tipped his chin up. "We'd just start using condoms again. No big deal."

Jesse swallowed hard.

"Does that bother you? Needing to use them?"

"No. In fact, I've, um . . ." He sighed. "I don't even know why I'm making such a big deal out of it. I've never even *gone* bareback with anyone. Not since my first." He cringed. "The one who . . ."

"The one who infected you?"

Jesse nodded. He met my gaze, his eyes full of shyness and uncertainty. "But I want to with you. Once my tests come back again, and as long as you feel safe doing it."

I laced our fingers together and kissed the backs of his. "I don't see why not. As long as it's just us."

He held my gaze, his expression so full of sweetness and hope. "I haven't even looked at anyone since we started doing this."

"Neither have I."

Some playfulness crept in, and the hopeful smile became a devilish smirk. "Don't lie, Garrett."

"Huh?"

He cupped the back of my neck and kissed me before he whispered, "I saw you looking at Levi."

I snorted. "Okay. Guilty." I wrapped my arms around him. "But I saw *you* checking out Hunter. So."

"Fair, fair." He met my gaze, grinning. "We're allowed to look, right?"

"Of course. To be serious, though, I'm only interested in you."

"Same." He sobered. "So, we'll talk about it when the results come back?"

I nodded. "Definitely."

And I couldn't wait.

CHAPTER TWENTY-SEVEN

JESSE

Things were better after that. Clearing the air and tangling up my sheets had brought us back to that easy place we'd been in before I'd gotten sick.

I still caught myself marveling at how his mind worked. It was weird how he could simultaneously worry himself crazy over me being positive, but then be completely chill about it. Not all guys were hung up on my status, but the ones who were always worried about getting infected. If Garrett had any concerns about that, he'd never let on. In bed, he gave a hundred percent. Never shied away from kissing me. Never freaked out if any of my cum got on him. Bottomed for me with no shortage of enthusiasm.

And besides, we *were* still using condoms. On top of that, my viral load was (usually) undetectable. We both knew that while the chances of me infecting him weren't *quite* zero, they were slimmer than a flea's dick.

No, his worries were about me. One sneeze, and I could still almost feel him having visions of me on my deathbed. I didn't like that, but I reminded myself now that it wasn't him genuinely thinking I was dying so much as his own PTSD about losing his husband. That would get better with time. He was trying. He really was. The next time some bug knocked me on my ass, I was confident we'd both handle it better.

So yeah, things were better now.

Except . . .

Garrett was distant tonight.

It had been almost a week since the night we'd talked and fucked things through, and everything had been fine right up until tonight.

Ever since he'd come over after work, he'd been distant. Hell, *distant* didn't begin to describe it. He was in another world entirely. We were on my sofa, both ignoring a TV show I couldn't even name. I watched him. He was . . . God knew where.

I gave his arm a gentle nudge. "Garrett?"

He jumped, shook himself, and turned to me. "Hmm? What?"

"You okay tonight? You don't seem like you're really"—I waved a hand in front of my own face—"here."

"Sorry." He put a hand on my knee. "Just . . . a lot on my mind."

I lifted my eyebrows, not sure if I should pry.

He stared down at his hand, watching his thumb trace the seam of my jeans. "I need to go out of town for a few days. The week after next."

I tried to read his face. His expression didn't offer much, but he didn't look or sound happy about the trip. "Everything okay?"

"Yeah. I need to go back to Seattle." He kept his eyes down as he took in a deep breath. "The thing is, that Friday is a year. Since Sean . . ."

"Oh. I'm sorry." That sounded so useless, but I didn't know what else to say. I put a hand on his knee, hoping the contact provided some comfort.

Garrett covered my hand with his. "I'm leaving on Thursday. Staying with my sister for a couple of nights. I, um . . ." Another breath, and then he turned to me. "I need to go visit him. I already feel guilty for being away as long as I have."

I nodded. "Yeah, I understand." I paused. "Do you want me to come with you?" I'd blurted the question before I could stop myself, and now I felt like a fucking jackass. Really? A grieving widower wanting to take his new boyfriend to—

"Would you *want* to go?" His tone suggested he wasn't against the idea. "It might be a bit, uh, emotional for me and weird for you."

I swallowed. "If you need me to, yeah. If you want to go alone, I can definitely understand, but if you need me . . ." I slipped my hand into his. "If you need someone with you, just say so."

His lips parted. "You're serious."

"Of course." I smiled cautiously. "You took care of me when I needed it."

That got a soft laugh out of him. "To a fault, maybe."

"Eh, who's keeping score?"

He laughed again, but sobered pretty fast. "It's going to be rough. At the cemetery."

"I know. I'm not expecting a party."

His eyes lost focus, and I wondered if he was considering my offer or trying to figure out how to gently say no. I was on the verge of giving him an out when he exhaled slowly, curling his fingers between mine. "Thank you. I could definitely use some company."

I brought our hands up and kissed the backs of his fingers. "Anything you need. Just say so."

He met my gaze, and though his smile was slow to form, it was sweet and sincere. "You're amazing, you know that?"

I can't think of anything I wouldn't do for you.

That thought was terrifying in ways I wasn't ready to unpack, so I pushed it to the far corners of my mind and lifted my chin to kiss him softly. "Will your sister mind me staying? Or should we—"

"She won't mind." He smoothed my hair, the tender gesture making my heart flutter. "I'll double-check with her tomorrow, but I know her. She'll be fine. Especially since she likes you."

"Well, I would hope so," I said as haughtily as I could. Buffing my nails on my shirt, I added, "I'm fucking *awesome*."

Garrett laughed with feeling this time. "Yes, you are. Now get over here . . ."

CHAPTER TWENTY-EIGHT

GARRETT

The carefully manicured lawn was wet beneath our feet. Last night's rain gleamed in the late-morning sun, on the grass and the polished headstones, but there wasn't a cloud in the sky now. Typical Seattle.

I hadn't been back here since just before I'd moved to Bluewater Bay, and it was surreal to follow these familiar paths again. Like I'd been gone forever and not long enough and too long and . . . fuck, but grief messed with my sense of time. Why not? It messed with everything else.

Beside me, Jesse was silent. He followed me as I followed the path, and I didn't have to think to find the plot I was looking for. My feet knew the way.

Like most of the stones in this cemetery, the headstone was flat, nearly flush with the grass around it. Raindrops beaded on the polished granite and pooled inside some of the engraved letters. And just like always, my breath hitched as I read the words.

Sean David Maillet-Blaine
Loving husband, brother, son, & friend.
Eternally a fabulous queen.

"'Eternally a fabulous queen'?" Jesse eyed me incredulously.

I laughed despite the tightness in my throat. "He made his mother and me swear on our lives we'd put that on his headstone."

"That's . . ." Jesse gave a soft, cautious laugh. "That's kind of awesome."

"It's very Sean, believe me." I crouched in front of the headstone, and Jesse did the same.

"It's still kind of weird seeing our names like that," I said. "Hyphenated, I mean."

"It is?"

"Yeah." I glanced at him and realized he didn't know the story. "Sean didn't take my name until after his diagnosis. He said . . ." The air was suddenly thick, threatening to choke me.

Jesse put a hand between my shoulders. The mix of sympathy in his touch and the curiosity in his expression were soothing in a way I'd never felt before. Not in a way that made my eyes stop stinging or my voice stop shaking. Instead, it was like unspoken permission to break if I needed to. And I didn't know if I needed to or not, but it was profoundly comforting to feel like I was with someone who'd let me.

My voice wavered as I tried again. "He wanted both of our names on his headstone. So that no matter what . . ." I cleared my throat. "It didn't mean we'd always be together. He insisted, time and again, that he didn't want me moping around until I died too. But he wanted some piece of us to last forever." I trailed my fingers over our hyphenated names. "So there it is."

"Wow," Jesse breathed. "He really put a lot of thought into this."

"That was his way." I smiled despite the sting in my eyes. "People thought he was flighty and ditzy because he was so boisterous, but he was really the opposite. As much as people gave me the side-eye for wanting to be with someone so young and immature, believe me—he was the mature one."

"Is this where I'm supposed to make a joke about not being surprised?"

He didn't laugh until I did. And from both of us, it was a quiet sound. Not uneasy, just not raucous.

"Fair enough," I said. "I mean, it wasn't one-sided. When we traveled, I was the one who had everything booked and organized, and being an accountant, I did our taxes. But he was the kind of guy who'd make a dentist appointment six months in advance, and remember it without needing one of those reminder postcards. He didn't even put it on the damn calendar."

"Bastard," Jesse muttered.

I laughed. "Seriously." Humor fading, I traced my finger along the sharp edge of the headstone. A memory tried to surface of Sean's steel-trap mind becoming less so. When the chemo brain had started to kick in, and later when it was more than just the drugs, but I forced it away. Even here by his grave, I wanted to hold on to the good parts. "He was something else, let me tell you. Once he got his head around being terminally ill, he focused almost all his energy on making sure the rest of us were ready for him to go."

Jesse turned to me. "Really?"

I nodded. "To be honest, I think he needed something to distract himself. Focusing on us and how we'd grieve for him and remember him—that was a lot easier than thinking about his own death." I released a ragged breath, my chest hurting at the memory. "He was scared. He knew he was going to die, and he made peace with it faster than I thought he would, but . . ." I chewed the inside of my cheek, struggling to find the words. "He made peace with the fact that his life was being cut short. It was the actual death that scared him."

"So, suffering."

"Exactly. I mean, none of us wanted to think about it. I'm pretty sure his family and I were all hoping for the same thing—either he'd go in his sleep, or we'd all be there with him, and he'd say goodbye before he went to sleep and didn't wake up." A weight started lifting off my shoulders. Had I never actually said any of these words out loud? "I don't think any of us actually believed that would happen, but you kind of hold on to whatever hope you can at that point."

Jesse nodded silently.

I absently ran my thumb along the edge of the headstone, the wet granite cool and sharp under my touch. "He was terrified that he'd be in horrible pain at the end. I can't even tell you how many times he begged me to do whatever I had to do if it got really bad."

Jesse was quiet for a few seconds, but then he tensed as if the pieces had come together in his mind. "Whoa."

"Yeah." More weight came off my shoulders. I didn't ask, and Jesse didn't say, but I felt like he didn't judge me or Sean for that. Like he knew that, yes, I would have done what my husband had asked, and he wasn't horrified by that. Or maybe I was reading too much into it, but the fact that I could say out loud what Sean had made me promise, and I didn't feel the need to defend *making* that promise? Fuck. What a relief. I exhaled and focused on the headstone again. "I think he poured all his energy into the rest of us because of that.

He really did care about all of us, and he was worried about how we were going to cope, but at least part of it was because he was scared."

"I'll bet he was." Jesse shifted a little, glancing at me like he wanted to ask something, but wasn't sure how. I had a feeling I knew what was on his mind.

"He went peacefully at the end," I said. "He was in a lot of pain there for a while, but once the doctors declared him terminal and shifted the focus to palliative care, he didn't feel much of it. The last few days, he was pretty much unconscious." I wiped my eyes and shakily added, "And then he just . . . slipped away."

Jesse put a hand on my bent knee. "Were you with him?"

I nodded, resting my hand on top of his. "Yeah. And I'm glad I was. And that he didn't suffer. It was the hardest thing I've ever been through, but given the circumstances, it was probably the best outcome any of us could have asked for."

Jesse didn't speak. For a moment, the only sound was his thumb brushing back and forth on my jeans.

After a while, I spoke again. "He used to—" I choked on a sound that was mostly a laugh but kind of wanted to be a sob too. Clearing my throat, I swiped at my eyes. "He used to tell us that if anyone wasted their time pining for him or moping about him, he'd come back and haunt us."

"Wow." Jesse shook his head, laughing quietly. "Did he plan his own funeral too?" He flinched like he hadn't meant to blurt that out.

Chuckling, I took Jesse's hand and gave it a gentle squeeze. "He had a few opinions on that subject."

"Seriously?"

"Mm-hmm." I pulled in a breath. "Early on, when he was between treatments and could stomach alcohol, he decided he wanted to get drunk. So one night, we got shit-faced. We started talking about the things he wanted at his funeral." I laughed, shaking my head. "Started writing it down and everything."

Jesse's eyebrows knitted together. "Dare I ask?"

I started ticking the points off on my fingers. "Bounce house. Chocolate fountain. He wanted a drag show, but only if I promised—in writing—not to include this one drag queen from a club we went to sometimes."

A laugh burst out of Jesse, and he nearly toppled forward. "*What?*"
I chuckled despite the nostalgic sting in my eyes. "Hand to God."
"Did . . . did you *do* all of that, though?"
Sobering a bit, I sighed and shook my head. "No. And Sean even
told me he understood that the funeral was for all of us to get closure.
He wanted us to do whatever we needed, as long as we got on with our
lives afterward."
Still working on that, Sean, but I promise I'm trying.
I rose, knees creaking from being in a crouch for so long. When
we were both on our feet, I put an arm around Jesse and kissed his
cheek. "Thank you. For coming with me, and for letting me talk about
Sean."
"You're welcome." He rested a hand on the small of my back.
"And you can talk about him whenever you need to. I'm sure it's good
for you, and I . . ." He shifted his gaze to the headstone.
"Hmm?"
Jesse took in a breath before meeting my gaze again. In a soft, shy
voice, he said, "I really do like hearing about him."
"You do?"
He nodded. "Sounds like he was a great guy, and he was obviously
important to you."
"He was." I swallowed. "But I don't want to be grim and depressing
all the time."
"You're not." He rubbed his hand up and down my back, the
gesture soothing in ways I hadn't realized I'd needed. "You talk about
the good stuff too."
"True." I searched his blue eyes. "And it's not . . . I mean, it doesn't
sound like someone obsessing over an ex or—"
"No, not at all." There wasn't a trace of insincerity in his expression.
Quite the contrary.
I wrapped my arms around him and kissed his temple. "Thank
you."
"Anytime." He held me tight, and neither of us let go for a long
time. As we stood there in the brisk morning light, embracing and
not speaking, I was suddenly beyond grateful that he'd offered to
come with me. I hadn't been sure I could do this alone, but I hadn't

anticipated how hard it would really be or how much comfort I'd find in Jesse's sure, quiet presence.

In a way I hadn't expected, coming here felt good. It was hard to see Sean's grave, but it was comforting to see it with Jesse. And it made me see my relationship with Jesse in a new light. I hadn't believed it was possible for me to feel anything for a man again, never mind that I'd find someone who understood what Sean meant to me. Someone who didn't resent him or feel threatened by him. With Jesse, I felt like I had a shot at falling in love again, and I could do it without hiding, ignoring, or rushing my grief. Jesse didn't just tolerate me talking about Sean—he encouraged it. He didn't expect us to live in some kind of vacuum where Sean had never existed.

Jesse was filling some of the space Sean had occupied, but he wasn't filling Sean's shoes. His presence didn't make Sean seem less gone. The similarities between them, those little things my mind kept pouncing on, were just grief looking for something that wasn't there.

Sean wasn't here anymore, but Jesse was.

Standing there beside Sean's headstone, I held Jesse a little tighter and kissed the top of his head. My worlds hadn't collided today. Instead, they'd seamlessly come together, the edges overlapping.

"You okay?" Jesse whispered without loosening his embrace.

"Yeah. I think so." We slowly parted, and I cupped his cheek. "I know I already said this, but thank you. For . . . all of this. Coming with me, letting me talk . . ."

He smiled and lifted his chin to kiss me. Just a soft, chaste kiss full of comfort and understanding.

As I drew back, I asked, "Ready to go?"

"We can stay as long as you need to."

I glanced at the headstone, then back at him, and smiled. "I think I'm ready."

Jesse nodded, and I wrapped my arm around him as we headed back toward the parking lot. There were a million emotions swirling in my chest, but I felt a lot better than I'd expected to today. I'd take it.

Someone else was coming up the winding rain-dampened strip of asphalt. As the distance between us closed, I realized it was my brother-in-law, Mark.

He recognized me a moment later. As we neared each other, I realized he was eyeing Jesse, and my stomach flipped. Shit. This wasn't how I needed Sean's family finding out I was seeing someone new.

But the cat was out of the bag now, so playing it cool was my only option.

"Mark. How are you?" I released Jesse and extended my hand.

"Garrett." He gave me a curt nod as he shook my hand.

Ignoring my nerves, I gestured casually at Jesse. "This is Jesse. Jesse, this is Mark. Sean's brother."

Mark regarded him coldly, but offered his hand. "Hi."

"Hi." As they shook hands, Jesse smiled uneasily, which gave me a chill. He'd picked up on the undercurrent of hostility too, hadn't he? Which meant I hadn't been imagining it. There'd never been a lot of love lost between me and my brother-in-law, but we'd been there for each other in Sean's final months. The frostiness radiating from him now was damn near visible to the naked eye, though.

He cut his gaze toward Jesse before looking at me again. "How are you doing?" The accusation was almost as palpable as the cold air between us.

"As well as can be expected." I kept my tone even. "One day at a time, right?"

He grunted softly. "Yeah. One day at a time." He gestured past us. "Well. I'd better . . ."

"Yeah. Yeah. We should get going. It was good to see you."

"You too," he said without a trace of sincerity.

Without another word, Mark continued up the path. Over my shoulder, I watched him go.

"I don't think he liked me," Jesse said.

"He's never liked me." I put my arm around him again, and we continued toward the parking lot. "Don't take it personally."

He was right, though—Mark was not pleased to see Jesse, and I didn't have to ask why.

Something tells me I haven't heard the end of this.

I didn't dwell on the issue, though. I was worried, but far too distracted. My mind was a tangle of thoughts, and as we left the cemetery behind, my emotions started going haywire. I'd felt pretty damn good while I was standing beside the gravesite with Jesse, but leaving . . . Christ, that ripped at my seams. It pinged the same nerves that had driven me to fresh tears when I'd left Sean's funeral. Nothing made his death more final than leaving him there in that quiet, empty park.

I didn't cry this time. The volley of feelings all seemed to try to cancel each other out. The relief that Jesse was beside me neutralized the pain at realizing Sean had been gone a full year. The crushing sadness over leaving the cemetery took the place where the previsit apprehension had been.

By the time we were back at Fiona's house, I was exhausted. From the visit, and also from the onslaught of contradictory feelings. I made it into the guest room, Jesse on my heels, and sank onto the foot of the bed as all the air left my lungs in a long sigh.

Jesse sat beside me. "You okay?"

I nodded, but I didn't look at him. I stared at the carpet, trying to get a grip on the flurry of feelings in my chest. There were places in me that had just been numb and empty for the last year, and now emotions were bubbling up and filling those voids. Suddenly there were words and feelings that needed an outlet.

"The last month or so before he died," I said without really thinking about it, "I'd wake up every morning hoping he'd gone in his sleep."

Beside me, Jesse's breath hitched, but he said nothing.

I swallowed, the mix of emotions trying to tear my chest apart. "It wasn't that I wanted him gone. I just . . . I couldn't stand . . ."

"You couldn't stand watching him suffer." Jesse's words forced a breath out of me.

Closing my eyes, I nodded. "There was nothing in the world I wanted more than for him to stay with me *except* for him to stop being in pain. Watching someone you love go through that?" I opened my eyes again, blinking a few times to clear my vision. "That's a kind of hell I wouldn't wish on my worst enemy."

Jesse took my hand and squeezed it, that small gesture full of more compassion and understanding than I ever imagined I'd get if I admitted out loud how I'd felt during my husband's final weeks. In a soft voice, he said, "You feel guilty for feeling that way, don't you?"

I laughed humorlessly, for lack of any other way to release this weird energy. "You think?" It came out with much more sarcasm than I'd intended. Gripping Jesse's hand harder, I wiped my free hand over my face. "I'm sorry."

"Sorry? Jesus, Garrett." His thumb ran along the side of my hand. "If I'd been in your shoes, I think I'd have felt the same way."

I turned to him, not sure how to respond.

He held my gaze. "I wouldn't want to watch someone suffer either. Wanting that suffering to end isn't the same as wanting the person gone. And wanting the person to hold on isn't the same as wanting them to suffer." He brought our tightly clasped hands up and kissed the backs of my fingers. "I'm not going to tell you I know how you feel or what it was like to go through any of that, but . . . what you're telling me right now?" He nodded slowly. "I get it. And it's not nearly as fucked up as you probably think it is."

I swallowed, relieved in ways I hadn't imagined I'd ever feel. I'd hated myself every time I'd woken up and realized Sean was still holding on, and I hadn't thought anyone would ever understand that feeling. What kind of asshole wished his husband would give up and die?

But Jesse got it. And that was a relief. Not just that someone got it, but that *he* did.

"You okay?" he asked.

I nodded. "I think so. Or at least, I think I will be."

Twin creases appeared between his eyebrows. He released my hand and touched my face. "Whatever you're feeling or needing right now? It's okay. If you need to be alone, or if you want to go out somewhere, or if you want to talk, or not talk . . ." He traced his thumb along my cheekbone. "If there's anything I can do, all you have to do is ask."

I put my hand over his, the warmth of his skin electric against my palm.

Eyes locked on mine, he whispered, "Tell me what you need."

The hand on my cheek was almost certainly meant to be reassuring and nothing more, but it sent something intense crackling along my nerve endings. Today had broken open the mostly numb shell of grief, reminding me how horrible my husband's final months had been and how lonely I'd been since he'd passed. The time I'd spent with Jesse, rekindling my ability to touch and connect with someone, put a wedge between the present and that painful past, though, separating me from those dark days and tempering the hurt that lingered. It was difficult to imagine how I'd feel right now if Jesse weren't with me. If he hadn't been with me for the last several weeks, and if he weren't sitting here beside me while my emotions flailed. If he hadn't been there today to listen to me and stand next to me.

I didn't think I'd ever been as grateful for anything as I was, in that moment, for the man sitting beside me.

Without a word, I curved a hand behind his neck and kissed him. Hard. Needy. No pretense whatsoever—this was going to end with us naked and spent.

Jesse didn't miss a beat. He grabbed on and returned my kiss with equal fervor. In a matter of seconds, we were panting, groping, rutting against each other. It seemed crude and crass, like this was the last thing we should've been doing after visiting the cemetery on the anniversary of my husband's death. But at the same time, it was perfect. It was exactly what I needed. The visit had awakened emotions I hadn't wanted to acknowledge, and it had pulled at parts of me that were still—and maybe always would be—numb, and I was suddenly desperate to feel things that didn't hurt. To feel *alive*.

And was there anywhere these days where I felt more alive than tangled up with Jesse?

Especially now. Holy shit.

All those emotions that had been bubbling up broke loose, tightening my chest and stinging my eyes, and I held on to him tighter. I was hungry for him, his touch, his moans. It didn't have to make sense. Nothing needed to make sense right now.

But he'd also been there with me today. Was this weird for him?

I broke the kiss and looked into his eyes. "You sure you're okay with this?"

He licked his lips. "Shouldn't I be asking you that?"

"I'm completely okay with it." I slid a hand up into his hair. "I want you so bad right now." *I need you. God, Jesse, I need you.*

Because you're you, damn it. Not a reminder of someone else. You.

Jesse grabbed me and kissed me again, and there was no stopping. He rolled me onto my back and straddled me, kissing me hard, and he groaned as I tugged at his shirt. The more clothes came off, the wilder he got. The wilder we both got, but especially him. Jesse was always aggressive, but right now, he had that aggression cranked up to a twelve, and I loved it. I reveled in it and drowned in it and couldn't get enough of it.

We grappled like one of us was trying to gain control, but we weren't. We were just needy and demanding, digging in fingers and raking nails across skin and throwing each other down, biting hard enough to bruise when we weren't violently making out. This wasn't how we usually fucked, but I didn't care. It was like the only way these emotions would calm down was to find an outlet, and the only outlet was hungry, feverish sex.

"Fuck me," I panted between kisses. Foreplay could wait until I wasn't this desperate.

He responded with a low, throaty moan and shuddered against me, rubbing my hip with his rock-hard erection. "We've got . . . lube . . . everything . . ."

"Yeah." I waved a hand in the general direction of my bag. "It's all—"

He lunged for the bag, grabbed it off the floor, and dragged it up onto the bed with shaky hands.

I pulled back the zipper. He went for the condoms while I went for the lube, and after he'd torn the wrapper, he growled, "Hands and knees."

Nothing—no amount of weed or booze or any goddamned thing—had ever spun my head as fast as it was spinning right then. Despite my light head and my shaking limbs, I did as I was told, and I bit my lip as I silently begged him to hurry the hell up.

He didn't waste time. Once the condom was on, he knelt behind me, and as soon as he'd slicked some lube on me and a lot more on himself, he lined his dick up with my hole. I shivered. Yes. God, yes. It was like he knew exactly what I needed. No prep. No gentleness. I wanted it rough, hard, painful, forceful—I didn't care if he made me cry as long as he made me come.

He didn't thrust in. He pressed his cock against me, and he stayed there, letting me lean back and take him. As he breached me, we both groaned. He wrapped his arm around my waist, quite possibly to steady himself, and exhaled hard against my back.

"This okay?" he panted. "Not . . . not too—"

"More." I squeezed my eyes shut as I rocked back to take him deeper. "God, Jesse . . ."

He grabbed my hips and withdrew a little. Before I could protest, though, he slammed back in, and the whole world went white for a second.

"Oh yeah," I moaned. "More of that. Fuck yeah."

He gave me more of that. So much more. He rode me hard, fingers bruising my hips as he forced his cock in again and again.

I dropped to my forearms, which shifted his angle inside me, and everything blurred as he hit that sweet spot *just* right. The sounds I was making weren't words anymore, but he must've understood them as encouragement because he didn't let up.

Distantly, I was aware that my head had been a confusing mess of thoughts and emotions, but all that was gone. Nothing existed except here and now and this, and nothing mattered except the steady cadence of *more, more, more,* punctuated by Jesse's brutal thrusts.

His rhythm faltered and he cried out as he drove himself in and stayed there. "Oh . . . fuck . . ."

I thought he might've come, but then he nudged me all the way down to the mattress and started riding me again.

"You feel so good," he panted, fucking me hard enough to rub my cock against the sheets. "God, Garrett . . ."

I murmured something that kind of sounded like, "So do you," but English wasn't high on my priority list. My priority list was blank except for lying there and taking Jesse's thick cock while his hot, sweaty skin pressed against mine. It was too much, and it was painful, and it was the most perfect thing I'd ever experienced in my life. I was on the brink of sobbing and I didn't even know why. Overwhelmed and . . . Fuck, he was just so good. So, so good.

Jesse moaned into my hair and thrust harder, his rhythm falling apart the way it always did when he was close. "Come, baby," he whispered. The combination of demanding and desperate in his tone was too much, and the shudder that went through me could've registered on a Richter scale.

"Oh God," I breathed as he thrust deep, my entire body shaking as he drove me over the edge. "Fuck, *yeah!*" Jesse groaned hard, and he pounded me for all he was worth as I came, and then he was coming too, dick pulsing inside my tender ass as his raw, raspy cries echoed off the walls.

One last hard tremor rocked me from head to toe, and I was still. I was already facedown on the mattress, but I felt like I'd collapsed anyway. Then he collapsed over me, shaking and panting. I loved it. The heat of his skin. The weight of him. The ragged gusts of cool breath across sweat. Somehow it all added up to everything in the world being right and perfect, even if it was just for a few minutes.

He kissed the back of my neck, and goose bumps prickled all over me. With a soft grunt, he pulled out, then flopped onto the bed beside me. "Holy fuck."

"Yeah." I turned on my side. "I was thinking the same thing."

Our eyes met. He was the very picture of blissed-out perfection. Tousled hair. Sweat dripping down his face. Skin flushed. Chest rising and falling with harsh breaths.

How are you mine?

I touched his cheek with a trembling hand, and he kissed my palm. Then we just gazed at each other and smiled.

After a long, sweet moment, we finally rose, cleaned ourselves up, and sank back onto the bed. He rested his head on my shoulder, and neither of us said anything for a while. The silence was hardly awkward or uncomfortable—just the two of us lying together and letting the dust settle. My body felt spectacular. Even my head seemed clearer, and I didn't care if it was temporary. It felt good right now.

"Doing all right?" he finally asked.

"Yeah." I pressed a kiss to his forehead, which was still warm and damp with sweat. "I feel pretty good, actually."

"Good." He tilted his head up to kiss under my jaw, then nestled back under my chin.

I stroked Jesse's hair and gazed up at the ceiling. Our hungry, needy fuck had scattered some of those overwhelming emotions and calmed others, but a few more were heading to the surface. Feelings I hadn't expected to ever have again. Some I'd only had for one person before now.

I tried not to compare him to my late husband, but the way I felt right now with Jesse was uncannily similar to the way I'd felt in the early days with Sean. There'd been a profound realization, a foundation-rattling epiphany when I'd looked at him and simply *known*. There'd never been any questioning or angst about it. I'd known the moment I'd started falling for Sean, and I'd surrendered to that fall like an eager skydiver. It wasn't something I'd experienced before him or after him . . . until right now.

I didn't say anything. This wasn't the time to think like this, never mind say it out loud, and I still had way too many emotions to sift through before I was sure-footed enough to make any big declarations, but I couldn't deny it—I was falling for Jesse. Falling hard for him.

And I didn't want to stop.

CHAPTER TWENTY-NINE

JESSE

We dozed for a little while. We were both emotionally exhausted and physically wrung out, so we gave in to fatigue.

I woke to Garrett snuggling up against me again, and I smiled into the pillow. We'd probably drifted apart like we always did when we shared a bed, but he'd found his way back to me.

Lacing my fingers through his, I murmured, "Feel better?"

"Much." He planted a kiss between my shoulder blades that sent a shiver straight through me. "Feel like moving?"

"Depends on what kind of moving we're talking about."

"Something that gets us to food."

"Mmm, I like that idea." I started to roll over, so he loosened his embrace enough to let me. "Want to order out or something?"

"Actually." He swallowed. "I want to take you to dinner. Someplace nice."

I pushed myself up onto an elbow. "Really?"

He nodded. "Yeah. It means a lot that you came all the way out here and went with me this morning. And . . ." He looked down, but I caught the blush on his cheeks as he added, "I want to anyway."

I smiled. "Okay. Where did you have in mind?"

The grin spreading across his lips made my pulse surge, and he leaned in for a kiss as he whispered, "You'll see."

An hour later, we were in the truck and wading through downtown Seattle traffic. We kept the conversation light, which was a relief. The heavy subjects had been necessary, but a break wasn't unwelcome.

The day had left my mind in a weird place. I'd meant it when I told Garrett I liked hearing about Sean, and it obviously did him a lot of good to talk about Sean. Still, going with my boyfriend to his late husband's grave was a weirdly intense experience. Like . . . momentous. One of those things you only did with someone you were getting Serious™ with. And maybe that's what we were doing. Maybe this was serious. Was it too much for him now? Was he ready? How the hell would I even ask him that?

More than ever, I was keenly aware of the differences between Garrett and me. The age gap itself wasn't a big deal, but the amount of living he'd done in his fifteen-year head start . . . that had been more noticeable today. This was a guy who'd been married. Who'd kept his vows all the way to the "until death" part. Garrett was grieving his husband, and I'd never even signed a lease with someone.

Garrett put on his turn signal, and I shook myself out of my thoughts as he pulled into a parking lot by the Seattle Center. He found a spot, parked, and turned off the engine. "Ready?"

"Ready for—" I looked outside, and realized we were near the base of the Space Needle. When I turned to him, he was grinning. "We're . . . Are we eating up there?"

"Yep." He pocketed his keys and leaned across to kiss me. "Got a reservation at a window table and everything."

I couldn't help laughing. "You really went all out, didn't you?"

"You better believe it."

We got out, and after I paid for the parking spot—I'd insisted— we walked to the base of the Space Needle. I'd never eaten up there before. I'd been up to the observation deck a couple of times—once as a kid and once with a boyfriend a year before I'd moved to Bluewater Bay—but the restaurant had always been too rich for my budget. I could afford it now, but Garrett had made it pretty clear dinner was on him tonight. Fine. Next time *I'd* take *him* someplace nice.

On the way from the elevator to the restaurant, he rested his hand on the small of my back, and I had butterflies like I'd never experienced. It was hard to believe this was still the same day we'd visited Sean's grave, and the fact that he could be this romantic and affectionate toward me even after this morning . . . Holy shit.

Even as we sat down, I barely noticed the view outside the slowly revolving restaurant. I was distantly aware of Mount Rainier glowing in the rich pink light of the sun setting over Puget Sound. Of a lit-up ferry lazily cutting a path through the sparkling water on the way to Bremerton or Bainbridge Island. It was all there, and I could see it, but I was mostly aware of the atmosphere. Of the way the warm light played on Garrett's features and in his dark eyes.

There was a menu I needed to read, and there was a stunning view outside, but neither registered. All I could do was stare at him and try to make sense of all the twists and turns and washed-out bridges our roads had gone through to bring us here. The last several hours alone had been a hell of a ride. This morning, we'd stood beside Sean's headstone. This afternoon, we'd had some of the most passionate, savage sex I'd ever experienced. Tonight, we were having a romantic dinner with a spectacular view. It didn't make sense, and yet I couldn't imagine being anywhere but here with him right now.

I'd expected the visit to Sean's grave to be difficult. Maybe even harrowing. Seeing that kind of pain on my boyfriend's face? My heart ached just thinking about it.

It had indeed been difficult, but I'd come away with feelings I hadn't anticipated. There was a hollow spot I couldn't explain.

No. That wasn't right. I could explain it. After visiting Sean's grave, there was a sense of grief, despite the fact that I'd never met him. There was a sense of loss. An empty space he should've been occupying. Logically I knew that if he were still alive, I'd never have met Garrett, but that didn't stop me from wishing I could have known him.

Over the rim of my water glass, I watched Garrett as he gazed out at the city and the water below us. For the first time, I truly felt the weight of Sean's death, and the travesty it was that he was no longer in Garrett's life except as a memory. I hadn't known Garrett before Sean, but I knew Garrett had to be a different man because of him. Everyone was shaped by their relationships. Even if I didn't know *how* Sean had influenced him or who Garrett had been before his husband had come along, there was no doubt in my mind that the man sitting across from me, bathed in the light of the vanishing sun, wouldn't exist if not for Sean.

Somehow, I found enough brain cells to peruse the menu, and when the waiter came, I ordered. My mind hadn't strayed far from its track, though. Once Garrett and I were alone again, I gazed at him and said, "Tell me something about Sean."

Garrett blinked. "Like what?"

"Anything."

He studied me for a long moment like he wasn't convinced I was serious. Then, swallowing hard, he gazed out at the city. "Well." He took a deep breath. "He dragged me to the top of Mount Rainier once."

"Did he? How was that?"

"Cold. Miserable. We sniped at each other until the air got thin enough that we couldn't walk and talk." Garrett laughed quietly. "Then we signed our names in the book at the top, and we laughed like idiots because . . ." His eyes lost focus, and after a moment, he shook his head. "I don't know. We were probably a little delirious by that point from the lack of oxygen and from waking up at three in the damned morning. But it seemed funny in the moment. We'd grumbled at each other most of the way up the mountain, and once we were at the top, everything was fine."

"Was it worth the hike?"

"Oh yeah. Definitely." He smiled as he turned to me. "It's one of those experiences that's miserable at the time, but once it's over, you're glad you did it."

"What made him drag you up there?"

"He'd always wanted to do it." Garrett shrugged. "He was like that. Got his mind set on something, and he did it. Hell, I did more in the five years I was with him than I did in the ten before we met. For someone . . ." He paused, exhaling heavily. "For someone who didn't get a lot of years, he checked off quite a few things on his bucket list."

I smiled. "Good for him."

"Yeah." He nodded. Then he took a breath as he thumbed the condensation on his water glass. "He was an interesting person, that's for sure. Loved musical theater, but lived and breathed for football. Couldn't walk past a bookstore. He was horribly allergic to cats, but always insisted on cuddling his mom's cats anyway." Garrett laughed softly, chin quivering a little.

I reached for his hand and squeezed it, and he squeezed back.

When he met my gaze, there were tears his eyes, but he was smiling. "I think you and he would've really liked each other."

A lump suddenly materialized in my throat. "Really?"

"Yeah." He sniffed, watching his fingers sliding back and forth on my hand. "If I ever turned the two of you loose in a store with smart-ass T-shirts or mugs, we'd have had to send in search and rescue to get you back out."

I laughed, and holy shit, I really was getting choked up. "What was his favorite one?"

Garrett's lips quirked and his eyes lost focus. Then he laughed again, the sound still sad but genuine at the same time. "It was a camouflage T-shirt that said *Ha! Now you can't see me!*"

"Oh, I love that one!"

"I'm so not surprised." He patted my hand and shifted his gaze out the window at whatever part of Seattle we were facing now. "And our boss was always getting on his case about his coffee cups being 'appropriate' for work." He rolled his eyes. "Took her way too long to figure out that the more shit she gave him, the worse the next cup would be."

I snorted. "Oh God . . ."

"Yeah. She finally gave up when he brought in a bedazzled chalice that said 'Queen Bitch' in bright-red sequins. I heard her tell someone she didn't even want to know how he'd top *that* one."

"Never a dull moment with him, from the sound of it."

"No. Never." He shook his head, still smiling. "Definitely not a dull moment." He paused, then looked in my eyes. "You really don't mind talking about him?"

"Not at all."

Garrett put a hand on mine. "I brought you here for a romantic dinner. We don't have to spend it talking about my past."

"But I want to talk about you. That means talking about him."

His eyebrows jumped, but then he smiled again, his expression so sweet I wanted to swoon. Running his thumb alongside my hand, he said, "I don't know what I did to get so lucky, but I'm sure glad I did it."

"You happened to be tending bar the night some asshole stood me up." I turned my hand over under his and gently clasped my fingers around his wrist. "And I've never been so happy to *be* stood up."

He chuckled. "I don't know if I want to kick that asshole's teeth in or send him a thank-you card."

"Either or." I shrugged, grinning playfully. "No skin off my nose either way."

He laughed, and . . . yeah. I would never stop loving the way he laughed. I loved the sparkle in his eyes and the way some of the lines in his face deepened.

I ran my thumb alongside his hand.

You're so fucking beautiful, and somehow, you're mine.

After dinner, we went out to the observation deck. Though it was practically summer, the night was crisp, a sharp wind blowing in off Puget Sound and keeping the air cool and comfortable.

The sun was completely gone now. Mount Rainier was invisible, and Puget Sound would've been too if not for the skyline reflecting off its mostly calm surface. Beneath us, the roads were colorful with amber streetlights, pale headlights, and glowing signs and displays from stores and businesses.

"I've always loved the view from up here," Garrett said after a while.

I turned to him, fully intending to agree, but froze. My breath stuck in my throat, and I just stared at him.

Like the lights in the Alehouse, the dimness out here smoothed over the lines in his face, but it also softened the white in his hair. He looked younger. No . . . less stressed. Like someone who hadn't been through hell and back.

My heart skipped.

It was almost like getting a glimpse of his face back before his world had come apart.

Garrett cocked his head. "Something wrong?"

Just the fact that the universe has been so, so unfair to you.

"No." I stepped closer and wrapped my arm around him. "I just like how that light looks on you."

He laughed softly, probably blushing. He pulled me close and kissed me, and then we gazed out at the city for a little while, letting the wind ruffle our hair as the quiet night settled around us.

When he turned back to me, there were tears in his eyes again, but more than that, some deeply intense expression that caught me off guard. Something sincere and vulnerable, genuine and raw, that the low light didn't begin to temper.

Swallowing hard, he freed himself from our embrace, and he pressed his hip against the railing as he faced me. Then he brought my hand up to his lips and kissed it. "I don't know how I would have coped today without you."

The words startled me as much as the expression. I mentally flailed, trying to find something to say, but nothing I came up with seemed right.

He rested our joined hands on the railing. "You've been a hell of a lot stronger than I've had any right to ask you to be, but don't think it's gone unnoticed. Being with someone like me, who's been through what I have . . ." He exhaled, shaking his head. "Just . . . thank you."

"You're welcome." It sounded so stupid and bland. Jesus. "You're worth it." It still sounded stupid, but the way his breath hitched said maybe he understood what I was struggling to say.

"Thank you," he whispered again. After a moment of taut silence, he cleared his throat. He was holding my hand almost painfully tight now, and I wondered if he was trying to keep his own from shaking. "When I met you, I wasn't even thinking about dating again. Hadn't looked at an app or a website or anything. But then you came into the picture, and it made perfect sense for this to happen."

I shifted, suddenly nervous. Suddenly full of things I *needed* to say, but things that didn't seem like they should be said *right now*.

Garrett touched my face with his free hand. "What's wrong?"

"I . . ." No, this wasn't the time. Burning thoughts or not, the man didn't need to be hammered with—

"Talk to me," he whispered. "Whatever it is."

I hesitated, staring out at the dark place where Mount Rainier would be when the sun rose. My heart was going crazy now, and I didn't want to ruin this intimate moment, but I wasn't going to relax until the words came out.

Finally I turned my hand over under his to clasp our fingers together. "I want to get this right, you know? What we're doing? But I'm not sure I know how. Like . . ." Staring down at our hands, I struggled to pull my thoughts together. When I looked at him again, my voice shook. "I've been a boyfriend before, and I think I'm pretty good at being someone's boyfriend. I've just never been a boyfriend to someone who's grieving a husband."

Garrett flinched subtly, fingers twitching between mine.

"I guess what I'm saying," I went on, speaking slowly so I could pick each word carefully, "is that I don't know *how* to be what you need, but I *want* to be."

His forehead creased, and his grasp tightened slightly as a smile began to form. "You. That's all you need to be." Caressing my cheek, he leaned in for a soft kiss before he said, "I'm really glad you came. And not just for the moral support. I . . . I *like* being with you, Jesse. All the time."

I covered his hand with mine, pressing his palm against my face. "Me too."

And wasn't that the understatement of the night? The longer we stood here, the harder my heart pounded. The restaurant below us was standing still compared to how fast my head was spinning. No one had ever looked at me like he was looking at me now, and I'd sure as hell never looked at anyone this way either.

In Portland, I'd had a feeling I was starting to fall for him. Now, it was a full-on free fall. Too fast and not fast enough. Weightless and heavy. Screaming toward the ground and rocketing skyward.

I didn't say anything, though. God knew if he was ready to hear it, and this was new territory for me anyway.

But I was pretty sure this was what being in love felt like.

Earlier today, we'd all but thrown each other down on this bed.

Tonight, we sank onto the guest room mattress, kissing lazily and running hands all over each other's clothed bodies. I barely remembered the drive back to Fiona's house. It had been a blur of stoplight glances and loaded grins and me silently praying for the late-night traffic to get the fuck out of the way.

Now we were here, and it was perfect. Even though we were both rock-hard, I didn't know if this would lead to sex—if we had anything left after today—but I didn't mind if this was as far as we went. Every time he ran his fingers through my hair or teased my lips with the tip of his tongue, it was as erotic as feeling and watching my dick slide into him.

For the longest time, we just lay there, Garrett half on top of me, clothes rumpled but still in place. I could get fucking drunk on the way this man kissed. He could be as aggressive and demanding as anyone, and I enjoyed that too, but right now he was sensual and soft. Like he'd never kissed me before and wanted to take his time tasting and exploring. Oh, he could have all the time in the world if he kept this up. I loved how his tongue could be so insistent without being invasive, sliding past mine and exploring without seeming like he wanted to lick my damn tonsils. And sometimes he'd go back to just his lips against mine, moving gently without any tongue at all, before he'd nudge my lips apart to taste my mouth again.

After a long while, Garrett lifted himself off me and turned on his back, but he didn't lie flat. Instead, he sat up against the headboard. Then he gave me a gentle tug, and I let him guide me onto his lap.

Oh, now this was nice. I loved the way his hips felt between my thighs and how my chest was pressed against his and, dear God, the way his hands ran all over me. Up and down my back. Over my thighs. Cupping my ass.

Then he slid a hand between us, and I gasped as he started undoing my pants. Yes. Fuck yes. I wanted his skin on mine, and my painfully hard erection was a damn good place to start.

After some fumbling, he freed my dick from my pants, and I groaned with relief. As he started stroking me, I couldn't help moving my hips, rising and falling in a pantomime of riding his cock, and . . . Fuck. That was a sexy thought, wasn't it? I didn't bottom often, but damn if the thought of riding his dick wasn't irresistible right then, and not just because he was probably sore from earlier. Except we still had clothes on, and the condoms and lube were . . . Fuck, we *had* brought them, hadn't we? Of course we had. We'd used them earlier.

"We have condoms left?" I asked.

"Mm-hmm." Garrett gave my cock a slow, tight pull. "I've always got *plenty* handy if I'm going to be around you."

"Mmm, good." I moaned and kissed him. "Because I want you just like this."

Garrett squirmed under me and dipped his head to skate his lips along my neck. "Might be kind of tough for you to top me from there."

"Who said anything about topping you?"

He whimpered against my neck. "You serious?"

"Uh-huh." I pressed against his clothed dick. "You like that idea?"

"*Oh*, yeah." He nipped under my jaw. "Might need to get some clothes out of the way, though."

"Good thinking."

We got up, stripped out of our clothes, and climbed back into the guest bed. Just like before, he sat up against the headboard, this time with a pillow tucked behind his back, and bit his lip as I straddled him again.

"You do like this position, don't you?" he murmured between kisses.

"I'll like it even better once you put a condom on."

He sucked in a sharp breath, then kissed me harder and held me tighter. "Assuming I don't come just thinking about it."

I sort of moaned, sort of laughed and broke the kiss to reach for the lube and one of the condoms we'd left on the nightstand.

Garrett took it from me, tore the wrapper, and started rolling on the condom. As he did, he glanced up at me. "I didn't think you bottomed."

"I usually don't." I poured some lube into my palm. "But sometimes . . ."

Garrett met my gaze. "Any time the mood strikes, you know where to find me."

"Uh-huh. Well the mood is striking me right now."

"And thank God for that," he growled, sliding his hands up my bare chest.

As I positioned myself over him, he steadied his cock with one hand and my hip with the other. I held his shoulders and eased myself down. As the thick, blunt head pressed against me, I hesitated, reminding myself to breathe and relax.

"I can finger you first," he said. "I don't want to hurt you."

I shook my head. "No, I'm good. I'm . . . I can handle it."

"I want you to enjoy it, not 'handle it.'"

I leaned in and kissed him. "I'm good. I promise. I *have* done this before."

"Okay. Anything you want, say the word. I mean it—I don't want to hurt you."

Our eyes met, and the sincerity in his was almost as palpable as the desire. God, no wonder I was willing—eager, even—to bottom for him. He was safe. He was kind and giving and considerate. He wasn't the first to say he didn't want to hurt me, but I believed him in ways I'd never believed any other man. In *profound* ways I was too dizzy and turned on and overwhelmed to comprehend right then.

And it just made me want him that much more.

I lowered myself a bit farther and bore down a little, and when the head of his cock slipped in, I couldn't help but groan.

Garrett's hand drifted up my thigh to my hip. "You sure you're okay?"

"Yeah." I licked my lips. "It's . . . just been a while." Maybe I should've had him finger me, but I'd done this before without much prep. Okay, so the last guy hadn't been as blessed as Garrett, but I was fine.

"Go as slow as you need to." His voice was as gentle as his touch. "I'm in no rush."

I nodded—but didn't speak—and concentrated on relaxing. I eased myself down, eyes watering as he stretched my hole. It didn't hurt or anything—it was just really, *really* intense. Conflicting needs scrambled my brain. Now that I had him in me, I wanted every inch, but at the same time, I wasn't sure I could handle any more. I wanted to ride him hard, feel him pounding me, but I also wanted to go slow so I could feel the smooth slide of his thick cock.

He slid across my prostate, and I sucked in air through my teeth.

"This all right?" he breathed.

"Uh-huh. So good." Now that I was relaxed enough, now that I could take him easily, I wrapped my arms around his neck, and he put his around my waist, and for a while, we just kissed like that— holding on to each other, his cock buried to the hilt inside me. My hips moved a little, but only enough to keep stimulating us both in the most deliciously mind-blowing way.

This couldn't have been more different from earlier, but it was no less intense. Every movement was gentle and subdued, and every nerve ending was alight just like they had been when we'd bruised and bitten each other.

We barely made a sound. I moved too slowly for the bed to protest. I claimed a deep, needy kiss and continued my easy, fluid motions, savoring every stroke as his cock moved inside me. We kissed too much to speak, and even our soft moans were swallowed up and muffled. Only the wet sounds of kissing and the whispers of hands running over skin kept the room from being completely silent.

Little by little, I picked up speed, but not much—just enough to make him gasp. Good thing we'd already gone one round today, or I'd have come by now, and I wanted this to last. He felt so good—not just his cock, but his body against mine, his arms around me, his lips teasing mine in between gulps of air.

Garrett shivered, fingers digging into my hips. "Oh, *fuck* you feel good," he whispered. "Jesus, Jesse . . ." He whimpered softly and shuddered. His fingers dug into my hips, and when he let his head fall back, I leaned down to kiss his neck. A hand suddenly materialized on the back of my head, and he gripped my hair as if to hold me in place as his throaty groans vibrated against my lips.

"You feel amazing," I breathed.

He just moaned again and ran his hands down my back.

I couldn't take any more. My orgasm was building quickly, and the need to let go threatened to drive me insane, so I sat up. Angling my hips *just* right, I rode him faster, desperate for relief, and now my cock was rubbing against his belly and oh *fuck*, I was going to lose it.

Garrett stared at me, wide-eyed and lips apart as if he'd never witnessed—never mind experienced—anything like this before. Maybe he hadn't. This level of *oh God yeah* was sure as hell new to me.

"Fuck, Garrett," I murmured, riding him for all I was worth. "Oh yeah, I'm gonna come . . . I'm . . . fuck!" I shot cum onto his stomach and even his chest, and he gasped just before he grabbed my hips, pulled me all the way down onto him, and shuddered again. Neither of us was quiet, but we were hardly saying anything coherent—just moaning and slurring as we rode our orgasms out.

I sank against him, slinging my arms around him, and he held me close as we both trembled and panted, the headboard holding us upright.

When the spinning room had slowed a little, I rested my hands on his shoulders and lifted my head so I could see him. My heart beat like crazy, and it wasn't from the exertion or the orgasm. It was the same feeling I'd had on the observation deck. That panicky exhilarated feeling like I was falling. Or like I already had.

You. I combed my fingers through his sweaty hair. *All I want is you.*

Garrett caressed my cheek, and his smile made my spine tingle. "Like I said before," he slurred, "anytime you want to bottom? You know where to find me."

I laughed, sounding about as drunk as I felt. "I'll remember that. Definitely."

I lifted myself off him, and we both staggered to our feet to get cleaned up. After he'd gotten rid of the condom and we'd both mopped up some of the cum I'd gotten on both of us, I started back toward the bed. I only made it a couple of steps, though, before Garrett caught me with an arm around my waist. I turned, thinking he was going to say something. Instead, he gathered me in a warm embrace and kissed me so tenderly, I thought my legs were going to melt out from under me.

How do you make me feel things no one ever has before?

"In case I haven't said it enough," he whispered, "you're amazing."

I smiled against his lips. "You're not so bad yourself, you know."

Garrett laughed softly and kissed me again. I held on and let myself get lost in that flying-falling-what-the-hell-is-happening feeling, which was back in full force as we stood there, sharing a lazy kiss while our bodies were still hot and sweaty from everything we'd just done. I wasn't turned on—not yet—but *something* in me was aroused. Something I'd never felt with anyone before.

As I drew back and met his gaze, my heart pounded.

Oh yeah.

I am definitely in love with you.

CHAPTER THIRTY

GARRETT

Compared to yesterday, the second morning at my sister's was amazing.

Since Fiona left early to go to work, we'd said our goodbyes over coffee, and then Jesse and I had the house to ourselves. The drive back to Bluewater Bay would only take us about three hours, and since neither of us had to be anywhere tonight, we weren't in a tremendous hurry to get on the road. We lounged in bed, enjoying the laziest, most languid morning sex the world had ever seen.

After we'd finally gotten up and showered, we both pulled on a pair of jeans, but we didn't bother with anything else. If the looks he kept shooting me were any indication, there would definitely be one more round after we'd had coffee and before we hit the road. No point in getting completely dressed, was there?

And besides, I thought with a grin as I followed him into the kitchen, what was the point of leaving all those bites and bruises and scratches if we weren't going to admire them? Because holy shit, we must've been rougher than I'd realized yesterday.

In the kitchen, Fiona had already done the dishes from the coffee we'd had earlier, so Jesse opened the cabinet to get two more mugs. He huffed as he perused the selection. "Your sister's coffee cups are boring."

"They hold coffee." I reached past him and took down two black mugs. "That's the only purpose they need to serve."

"*Pfft.*" He closed the cabinet. "I demand entertainment *and* caffeine from my coffee cups."

"Of course you do." I poured us each a cup. Then we leaned against the counter and sipped in companionable silence.

"So," Jesse said after a while. "What's the plan for today?"

I shrugged. "Anything, really. As long as we're on the road by four or five, we're good. Especially since it's a weekend and the Mariners aren't playing at home, so the traffic shouldn't be too bad."

"Okay." He sipped his coffee and set the cup on the counter. Then he wrapped his arms around me. "Last night was amazing, by the way."

"I know." I flashed him a grin. "I was there."

He laughed, rolling his eyes, and lifted himself up for a soft kiss. "And thanks for dinner. I've never eaten there before."

"It's a lot better than it used to be." I put my coffee aside and smoothed his disheveled blond hair. "I know a few other places we can try next time we're in town."

"Me too." He lifted his eyebrows and offered the sweetest little smile. "So does that mean there's going to be a next time?"

"Of course. Maybe under, you know, happier circumstances."

The smile faltered a little but then came back to life as he touched my face. "Anytime we're in town and you want to go see him, we can."

Oh. My heart. This man.

"Really?"

"Of course." He shrugged.

I wrapped my arms around him. "You really are amazing." I paused. "Sorry. You're fucking awesome."

He chuckled as he hugged me back. He took a breath like he was about to speak, but right then, Fiona's doorbell rang.

"What the hell?" Jesse drew back, glaring in that direction as he released me. "Seriously? Right when I was getting all kinds of adorable?"

"You're always all kinds of adorable." I kissed his forehead. "It's probably just a delivery. Fiona's got an itchy trigger finger when it comes to Amazon's one-click function."

"I can relate." Jesse gave me a wolfish grin. "You gonna show off all those bite marks to the poor guy?"

I glanced down at the many nips and bites visible on my bare torso. Part of me wanted to grab a shirt and cover it up, but to hell with it. I was feeling too damn good today, all things considered, and decided the UPS guy could cope with a shirtless, well-nibbled man signing for Fiona's packages.

When I pulled open the door, my breath caught. I'd been expecting the UPS driver or . . . well, pretty much anyone.

Anyone except Sean's older sister.

Courtney glared at me across the welcome mat, arms folded tightly across her blouse. Her eyes did a slow down-up, and her lips bleached as her glare slid over the bite marks that were suddenly way too conspicuous.

Feeling exposed and without a shirt in sight, I shifted uncomfortably. "Courtney. I—"

"We need to talk." She brushed past me into the living room—and halted. The whole city probably felt the moment her eyes locked on Jesse. He'd appeared in the doorway between the kitchen and living room, low-slung jeans hugging his hips and, like me, no shirt.

Uneasy, I shut the door behind me, the click startling all three of us like a gun had gone off. "I, uh . . ." They both stared at me, and my heart thumped against my ribs. "Courtney, this is Jesse. Jesse, Courtney."

Jesse took a cautious step forward, brushing his hair out of his face as he extended his other hand. "Hi." He didn't sound nearly as confident as he usually did.

She eyed his hand warily but didn't accept it. After a couple of tense seconds, he withdrew it and retreated a step. Slowly, she turned to me.

The last three years had aged her. Hell, they'd aged all of us. Neither of us had really started to gray until Sean's diagnosis. A not-insignificant amount of my hair had turned white, and her blonde hair was mostly gray. We both had more lines—worry and grief permanently etched into our skin, especially at our eyes and mouths.

She did look better than she had a year ago, though. She'd been dangerously gaunt at the funeral, but she'd gained back some of the weight she'd lost. There was a little more light in her eyes. She stood straighter, almost as straight as she'd had when I'd met her.

So yeah, she was looking better, but that didn't explain why she was *here*.

"Um." I swallowed. "What's this about?"

Courtney set her jaw and lifted her chin, glaring at me. "Mark said he saw you at the cemetery yesterday." She glanced at Jesse. "With a *man*."

I opened my mouth to speak, but she jabbed a finger at my chest.

"Is it true? Did you really—" She cut her eyes toward Jesse again and gave him a slow, disgusted down-up. Lips curled, she faced me again. "Don't even try to bullshit me, Garrett." Her voice wavered and her eyes flashed with pain and anger. "Did you bring your new *boyfriend*"—she spat the word like it was poison—"to the cemetery?"

There was no point in trying to dodge the question, and I hadn't intended to anyway. Mark had seen us. Besides, I wasn't ashamed of Jesse.

"Yes, it's true." I kept my voice as level as I could. "I've started seeing someone." I nodded toward Jesse. "And yes, he was with me yesterday."

Her eyebrows climbed her forehead and her arms tightened across her chest. Eyes flicking toward the kitchen, she growled, "You've been seeing someone long enough to take him to *my brother's grave*?"

I clenched my teeth. "I've been seeing him long enough to accept his support when I'm visiting my *husband's* grave, if that's all right with you."

"Uh-huh." Her nostrils flared as she growled, "Is he the reason you didn't have the decency to visit our family while you were in town? You couldn't come see us and see how my mother is doing after losing her *son*?"

I winced and broke eye contact. I'd hemmed and hawed about seeing the family when we came to town, and yes, I'd been afraid of visiting them with Jesse. But Jesse would have understood if I'd needed some time to go visit them alone. Truth was, I'd been brittle enough over the prospect of going to the cemetery. I didn't think I could cope with seeing my in-laws. There'd been enough bad blood before Sean had gotten sick, and I hadn't wanted to see if they'd still be as charitable toward me as they had in his last days.

If that made me a coward, then so be it.

"Courtney," I said as calmly as I could. "I'm not trying to be disrespectful to your family or to Sean."

"So you couldn't even wait *a year* before you had to start fucking someone else? What is wrong with you, Garrett?"

I gritted my teeth. "I met someone, and I clicked with him. Yes, it happened sooner than I thought it would, but your brother even told me he didn't want me to wait if—"

"Of course Sean told you that!" She swiped at the tears that were starting to stream down her red cheeks. "He didn't want to be an asshole. He didn't actually think you'd go running out and dive into another man's bed before he was lukewarm in his grave. And I mean . . . look at him." She gestured sharply at Jesse, who jumped.

Eyes wide in shock and horror, he glanced back and forth between us.

I nodded toward the kitchen, and he happily took the suggestion and left the room. Facing my sister-in-law again, I said, "What about him?"

She blinked. "Really? You don't see it?"

"See what?" I snapped, my patience fraying rapidly.

She rolled her eyes. "Mark said he reminded him of Sean. And yeah, I can see it."

I scoffed. "He looks nothing like Sean."

"Oh, for God's sake." She gestured toward the kitchen. "He's . . . I mean, you and Sean used to *joke* about that, Garrett! Remember?" Her voice shook. "Remember how you used to say he was the only queen who could win your heart?"

My gut clenched. It had only been lighthearted silliness—something Sean had so effortlessly brought out of me—but the words hit me hard now.

"So now my brother's been gone *a year*, and you've already got . . ." Another sharp gesture toward the kitchen. "So much for the only queen, huh? Or do you just have a thing for blonds?"

Guilt and anger were fighting for dominance in my chest. Mark and Courtney had seen it? Scott and Fiona had seen it? What if they were—

"Jesse has nothing to do with Sean," I snapped. "He has—"

"Whatever helps you sleep at night, asshole."

"Courtney, what the hell? This is—"

"Save it." Her lips pulled back in a sneer. "I *never* trusted you because I knew you were just looking for some guy to depend on you. For some reason, my brother was head over heels for you, but I figured you'd at least have the decency not to go out and replace him so soon." She laughed humorlessly. "But hey, what do I know?"

Shock kept me mute for a long moment. When I finally found some breath, I said, "I loved Sean, Courtney. I will love him until the day I die. But I'm not going to ask someone else's permission before I decide I've grieved enough to—"

"Grieved *enough*?" She stared at me like I'd just insulted the entire family. Waving toward the kitchen, she demanded, "How long has this been going on, anyway? Did you at least wait until after the funeral to open a Grindr account?"

I clenched my teeth to keep the anger in check. "I met him after I moved to Bluewater Bay. And no, I wasn't out looking. We met, and we clicked, and he came with me yesterday because I needed the support."

"And it never dawned on you to talk to us?" She put a hand to her chest, the rage tipping slightly in favor of hurt. "Sean's family?"

Sean's family, who couldn't stand me until he was dying? No, thanks.

But I didn't want to pour gas on the fire, so I calmly said, "You were all going to be struggling as much as I was yesterday. Why would I compound that?"

"Oh, bullshit." Courtney's expression was definitely moving back toward anger now. "But I can see why you wouldn't want to come around if you had something to hide."

I forced out a breath and managed to not roll my eyes. "I wasn't hiding him. I—"

"Yeah, okay. Listen, if you want to run out and replace Sean, be my guest." She stabbed a finger at me. "But you have no right to bring him—"

"I'm not sure how that's your decision," I snapped.

She straightened a little, as if startled that I'd gotten in her face, but when she recovered, icicles hung from every word. "Look at him, Garrett." She gestured in the direction Jesse had gone. "He's a kid. Another naïve young boy for you to take under your wing and take advantage of."

My jaw fell open. I'd known what they thought of me, but they'd never said it out loud to my face.

Her glare dared me to suggest she was wrong.

"I *loved* your brother, Courtney," I said through my teeth, voice shaking anyway. "I wasn't taking advantage of a naïve kid."

"Sure you weren't. And as smart as Sean was, he fell for it hook, line, and sinker no matter how much we all tried to warn him."

The words tore at me, ripping open fresh wounds to go alongside the old ones.

And she wasn't done. "If he'd lived longer, maybe he would have opened his eyes and seen. Hopefully before you found something younger and shinier to replace him." Another pointed glance toward the kitchen. "Nice job finding one who's a younger, *healthier* clone of my brother, you fucking—"

"That's enough!" I bellowed. "Get the fuck out, Courtney. Now."

She eyed me coolly. "That's what I thought." She turned to go, and I was too shocked by the avalanche of accusations to counter any of them. At the door, she paused and looked back. "We tried to warn Sean, and I sure as hell hope someone's warning this new boy toy about the same shit." She shook her head, lip curled. "If you're so desperate for something to depend on you and blindly love you, just get a fucking dog and save the rest of us the heartache."

And with that, she was gone.

I thought I was going to be sick, but my knees were shaking too much to carry me to the bathroom. Instead, I sank onto the couch, swallowing hard and hoping my stomach stayed put. My ears rang and my mind reeled. It didn't matter that I'd known how Sean's family felt about me. Hearing it . . . Fuck. They'd tried to warn him away from me. They'd thought . . . thought I was *taking advantage* of him. Even after we'd made peace—sort of—while Sean was dying . . . this? Did my in-laws really believe I'd had Jesse on the side before Sean had died?

And what was I supposed to make of yet another person noticing the similarities between Sean and—

A hand on my shoulder had me back on my feet with a gasp.

Jesse showed his palms. "Hey. Easy."

"Sorry. I . . ." I sank back down. "Didn't hear you come in."

He sat beside me. "You okay?"

Not even a little.

I turned to him, and I couldn't help looking him up and down. As I did, the sick feeling worsened. It was impossible not to see everything Fiona and Courtney had seen. A young guy unabashedly embracing—not just in touch with—his femininity. So different from anyone I'd ever dated . . . with one exception.

Jesse's hair was different. His face. His eyes. His voice. But somehow, gazing at him now, I could only see Sean in him. All the pieces of him that I'd found in Jesse. The sarcasm. The sense of humor. The feistiness. How he so effortlessly switched between adorable and devilish.

Fuck. *Were* Fiona and Courtney right? *Had* I been right when I'd second-guessed myself? *Was* Jesse just a substitute? Someone to fill the role Sean had vacated? *Was* that why I'd fallen for him so fast and so hard?

It sounded ridiculous, and yet it made sense. As much as anything could make sense right then. Holy fuck, I didn't think I'd ever been this confused in my life. This *lost.* I'd thought I was making leaps and bounds with moving on, and now I was afraid I was not only back at square one, but dragging someone else's heart along with me. Was this why everyone had told me to wait a year before making any major decisions? Because even when I *felt* like I was ready to move on, there was still so, *so* much further to go?

"Garrett?" Jesse's gentle voice prodded me out of my thoughts, and he touched my shoulder. "You still with me?"

"Yeah. Sorry." I stood up on shaking legs and tried to roll some tension out of my shoulders. "You okay with just hitting the road?"

He nodded. "Yeah. Let's go home."

CHAPTER THIRTY-ONE

JESSE

Awkwardly silent car rides were always miserable. They always made me twitchy and uncomfortable. When the awkwardly silent car ride was three goddamned hours, it might as well have been my own private circle of hell.

We'd left Fiona's house half an hour or so after Courtney had stormed out, and the silence had already settled in before we'd even taken our stuff out to Garrett's truck. All the way out of Seattle and up into Edmonds, the only conversation was about whether we should stop for lunch (neither of us was hungry) and if we should get gas before we got on the ferry (we did).

We took the ferry from Edmonds to Kingston, and we both made our excuses to not stay in the truck. I went up to use the bathroom. He stepped out to get a soda. With some expert-level foot-dragging on our respective errands, we managed to avoid each other for about twenty-five minutes of the half-hour boat ride.

While he drove us off the ferry and back onto the highway, I stole a few surreptitious looks at him. The quiet was killing me, and I didn't know what to say. We hadn't fought. He had no reason to be pissed at me, and I knew he wasn't, but the spat he'd had with his sister-in-law had rattled something in him. Something he didn't want to talk about. Now he'd withdrawn into himself, leaving me out here with no idea if or how to break the silence. What did he need from me? Space? A shoulder? Reassurance that Courtney was wrong?

Talk to me, Garrett. I want to help.

And there was a selfish angle too. I didn't want to make what happened this morning about me, but what was happening *now* sure as shit affected me. He had every right to be upset, and maybe that meant he had every right to shut me out too, but . . . there had to be some middle ground here somewhere. Something between *I need to sort this out in my head* and *you don't exist.* At what point did I have the right to say, *Hey, bruh, I'm still here,* and get pissed if he kept the walls up? Especially when I had a few questions about his sister-in-law's accusations.

He'd told me about the strained relationship he'd had with them, so that much hadn't been a surprise. That part about me being like Sean, though? Uh . . . ?

"But if you're asking who I've been wanting for the last few days, and who I hope is coming in whenever the Alehouse door opens . . . no question. It's you."

"That's all I need to know, then. I don't want you to forget him or not think about him. Just as long as you're thinking of me as me and not 'that guy who's kind of like him.'"

"Not at all. Pretty sure you're one of a kind anyway."

My throat tightened around my breath. *You sure about that last part, Garrett?*

But what was I supposed to say? And shouldn't *he* have been saying something? Did I have any right to be pissed? To demand answers? Did *he* have any right to shut me out?

I watched him from the corner of my eye, trying to gauge him, but that was impossible right now. He wasn't one to wear his thoughts on his sleeve anyway, but his poker face was rock-solid today. If I had to guess, he was replaying the argument over and over in his head. If he wasn't, I sure was. Her words kept echoing in my ears, and I kept seeing him flinching every time they hit their mark.

Somewhere between the Hood Canal Bridge and one of those tiny Olympic Peninsula towns I couldn't name, an epiphany ratcheted up my discomfort by about five hundred percent.

"You and Sean used to joke *about that, Garrett! Remember? Remember how you used to say he was the only queen who could win your heart?"*

"If you want to run out and replace Sean, be my guest."

Acid burned in the back of my throat. The things he'd said up on the Space Needle observation deck repeated ad nauseam in my head, their real meaning becoming clearer each time.

"I guess what I'm saying," I heard myself cautiously venturing, *"is that I don't know* how *to be what you need, but I* want *to be."*

"You," he'd said with certainty. *"That's all you need to be."*

A lump rose in my throat. In light of everything his sister-in-law had said, and this painfully long silence, it was impossible not to put the pieces together.

It wasn't me he needed. Well, it was, but it wasn't. Garrett needed someone who wasn't here anymore, and I was the closest thing he could find to fill that space.

What did he need from me? Sean.

That lump rose higher, my eyes stinging, and I stared out the passenger-side window so he wouldn't see. Not that he seemed to even remember I was here, but whatever.

I shouldn't have been surprised, and maybe I wasn't. Disappointed? Oh yeah. Devastated? Probably would be when the numbness finally cracked. Surprised? I . . . wasn't sure.

Hopeless? Oh yeah. Big time. Because while I could be a lot of things for Garrett, Sean wasn't one of them. He was gone. I was me. So where did that leave us?

We crossed into Bluewater Bay, and I was both relieved and apprehensive. The long, excruciating drive was about to be over. But . . . now what?

"Damn it," Garrett muttered and started slowing down.

"What?"

"Missed the turn." He laughed humorlessly as he pulled into the bank parking lot. "You'd think I'd know my way around town by now."

I chewed my lip, once again at a loss for what to say.

Garrett turned the truck around and continued toward the complex. Neither of us spoke. The silence followed us up the stairs to his apartment, broken only by him quietly offering me a drink and me just as quietly declining.

In a matter of minutes, the quiet had overstayed its welcome, and I was starting to wonder if I had too. He'd folded in on himself after his sister-in-law had left, and he wasn't exactly opening up now.

And even if he did, what could I do for him? What in the world did he need from me?

Something I can't be. Someone who isn't here.

The lump was still in my throat, and it was bigger now. The fact was, I could be with a man who was still grieving. I could love a man who still hurt over someone he'd lost too soon.

But I couldn't replace Sean. Be a companion, a lover, a boyfriend? Yes. But *be* Sean? No.

And after the things Garrett's sister-in-law had said and the things Garrett hadn't said, it was getting too hard to believe he wanted *me* and not just the nearest guy who kinda resembled the man he'd lost.

Fuck. Fuck, fuck, fuck.

Finally, I couldn't take the silence anymore. "She's right, isn't she?"

Garrett turned, brow furrowed. "Huh?"

"Your sister-in-law." I pushed my shoulders back. "What she said."

He lowered his gaze, and his shoulders sank just as slowly and unmistakably as my heart. Neither of us spoke. I'd expected him to get defensive, but . . . not this. Not quietly resigned. I didn't know how to respond. It would've been irritating if he'd snapped at me or told me I was imagining things, but he didn't even fight it. Maybe I was hallucinating, but if anything, I swore he was relieved by the accusation. Like now that I'd said it, he didn't have to try to hide it anymore.

So what was the point in continuing the conversation? I had my answer.

Fighting to keep my voice even, I stood. "I think I'm gonna go."

No response.

I chewed the inside of my lip, fighting back nausea and tears and way too many emotions. "Like, I'm going to *go*. I don't think I can do this."

That at least got him to look at me. "What?"

"I can't be what you need. I think that's—" My voice tried to break, and I cleared my throat as I took another step toward the door. "I just need to go before I get in any further over my head."

He studied me, but then he dropped his gaze and wiped his hand over his face. He didn't speak, though, and if I stood here much longer, I was going to lose it.

So I started to go.

Hand on the door, I paused. Garrett hadn't fought my accusation, and now he didn't try to stop me from leaving. If I'd been right, then fine, but didn't he *care* that I was leaving? Wasn't he going to lift a finger to keep me here? Fuck. All those romantic comedies I'd watched over the years and all those sappy novels just made this moment worse. Too many visions of the hero running out and yelling, "Wait! Wait!"

The hero wasn't chasing anyone this time.

Hero, my ass.

And just like that, I was pissed. I spun around and faced him. "What the fuck, Garrett?"

He jumped. Hell, so did I.

I recovered, though, and strode back across the room to stab a finger at him. "Seriously? That's it? You're just . . . *That's it?*"

He sat back a little and showed his palms. "What do you want me to say?"

"I just want—" I almost choked on the words, and my voice wavered when I finally ground out, "Do you even *care* if I stay or go?"

"Of course I do." Garrett held my gaze, his expression unreadable except for the bone-deep fatigue. "But for God's sake, do I look like I have any fight left in me?"

A pang of guilt tugged at me, but it was quickly eclipsed by hurt and anger, and my voice was a shaky mess as I ground out: "If this isn't worth fighting for, then just say so."

"I'm not even sure why we're fighting." He rose so we were more or less eye to eye. "I'm sorry if I didn't talk much on the way back, but—"

"No, that's not why I'm upset. For fuck's sake, I had to listen to your sister-in-law telling you all the reasons why I'm nothing more than a surrogate for Sean, and you've had hours to say something to make me believe she was wrong. *Is she wrong or not?*"

Garrett flinched, avoiding my eyes, and I couldn't read the tension in his jaw. Was he pissed? Hurt? Had I hit close to home?

Now it was my jaw getting tense, and my teeth ached from grinding them. Barely keeping my voice even, I repeated, "Is she wrong or not, Garrett?"

"You . . ." He swallowed, and he couldn't quite meet my gaze. "You're pissed because I haven't reassured you that you're not a replacement for my husband?"

"Well." I threw up my hands. "Am I?"

His lips thinned. "You're not Sean, Jesse."

"You don't fucking say." There was more bitterness in my tone than I'd intended. I made no apologies. Especially since I couldn't tell who he was trying to convince—me or himself.

Garrett finally looked me in the eye. "What do you want from me?" He shrugged, but it was a taut, irritated gesture, not a flippant one. "The point is that I've told you this before—you have *never* been a replacement for Sean."

So why don't you sound convinced this time?

"Doesn't sound like I could fill his shoes if I wanted to," I growled.

Garrett jumped like I'd punched him. Then his eyes narrowed, and he set his jaw. "Have I ever compared you to him?"

"Out loud?" I folded my arms. "No."

"For God's sake." He threw up his hands, then raked one through his hair. "I can't fucking believe this."

"Because you did mention how you were never into my *type* before him, so after everything Courtney said, if you've got a reason for me to think differently, I'm all ears."

"And would you actually listen to me?" he snarled. "Or are you going to get in line with everyone else and tell me what I want and what I feel?"

The fury in his usually calm voice startled me, but I recovered quickly, tightening my arms over my chest as I glared across the narrow space at him. "I've done everything I can to be what you need, Garrett. I don't think I'm asking too much for you to give me some sign that you want *me* and not someone else."

"Do you want me to tell you I'm over my husband and don't wish every goddamned day that I didn't have to watch cancer eat him alive for a year and a fucking half?" he asked through clenched teeth. "Do you want me to tell you that I didn't love him so much it hurt and that he didn't leave a gaping hole in my life?" His voice started to waver, and his eyes gleamed with a hint of tears as he growled, "Tell me what the fuck you want to hear, Jesse, because I've got nothing."

We stared at each other. The words hung in the air, fury still thrumming from every syllable just like pain still reverberated in my bones.

"Oh hey. Look at that." I forced back the tears. "Guess you had some fight left in you after all."

Garrett closed his eyes and sighed. Then, shaking his head, he looked at me, and his tone was gentler. "Jesse, I'm sorry. I don't want you to leave."

"I'm just not sure I understand why you want me to stay." I fucking hated the shakiness in my voice.

"Are you really going to make me spell it out?"

I tightened my arms again, this time to steady myself. "After today, I think you might need to. I don't . . . I don't know what I'm supposed to be for you."

"Have I ever asked you to be anything but you?"

"No, but you have mentioned how much I resemble someone we both know you've been missing."

Garrett winced, looking away.

Much more of this, and I was going to break down in tears. I'd been on shaky ground since Seattle, and now just the sight of him— especially as he refused to deny what I'd said—threatened to split me in half.

I took a deep breath to pull myself together. "I can't do this. I need to go." I started toward the door again, jaw clenched as I willed the tears to stay back just a little longer.

"Jesse, I love you." He blurted it out. Quickly, almost as one syllable. Almost like he hadn't expected the words to come out at all, though he didn't take them back.

I halted. As I turned to face him, the sincerity and pain in his eyes almost broke me, but I shook my head anyway. "No, you don't."

"Jesse . . ."

I put up a hand, scared he'd keep talking and convince me to stay. This had to stop. Right now. No matter how much the truth hurt, it was still the truth.

"I know you care about me, but you're not in love with me. You're in love with something that feels better than that empty spot where Sean used to be." My voice was shaky, but mostly it made me sound tired. Really tired. Because holy shit, I *was* tired. "I don't want you to be lonely, and God knows I don't want you to be in pain from losing him." Exhaling, I shook my head. "But I can't *be* him. And I can't be with someone who needs someone else."

Again, Garrett dropped his gaze.

Again, he didn't argue.

And again, he didn't stop me from leaving.

CHAPTER THIRTY-TWO

GARRETT

S cott watched me silently from the other chair on his balcony. Neither of us were smoking. My head was already clouded and didn't need to get worse. Scott hadn't said a word about it, and there was no lighter, no weed, and no paper on the table between us.

It had been five days since Jesse walked out of my apartment. I'd thrown myself into the longest shifts Don would allow and found every excuse imaginable to stay away from my place. At least until the echoes of our fight had faded enough to let me sleep.

I'd avoided Scott too. I'd known he would take one look at me and turn into my therapist instead of my friend. But when he'd texted this morning to ask if I wanted to come by, the loneliness had won over my need to avoid being analyzed, and I'd come over.

Sure enough, I hadn't fooled him.

I'd told him everything. The visit to Sean's grave. My sister-in-law tearing into me. The fight before Jesse had walked out.

I'd finished a good fifteen minutes ago, and we'd both been quiet since then. I didn't know if Scott was waiting for me to speak, or if he was running my story through his therapist gears, but neither of us had said anything.

Scott drummed his nails on the armrest of his chair. "Have you considered talking to him?"

"I don't know what to say to him." I gazed up at the trees to avoid his scrutiny. "I mean, maybe he's right. Maybe I *was* looking for Sean."

"Do you really believe that? Or are you just trying to justify letting him go and not putting yourself out there again?"

I gritted my teeth. "I don't know what I believe. I know how I feel about Jesse. I just . . . I don't know if . . ." Sighing, I rubbed my eyes with my thumb and forefinger. "Am I using him to replace Sean? I mean, how do I . . . how do I know if it's real, or if it's just a Band-Aid for someone who's missing? I can't gamble with his feelings, you know?"

"You obviously care about him."

"Of course I do." I finally made myself look at him. "But now I've got my sister and Sean's sister and Jesse himself thinking he's just a substitute for Sean, and I . . . How do I know he's not?"

Scott watched me silently for a moment. "Who do you think of when you're with Jesse? Him or Sean?"

"Him." I paused. "I mean, Sean's on my mind a lot. Not as much as he was a year ago, but he's definitely there."

"But when you're looking at Jesse, who are you seeing?"

"Jesse." I didn't even have to consider the answer. "Always."

"Then I don't think you have anything to worry about."

"Except convincing Jesse."

"Sounds like you needed to convince yourself first."

And I still wasn't so sure. Except I was. And I wasn't. Fuck—what was wrong with my brain?

I stared up at the trees again, not sure what to say.

Scott took a breath. "Look, Sean's death was a massive upheaval in your life. And before the dust had even settled, you gave up everything else. Your job. Your house. The city you lived in. You walked away from everything familiar before he'd even been gone a year." Scott paused, as if to let it sink in. Or maybe wait for my reaction. When I said nothing, he softly added, "I know how much it hurts to lose someone you love. And I know how hard it is to move on and how easy it is to second-guess every step you take. It doesn't help to have your sister-in-law come along and step on some raw wounds, but that doesn't mean she's right."

"Doesn't mean she's wrong, either."

Scott sighed like he was starting to get impatient. "That's bullshit, and no matter how much you don't want to admit it, you *know* it's bullshit. Look, I don't care what the fuck that woman says. Anyone who paid attention for five seconds knows you loved Sean, and anyone who's been within a mile of you lately knows you love Jesse."

"But what about—"

"Listen to me." His voice was firm, but still gentle. "You have every right to move on in your own time and in your own way."

"Then why do I feel like I was using Jesse?"

"I don't know. But I don't think you were."

I turned to him, furrowing my brow.

Scott leaned forward and rested his elbows on his knees as he locked eyes with me. "I've known you for a long time, Garrett. I know you. And whenever you mentioned Jesse, you got a look in your eyes I've only seen you get for one other person."

I winced. "And you don't think that's because Jesse was replacing that other person?"

"Not at all." He reached over the small table and touched my arm. "Listen to me. Yes, you've got a lot of grief to work through. And yes, you're still going to be hurting for Sean for a long time. But for God's sake, don't let that blind you to what you're feeling for Jesse."

"Jesse, I love you." The words had tumbled off my lips, unexpected but sincere.

Jesse had halted. The second he'd turned to face me, my heart had sunk lower than I'd thought possible, and lower still when he'd shaken his head. *"No, you don't."*

"Jesse . . ."

He'd put up a hand. *"I know you care about me, but you're not in love with me. You're in love with something that feels better than that empty spot where Sean used to be."* There'd been no malice in the words. They hadn't been meant to hurt, simply to state—sadly and softly—a fact. *"I don't want you to be lonely, and God knows I don't want you to be in pain from losing him. But I can't be him. And I can't be with someone who needs someone else."*

The memory made my eyes sting. No matter how many times I'd heard those words in my head, followed by the click—not slam—of my front door, they still hurt. They hurt bad. And I couldn't compare the pain of losing Sean to Jesse. It was like comparing a broken rib to a tooth in desperate need of a root canal. Both hurt like hell in their own ways, and when they were at their most intense, they each seemed like the worst pain ever. The pain of one didn't negate—or have a damned thing to do with—the other.

I released a ragged breath. "I don't know what I feel anymore. And even if I do figure it out, I'm pretty sure Jesse's done with me."

"Have you thought about—"

"I've thought about talking to him every minute of every day since he left."

The unspoken question hung in the air. *So why haven't you?*

Because it hurt too much to watch him go once.

Because I'm scared I'll hurt him more than I already have.

Because I don't know if I can honestly tell him I'm ready to be in love with him.

Scott blew out a breath. "Look, I know this is hard, and facing him isn't going to be easy. But if you don't tell him everything you just told me, I have a feeling you're going to regret it for a long time."

I closed my eyes. Wasn't like I could argue with him, but that was hardly enough to magically give me the courage to face the man I'd hurt. "I know I should. I . . . I mean, what if I'm not ready for something with him? It's just so . . ." I cleared my throat, but it did nothing to steady my voice. "It's too soon. Sean's barely been gone a year."

"You've been grieving for longer than a year, though."

I eyed him. "What?"

"You didn't start grieving the day Sean died," Scott said softly. "You started the day he was diagnosed."

I stared down at the pine-needle-covered boards beneath our feet.

"You can let yourself grieve for Sean," he went on, "and still let yourself be in love with Jesse."

"Except he's so worried about not being enough for me. Because he isn't Sean." I wiped my eyes, long past caring if Scott noticed. "And I don't know if I can be what he needs, you know? Because I've got so much shit to—"

"Garrett." His voice was firmer now, but not hostile or chastising. "You're an amazing guy. Any man would be lucky to have you. The fact that you're going through hell doesn't change that." He put a hand on mine and squeezed. "You're still climbing out of all that grief, and you will be for a long time, but you're still *you*. And take it from the man who's known you longer than most people—if you're half as good to Jesse as you were to Sean, you'll be more than enough for him."

With that, I broke.

Scott moved his chair closer and wrapped his arms around me, and I buried my face against his shoulder as the tears came harder than they had in a year. Dams broke inside me. I realized how much the loss of my husband still hurt, and how much I loved Jesse, and how badly I wanted both of them back in my world. One was gone forever, and the fear that the other was too cut me right to the bone. But did I have any right to ask him to come back when Sean's absence was still more raw and painful than I'd realized?

When I'd collected myself, I drew back, wiping my eyes with a shaking hand. "How the hell do I even pull off another relationship right now? I'm a fucking wreck."

"One day a time. Same as any of us."

I coughed to get some breath moving. "And what about the things Courtney said . . . I mean, when she pointed out how similar Jesse is to Sean, I—"

"So what if he is?"

"I . . ." I had no answer.

"First, quit making excuses. You love him. You're hurting for Sean, but you're hurting for Jesse too. You can fix one of those, Garrett."

I winced.

"Facing him won't be easy, but neither will living without him." He took my hand again. "And as far as what your sister-in-law said? Look, even if there are things about him that remind you of Sean, and even if that's what attracted you to him, he's not the same person." He gave my hand a firm squeeze. "I suspect if you dig deep enough, you'll find all the reasons you fell in love with him, and they won't have anything to do with Sean."

The words tore at the wounds I'd already been nursing. I'd been avoiding thinking about what had drawn me to Jesse and made me fall so hard for him, and Scott's comment was like an incantation that turned all those things loose in my mind. The last couple of months flashed through my head, from the silly moments to the quiet ones. Jesse's passion for everything from a card game to his job to *me*. His fearlessness and his sweetness.

Oh God. What did I do?

"You can fix this, Garrett," Scott said as if he could read my thoughts. By now he probably could. "You just need to talk to him."

"That's easier said than done."

"So is anything worth doing."

"Point taken." I exhaled. "I'm not going to lie—I'm terrified. And not just of talking to him. I'm scared of being with him."

"You're a widower," he said softly. "I'd be surprised if you weren't scared to be with someone new. Especially someone who, I'm assuming from things you've said before, has HIV."

I blinked, but hell, I shouldn't have been surprised Scott had been able to read between the lines. I sighed. "You know what's crazy?"

"Hmm?"

"Most of the time, I don't even think about him being positive. Except when . . ." My face burned.

"When, what?"

I stared out at the trees for a long moment, then took a deep breath. "Most of the time, it's a nonissue. He's taking medication that keeps it from . . . well, so it really doesn't do anything to him. But then he had the flu a while ago, and it took me back to when Sean was sick. Ninety-nine percent of the time, I don't think about it, but one cough and I'm scared out of my mind." I sagged back in the chair, releasing a heavy breath. "Rationally I know it's not what it was when we were growing up, but . . . for God's sake, I've already lost Sean. I can't . . ." I lowered my gaze, and my throat tightened as I tried to pull myself together enough to speak. "I can't lose Jesse too."

"Garrett. You already have."

My head snapped up.

Scott looked me in the eyes, expression completely serious. "Of course, he's still alive, but you've lost him. You were so scared of losing him, you went ahead and pushed him away."

"More like I didn't stop him from leaving."

"And why did he leave?"

"I already told you."

"That was rhetorical." He sighed. "I'm serious. You've got to stop making excuses and just *go get him back*. You let your fear of losing him make you lose him anyway, and now you're hurting just like you were afraid you would."

Oh, wasn't that an understatement.

"You can't just avoid loving someone because you might lose them," he went on. He studied me, then folded his hands in his lap. "Remember when Sean was really sick, and I came out to help on the weekends?"

I nodded. "Yeah, you were a lifesaver."

A smile flickered across his lips. "Well, when I was there one weekend, his mom pulled me aside. And she told me what her biggest fear was."

I raised my eyebrows.

Scott locked eyes with me. "The thing that scared her the most while Sean was sick was that something would happen to *you.*"

I blinked. "What?"

"She was terrified, Garrett. Absolutely terrified you'd get into a car accident or something—anything—would happen and take you away from Sean when he needed you the most. She knew she was losing her son and that there was nothing she could do, but she prayed every single day that *he* didn't lose *you.*"

I stared at him.

"Because she knew Sean needed you and that you loved him. I know your in-laws have said a lot of shit over the years, but when it counted?" He swallowed. "His mom knew. And she was terrified he would lose you because—and this is the important part—nothing is guaranteed for any of us. Any of us could live to be a hundred or be run over by a truck on our way to the grocery store. One of us could get cancer like Sean did or take a bullet like Nathan. You just don't know. All you know is who you have right now. Which means every minute we're sitting here talking is one less minute you're with the man you so obviously love." Scott's brow pinched. "Do you want to waste your life worrying that he might be gone? Or do you want to enjoy every single minute you have with him just like Sean enjoyed them all with you?"

A comment about how Sean definitely didn't enjoy every minute stopped at the tip of my tongue. Even those minutes when we'd been fighting or I'd been a pain in the ass were minutes I'd have sold my soul to have back. Struggling with my composure, I leaned over and hugged him again. "Thank you. I needed this."

"I know you did. And I'm sorry it's been so rough."

"Thanks."

All I have to do now is find the courage to go talk to him . . .

CHAPTER THIRTY-THREE

JESSE

"Jesse Connelly." Lydia gave me one of those looks that said I was in deep shit, as if my full name hadn't already given that away. "We need to have a chat in the office."

Aw, crap. Preemptive guilt swelled in my gut. I didn't know what I'd done, but with as out of it as I'd been for the last few days, I wasn't surprised I'd fucked something up.

So, I put aside the inventory sheet I'd been entering into the computer and followed her into the back. As we walked, I glanced at Dexy, and she grimaced like she thought I was about to get reamed. Did she know what was going on or what I'd fucked up? Because I sure as fuck didn't. All I knew was Lydia didn't usually raise her voice at anyone unless something was really, really fubar. Not that she'd raised her voice yet, but anytime I got called back into the office, I expected an ass-chewing like I'd occasionally gotten at my previous jobs.

Steeling myself, I stepped into the office with her.

She shut the door and leaned against Simon's desk, arms folded loosely across her Wolf's Landing T-shirt, and inclined her head. "What's going on?"

I fought the urge to shift my weight. "With what?"

"With you, hon. You've been a wreck since you came back from Seattle, and I'm not buying the explanations that you're tired from the trip. Not after almost a week."

I avoided her gaze.

Her tone was softer as she asked, "What happened in Seattle?"

Oh. That.

Fuck.

Can't you just scream at me for something I screwed up? Do we have to talk about this?

But I sagged against the door and sighed. "We split up."

"That doesn't answer my question."

I pressed my fingers into the bridge of my nose. "Everything was going great. I mean, when we went out to dinner the last night, it was . . ." I dropped my hand and let my head fall against the door. "God, it was perfect. Seriously the most romantic night of my life. And the next day it all went to hell."

"How? Why?"

I took a breath and told her, my voice cracking more than once as I relived the fight between him and his sister-in-law. Even more when I told her about the one between him and me. I was genuinely shocked I hadn't broken out into a sweat by the time I was done.

"Then I told him I couldn't do it anymore," I said. "He needed someone I'm not, and I . . ."

"What did he say?" She cringed like she was already playing it out in her mind.

I deflated. "He told me he loved me."

Lydia's teeth snapped together, and her eyes widened. "Come again?"

I stared at my feet. "He said he loved me."

"And?"

I looked at her. "And . . . it was after what his sister-in-law had said. And I mean it wasn't even twenty-four hours after we'd visited the cemetery where—"

"So what? You were there for him and being supportive when he needed you, and then you had a nice romantic evening together. He'd damn well better love you!"

"I don't want him to love me just because I was there for him when he was grieving."

Lydia pinched the bridge of her nose and forced out a long breath. "Jesse. Sweetheart. Don't make me smack you."

"For what?"

She groaned as she flailed her hand. "For fuck's sake. Are you being deliberately obtuse?"

I blinked.

Lydia rolled her eyes and started ticking points off on her fingers. "When he was at his most emotionally vulnerable, he took you with him because he trusted you enough to lean on you when he needed you. When you guys were at the con together, he was practically swooning over you every time he saw you. When you were sick, he took care of you. And I know that last one drove you nuts because you're you, but the fact is, he did it because he cares about you, and you damn well better not take that shit for granted." She lowered her hands. "What more do you need?"

I didn't answer.

And she wasn't done, apparently. "When you two fought and you walked out, how long had it been since his sister-in-law tore into him?"

"I don't know. We'd just gotten back to Bluewater Bay, and we left Seattle like an hour after it—"

"Yeah, yeah, yeah. I'm not asking if a train leaves Bluewater Bay and a fight happens in Seattle." She waved her hand. "Point is, it was the same day, yeah?"

I nodded.

"And it was after a pretty emotionally intense weekend, wasn't it?"

The weekend flashed through my mind—the visit to Sean's grave, our romantic evening at the Space Needle, the fight with his sister-in-law—and I gulped. "You could say that."

She held my gaze, tilting her head slightly. "Don't you think that *maybe* you should've cut him a *little* bit of slack? He's a grieving widower who'd just been verbally bitch-slapped by his dead husband's sister." She threw up her hands. "Would *you* be able to process or express your feelings after something like that?"

Well, shit. When she put it like that . . .

"God. Now I feel like a dick." I banged my head back against the door and cursed. "But I mean, how can I tell if he *does* want me or . . . someone who isn't here anymore?"

"At some point, you're going to have to trust him when he says what he wants."

"But it's only been a year."

"Yeah, and people grieve in their own way and in their own time. The fact that he met you while he was still grieving—that doesn't mean he doesn't love you."

"But how do I know I'm not just filling in until he's strong enough to move on from his husband?"

Lydia's eyebrows climbed her forehead. "Have you *seen* the way that man looks at you?"

My composure was threatening to crumple, but I managed to say, "Yeah. And do you know how much it hurts to think of who he's really seeing when he looks at me like that?"

Her lips parted. "Do you actually believe that?"

"I . . ."

I don't know what I believe.

I want to be wrong.

I'm terrified I'm right.

"Jesse."

I met Lydia's gaze.

"Do you love him?"

Instantly, my vision blurred, and I looked away as I swiped at my eyes. "So much."

The desk creaked and her shoes scuffed across the floor. When her hands met my shoulders, I thought I was going to crack. "Go talk to him, hon."

"What do I say?" I met her gaze and fought to keep my voice steady. "I was such an asshole to him, and . . . I mean, even if I hadn't been, what if his sister-in-law was right?"

"What if she wasn't?"

I bit my lip.

"You want to spend the rest of your life wondering if you let a great guy slip through your fingers because of what someone *else* said to him out of anger and grief?"

Fuck if she didn't have a point.

"Go." She tugged me away from the door and gently turned me around to face it. "Go talk to him."

"But I've got work to—"

"Honey, you're not getting anything done until you sort your shit out with him. *Go.*"

I laughed. "Okay, okay. And thanks for the pep talk."

"Anytime."

I clocked out and headed straight for the Alehouse. I was tempted to go home and grab a shower, change clothes, eat something—basically anything to put off the inevitable. But I knew myself, and I knew if I procrastinated, I'd never go talk to him. I needed to go now while Lydia's words were still ringing in my ears.

Outside the bar, I paused to collect myself and take a deep breath. I could do this. Even if the outcome wasn't good, we couldn't leave things the way they'd ended the other day.

Panic and a million reasons to be anywhere but here were starting to claw their way into my brain, so before I could give them any attention, I pushed open the door and strode inside.

My gaze went right to him.

And his was right on me.

His eyes widened. Across the dim room, we stared at each other. Well. I was here. He saw me. No turning back.

Heart thumping and nerves going apeshit, I started across the bar. If one of the lumberjack-holes at the bar was giving me the side-eye again, I didn't notice. For all I knew, the place was empty except for me and Garrett and all the shit we needed to sort out.

I stopped in front of him. "Hey."

He moistened his lips. "Hey."

"Um." I fidgeted uncomfortably. "Can we talk?"

Garrett eyed me uneasily. "Maybe we should."

My mouth was dry. "So, uh . . ."

He glanced over his shoulder. "I've got about forty-five minutes left on my shift." He met my eyes, eyebrows up. "You're welcome to hang here until I'm off, or I can meet you—"

"This is fine." As if for emphasis, I pulled out a barstool and slid onto it. If I left now, there was no guarantee I'd be wherever we promised to meet up later. This was now or never.

"Okay." He looked at me with a cautious smile. "While you're waiting, you, um, want a Coke on the Rocks?"

I actually laughed, if a little halfheartedly. "Sure. Why not?"

He poured the drink and handed it to me, and a sinking feeling in my gut almost made me hand it right back. It was weird, sitting here in the Alehouse with that gorgeous bartender and feeling a million miles away from him. We knew each other too well for this kind of distance, especially when conversation had come so easily while we'd still been strangers. Back when we'd still had huge cards against our vests, and we'd been feeling each other out, pulled in by a magnetic attraction and scared shitless of how things might play out.

Had it really been less than a week since I'd looked in his eyes on the observation deck of the Space Needle and known without a doubt I was in love with him? How could one fight and five days put so much cold air between us after we'd been so intimate?

Garrett continued working. I sipped the Coke I didn't really want. We didn't talk. Didn't exchange any banter or looks.

Finally, his shift was over. I paid for my soda, he clocked out, and we left the Alehouse in uncomfortable silence.

We didn't go far. A block or so from the bar, away from potential eavesdroppers, we stopped under the pasty glow of a streetlight.

And surprise, surprise... the silence lingered. Somewhere nearby, a cricket filled in the background, emphasizing how quiet it was under this light. We needed to talk, and we'd come out here to talk, and there was so much shit we needed to talk about, but I had no idea how to start.

Garrett spoke first. "Listen, you have every right to be pissed. And I'm ... I've thought about a million things to say, and it just keeps coming back to *I'm sorry*. That's ... that's really it. I'm sorry."

"Me too." I swallowed. "I ... As shell-shocked as you were after your sister-in-law's tirade, I shouldn't have come at you sideways. I should've waited before I lost it like that."

"I don't think I can really blame you." He avoided my eyes. "That ... Everything that day was a fucking mess. And I'm sorry you got caught in it and..." He exhaled. "Just... I'm sorry. For everything."

I watched him, not sure what to say. "So where do we go from here?" There was probably more to talk about, more to pick apart and scrutinize until we'd really apologized for everything we had and hadn't said, but I needed to know what happened next. What was the point of dissecting it all if we were just going to walk away?

He slid his hands into his pockets and stared at the pavement between us. "Is there any going back to where we were before?"

In an instant, my throat was tight and achy. God, I wanted to do exactly that—go right back to where things had been until moments after his sister-in-law had rung Fiona's doorbell. But I didn't know if we could. If either of us could.

"I don't know," I said. "I've never done it before."

Garrett lifted his gaze. "Which part?"

"Any of it, to be honest. I've dated guys, but never someone who's lost a partner like you lost Sean. And never . . ." I swallowed. "Never someone I felt this way about." Moistening my lips, I shook my head. "I want to do right by you, but I won't pretend I have a clue what I'm doing."

"This is new for me too. I wish I could say I knew more than you about what we're doing, but I don't." He gulped hard. "Maybe we can figure it out together."

I flinched. Silence fell. And lingered.

"Talk to me," he pleaded softly. "I don't know what to say except that I miss you and I want you back."

"Me too." I wiped a hand over my face. "And it . . . it wasn't fair for me to expect you to be over Sean. Or to hold it against you that you weren't. The thing is, if there's room in your heart for both of us, even if you're not ready for something more than friendship, I still want you in my life. I'd rather have you as a friend than not at all. Playing Magic, geeking out over stuff, just hanging out—I want all of that as much as I want the sex and whatever else. I . . . God, I seriously miss you."

"I miss you too. But as a hell of a lot more than a friend."

My heart flipped. "Are you . . . I mean, are you in a place where . . ." I bit my lip, not sure how to proceed.

"I won't lie. I'm not over Sean, and I may never be." Garrett swallowed. "But that doesn't mean I can't love you."

It wasn't supposed to hurt, hearing those words. Every time he'd said them so far, though, it had been like a kick in the balls. I believed he meant them. It just hurt to think he might be in love with the space I filled, not *me*.

I ran a hand through my hair and avoided his eyes. "What about the things your sister-in-law said?" I didn't have to look to know he'd flinched. I swore I felt it.

"She gave me a lot to think about," he said.

Steeling myself, I looked at him. "And?"

"And I think I've got a lot more grieving to do than I realized. I'm going to look into talking to a counselor. Someone who specializes in this kind of thing." He sighed. "It's something I probably should have done a long time ago."

"That sounds like a good idea." But the question lingered—*where does that leave us?* I was thrilled he was getting a handle on his grief, but I had no idea where my place was in his world, or if I had one at all.

Then Garrett pushed his shoulders back and looked right in my eyes. "The last time we talked, you were upset because you didn't think you could fill Sean's shoes."

Jaw tight, I nodded.

"And the more I've thought about it the last few days, the more I've realized you were right. You can't fill his shoes."

The bluntness caught me off guard, and my breath hitched.

"You can't," he said again. "And if the roles were reversed, he'd never be able to fill yours."

I blinked. "What?"

Garrett exhaled slowly. "You're not Sean. You couldn't be if you tried, and I don't *want* you to try. I loved him, and I always will, but he's gone." He paused like he needed to pull himself together. "And yeah, I'm still coping with that. Apparently not as well as I thought I was, but I'm getting there." He chewed his lip. "None of that changes the fact that I met you, though, or that I was attracted to you from day one. And it doesn't change the fact that I fell in love with you."

My heart skipped, but he wasn't done.

"The fact that there are things about you guys that are similar? I don't know. Maybe that's why you caught my eye, but I never factored in those similarities when I fell for you. I fell in love with the sum total of *you*." He paused. "I mean, you have things in common with guys I dated before Sean too. Jackson was into comics and Magic. Miguel had taste in music that was a lot like yours. Sometimes when you laugh, you remind me of Cory." He gestured dismissively. "It doesn't mean you were a replacement for them any more than you're a replacement for Sean."

I leaned hard against the brick wall, my knees unsteady and my head spinning.

Garrett looked in my eyes. "I love you, Jesse. I love how excited you get over all that stuff you think is geeky and dorky. I love how we can't play Magic without winding up in bed. I love . . ." He paused again. "When I look at you, I don't see someone who can fill the void Sean left. I see someone who can fill a void I never knew was there."

I was afraid to ask, but did anyway: "What void is that?"

He hesitated, then came a little closer and dropped his voice to nearly a whisper. "The one that was waiting for you."

My lips parted, but no air and no voice moved between them. I just stared at him, disbelieving.

"It seems contradictory, but it's not," he said. "Part of me still hurts and will probably always hurt over losing Sean and not getting to spend my life with him. But the other part is thrilled and grateful that I found you, and that—" He snapped his teeth together.

I studied him. "And that . . . what?"

Garrett took a deep breath. "That there might be some chance of spending my life with *you*."

I pushed myself off the wall and moved toward him. "I'd say there's more than a chance." Then I grabbed him, nearly bowling him over, and kissed him. Tears burned my eyes, and when he threw his arms around me and held me tighter than he ever had, a few slipped free. I didn't care.

Garrett touched his forehead to mine as he brushed his thumb across my damp cheek. "I'm sorry about what happened in Seattle. It . . ." He sighed, warm breath gusting across my lips. "I shouldn't have shut you out after that, and I shouldn't have put you in that situation in the first place."

"But you didn't want to be alone."

"No. I didn't." He cupped my face. "That doesn't mean I had any right to drag you into it."

"You didn't drag me into anything." My voice was shaky, and I prayed like hell it didn't break. "No, it wasn't the most comfortable thing I've ever gone into, but if you needed me with you to go visit Sean, then of course I was going to be with you." I ran trembling fingers through his hair. "I want to be there for you even when it's hard or uncomfortable because I love you."

Garrett exhaled, and when he sniffed, I realized his face was wet too.

Brushing a tear from his cheek, I whispered, "I've never loved anyone like I love you. I don't know *how* to be in love with someone like this, especially not someone who's still grieving for someone else, but if you'll be patient with me, I'll figure it out." I cupped his face. "I just don't want to lose you."

"You won't," he whispered. Then he smiled and kissed me again. "You're amazing, you know that?"

"No." I pulled back and met his eyes. "I just love you. So much. I should have been more patient and just . . . not such a raging dick. I'm so sorry."

"It's okay." He pressed a kiss to my forehead. "You had every right to be pissed, and God, I love you. I meant it when I said it before, but damn, I didn't realize just how much until you were gone."

"I know you meant it then. I was just too pissed off and stubborn to—"

Garrett cut me off with a tender kiss. "I'm serious—you had every right to be. And I mean, maybe we needed to go there so we could get here."

I looked into his eyes, and the resounding truth in his words settled something—everything—in me. There'd been nagging doubts and second guesses from the start, but they were all quiet now. Neither of us could predict where things would go or what the future held, but right here, right now, I knew what this was. What we were to each other. Who I didn't have to be and who he didn't want me to be.

Forcing back that stubborn lump in my throat, I nodded. "I think you're right." Pulling him closer, I smiled. "You asked a few minutes ago if we could go back to where we were before. I'd say the answer is no."

Alarm widened his eyes.

I lifted my chin for a soft kiss. "We're going to somewhere so much better."

He grinned, and he kissed me. "You really are amazing."

"Garrett. We've been over this." I buffed my nails on my shirt. "I'm fucking awesome."

He laughed. Like, for real. With feeling. And he gathered me in his arms and just hugged me close. "Don't ever change, baby."

I smiled against his shoulder, closing my eyes and basking in his strong, warm embrace.

"You know," he said after a while, "that bed in my apartment is awfully big with only one person in it."

Struggling against a laugh, I looked up at him. "Is it?"

"Yeah." He smoothed my hair. "Any chance you might help me out with that?"

I grinned, electricity zinging along my nerve endings as relief met arousal. "Yeah. I think I can help."

CHAPTER THIRTY-FOUR

GARRETT

We staggered in through my front door, and God only knew how, but we made it down the hall to the bedroom. Somewhere along the way, I'd lost my shoes and Jesse's shirt was gone. As Jesse toed off his shoes, I fumbled with the buttons on my shirt, and we kept right on kissing as much as we could.

I gave up on unbuttoning the entire shirt. Instead, I broke away for a second to pull my shirt up and off, and it probably hadn't even hit the floor before I was kissing Jesse again. His hands ran all over my newly bared skin, igniting nerve endings that had been aching for his touch for what seemed like forever.

"I want you so bad," he said between kisses. "I've . . . I've been going out of my mind."

"Me too. I missed you."

He whimpered softly, then kissed me harder, gripping the back of my neck painfully tight. Christ, I could've stood there like this all damn night, but there were still far too many layers between us. Time to do something about that before something caught fire.

As I unbuckled his belt, he groaned. Or maybe I did. All I knew was the room was filled with the sounds of two men who needed each other so bad it hurt, and it didn't matter whose voice was whose.

The buckle finally gave. I unzipped and unbuttoned his pants, and as I slid them down, my hand brushed over his thick erection. A curse slipped off my tongue, barely audible against his lips, and I couldn't resist—I dropped to my knees in front of him. Gripping his partially rucked-down jeans, I took his cock as deep into my mouth as I could.

"Ooh, yeah," he moaned, sliding both hands through my hair. His hips rocked almost imperceptibly and pushed his dick just a little deeper into my throat. I took him eagerly. I loved the taste of his skin, the way he moved, the sounds he made—he was fucking addictive.

I hummed around his cock, and he rewarded me with breathy curses. The jerky movements of his hips intensified. Not enough to choke me, though—just enough to let me know he was definitely enjoying himself. I grabbed his ass and egged him on, taking him as deep as my well-trained gag reflex would allow, and the whispered swearing became throaty groans of inventive profanity that might've made me laugh if I hadn't been so aroused.

His fingers tightened in my hair, slowing the movements of my head. "You want me to fuck you?" he slurred. "'Cause I'm . . . I'm not gonna last if you keep . . ."

I gave the head one last lick before I sat back on my heels and looked up at him. "What kind of question is that?"

He laughed, combing his fingers through my hair. "Then you'd better get on the bed."

"Bossy." I grinned as I stood, and he pulled me into a deep kiss.

It didn't last long. He broke away and nodded for the bed. "Now."

Oh, yeah, he was feeling bossy today. I loved it.

As we stripped off the last of our clothes, he said, "Grab the lube?"

I nodded—I was closer to my nightstand, after all—and reached into the drawer. I took out lube and a condom, but as I sat on the bed, I paused. I looked at the condom between my fingers, then at him. "Do we need this?"

Swallowing hard, Jesse joined me on the bed. His eyes flicked back and forth from me to the rubber. "You tell me."

I shrugged. "Why not?"

He studied me, his expression unreadable. I considered dropping the thought—we could discuss it later when we weren't both hard. Before I could, though, he plucked the condom from my hand.

And tossed it away.

Then he wrapped his arms around me and kissed me, and we both sank back onto the mattress. I parted my legs for him, and his hips settled between them, and we just held on and kissed. As impatient as I was for him to fuck me, this was just too good to pass up. Any chance to have his body against me and his tongue sliding past mine? God, yes.

"I want you just like this," he murmured against my lips. "On your back so I can see you."

I moaned in agreement. I wasn't going to say no to watching his face while he took me without that layer of latex between us.

He picked up the lube and poured some on his hand before dropping the bottle on the mattress—out of the way but still within reach. I spread my legs wider and held my breath as he pushed a couple of slick fingers into me. I was relaxed enough to take them easily, but I was so turned on I was afraid I'd come if he kept this up for long. He didn't—he slid them in and out a few times, then withdrew them and put some more lube on himself. I couldn't help squirming as I watched him stroking himself. It hadn't even been that long since the last time we'd had sex, but I needed him like it had been *years*.

Jesse lined himself up, and as he started to push in, his eyelids slid shut. "Fuck . . ."

As the head pushed inside, I nearly closed my eyes too, but like hell was I missing one second of Jesse's expression. Topping with a condom felt good. Topping bareback? *Fuck* was right.

The furrows between his eyebrows were deep, his eyes screwed shut, but his lips were apart, almost forming an O. Withdrawing a little, he pushed back in, and a low, guttural sound escaped his throat as he worked his cock deeper. "You . . . mind if we go slow?"

"Mind?" I ran my hands up his back. "I *love* this."

He made a pleased noise—somewhere between a hum and a moan—and took another long, slow stroke inside me. "Oh *Jesus*, you feel good."

So did he. I was already in heaven as he started to fuck me, and watching him took this to a whole new level because, oh God, he was beautiful. His usually meticulous hair had been disheveled well before we'd made it into bed, and now it was tumbling into his eyes. His fair skin was flushed, smooth features taut with exertion and sensation.

I couldn't resist—I reached up to touch his cheek. At the first brush of my fingertips, he sucked in a sharp breath, and then he opened those amazing blue eyes. Holy fuck. His pupils were wide, and there was a gleam of lust and love and need and relief, and suddenly it wasn't his thick cock making it hard to breathe.

A prickle of panic reminded me how easily this all could have slipped through our fingers, how many ways we could have gone that didn't result in us landing here in bed, and suddenly he wasn't close enough. Deep inside me, but still too far.

"Come here," I whispered, and drew him down.

He didn't resist. He lowered himself onto his forearms and met my lips in a breathless kiss. I held him tight, fingers splayed in his hair and in the middle of his back. We were utterly locked together. As intertwined as two bodies could be. The deliciously invasive feeling of his dick sliding in and out of my sensitive, stretched hole made me dizzy, and so did the heat of his skin and the taste of his demanding kiss.

How he had the presence of mind to keep moving his hips, I had no idea—maybe they were just moving on their own—but it was spectacular. His slow, fluid strokes started mimicking our kisses—harder, more frantic. There was no finesse, no precision, no rhythm to speak of at all except an uneven cadence made of primal desperation.

I reached between us, partly to stroke myself and partly to keep my cock and balls from getting trapped between us and killing the mood. The second I started stroking myself, my entire body tensed, and we both gasped as I clenched around him.

Jesse broke the kiss with a low moan. A tremor rippled through him, pushing him deeper as his muscles quivered between my thighs, and he cursed, the sound so strained it inched toward a sob. "Fuck . . ."

"You feel so good, baby," I murmured. "Holy shit."

Jesse brushed his lips across mine, but only for a second before he let his head fall beside mine. Burying his face against my neck, he slid his hands under me and hooked his hands over my shoulders. His thrusts became even harder and more frantic than before, shoving the air out of my lungs each time he bottomed out.

I closed my eyes and let myself get carried away by the sensation of being soundly fucked. By the heat of Jesse's body. By the very presence of him. By his cock inside me and his palpable need for more.

"I'mma come," he slurred. "I'm . . . Do you . . . you want me to pull out, or—"

"No. Come." I gripped his shoulder tighter and pumped my cock faster and rocked my hips as much as I could to complement his movements. "C'mon, baby."

He groaned, thrusting harder, and the air seemed to thrum around us with the tension building inside him. I could feel his orgasm closing in as surely as I could feel my own.

All at once, the tension snapped. My entire body seized with the force of my release, and before the first drop of semen had landed on my stomach, Jesse cried out and shuddered. His hips jerked and tried to push him deeper, and we both gasped and moaned and fell to pieces in each other's arms.

I slid my hand out from between us and slung it over him. There was cum all over both of us and on his back now, but I didn't care. He didn't seem to either. We were messy and spent, sweaty and shaky, and everything was exactly as it needed to be.

"I love you," he murmured against my neck.

I lifted my head just long enough to press a kiss to his shoulder. "I love you too. And thank you again. For understanding and for giving me time."

"You can have as much time as you need. I'll be here."

I smiled. "You really are fucking awesome."

"Uh, yeah? No shit?"

I snorted, and we both started laughing. It felt good. Hell, it felt great. Despite plenty of stubbornness and stupidity on both sides— despite everything—we'd found our way back to this. To each other's arms and to the easy banter we'd shared since day one.

I fully expected more bumps in the road after this, but I was confident we could make it past them now. The rough patches and fights and whatever else came our way were things we could work through. We knew how to talk things out, and I damn sure knew that it was worth the effort because of what we'd be saving every time we pulled ourselves through something.

We could do this.

We *would* do this.

Because we were fucking awesome together.

GARRETT

The Following December

When Scott and Jeremy's wedding venue had fallen through, they'd decided to hell with booking a facility—they were getting married outside. That was a gamble in Western Washington, of course. Rain shadow or not, the Olympic Peninsula *did* get rain, and this *was* December. In fact, it had rained for a solid week leading up to the wedding.

The day of, though, there wasn't a cloud in sight as everyone trekked from the parking lot to the gorgeous—if slightly damp—lawn of the winery they'd rented in Port Angeles. Despite the shitty weather for the last few days, this was going to be a gorgeous afternoon.

And it turned out Scott hadn't been kidding—his wedding was *huge*. Both of their families had shown up in droves. Even Jeremy's ex-wife and his kids were there, which spoke volumes about the progress that family had made. When he and Scott had first started dating, things had been strained to say the least. His daughter had refused to speak to him. But with some patience and counseling, things were better. Much better. I wasn't sure if Jeremy approved of his daughter's visibly pierced and tattooed boyfriend, but he didn't say anything. Not where I could hear it, anyway.

In addition to family and friends, there were a ton of people from Wolf's Landing, many of whom I knew now thanks to Jesse. Hunter and Kevin. Levi and Carter. Of course Anna Maxwell—who had a different bodyguard so Jeremy didn't have to work at his own wedding—and her fiancée Natalya.

Spirits were especially high among that particular crowd. For months, there'd been some rumors about possibly canceling the show, but given the sky-high ratings, everyone had mostly brushed that off as gossip. *Mostly*. Recently, though, the announcement had been made that the show was renewed for at least two more seasons, and Hunter and Kevin were apparently hard at work on the next book. That would keep everyone in Bluewater Bay busy and employed for a good long time.

At that, everyone on the set and in town had released a collective sigh of relief. It was funny how even the locals—the ones who hadn't been thrilled about the arrival of *Wolf's Landing*—were relieved that it was continuing. Sure, the culture and the landscape of the town had changed dramatically, but everyone seemed to agree that the change was for the better.

Maybe that was why I'd been drawn to this place. I'd visited Scott here in the days before *Wolf's Landing*. Back when it had been a sleepy fishing and logging town in the middle of nowhere. It had been largely unchanged for decades before suddenly being hit with massive upheaval. There'd been some backlash and a period of adjustment, and it hadn't always been easy for the little town to weather the influx of Hollywood and its people, but in the end, Bluewater Bay hadn't just adapted—it had thrived. It had a whole new heartbeat now, and something told me that even when the day came that *Wolf's Landing* moved on, the town would continue to be this vibrant, resilient place.

So when my own world had been tossed on its head, I'd come to Bluewater Bay in search of a new start, and I'd found it. My life barely resembled the one I'd had before leaving Seattle. I'd gotten to know everyone at End O' Earth, and sometimes I went in and helped out when a new release promised to swamp them. Simon and I had become especially good friends, particularly after I'd helped him revamp his bookkeeping system to be more efficient. That had actually annoyed Jesse—now that Simon didn't have to devote as many hours to the shop's finances, he had more time on his hands for creative things. Apparently, those were not his strong point, and Jesse usually wound up doing damage control.

"Should we go sit?" Jesse's voice pulled me out of my thoughts, and I shifted my gaze from the mingling guests to the man I'd been in love with for the past several months.

Good God, he was gorgeous. He'd gone with a perfectly tailored dark-gray suit, and his recently bleached hair was flawlessly arranged. He did look a little tired, and he had some faint circles under his eyes, but that was my fault. What could I say? We'd only been living together a month, and the novelty still hadn't worn off.

I kissed his cheek and wrapped an arm around his waist. "Sure. Looks like people are heading that way."

We followed the crowd's steady migration toward the rows of white folding chairs. There, we ran into Levi and Carter and ended up sitting beside them.

There was still something incredibly surreal about being friends with an actor I'd had a crush on for ages. That novelty hadn't begun to wear off either. I could chat casually and easily with Levi now, but sometimes I still had to stop and ask myself if it was real.

Magic: The Gathering nights had become regular occurrences. Enough that I was used to finding Maine Coon fur on my clothes, since Levi's cat Zelda had taken to perching on my lap while we played. She didn't stick around much when it was *Call of Duty* night, though. The yelling annoyed her.

I'd never thought I'd have Levi Pritchard and company lounging in my living room—or that I'd be lounging in his living room with his cat on my lap—shit-talking and laughing over cards or controllers, but such was my life these days. Carter, Jesse, and Hunter had even gotten me into *Space Villager*. Despite some grumbling about trendy shit and time vampires, Levi and Kevin had grudgingly given it a try too . . . and promptly gotten hooked.

Somehow, in the course of a year, this had become my world. A group of friends who'd welcomed me into their fold. Having my high school best friend nearby. Falling in love. A new town. A new job. It was my new normal, and I loved it. All of it.

I'd expected to tend bar for a few months until I figured out what I wanted to do long-term, but I was still working at the Alehouse. I liked it. The job was fun. The people were generally nice. The hours weren't bad. Maybe I'd still be doing it in a year, maybe I wouldn't, but I wasn't in a big hurry to find something else.

Sometimes I had that itch to go back to the more analytical work of accounting, but I scratched that by offering to handle taxes for my friends. Word of that offer had apparently gotten around, and it sounded like I was going to be doing tax returns for half of the *Wolf's Landing* cast and crew this year. There'd even been some noise about a full-time accounting gig with the studio, but I'd wait to see something in writing before I got excited about it.

So yeah. Life was good.

It wasn't all smooth sailing, of course. There were still days when Sean's absence cut to the quick. The grief could hit me out of nowhere and pull me back to that dark place.

Through it all, Jesse was a saint. He somehow seemed to know when I needed space and when I needed a shoulder, and he always gave it to me. I'd apologized a million times for letting my grief interfere with our relationship, but he'd insisted it wasn't interference.

"You were a package deal when I met you," he'd told me hundreds of times. *"I don't want you to pretend Sean didn't exist or that it doesn't still hurt that he's gone."*

He meant it too. When I was on a more even keel, sometimes he'd ask about Sean. About when we were dating. Our wedding. Trips we'd taken together.

One day, I'd caught him gazing at the small framed wedding photo I kept on my dresser, and I'd thought he'd been upset that it was still there. But when I'd asked, he'd just offered a sad smile and said, *"With everything you've told me about him, I just wish I could've known him."*

Just thinking about it now made my eyes sting.

"Hey." Jesse nudged me with his elbow. "You okay?"

"Yeah." I made the most casual gesture I could about wiping away the tears before he saw them.

He laughed and kissed my cheek. "You're not supposed to cry until the ceremony starts."

"Shut up." I wrapped an arm around his shoulders. He leaned against me, and . . . God, this was perfect. We fit so well together in every way. I tried not to think about how easily this could have slipped through our fingers, and I just focused on how grateful I was that it hadn't.

A few minutes later, the ceremony started. Scott and Jeremy stood at the front in matching black tuxes. As they joined hands, they both smiled, and I didn't think I'd ever seen Scott looking this happy. He'd been through hell and back. He'd suffered a loss most people couldn't fathom. But here he was—gazing at the man he loved, saying the words he'd never thought he'd say to anyone else.

I swallowed hard as I listened to their vows. Was that in my future with Jesse? The thought of marrying him didn't feel like a betrayal to Sean, but it wasn't something we needed to do yet. *Yet.* The more I watched the happy grooms, though, the more I wondered if this was something we should start talking about. We'd moved in together, and we'd made noise about buying a place in the next year or so, but what about this?

I clasped our fingers together. We'd talk about it. And … maybe …

This was so surreal too. A year ago, I couldn't have begun to imagine this. Just the thought of coming to Scott's wedding had filled me with dread because I hadn't been sure I could cope. Being here with a new love? Considering the idea of standing up there and reciting those vows myself? Unthinkable.

But here we were.

Life had, despite my fears, gone on. There'd be ups and downs in our future, and there were no guarantees, but I was okay with that. A chapter had ended, leaving me aimless and hurting and certain there wasn't life after the man I'd loved, but as cruel as the world could be, it wasn't *that* cruel. There was more. When one chapter ended, there was heartache and emptiness, but it wasn't the end of happiness either.

I would always love Sean, and I'd miss him for the rest of my life. But I loved Jesse too, and I was excited about where life would take us. Nervous and scared for a lot of reasons, but excited too.

My world would never be the same. Bluewater Bay was my home now. So was Jesse. Though a piece of me would always be missing, I wasn't in pieces anymore.

I clasped Jesse's hand tighter, and we exchanged smiles before shifting our gazes back to the ceremony. I kept smiling as I held his hand and watched my best friend get married.

I promised I'd be okay, Sean.
And I am.

Starstruck
L.A. Witt

There's Something About Ari
L.B. Gregg

Hell on Wheels
Z.A. Maxfield

Lone Wolf
*Aleksandr Voinov and
L.A. Witt*

The Burnt Toast B&B
*Heidi Belleau and
Rachel Haimowitz*

Lights, Camera, Cupid!
A Valentine's Day Collection

Wedding Favors
Anne Tenino

The Deep of the Sound
Amy Lane

When to Hold Them
G.B. Gordon

Rain Shadow
L.A. Witt

Stuck Landing
Lauren Gallagher

How the Cookie Crumbles
Jaime Samms

Selfie
Amy Lane

All the Wrong Places
Ann Gallagher

Bluewater Blues
G.B. Gordon

No Small Parts
Ally Blue

For a Good Time, Call . . .
Anne Tenino and E.J. Russell

All Wheel Drive
Z.A. Maxfield

Get a Grip
L.A. Witt

Three Player Game
Jaime Samms

Operation Green Card
G.B. Gordon

Outside the Lines
Anna Zabo

Dear Reader,

Thank you for reading L.A. Witt's *New Hand*!

We know your time is precious and you have many, many entertainment options, so it means a lot that you've chosen to spend your time reading. We really hope you enjoyed it.

We'd be honored if you'd consider posting a review—good or bad—on sites like **Amazon, Barnes & Noble, Kobo, Goodreads, Twitter, Facebook, Tumblr,** and your blog or website. We'd also be honored if you told your friends and family about this book. Word of mouth is a book's lifeblood!

For more information on upcoming releases, author interviews, blog tours, contests, giveaways, and more, please sign up for our weekly, spam-free newsletter and visit us around the web:

Newsletter: tinyurl.com/RiptideSignup
Twitter: twitter.com/RiptideBooks
Facebook: facebook.com/RiptidePublishing
Goodreads: tinyurl.com/RiptideOnGoodreads
Tumblr: riptidepublishing.tumblr.com

Thank you so much for Reading the Rainbow!

RiptidePublishing.com

ACKNOWLEDGMENTS

Hat tip to Annabeth Albert for the *Space Villager* Easter egg, and also helping me figure out a title for the book!

ALSO BY L.A. WITT

Anchor Point series
Just Drive
Afraid to Fly
Chief's Mess
Rank & File

Bad Behavior series, with Cari Z
Risky Behavior
Suspicious Behavior
Reckless Behavior (coming soon)

Starstruck (a Bluewater Bay story)
Finding Master Right
Static

Writing as Lauren Gallagher
Stuck Landing (a Bluewater Bay story)
Razor Wire

Writing as Ann Gallagher
Lead Me Not
All the Wrong Places (a Bluewater Bay story)

Writing as Lori A. Witt
The Tide of War

See L.A. Witt's full booklist at: gallagherwitt.com

ABOUT THE AUTHOR

L.A. Witt is an abnormal M/M romance writer who has finally been released from the purgatorial corn maze of Omaha, Nebraska, and now spends her time on the southwestern coast of Spain. In between wondering how she didn't lose her mind in Omaha, she explores the country with her husband, several clairvoyant hamsters, and an ever-growing herd of rabid plot bunnies. She also has substantially more time on her hands these days, as she has recruited a small army of mercenaries to search South America for her nemesis, romance author Lauren Gallagher, but don't tell Lauren. And definitely don't tell Lori A. Witt or Ann Gallagher. Neither of those twits can keep their mouths shut . . .

Website: www.gallagherwitt.com
E-mail: gallagherwitt@gmail.com
Twitter: @GallagherWitt